GRIM

HAVOC OF SINS

GRIM
HAVOC OF SINS

First edition: 2024
ISBN: 978-1959194675

Cover & Interior Design by Spellbinding Design
Photography by Jody Wright
Edited by Lori Whitman

Again, to my dark side that's been begging to be let back out.
Run free, little spawn.

LETTER TO MY READERS

Here we are again, in the middle of a tangled web. Oh, how I love to spin! *Rubs hands together * I have provided you with a character guide with old and new characters just to help when I toss you into this whole new world. I suggest you grab a notebook and pen to jot down names as you go, but I'll leave that up to you.

This book is heavily laced with characters from the Devil's Reach motorcycle club and as we dive further into the series, you may find it a better read if you were familiar with my Dark Water Series and Quiet Mafia Series. Of course, you can read this story as is, but holy shhh you just might miss some fun easter eggs that will answer some of those things you caught from books ago and even some things to come.

As my faithful readers know, I don't write light storylines, so find a quiet room, grab your favorite drink, and meet me between the pages for another adventure.

Happy reading friends.

Jodi

CHARACTER GUIDE

<u>**Gates Family**</u>

Jim Gates: Grim's father and owner of Indulge Hotel

Laurel Gates: Grim's mother

Grim Gates: Owner of Secrets and oldest of the brothers

Leo Gates: Middle of the three brothers

Knox Gates: Youngest of the three brothers

Leal and Zhar: Grim's Doberman Pinschers

Darcy: Dog walker

<u>**Extras to the Gates Family**</u>

Jesse: Grim's right-hand man

Cartwright: Grim's main driver

Louis: Grim trusts him to ride his bike

Janelle: In love with Grim

Deborah: Real estate advisor

Tayla Canos: Cartel daughter (Dark Water Series)

Jerry and Elva Canos: Tayla's parents (Grim lived with them for 10 years when in Mexico)

Tame Family

Cameron Tame: Kenna's father, Lawyer to Jim Gates

Claudine Tame: Kenna's mother, travels the world for work

Kenna Tame: Goes by Lodge to keep her job separate from her family

Calli Tame: Kenna's younger sister, doesn't get along with Kenna

Extras to the Tame Family

Simon Gable: Private Investigator, works for Cameron

Zara: Cameron's secretary

Extras

Jayden Wallace: Manager to super hosts

Mr. Salazar: Client of Kenna's

Yen Hong: Client of Kenna's

Elio Capri: Head of the Capri mafia family in Italy (Quiet Wealth Series) and friend of Grim

Vinni and Niccola Capri: Elio's cousins

Martin Castillo: Head of Cartel (Dark Water Series)

Hannah: Kenna's old friend

Gavin: Elevator operator at Indulge Hotel

Shore: Kenna's favorite driver at Indulge Hotel

<u>Devil's Reach Motorcycle Club</u>

Location of official clubhouse: Santa Monica, California

Trigger: President, married to Tess

Brick: Vice President, Minnie's longtime boyfriend

Tess: Married to Trigger, best friend to Brick and Minnie and owner of Dirty Deeds Club

Minnie: Kenna's best friend and owner of a sex house and Dirty Demons strip club.

Rail: Good friend of Kenna's and dates whoever he can

Morgan: Good friend of Kenna's. Holds the rank of Sergeant of Arms

<u>Stripe Backs Motorcycle Club</u>

Rival club to Devil's Reach

Location of official clubhouse: Venice, California.

Club weak and scattered as many members were killed over the years. Power struggle within the membership as they try to rebuild.

ONE

GRIM GATES

Flashes of green lit up as I gained on the bike ahead. I pulled a knife from my boot and swerved right then immediately went low and leaned left, and my knife flashed as it sliced through the tendons on the Stripe Back's calf like butter. His body jerked at the pain, and I steadied my bike and kicked at him to send him off the road. I glanced over my shoulder to see him bounce and run headfirst into a cactus.

Bang! Bang! Shots came from somewhere. I pulled ahead and got between two trucks for protection. When one of the drivers started to use his radio, I pulled my gun and pointed it at him. He raised his hand, and his shoulders went high as he put his radio down and kept the truck steady. It took me a moment to settle my bike in the airflow between the trucks.

The other driver on the right caught my attention and indicated that there were two bikers in front of him.

I waited for the right time and jumped ahead of the trucks behind the bikers. I drilled a bullet into one guy's head, and the other fired a shot at me. It just missed my shoulder.

I popped a couple in his direction, and he suddenly let go of the gas, and his bike was sucked under the truck's massive wheels.

I spotted the exit up ahead and threw back my head and laughed. Exhilaration filled me. God, I loved this.

"They've turned off," Trigger called through the speaker in my helmet, and I waved as he pulled onto a side road. I grinned and flexed my fingers on the throttle to drop my speed a little, and the trucker was suddenly on my tail. I cut him off as I swerved across in front of him and down another side road.

"There's two ahead of you, Trig." Brick's voice filled my helmet. "Looks like you're clear for now, Grim."

"Any idea who has it?" I shouted.

"Not yet," Brick answered.

The sun was setting, and it would be completely

black soon. The desert had no mercy for those foolish enough not to pay attention to it. That was exactly why we'd lured them from the 15 freeway down onto a narrow road.

"I'm three miles ahead of you." Morgan's husky voice filled the radio. He'd been our decoy up ahead in a van. "I've got four following me, but they're keepin' their distance. My guess, they don't have it."

"Head home, Morgan," Trigger ordered. "They'd never think you'd leave us alone out here."

"Will do."

Pfft! A bullet whisked past my ear.

"Shit, where'd he come from?" Brick cursed over the radio.

I ducked as he closed on my bike and whirled around in one fluid motion to whip my knife into the side of his throat that showed under his helmet. He went down in a puff of white. I laughed as the white powder filled the air.

"There it is," I called into my mic as I shortened the distance between me and Trigger. He held up a fist as I moved to ride next to him.

"Brick and Rail are in position." Trigger's voice was thick with excitement. We started up the steep hill and our engines roared, filling the desert air with fumes and the stench of revenge.

Once at the top, we cleared the bend and could see

the last of them. Four fuckers left. They were about to pay the ultimate price. No one stole from me.

My adrenaline ran high, and I grinned as the rush went through my body.

"My turn to play," I called into my mic and sped up. I could hear Trigger's dark laugh. He understood the need to get a fix. He had his own demons that fucking wanted to come out to play. I knew he needed to ease the darkness inside. We both had our reasons, and I was happy he respected mine.

One of the Stripe Backs took aim, but I shot his hand and made him swerve. He dropped his gun but gained control of his bike again.

Good.

His bike had nothing on mine. I straddled an MTT 420-RR which topped out at two hundred seventy-three miles per hour, making her the world's fastest bike. She was slick, black and red in color, with a Rolls Royce Allison turbine engine and aerodynamic carbon-fiber fairings. They only made five of these bikes a year, and I had the very first one that hit the market this year.

I moved into position and hit the gas then swung my leg out to kick the side of his bike and sent him spiraling into the bushes. I breathed in the rush that came with the knowledge he'd feel his bones break before he came to a stop.

I slowed, dropped my foot, and swung my bike

around. I headed back as Trigger and the others sped by. I cut the engine and leaned the bike on her stand, then angled it so the headlight lit him up. He moaned as I made my way toward him. My boots crunched against the packed dirt, and the sounds of scorpions as they scurried away made me briefly wonder if I should use one of them instead of my fists. *Not a chance.*

"Please," he held up a hand as I pulled out my gun. "No, please," he begged, and I noted his leg was bent to the side, obviously broken.

"This?" I held it up. "It's too kind." I tossed it on the ground and peered down at him. "I think it's time we had a chat." He flinched as I bent down to shine my phone on his leather cut. "Mm, seems I got myself a washed-up VP." I took note his patch had been removed, but the evidence was still there. I raised my eyebrows at him. Though I'd known these guys from an earlier time, I'd been gone far too long to keep up with who was who anymore. Not that it mattered. They were all the same—stupid, reckless, and a pain in our fucking asses as they often crossed over territory lines and messed with other people's business. I knew there'd been some changes in their ranks, and they'd gotten a new president, but until they sorted out their shit, I was going to deal with them my way.

"Fuck you!" he spat as his demeanor went from fear to fierce. "You wear the cut," he glared at the

Devil's Reach cut I wore, "but it doesn't mean shit if you can't back it up."

"This is true." I rubbed my chin to savor the moment. "One busted leg, you can survive," I shifted my weight, "but two?" I wrapped my arm around his good leg and lifted it as if I was about to twist the knee. "What the fuck were you doing at Dirty Deed and stealing my shit?" It was bad enough they'd stolen from me, but now my product was wasted, smeared all over the pavement mixed in blood and guts. The ultimate insult was they'd stolen it from Minnie's club.

"Do it!" he rasped. His face was red and sweaty as he dared me to show my hand.

"Happy to oblige." In a flash, I lifted and twisted his knee and popped it out of its socket. As he screamed, I stood with one foot on the knee and pressed down as I yanked his leg upward and heard the snap of the ligaments. He cursed and flailed about while I fed off his pain. "Answer my question."

"That all you got?" he managed to spit out, his mouth dripping with saliva.

"Oh, fuck no, there's two hundred and six bones to play with, and the night's still young." I used the heel of my boot to crunch down on two of his fingers.

"Ahh!" he cried out.

"Shall we count as we go?" I rolled his ankle and snapped the bone, and the sound mixed with his screams. "All you have to do is answer one question and all of this can be over."

"Bones heal," he hissed and tried to find his breath. I spotted something with my phone light, and inspiration struck.

"Wait here." I picked up my gun as I headed back to my bike then removed a plastic bottle from my bag. I used my knife to cut it in half.

"Fuck you, Grim Gates!" he managed to yell through the pain. I knew shock was already beginning to set in. I didn't like that idea; it could end things too fast. I hurried back over.

"You know," I looked around as I squatted next to him, the bottom half of the bottle in my palm, "Trigger told me this story once where he tied a man's feet to one end of his bike and his arms to another bike and they drove off in different directions." I kept my voice conversation-like. "The guy's body just ripped in two." I made the motion with my hands. "I've done a lot of things," I pulled out a joint and lit the tip, "but I haven't done that yet." I let out a relaxed breath and sent white smoke into the air. "Or maybe I should just utilize mother nature." I reached over and scooped the half bottle through a fire ant hill. Thousands of pissed off ants poured out of the top. Quickly, I opened the man's pants and tossed the lot on his junk.

"Holy shit!" Panic broke over his face as his brain tuned in to the fact that he was being stung in his most protected area. "Ah! Ah! Ahh!" His mouth opened wide as the angry ants had their way with him. The pain from his broken bones had nothing on what he now experienced. The desert was as ruthless as I was; perhaps that's why we got along so well.

I snapped my lighter and held the flame out as an offering if he'd just tell me the truth.

"It was just a distraction," he screamed.

"From what?" I ignored his distress.

"From, from, ah-ah-ah..." He tried to speak as he rolled around like a whale out of water. "He wanted us to find out what she knew..." His screams took over again as the ants did their thing.

"What *who* knew?" I puffed on my joint and felt it line my lungs with sweet relaxation.

"The girl."

"You already said that, asshole. Who? Minnie?"

"No." His eyes rolled back as he passed out. I slapped his face, and he came to again, but only for a second.

"Who sent you and what girl? Fuck." I pulled out my phone, but before I could press in any numbers, Trigger and the guys pulled up.

"We got jack shit from the others." Rail hopped off his bike and removed his helmet.

"Well, a bullet in the mouth'll do that." Brick rolled his eyes as he admired the man at my feet. "Are those fire ants?" He stepped back quickly, and Rail covered his crotch with a curse.

"Morgan's got a few snakes behind him. They took the bait." Trigger was the last to get off his bike. "Anything?"

"Why do you look like that?" Brick's finger made a circle at my expression.

"Because they only took the drugs as a distraction." I stood. "He said they wanted to know what the girl knew."

"Who? Minnie?" His eyes darkened.

"No, someone else." The tension in Brick's shoulders lifted. "He mentioned they wanted to know what *she* knew."

"Who?" Trigger flipped his mohawk out of his face. "One of the girls they messed up?"

I shook my head. "I don't know, but they sent enough snakes to make me think she's important."

"I'd ask Minnie if any of her girls have been acting weird or off in any way." I could tell that comment hit too close for Brick's liking. He'd hate anyone to mess with his girl. He and Minnie were joined at the hip.

"Didn't give up anythin' else?" Trigger chin pointed at the guy on the ground.

"Nah, the ants got enthusiastic at that point." I sucked back the last of the joint and dropped it on the fucker's face then used my boot to snuff it out. Then I checked my watch and noted the time.

"Cooper's scraping up what's left of the shit on the road. He's covered in coke." Brick spat. "We'll dump him at the Stripe Backs' club, so they know we got 'em."

"Good." I nodded and wished I had a little longer with my guy.

"We got one left," Trigger huffed and pointed over his shoulder, "strapped to my bike. Got time for one more?"

I smirked and sent a text to my driver.

Grim: Hold plane. I'll be late.

A couple hours later, I turned off my bike and removed my helmet. I swung my leg over the saddle and stretched my back as Louis took the helmet from my outstretched hand. He handed me a wet wipe, and I mopped my face. The driver stood next to the car, patiently waiting. Trigger pulled in next to me and turned off his engine. He stayed seated.

"Louis." Trigger nodded as a greeting, and Louis quietly greeted Trigger in return. He knew better than to offer his hand. Trigger was the President of the Devil's Reach MC in Santa Monica, California. He had one hell of a dark past, and at one time it had clashed with mine. Things worked out, and we've been friends ever since. We shared a healthy respect for and rather enjoyed the darker side of life.

"See you back at the hotel?" Louis turned to me. I nodded. He was to ride my bike back to Vegas. He pulled on the helmet, climbed on my bike, and carefully started the engine. He knew if anything happened to her, he shouldn't return home.

"That's just what I needed." I grinned at Trigger as Louis drove off. The amped up feeling I couldn't seem to shake had fizzled away.

"By the way, just a warnin'." Trigger gave a *come close* nod and lowered his voice. "After the takedown in Mexico, we went back in after Blackstone left." He spat and looked at me, his eyes in slits. "We had a bit of fun then burned the fuckin' place to the ground. Charred the lot of 'em."

He referred to a few weeks before when a US military team we had connections with had been given the green light to take down a tier one Mexican Cartel. The Team had pulled in some favors, and the Devil's Reach Club and the head of the Italian Mafia had stepped up. They all had their own reasons for wanting in on that action. I had the pleasure of killing the Cartel kingpin himself, Martin Castillo, but for very different reasons that I held close to my chest. Only a few knew the truth, and I intended to keep it that way.

"Guess I missed a good light show, then." I grinned at him. "We probably made history on that one." I was sure it was one of the most successful takedowns in Mexican history.

"Indeed," he growled then leaned back on his bike. I could tell there was more. He spat then looked at me. "The fire held things up a bit, but we got word they identified Castillo's body. The shit will soon hit the news."

That should be interesting. "I appreciate the heads up."

"You should have let me kill him."

"Nah, it needed to be me."

"Mm." He rolled his neck and shrugged. "We had history. It would've felt good to slice his fuckin' throat." But I could see he'd already accepted that I'd taken his kill and he'd let it go.

"I owe you one." I pulled out my phone, and Trigger chuckled in agreement.

"Now you're back, you should join us more often." Trig flipped his Zippo lighter open and closed. "Keep things normal." His voice remained low so the others couldn't hear. Trigger was a private man and rarely let anyone into his world. My mind swung to his wife, Tess, and I almost laughed. She was a rare one for sure.

"Yeah, I might just take you up on that. I'm here now, permanently. It's been too long since we've had a good ride."

"Agreed." He started up his bike and left a trail of dust as he sped away to rendezvous with his men.

I headed toward my driver, who opened the door for me.

"Good evening, sir." Cartwright held up a garment bag. "Shall I take your cut?"

"Yes, thank you." I slid the MC leather cut off my back. He nodded at my bloody hands and handed me another wet wipe.

"Was your evening eventful?"

"Very."

"Do you feel better?"

"I do." I flashed him a wicked smile as I climbed into the back of the limo and changed from jeans, a t-shirt, and boots to a well-crafted suit and soft leather shoes.

Just another day of living my kind of life.

"Yes?" I answered a call as I secured my cufflinks.

"I thought you were going to take the meeting at nine via Zoom?" my father asked in his no-nonsense tone.

"My last meeting ran long." I checked my hands and rubbed my swollen knuckles. I fished out some ice cubes and dropped them into a glass and pressed my knuckles against it. "Not to worry. I let them know, and we re-scheduled for tomorrow at two."

"Oh, I guess my calendar didn't update." I heard some hard taps to his keyboard. "Cameron has a new client coming in, tomorrow morning at eleven. The guy owns Imalta Oil Industries, and Cameron wants you there since you're so tight with," he paused, and I heard him speak quietly to someone, "with Italy."

"I'm sure Cameron does." I rolled my eyes. "Is he aware I'm here in person and that it won't be a video call?" I couldn't help but grin at the thought that my unexpected early arrival would fuck with his head. Cameron Tame was a ruthless lawyer and had worked for our family for the past ten years. He'd come in just as I started to work internationally. Though he was great at what he did, we were oil and water, plus he sometimes forgot he worked for us and not the other way around.

"No, I figured it would be more fun to witness that in person." He chuckled along with me. "But truth be told, son, we're all looking forward to having you back permanently." I knew he wanted to say more, but he knew it wouldn't be wise.

"I am too." I fixed my tie and thought how nice it was going to be to work from home. I'd been traveling so much over the past ten years, mostly in Mexico and Italy, that I was more than ready to settle into life in Vegas again.

"A lot's changed since you left eighteen months ago, and Lord knows Knox wants out of dealing with your hotel build. That boy has his head in other places, and being in charge of building a hotel isn't one of them."

"Mm." I rolled my eyes. My baby brother didn't

have much interest in any of our businesses. The only thing he enjoyed was spending the money they brought in. Dad thought since I had so much going on in Mexico that it might spark Knox's interest if he took the lead on the project. The land was already purchased, but he would be my eyes and ears and make some of the early decisions with the developer on my hotel. I'd been skeptical but went with it. We both soon realized it wasn't his thing, but at least he'd hung in there. I kept him going with constant contact and regular visits. The last stretch of time in Mexico had been long, and I knew Knox was happy I was on my way back.

Taking out the drug lord Martin Castillo had served me well. I could continue to move the highest quality drugs from Mexico through the US and straight to Vegas without his interference. It was incredibly important to make sure I could provide this for my guests. The alternative would open the gate for others to come in, and I'd lose that income. Though I had my thumb on many business opportunities, the drug trade was the most lucrative. Besides, any loss of control in one area would affect our bottom line overall, and it wasn't in my nature to lose control of anything.

"Where are you now?" Dad broke my thoughts.

"I'm on the way to the plane. I flew into LA last night but stopped to help out Trigger."

"And?"

"And it was a much-needed visit." I glanced out the window and saw we'd arrived. "We're at the plane now."

"Do you see Leo?" I smiled as I saw my other brother Leo in the plane's window.

"I do."

"Good." I heard him tap away on his keyboard again. Dad might be a ruthless businessman, but he sure as hell loved his sons.

"Dad, I'll be home shortly. Can we talk then?"

"Looking forward to it." He paused. "Remember to change into your jacket."

"Already done." I hung up and stepped out as the driver opened my door.

Cartwright filled me in as I walked toward the steps of the plane. "Jet is fueled. It'll be a nice, short flight to Las Vegas. The skies are clear."

"Great, thank you."

He handed me my personal bag. "Safe flight, sir." With that, he turned and headed up the stairs.

Just as he disappeared inside the plane, vehicles could be heard.

"Grim?" Jesse, my right-hand man, stepped quickly to my side as two blacked out limos approached. "Were we expecting company?"

"Yeah." I gritted my teeth and tried to pull up the energy this was going to take. "Sorry in advance."

"Ah, fuck." Jesse dropped his head.

"Yeah."

I glanced back at the plane and saw my brother look in my direction. He must have heard the limos pull up. I waved to show him it was okay.

"That's not who I think it is," Jesse moaned.

"It is."

"Fuck me, there isn't enough whiskey on this flight, Grim," he muttered as we saw a hand appear. I watched the light flicker off the multi-bracelets on the wrist above that hand as it reached out to take the driver's.

"Hello, darling," Jenelle Borrows purred as her hungry gaze slid down my body and back up again. "I'm so glad Daddy called you and you had space for me on your flight. I hope it wasn't too much trouble."

Jesse slowly shook his head; I knew he was no fan of Jenelle's. My brothers and Jesse only tolerated her because they knew I had to.

"Not at all." I allowed my eyes a quick look at her long legs and thought about how I wouldn't mind going a few rounds with her even if she liked to keep it pretty tame.

She took my left hand and rubbed her thumb over my ring finger. I shot her a look. She could hitch a ride, but I wasn't going to put up with her usual bullshit on her imagined future with me.

"A hundred she's picked out the wedding invites already," Jesse muttered behind me.

"When Daddy said you were flying out of John Wayne airport, I moved my girls' weekend down here so I wouldn't miss you." Jenelle's father, Bruce, was a powerful man in the business world and one who was important to know. He did business with our family, and it brought a lot of clients to our hotel. Indulge had benefited just recently when he brought a high roller into our casino who dropped a magnitude of money in just twenty-four hours.

I knew he was great for our business, but it came at a personal cost. I knew he wanted to see me marry his baby girl. He wasn't the only businessman we had to tolerate who had ulterior motives when it came to their daughters. A future that included one of the Gates brothers brought dollar signs to their eyes. So, when I got an unexpected call from him, that she needed a lift, I didn't doubt he already knew I was on my way home and had checked out my flight plan.

She pressed a hand to her cleavage and looked up at me from behind her long lashes. "What can we possibly do in that huge plane all to ourselves?" She smiled wide and fanned herself as she headed toward the plane.

Jenelle, at five foot ten, worked as a model. Her straight blonde hair fell to her shoulders, and her body was rail thin without a single imperfection. Her high cheekbones and full lips looked sexy as hell in her photos but less so in person. I wish she hadn't had them filled. They'd looked better natural, but I knew the pressure the industry put on them to look a certain way.

I'd made the mistake of dating her a few times since we met on my twenty-third birthday. I should have known I was tempting fate, but I loved sex, and she was willing. She was fun between the sheets, but I didn't want fun. What I craved, she could never deliver, so I held back. She'd made it known she wanted to be Mrs. Gates someday. I wasn't totally against the vision, but I had a lot of life to enjoy before I hung up my balls for good.

"Slippery slope, man," Jesse warned with a curled lip. He'd seen me adjust my erection.

I studied her backside as she walked for a brief second, then side-eyed Jesse. "I could use a little reliever, and sounds like she feels the same." I grinned at him and waved for her man to bring her luggage.

"Give me five to freshen up, and I'll be all yours." Jenelle swung her Prada bag over her shoulder and walked with a swing in her hips down the aisle.

"Seriously?" Jesse snickered behind me. He wasn't going to give up easily. "I thought you left Malibu Barbie months ago."

"I just need a little nightcap," I shot back at him. "What's the harm in that?"

"She's probably friggin' chipped you, or even worse, her father did. It's why he knew where you were." Jesse shook his head. "Ten grand that this time she'll have you shopping for wedding rings."

"She's good for one thing, Jesse, and that's where it ends," I assured him as I felt my pants strain. I knew he was right. Jenelle had a way of getting what she wanted, thanks to her father.

"Seriously, Grim, she's smart." He put a hand on my arm. "She and her father would love nothing more than to cement your family name to theirs."

"You done?" I glared, but he knew I heard him. I didn't give a shit right now.

"For now." He had to laugh as I swaggered down the aisle after her and it lightened the mood.

"Grim." My younger brother, Leo, barred my way. He stood with folded arms and a look of distaste on his face. "Why's she here?"

"She needed a ride," Jesse replied for me.

"How, I mean, seriously?" Leo rolled his eyes. "She's like a piranha when it comes to you, Grim."

"Maybe, but I could use the welcome home gift." I shrugged.

"I was your welcome home gift." He owl-blinked at what he'd just said. "Okay, well, that came out all wrong." He rubbed his face, and I pulled him in for a hug.

"It's been too long, little brother."

"It has." Leo grinned and slapped my back, and we

both took a moment to rejoice being together again. "Grim, we really need to talk before we land."

"We do." I turned to Jesse. "I need you to preoccupy Malibu."

"Yeah, yeah." He knew better than to push back again.

We both sat in the plush ivory seats. I took a moment to enjoy the beauty of the plane. The stitching in the seats matched the mahogany table between us. God, I loved my life.

"Did you and Trigger fuck up?" Leo pointed to my battered knuckles, and I gave him my full attention.

"Just some asshole with a death wish," I huffed as I took the single malt from the flight attendant. "Some Stripe Backs caused shit at Minnie's club. Ended up with two battered girls." He gave me a look of shock. "Yeah, black eyes and one with a broken jaw. They stole some of my coke, but we caught them on their way back to LA."

"Oh, shit." He shook his head in disbelief. He knew I looked out for Minnie. She did the same for me, so this hit close to home. "How much coke did they get?"

"Not much, but that wasn't the real reason they were there. Sounds like some girl caused trouble, and they were really looking for her. Whatever the hell it was, we'll find out soon enough."

"And now you and Trigger have dealt with them. Will this blow back on you?"

"I doubt it." I shrugged. I knew Leo had been stressed enough the last while, and I didn't want to add to it. "If it does, we'll shut it down pretty quick."

"Good." He rubbed his lips then leaned down and ran a hand through his mop of hair. He seemed ready to change the topic. He started to speak, but her voice stopped him.

"Grim?" Jenelle pushed by Jesse, who threw up his hands behind her. She looked impatient.

Fuck.

"Can't family time be over?" Jenelle stuck her lip out like a child, and I rolled my eyes. "It's Nellie's turn." Leo bared his teeth at her nickname for herself.

"Go back to the room, Jenelle. I'm almost finished."

"Fine." She turned and made a motion for Jesse to move. "This plane's much too crowded."

"Remember that the next time you fly with us," Jesse grunted, and I cracked my knuckles.

"Give me this, then we'll talk." I shrugged at Leo as I propelled her toward the bedroom. I knew I needed time to talk with my brother, but I needed sex more.

Jenelle liked sex to be romantic. Lots of give and take shit. I didn't do well with that.

"Time to savor me." She put a pink coated fingertip to her lips then opened the first few buttons on her low-cut blouse. I knew she wanted me to undo the rest of the buttons and go slow. I tossed her on the bed and made an effort to give her what she wanted. A short time later, I got some relief, but my blood still pounded in my head. I tried to tamp down the flair of anger at how I had to hold myself back.

I reached for her, incredibly pent-up, and tried to get my head back in the game. It didn't help that she rolled on her stomach and began to tell me about her girls' weekend.

Christ, it was how I imagined married sex would be. I looked down at her and wanted to scream. She yawned sleepily, and I wanted to put my hands around her throat. This had been one big fucking mistake.

"Fuck." I quickly changed and left the room to join the others.

"You look…" I glared at Jesse, who shut his mouth.

"She's fuckin' asleep." I wasn't in the mood, and Jesse looked away.

"Deborah called." Leo changed the topic, and Jesse got up and took a seat a bit away from us, grumbling something about e-mails. Good. I wanted more time with my brother before we landed.

"Oh?" Deborah was my eyes and ears for any property that came up for sale on the strip. There was one I particularly wanted, and she knew I'd do whatever was necessary to get it. She was also someone who had her ear to the ground and would often pass along information she thought I might need to be aware of. Deborah was extremely important to my business.

"She wanted you to know she's coming to Vegas in the next few weeks. She'll confirm the dates shortly."

"Good." I checked my calendar and was pleased to see my secretary had already added that she was tentatively coming on my calendar. "Did she give you anything?"

"No, she kept the call vague."

"Excellent." Less was more when it came to our kind of business. If Deborah was quiet, it meant she knew something.

"Are you lookin' forward to coming home?"

I nodded. "I am." I wanted to spend more time with my family.

"Happy to hear it."

"How do you really feel about taking over the Mexico account for the next six months?"

He looked away and pressed his lips together. "I won't lie, stepping into your shoes isn't something I take lightly, but I need to prove to you and the family I can do it."

"You don't need to prove anything to me." My phone buzzed, but I ignored it. "You got this, Leo. Just keep your head up, watch your back, and remember what I taught you."

"And when in doubt, shoot first then call you." He smiled, but it didn't quite reach his eyes. I looked at him and wondered what I was missing.

"Remember, you only need to go to Mexico twice, and the rest can be handled from Vegas."

That seemed to settle his nerves, at least for the time being. I wished I hadn't had to come back early and have Leo finish things up for me, but it was necessary, and he'd been adamant that I go home and let him finish up. I figured he wanted the experience.

Leo, at twenty-seven, was three years younger than I was, and by all accounts my favorite in the family. I considered him my understudy, as he was just as eager to learn the business as I had been. Leo just needed to embrace his darker side more often when he had to get things done. I knew he would find that out on his own soon enough.

Our brother Knox, on the other hand, couldn't be more different than Leo or me. At twenty-five, he was a lover, not a fighter. Where I craved breaking bones and bloody knuckles, he just wanted to sit poolside in his designer sunglasses with a fancy drink while he studied the ladies. Knox wanted to live life on the high side. He wanted to party first and worry about the business later. I couldn't understand it, and Leo and I often talked about it, but it didn't mean we loved him any less. I'd always been close with my siblings, and my being gone so much over the past ten years had put a strain on all of us. We knew it couldn't be helped; it was just the way we had to live our lives. Everyone had to sacrifice something. I thought again how happy I was to have a chance to reconnect.

"Good," he answered, sounding relieved. As I sipped my drink, a feeling came over me as he started to tap his ring on the table. It was an old nervous habit he had. Something else was on his mind.

"Out with it." I waved, and his gaze shot to mine. A sudden heaviness filled my chest at his expression, and I knew something wasn't right. "What?"

"Dad's sick again," he blurted, and I stilled. "Sorry I lied." He let out a shaky breath. "I know I said I wanted to learn how to close some accounts down and finish things up for you, but I couldn't risk anyone hearing the truth. I didn't know how to get you back sooner."

"I see." My stomach took a nosedive as I digested Leo's words and what they meant. "And Dad told you this?"

"Well, no." I looked across at him. "I saw an email from his doctor. It came in when he needed me to fix his Excel spreadsheet." We both rolled our eyes at that; dad was always messing up his spreadsheet formulas. I could see the pain of what he told me weighed heavily on his chest. "I, ah, need you to come back, Grim." I reached over and grabbed his arm, and we both took a moment. I knew there was a lot to consider, what this could mean to all of us. When I tried to pull my arm back, he grabbed it, and I felt a chill pass between us.

"What is it, Leo?"

"There's something else. I think I'm seeing something, but I'm not sure."

"Okay." I caught Jesse's eyes on me. He seemed to sense something, but he didn't dare interrupt. "What do you mean?"

"Just," he lowered his voice as the attendant walked by, "keep your eyes open, will you? Things seem one way, but call it a gut feeling, I'm not so sure they aren't going the other." He looked into my eyes.

"As in something bad is coming?"

"Or is already there."

Leo had never been one for dramatics. He never embellished things. In fact, he underplayed most situations, so for him to behave this way was totally out of character.

"Can you elaborate?"

"No. I want to see if you get the same vibe I do. If you do, it should stay between us until we figure out a plan, okay? I need you to promise that Dad's news, what I'm feeling, all of it stays here. Everything has to stay the same, like normal. Promise?"

"I promise." He had my word. "And what if I don't see or feel what you did?"

"Then I'm wrong."

"Your gut is never wrong, Leo."

"Up until now, no." He shrugged and slowly let go of my arm as he leaned back in his chair. Usually, I'd demand Leo tell me exactly what was going on, but I respected what he was trying to do. He thought he'd sensed or seen something and wanted to bring me in with fresh eyes and a clear head so as not to set me up to look for something that might not be there. I was proud of him. It was important to make sure we all stayed alert, especially now.

"All right, I'll keep my eyes and ears open, watch and listen. If there's anything there, I'll pick up on it." I nodded. He put a finger to his lips as the captain came on and announced we were about to land in Las Vegas.

"Jesse, go wake Jenelle."

"With pleasure." He smirked, and Leo chuckled as we made our way down the stairs.

"Tell me she's not driving with us too."

"No," I shook my head as Jesse hurried past us, "I made sure her driver would be here." I pointed across the way to where her car was parked.

"Everything okay, boss?" Jesse asked as he opened the car door for me.

"Not sure yet. We'll talk later," I said quietly, and he glanced at Leo, who opened the opposite door, about to get inside.

"Grim!" Jenelle carefully picked her way down the plane stairs in her heels.

"Your driver's here." I pointed to the limo.

"Oh," she looked disappointed, "okay, well, call—"

I slammed the car door and let out a heavy sigh.

"You invited her," Jesse muttered from the front seat.

"Not by choice." I looked over at Leo, who now smiled like everything was fine and back to normal. We were good at pretending; it was how our world was, how deals got made.

I wasn't ready to go directly home when we arrived. I needed to drop in to check the progress of my baby. I'd been working on my dream for the past few years—a hotel of my own on the Strip. The ground had been broken while I was away, and although I'd been back several times to check on the progress of the construction, Leo had mentioned a few things, and I needed to see it for myself. I dropped Jesse and Leo off at Indulge and had Cartwright take me to the site.

"Sure is nice to have you back, sir." Cartwright had been my driver since I was ten. I smiled at him as he looked at me in the rear-view mirror. I trusted him with my life, and he trusted me with his. "Life's been a bit dull without you."

"Somehow I doubt that." I laughed and waited for him to stop the car near the entrance.

"Take your time and enjoy your work. It's truly the finest," he said as I exited the vehicle. He held out a bottle of my favorite whiskey and a joint. "I have a sudoku that I'm determined to finish."

"It's good to be back." I lit the joint from the flame he held up and took the bottle from him. Taking the steps three at a time, I pushed through the heavy plastic and took in the massive space. A rush of excitement filled me. This project was to be the sister to my father's hotel Indulge. I planned to call it Secrets.

I headed toward where the bar was going to be and slid the cork from the bottle as smoke circled around my fingers.

I could almost hear the music, the liquor flowing, and the excitement of those approved to be here. I took a swig of the whiskey and let it warm my insides.

It's good to be home.

Suddenly, a scream from somewhere up above stopped me cold.

TWO

KENNA LODGE

Bang! The kickback on the gun snapped me into a parallel universe where everything went still. I felt my soul leave then slam back into my body at the speed of light.

The now wide-eyed man lay on top of me. Those eyes locked onto mine, then the light fizzled from them and he went limp. The smell of expensive brandy and gun smoke nearly made me vomit, and I thrashed about as my brain fought to catch up.

"Get off me!" I pushed with all my might and rolled his heavy body off mine. I leapt to my feet and dropped the gun I still held like it was on fire. I side-stepped the patch of oozing blood. "No, no, no." I looked down at my outfit and was thankful my skirt was black. I could feel the wetness of the man's blood, but it wasn't obvious.

"Kenna, what the fuck, are you—" Minnie gasped. "What the hell's happening today? Is my fucking club cursed?"

"Minnie, I…" My words trickled off, and I wondered how much I should share. "I didn't mean to kill him." I wasn't sure what I came here to do.

"Jasper, bring Duggy!" Minnie called, and a moment later, two of her bouncers came in. They dropped a tarp, put the dead body on top, and rolled him up like a burrito. Then he was gone. All that could be seen now was a puddle of blood on the floor. I knew that would soon vanish as well. I didn't have time to appreciate just how fast it had all disappeared.

"Tracy," she said into her radio, "go check the dancer for room three." She looked over at me, and I took a moment to meet her eyes. "You want to tell me what that was about?"

"Nope." I grabbed my bag that had been thrown across the room then marched up to her and took her hand. "Thank you for letting me know he was here."

"Who is he, exactly?"

"I need you to do one more thing, Min. Take this to the grave." I searched her eyes. "Not even Brick can know."

"Kenna, this isn't my first rodeo. Disposing of

assholes may be a skill I have, but I deserve to know what's going on."

"Yeah, you do. I know you do, but for now—and I'm a shitty friend for asking this—but for now, I need you to trust that I got this." She pursed her lips and slit her eyes as she studied me.

"Fine, I got you until you don't."

"Thanks. I love you." I peeked out the door and hoped to hell his buddies were still enjoying the other rooms. Minnie's club offered a lot of options. "Talk later." I hurried away before she could ask any more questions.

I tried not to think about my tacky shoes as I rushed down the hall. I suddenly bumped shoulders with someone, I didn't look up to see who it was. I turned my face away and was out the back door almost at a full run. A bouncer I recognized looked me up and down.

"You good?"

"I'm okay, Nate." I hid my hands in my pockets. I walked around the corner and saw a town car with three huge men standing around it. One was bald, and he stroked his bushy mustache. I backed up then broke into a full sprint across the parking lot toward the lights of the Vegas strip. I felt weightless as my mind moved in slow motion as though it had to buffer what just happened. My mind might have been slow, but not my body, as everything around me blurred as I ran like the wind. My heels beat the pavement, cars zipped by me, until I came to the sign that read B&P's Construction. I pivoted by the sign, through the giant piles of dirt, to the seven-foot chain link fence that separated me from my alibi. I pulled back the corner of the fence by the light post and slipped through. I gulped in a few breaths as a small sense of security washed over me.

"Oh, Jesus, Jesus, Jesus," I repeated to myself as tears pricked my eyes. I felt the rush of what just happened slam into my body, the air squeezed out of my lungs with every beat of my heart. A roll of nausea broke over me, but I forced it back down with sheer will. Adrenaline and panic were a bad combination when you needed to think straight. I closed my eyes, but the moment I did, I began to relive it. "No!" I mentally kicked myself back in shape. I had no time to waste.

I pulled out my phone, took a deep breath, and with slippery fingers I called the one person I knew wouldn't question my story. I really wished I could call Morgan, but I couldn't, not for this. *Deep breaths, Kenna.*

"Ew!" In the low lighting I could see my blood-stained hands. I grabbed a couple tissues from my purse and did my best to wipe them as the phone rang.

"There she is," he chuckled, "I know you hate the Dave Matthews Band, but they covered some KISS songs too."

"Any band that covers those two bands in one set

should be sold on the black market," I joked as I tried like hell to conceal my heavy breathing. "Besides, I did tell you I wasn't going to stay out late tonight." I made my way toward the hotel as I prayed Bobby the security guard wasn't doing his rounds.

"You just left so quickly. I thought something was wrong."

"Nope." I dodged the construction on the ground level. I had made it this far in my new shoes and didn't want to break a heel at this point. I took a moment to pat myself on the back that I hadn't put on my stilettos.

"You're the only one I know who would leave a bar to go design." I could sense Dale's eyeroll through the phone.

"When inspiration hits, it hits." I pushed the sheet of plastic back to step inside the soon-to-be hottest, most posh hotel on the Vegas Strip. I leaned my back against one of the walls and felt my heart pound against my chest. *Focus.* "Besides, I can't be a hostess for the rest of my life."

"You're hella talented and drop dead frickin' gorgeous. You can do both."

"Says the guy who couldn't stay faithful with me for three months."

"I might be a hoe with shitty morals, but I can appreciate a fine-lookin' woman when I see one."

"Thanks." I forced a chuckle as I hurried up the unfinished steps to the third floor. I stepped into the dining area that would look over the Strip. An unfinished structure such as Secrets Hotel was a happy place for me. As I spoke to Dale, I readjusted my focus and forced my head back on straight.

"You know Minnie's going to want you."

"Doesn't mean I should automatically expect her to." Minnie had told me to show her what I would do if she owned this hotel. She was considering an expansion to her club and maybe even to Trigger's underground fight ring. This hotel only had some walls up. It was still very much a skeleton, and that meant a clean slate, no influence of any kind to mess with my head.

"Just be careful. I hate you going there alone." I closed my eyes and fought off the shakes.

"You know I'm here, and Bobby, the head of security this month, will be doing his rounds soon, so I'll touch base with him then."

"Good. Text me when you get home, though, okay? I also sent you up my latest dish, so I expect feedback sooner rather than later."

"I will. You know I will." I rolled my eyes but loved that he cared for me in his own jacked-up way. Dale was the head chef at Indulge and was known worldwide for his wagyu steak, always seared to perfection. A few years ago, he discovered my refined palate and awarded me the pleasure of taste testing the many new dishes he developed in his kitchen. Too bad his dating skills didn't match his culinary skills.

I needed everything to be just right; my alibi had to be flawless.

When I got to the perfect spot, I rubbed my still-sticky hands on the underside of my skirt then pulled my sketch pad out and nibbled on the end of a pencil as I forced myself to let my ideas flow for how I would set the lighting in this place. Dale would ask to see what I'd done. I loved that he was supportive, but tonight I really wished I could just go home. Straight lines were nearly impossible to do with shaky hands, so I did more shading.

I forced my head to clear. I wanted it to be seductive with a smidge of questionable seediness, so it needed a dark undertone. I wanted a feeling of "just by being here, you're committing a sin." I shivered at the idea. It was a simple word for me to play off.

Sinful.

I jumped when a police siren bounced off the walls and went straight through my nerves. I moved to the ledge and peered over to see it wasn't heading in the direction I'd just come from.

"Come on, Kenna, you need something to prove you were here." I talked my way through my panic, knowing my phone was tracking my every move.

I pressed pencil to paper and began to sketch out the lines of the room. The lights from the nearby hotels lit the room perfectly for the task. They cast just enough light for me to see the page and the room. I tucked the pencil away in a makeshift bun to keep my hair back from my face and fished around for my colored pencils. I found a deep orange and lined the bottom of the windows with a warm under glow. I moved to a black and made marks on the wall to show where the leather would connect. The walls would be made to look like leather headboards, and photos would dangle from chains to add a BDSM illusion without it being too obvious. Cast iron rods would display goblets that would hold real fire encased in glass bowls. I could see it all.

Between the jacked-up adrenaline and my drawing, I found myself getting turned on at how sexy the room would be. *Shit, if Minnie didn't use this idea, I might use it for myself.*

A strange feeling passed through me suddenly. I wasn't alone. I covered my mouth with my hand, but the moment I smelled the blood, vomit crept up and threatened to show itself. *Focus!* I pivoted on my heel to scan the room. The plastic fluttered in the breeze and made a soft sound, but that was all. I squinted to look into the dark areas, but I couldn't see anything. I shook it off after a moment and went back to my drawing, but my hands shook too much. A moment later, movement caught my eye. *Bobby?*

"Bobby?" I called. Nothing. "It's Kenna. I won't be much longer," I reassured him in case he didn't hear me the first time. I slid my book into my bag and tossed the pencils in the flap and went to find him.

I jumped as something fell, and then I saw him. He was dressed in a zip-up jacket, and it was pulled up over his mouth. It took my brain half a second to process who it was.

No.

My blood went cold, and my muscles locked in place as a feeling of dread went through me.

Run.

I backed up a few steps, then darted toward the plastic sheet that would be kitchen doors someday. As my hands tore at the plastic, I felt him and knew he was close.

I looked for something to use as a weapon. I wished to hell the construction workers had left a hammer or nail gun laying around.

My heart was in my throat; it beat so fast I could barely breathe.

"Come here, you bitch!" he screamed, and I looked around for something, anything to use, but there was nothing. His hand swiped at my arm, and my bag caught in his hold. I released my grip on it as I let go an ear-piercing scream. He threw my purse aside with another curse and lunged for me. I screamed again as loudly as I could.

"No!" I planted my hands against a workbench and

drilled my heel into his stomach. He doubled over, and I saw my keys on the floor. I scrambled for them, and once I felt the cold metal in my hands, I bolted for the stairs. My heels clicked loudly on the marble floor. "Bobby!" I called, hoping he was nearby. Normally, he wouldn't be far when I was on site, but of course this time he didn't know I was here. "Bobby, please help me!"

I came to a halt as the man blocked my path. What little light there was soon faded as I dodged him and ran to my left where the service elevators would be. A huge, dark hole greeted me, and I realized my mistake. The open walls and darkness below allowed the wind to swipe at my face and reminded me I was still two floors above ground level.

"Shit." I heaved to breathe as a hand covered my mouth and another wrapped around my stomach. I cried out again and drove my heel into his sneakered foot. He jerked backward and let go of me but only for a brief second. As quickly as I was released, I was whirled around and pushed hard against an exposed beam.

"There's nowhere to run, baby girl." He pulled out a gun and ran his hand down my bare thigh. I batted it away as my chest heaved in despair. He pointed the gun at my face, and I noticed the small edging of a tattoo on his chest when his shirt moved. "You think you're so smart? That you're some badass!" he screamed in my face. "You're nothing but a daddy's girl who had a stroke of luck!"

"I'm sorry." I could barely get the words out, I was so scared. "I'm sorry. I didn't mean to—" His hand moved up and a brand-new dose of fear coursed through me.

"What do you want?" I managed to choke out.

"Just a taste, or…" He came closer, and I somehow lifted my chin. "I like your fight."

"Screw you!" I hissed, and he backhanded me across the cheek.

Ouch. I blinked back the fuzzy spots as I absorbed the pain. When our eyes met again, I knew this could be the moment all women, particularly in Vegas, feared.

The fact I came here to give myself a damn alibi almost brought out a hysterical laugh, but it sounded more like a hiccup when it escaped my lips. Why hadn't I just gone home?

Suddenly, something shiny flashed, and the next moment his grip on me relaxed. I stepped back in confusion and saw a knife stuck into the side of his neck. His eyes were wide with shock as he slumped onto the concrete floor.

My arms locked in place around my middle as I forced myself to lift my head. I met a pair of steel-colored eyes. The smell of weed found its way past my tangled thoughts. A small cross below his eye stood out in the light as he squinted at me. My breathing hitched as he reached out to take my chin. He tilted it up slowly and turned my head to inspect my battered cheek. As hard as it was, I didn't break down. I couldn't. My chest heaved as I tried to get my wits about me.

It was too dark to see, and before I could say anything, those eyes turned away and he let go of my head. I felt strangely adrift at the loss of contact. In an instant, he was gone in the darkness as if he'd dissolved into thin air. I was utterly alone and terrified, unable to think. I didn't waste another moment. I ran from the place like the hounds of hell were at my heels until I reached my car that was parked down the street from Minnie's club. My fingers shook as I fumbled with my keys. I didn't even remember the doors would unlock without having to push the button. I opened the door, stumbled inside, and tore off down the road. As I raced by the security hut, Bobby poked his head out, clearly unaware that I was there or what had just happened.

"You're fine, you're fine," I told myself repeatedly as I got ready for work the next day. I'd barely slept. I patted my face with the cotton towel and looked in the mirror. I knew I couldn't tell a soul about what happened or… I squeezed my eyes shut but winced at the pain in my cheek. I'd popped a pain pill, but it still hadn't kicked in.

I should've known better, but what choice did I have? If I hadn't…*stop.*

I should've come up with a better story of my whereabouts. I knew they could ping the location of my call to Dale and see I hadn't lied, but the thought of what could have happened mixed with what did was all too much. I tossed the towel with a small sob.

I could have been killed just from being reckless and alone on private property, and who the hell was the man who'd saved me? He'd make a good witness, one who could testify I was there. But oh, yeah, he'd just killed someone, so that wasn't going to happen. Though, that wasn't someone random he was with …

Breathe, Kenna. I pushed my freakout back into the box in my head and slammed the door shut. In my line of work and with my kind of family, you saw a lot of things that might stay in your head, but you had to shove it out the back door if you wanted to survive. The people I was surrounded with had the kind of money that made them untouchable.

I popped open my concealer and dabbed the brush to my face, trying my best to hide the red mark. I thought I did a pretty good job. It wasn't the first time I'd ever been hit, and it probably wouldn't be my last. Life in the fast lane had its challenges.

Though I had my own house outside the city, I spent most of my time living in the hotel just below the owners' floors. Given the hours I worked, the drive to and from my home simply wasn't feasible. Plus, I felt safe there. You had to have special clearance to access my floor, and even higher clearance to go to the owners' floors.

I flicked through the outfits in my walk-in closet. Most of my clothes were really just scraps of fabric because this was Vegas and less was everything. As hostess for one of the hottest hotels on the Strip, my kind of clientele came with a cost, and that cost was my body up for show.

Annoyed I couldn't find anything I liked, I pushed a button, and the rack of clothes slid into the wall and another came forward. It was the start of summer, which meant I could wear my favorite color. White. Perfect. I spotted an outfit I liked and inspected the neckline then folded it over my arm. Now for some panties and a pushup bra. I was blessed with double D cups, no surgery needed, thanks to my mother's fabulous figure. She took the time to teach me from an early age how to care for my body. Eat right, work out, look after my skin, etcetera… and though it might seem vain to some, it had helped me in this industry. Now if only I didn't have to work under my father's best friend, Walter Wallace, I'd be a happy woman. Working for Wallace was just as difficult sometimes as working for my father, just in a different way, and his son Jayden made my head hurt.

My phone rang, and I tapped the screen.

"Good morning, Kenna." Zara, my father's secretary, sounded upbeat today.

"Morning, Zara. What's the shitstorm today?"

"Your father needs you in a meeting on the twentieth in fifteen."

"The twentieth?" I questioned. That meant he had a client coming in, and we were meeting with the hotel owners.

"The twentieth," she repeated to put emphasis on it. She lowered her voice. "A new client is here, and holy shit, Kenna, he's at least an eight."

"Really?" We hadn't had an eight in a very long time. She and I had our own sexy scale with clients. "Age?" I stepped into my dress and slid it up over my smooth skin then wiggled the girls into place.

"Forty-six, maybe."

"I can work with that." I flinched as I touched the tender spot on my cheek. *Mind over matter.*

I readjusted the girls and checked out the dress in the mirror. It was skintight right down to my knees, and I once again thanked my mother for all her coaching over the years.

"Trust me," Zara continued, "after the last one, who touched my boob as an introduction, I'd take a friggin' four. At least they aren't usually so full of themselves."

"Gotta love our industry." I swapped out my iPad case for one that matched my outfit then slipped on a pair of sparkly heels. *There.* I looked in the mirror again. *That's better.* "Okay, Zara, I'm ready." I put my ear bud in and grabbed my purse. "Give me the goods on Mr. Eight."

As she told me the details, I headed to the elevator and tapped my ID against the black pad then hit number twenty. I had a pretty good memory and quickly soaked up the important details she shared. By the time I hit the floor, the pain had subsided, and I was ready to go.

"Morning, Kenna," one of the security officers on the floor greeted me, and I smiled warmly at him as I went by. I moved down the long hallway that led to a set of big steel doors. The owners were among the wealthiest on the Strip, so I understood their need to be over the top with protection.

I scanned my badge at the door, and the doorman opened it.

Well, hello, Mr. Eight.

A tall man, with broad shoulders and a trim waist dressed in what I knew were some of the best Italian fabrics there were, stood looking out the window. His hands were tucked in his pockets and snugged his pants across his ass.

Jesus, if that's what his back looks like, I can barely wait for the front.

"Good morning, Kenna," Jim Gates, Sr. cooed from somewhere in the room.

"Morning, sir." I smiled as I continued to admire the view in front of me.

"Kenna," my father's voice pulled me from my thoughts and brought my attention to a second man I hadn't even noticed, "this is Mr. Salazar. He just flew in from Miami last night and will be staying for a few weeks while he conducts some business."

So, if Mr. Salazar is Mr. Eight, then who owns that fine ass by the window?

Mr. Salazar might be an eight, but his gorgeous lips twisted as he stared at me, and I immediately felt the burn in my gut. That happened a lot. People saw my large breasts and my figure and immediately misjudged me. They assume there was nothing there to back it up. I hated it, but at the same time I often found it amusing to toy with them. I knew I had a sharp mind, and I also knew pretty much whatever there was to know about Vegas.

"Lovely, to meet you, Mr. Salazar." I reached out and shook his hand. "Please take a seat so we can get to know one another."

"How old are you?" His voice was polished.

"Old enough to know not to answer that question," I shot back but sent a killer smile his way. I sensed the man by the window had turned slightly, but I didn't dare look. I needed to impress the man in front of me.

"So, I see you're to be in penthouse four. That has a lovely view of the rose terrace."

"I asked for the pool view." He cleared his throat. "And I asked for a bottle of my favorite bourbon and my suits to be pressed and ready for—"

"Your four p.m. meeting, yes." I nodded. "They've already been sent down to our laundry service and will be ready and in your room by two p.m." I held his gaze, not looking at my iPad. "Regarding your request for the pool view, you did indicate on your booking information that you wanted the rose terrace since the last time you stayed at the Mystic Hotel you felt the pool was too loud. But I'd be happy to make the arrangements for you to have a spectacular pool view here at Indulge Hotel. We provide only the very best for our clients and our pool view includes triple-paned glass to help lessen the sound."

He blinked at me, and I caught my father's smirk behind him. If only that brought me comfort.

"No, that won't be necessary. The rose terrace is fine."

"Excellent. I have dinner reservations for you at Villains Vines at six and a table reserved at our famed nightclub, Sinful Sweets, for ten."

"And my bourbon?"

"A bottle of Martin Mills is in your room, ordered for your table, and another sits on the top shelf at the club."

He leaned forward with an impressed look, and I held his gaze.

"And you?" he asked, and I smiled as his phone instantly pinged with my contact information.

"She's available twenty-four-seven," my father cut in, and I eyed him to back off.

"I think I made the right choice staying here."

"Not think," I winked, "did." I rose and extended my hand. "There's a masseuse waiting for you in your room."

"Lovely." He sent me a warm smile, and I saw I passed his test. "Thank you, Kenna."

"My pleasure, Mr. Salazar."

My father escorted him to the door, and once the door shut, he grinned at Jim. "We did it." Dad slapped Jim on the back. I felt my stomach twist. It would be so nice if just once in a while my father would express his appreciation for my part in something.

"Nice job, Kenna." Jim Gates, Sr., being the kind-hearted man he was, tossed me a bone. Though the Gateses were well known as notorious bastards in all things business and personal, when it came to their staff, I had to say we were treated well.

"Gotta run. Have an appointment in ten," my father called. I tried not to sigh as he left the room. I wondered if he even saw me as a daughter anymore or if I was just another employee. Sadly, I had to go with the latter.

"Kenna?" Jim stopped me as I was about to leave. I turned and realized I'd completely forgotten about the man who stood by the window. I could feel him as he studied me. My father's attitude still stung, and I didn't feel like talking, but I knew I had to rally. It was what I did. "I know it's been years, but I'd like to reintroduce my oldest son, Grim. He's come back to work with us in Vegas."

I'd noticed earlier he was tattooed right up to his hairline at the back of his head. The black and white art showed as it curled around the line of his chin and down his throat then disappeared into his crisp gray dress shirt.

I wondered how much more of him was covered in tattoos. His muscles were obvious through his suit and drew the imagination. A light beard dusted his face and outlined his sinful mouth. His stone-cold eyes latched on to mine like a magnet. I felt my heartrate speed up. His brows were tilted into a scowl that deepened the coldness of his gaze. A tiny Roman cross sat on the top of his cheekbone, and I saw it twitch as his gaze darkened.

A flashback of last night flickered through me, and I drew in a sharp breath that caught in my throat.

Oh, Shit.

THREE

GRIM

The small sound she made caused the corner of my lip to twitch. Was she scared? Staying where I was, I tucked my hands casually back into my pants pockets. I was aware it emphasized what I had to offer a woman.

"Yes, I remember we've met," I drawled casually as I kept my gaze locked on the gorgeous bombshell in front of me. Yes, *I'm the one who killed a man in front of you last night.* I also knew full well who she was. I'd never forget the heated conversation I'd had with one of her friends in the hotel spa years back when Kenna walked in on us.

"Yes, I do believe the last time I *saw* you, you were giving my potential client a private tour of the sauna room. Evidently, it wasn't an enjoyable tour for her. I lost that client because of your lack of," she paused, "communication skills." She rolled her eyes but smiled at my father.

"I see there's a story there." Dad muffled a chuckle. "Well, nevertheless, Grim is back and will be handling things here at Indulge and at his new hotel, Secrets. I'm sure you'll be running into each other a lot—"

"Aren't I lucky?" She dripped with sarcasm.

"You are." I shot back and made her glare at me.

"Grim will be on his best behavior." My father eyed me, and I raised a brow.

"I make no promises." I didn't break eye contact with her.

"No need to worry. My clients are all men." She smiled wide. "Have at it."

I shot her a look to be careful with her tone, but she dismissed it. When I looked at most people that way, they immediately backed down, but she showed no sign of that. I forced my temper back.

"I see you have a mouth."

"Yes, and this mouth has helped get *your* hotel some very high paying guests." Her phone vibrated in her hand, and she glanced at the message. "Point to make my case." She turned her phone around to show me the caller ID. "It seems Mr. Dean needs me," she said to my father. "Do you mind?" She failed to address me.

"Not at all." Dad smiled at her. I noticed she flinched slightly when she pressed the phone to her cheek. She may have hidden the bruise with makeup, but the swelling was still evident. The tips of her fingers grazed over it as she switched hands with her phone but dropped when she caught my stare.

"Could you please hold for a moment?" She spoke in an even tone then lowered the phone and looked at me with a cool expression. "Was there anything further?"

"I do believe we still have something to discuss." I pointed to my cheek in reference to last night.

"I'm afraid I have no idea what you mean."

"It's fine, Kenna. Please attend to Mr. Dean." My father pointed toward the door for her to leave.

I leaned against the conference table. "I'm looking forward to seeing you around, Kenna."

"Trust me, the pleasure is *all* yours," she tossed over her shoulder, and I took in her tight-as- hell dress that instantly intrigued me and pissed me off as she disappeared out the door.

"Careful, son. Every damn owner in the United States wants her. She's that good." His voice was low as the door closed behind her. "It took a lot of convincing by her father to get her to work here. She was set to stay in Dubai and work her way up at Buji Al Arab." He looked at me from behind his reading glasses. The Buji Al Arab was one of the top hotels in the world, next to us, of course.

"What changed her mind?"

"You'll have to ask her."

"She needs to lose the attitude first."

"It seems to work for her. She's been here for just under a year and has signed an impressive number of clients already. Not only that, but she poached Yen Hong for us from The Wynn. He lost five million in our casino the first night. She's on the verge of signing Sonny Conti as well."

"Seriously?" I scrunched up my face. "Sonny Conti, as in Victor Conti's son?"

"That would be the one."

"As in Sonny who nearly shot me in the fucking chest when he was dickin' around in front of a girl a few years back?" Dad nodded like what I was saying wasn't a huge red flag. "As in Sonny who did a line of coke, downed a bottle of Fireball, ate a handful of gummies, then proceeded to participate in that monstrous hit behind Circus Circus?"

"Yes." Dad huffed as though he'd already heard this story ten times. I threw him an incredulous look.

"Dad, Conti's a loose cannon. Don't you remember that night? If it wasn't for me, Trigger, and Morgan, he'd be dead and buried in the desert with the other guys."

"And no one can know you were there." He eyed

me. It hadn't been Trigger's hit, and if anyone knew we'd even been there that night, we'd all have a target on our backs.

"Mobsters and guns are bad for business." I put my hands on my hips and shook my head. "Unless they work for me," I had to add at his lifted eyebrow.

"I agree, son." He huffed again. "But Cameron and I have discussed it." He gave me a pointed look. "Sonny Conti came into a lot of money from that hit." He waved at me to calm down. "Grim, think about it. A woman who knows what she's doing, someone like Kenna, could bring him in and increase the revenue at Indulge thirty percent in a year."

I shook my head and thought how glad I was that I'd come back home. My father's level of thinking was off the wall.

"Or have a bloodbath." I tossed my hands in the air. Sonny was reckless with his money, and having someone who could guide him to the right place to lose it would be huge for Indulge, but Sonny wasn't that client.

"This deal's been in the works for quite some time now." My father removed his glasses and pinched the bridge of his nose. "Kenna has worked very hard for it, and Cameron agrees he would be a good fit. Maybe right now you don't see the benefit, but someday I'm sure you will. I've got this, son."

"I don't agree." I shrugged. "I know Sonny better

than you and Cameron, and I'm telling you it's a horrible idea bringing him on." He went to speak, but I held up my hand to let him know I wasn't finished. "But this is your deal that you started before I came back, so I'll back off for now." I shook away my urge to end the very notion of what they had in mind, but I respected my father enough not to undermine him at this point. Plus, I didn't want to butt heads with him my first day back.

"Good." He pushed his glasses back on, and the tension slowly lifted between us. We were two strong-headed males; it was what made us so good at this business. I studied my father's face and noted he looked tired. The last few years had taken a toll on him. I only hoped it was that and not the illness that made him look that way. I was glad Leo did what he did to get me to come back early. I might not have appreciated the lie, but he'd done what he felt he needed to. Time with my father was something I could never get back.

"I thought Cameron was going to trip over his fucking feet when he came in and saw me in the office." I chuckled as I changed the topic. I'd returned home the previous night and had showed up in the office early in the morning without warning. Only my family knew I was back. When Cameron caught sight of me behind the desk, he was so taken aback he'd become a stammering mess when he tried to get his words out. We'd never seen eye to eye and probably never would. I had asked Dad to keep my return home quiet, mainly because it was fun to fuck around with him. The look on Cameron's face was worth it and then some.

"He was pretty shocked you're back." He tossed some papers on his desk and sighed. "Although I'm not looking forward to the two of you constantly fighting."

"If he wasn't such an arrogant asshole with little to no boundaries when it comes to our business, we wouldn't have a problem." I stood and went to look out the window.

"He's only trying to help."

"That's the one argument you and I will take to the grave, Dad." I watched the cars move below us along the strip.

"Indeed."

"So," I took a deep breath and changed the topic once again, "you really think Kenna is capable of pulling off a deal with Sonny Conti?"

"I do, Grim," he sounded like his old self, and it made me turn to face him, "and Kenna's staying put, so find a way to handle her attitude or head back to Mexico. We need her." He chuckled, and I huffed as I took a seat at the table.

"So, I'm supposed to deal with that mouth?"

"You've dealt with worse." He shrugged me off as he took a call and mouthed it was from Mom.

I couldn't help but wonder if Kenna would mention what happened at the hotel the night before to anyone. I'd never really paid much attention to Cameron's daughter in the past, and it had been years since I'd seen her. I knew she'd grown up in LA and that she'd traveled a lot with her mother before she took a job somewhere abroad. I'd maybe seen her a handful of times in my life, which was odd, considering our fathers had been close for over a decade.

I remembered that although she was Cameron Tame's daughter, she went by a different last name. Maybe she wanted to keep her privacy or something. I did know her sometimes nasty younger sister, Calli Tame. Calli worked at their father's law office just off the Strip, and she definitely used her father's last name to her advantage whenever she could. I could already see the sisters were very different.

Cameron worked for our hotel. He and Dad had met years earlier when Dad's cancer first came up. He had his own practice as a criminal defense attorney and was very well known and successful. I knew Cameron was a good friend because when Dad grew ill, and we almost lost him, Cameron found one of the best doctors in the world and was able to get Dad in to see him.

While the good doctor worked with him to get him

healthy, Cameron worked hard to get Dad out of a sticky court case that could have landed him in jail for over a decade. Dad had a lot of faith in him. For a time, he and I had gotten along. I tried hard to remember all he'd done for our family, but over the years, his ego irritated the fuck out of me, and we'd started to butt heads. Luckily, up to this point, I hadn't had to engage with him that often.

I'd been warned by my father to be nice to Kenna before. I was sure my reputation of being a controlling asshole had made them nervous she wouldn't want to work here. She hadn't quit yet. *There's still time.* I hadn't seen her enough to form an opinion of her, and after the incident in the sauna room, she'd avoided me like the plague. My dealings in Mexico had pulled most of my attention and didn't leave much time for anything else. Now, I just hoped she was nothing like her father and kept her mouth shut and followed my orders.

I interrupted Dad briefly and told him to say hi to Mom. "I have a meeting with Jesse. I'll touch base later." I waved as I left the conference room to get on with my day.

The only real highlight of my day came later that evening. I watched a man on the floor who thought he could cheat at blackjack. Of course, several cameras were on to him, the dealer was just buying time, so I thought I'd have a little fun.

I eased into the chair next to him and dropped

some chips on the table as I took a glass of whiskey from the server's outstretched tray.

The man looked at me and studied my tattooed neck then my hands. His huge cowboy hat, flannel shirt, and conference lanyard confirmed he was indeed from out of town.

"Tell me something." He turned to look at me. "How's a boy like you gonna get a job with scribbles like that on your body? It's a disgrace if you ask me. A man all doodled over."

The dealer glanced at me, but I shook my head, and he backed off. My men, who had quietly placed themselves close to the table, would do nothing unless told to.

"And ignorance will land you a job as well?" I arched a brow and gave him a cold stare.

"It's just a little much, don't you think?" He snickered, and I smiled. He rolled his eyes. "Why would anyone do that to their skin?"

"It helps hide things," I muttered around the lip of my cup.

"Such as?"

"Scars, bullet holes, burns." I tapped the table, and the dealer snapped over another card.

"Is that right?" He mocked me like he didn't believe me. "Y'all know what I think?"

"I'm sure you'll enlighten me."

"I see a rebellious teen trying to get Daddy's attention, gets pictures drawn all over his skin, drinks eggs for breakfast," he pointed to my arms, "and thinks his fancy body'll help to get him a job."

"Twenty-one." The dealer spoke over the noise, and I nodded for him to deal again.

"Dammit." The man turned his attention back to the dealer.

"I bet you I'll win again." I pointed to the deck, and he squinted at me as the dealer's quick hands dealt the cards one by one.

"Twenty-one," the dealer repeated.

"And I'll win again." The dealer repeated the game. I won again, twenty-one.

"How?"

"Here's the thing, I've worked since I was thirteen. Got my first tatt *with* my dad at sixteen. Ran two successful companies and am launching my third later this year." I leaned forward. "How I won is because I own this hotel, and I know you've been cheating for the past two hours." His face paled. "As I see it, you have two choices. You can be escorted out the front or the back, but either way, you'll have to deal with me alone."

His mouth dropped open as he suddenly stood, and at my nod my men were on him like a fly in a shithouse.

"Go." I flicked my hand as they dragged him off. I

tossed a grand at the dealer for his time and nodded. "Stevie."

"Mr. Gates." He nodded back.

His screams as I snapped his fingers brought a smile to my face.

"It behooves me to remind you of the appropriate behavior while at a blackjack table." He screamed again, and to quiet him I punched him square in the jaw. After all, he had tried to steal from our casino.

"Please, I've got a family!" he screamed, like that was going to help his situation. "I have a son."

"Well, that really changes things, doesn't it?" I rolled his shoulder then kicked his elbow in the opposite direction. His screams turned into sobs. "Do you treat your son with the same disrespect you treated me? A stranger?"

"I, I, I can't." He tried to think, but the pain was too much. I yanked him to his feet, and Jesse held him up for me, and I plowed my fist into his stomach.

"Don't fuck this world up any more than it already is!" I snapped his other wrist, but sadly, he'd passed out, and my fun was over.

Once my men took his information and dragged his ridiculously clad body from my sight, I made sure he was banned from the hotel and all the money was returned plus a fee for his crimes. He would be unceremoniously dumped at the airport with his belongings in garbage bags. He should count himself lucky. In the old days, he'd have ended up in a dumpster in the alleyway behind the Wolverine Strip Club. That rarely happened today. Not to say never.

I used my handkerchief and applied pressure to my knuckles. The last thing I needed was a bloodstain on my suit. When the elevator doors opened, I tossed the silk fabric in the trash and headed toward Desires where I was to meet my family for dinner.

I was pleased that some of the tension from earlier in the day had eased.

Normally, when I came back from being away, I liked to dine alone upstairs with my private chef, but I needed to show people I was back, and the best way to do that was to be visible.

I climbed up to the second platform where my family often ate. The rich and famous of the world dining together gave our guests a thrill and helped make them dream big.

"There he is." Dad stood and gave me a hug. "I heard you dealt with a little problem?" he mumbled.

"I did."

"I bet you feel better."

"Mildly." I appreciated that my father knew what fed my cravings.

Hardly visible, but always near, our security team

kept a close eye on the family. It was important to be seen, but we kept the risk to a minimum. You never knew who lurked in the shadows to take us out. We did, after all, dabble in the darker side of things. When we were home, we had an entourage of about four men around us. When we traveled, that number would double.

"Cameron." I nodded at the man who did his best to look like someone important by the way he watched the room. His expression made it seem like everyone else was less important. I shook off my distaste and took a seat next to my brother.

"Minnie was lookin' for ya." Leo pointed over his shoulder.

"Where?" I craned my neck and saw her talking to Kenna.

Great.

Minnie reached over and touched her cheek, but Kenna shook her head and slapped a smile on her face. I wondered what was said.

"Well, Salazar's happy. Just look at him at his table." Cameron huffed as he rubbed a hand through his gray hair. "He's one friggin' high-ass maintenance client."

"When are they not?" Leo replied to Cameron's comment. "Let Kenna deal with him."

"I suppose so. If you see her, let her know I'm looking for her."

"She's once again avoiding my calls," he complained. I failed to mention she wasn't far from us.

"Sure," Leo assured him and sent a smirk my way.

"Anyway, I never said welcome back, Grim." He moved to pat my shoulder but caught my glare and thought better of it.

"Thanks." I hopped up and pulled out Mom's chair as she approached. Her purse wiggled, and I eyed the little shit inside. He was cute, but pocket-size anything didn't make sense to me. Mom, however, thought it was hysterical to own a fun-sized version of my two dogs.

"Nice to have you home, son. For good." She kissed my cheek to solidify her words and slipped into her chair. The pup's face peeked out of her purse, and I rolled my eyes.

"You look as beautiful as ever, Mom." I hugged her then sat. Even at her advanced age, she was a woman who drew the eye. She reminded me of that Italian actress, Sophia Loren. Dad's eyes lit up as he admired her and leaned in for a kiss.

Minnie's laugh drew my attention, and I saw she and Kenna had their heads together as they looked at a cell phone. I excused myself from the table and headed toward them.

"Girl, those tits of yours would look phenomenal in this two-piece." Minnie laughed again as she gawked at Kenna's chest then back at the phone. She looked up at me as I approached.

"Ladies." I nodded and saw Kenna's face twist with annoyance.

The feeling's mutual, sweetheart.

"Grim!" Minnie squealed as I leaned in for a hug. Sometimes she really did sound like Minnie Mouse. "I heard you were back." She hugged me harder.

"I am."

"For good this time?"

"Yes, Leo will be taking over for me in Mexico—for a while, at least—then he'll be back."

"I have something less painful to do at the moment," Kenna murmured and kissed Minnie's cheek. "Order me two." She winked as she tapped Minnie's cell phone and left. I found myself curious as to exactly what they'd been looking at.

"I'll be sad to see Leo go," Minnie pulled her gaze from Kenna's retreating backside and looked at me, "but I'm so fucking happy you're home." She beamed. "You bring out a fun side in Brick, and I, for one, am dying to see that back."

"Everything good?" He'd seemed fine to me before the desert ride. He'd been as excited as the rest of us to take down those snakes.

"Well, I'm living here full time, and he's in Santa Monica, so you tell me." Her face fell for a half second, but she slapped a smile back on. "Whatever. I get you back, I see Brick whenever he comes into town, and I have my girls, so I'm livin' my best life."

"By girls, you mean Kenna?" I needed to know who fit where.

"She's my main girl, yeah. Do you remember her?"

"Not really."

"*Pfft*. Oh, yes, you do." She eyed me. "You know perfectly well. You lost her a big client she brought in from Mulan, remember?" She eyed me harder when I didn't react.

"Not that I need to explain myself," my voice was sharper than I intended it to be, "but that was a misunderstanding."

"So, you do remember." She bristled. "Maybe you should share that with her."

"I don't owe her shit." I tried to hold back my temper, so I changed course. "I didn't even know you guys knew each other."

"Not just me, Grim." She chuckled. "She's tight with all of us, and super close with Rail and Morgan."

Seriously?

"When did that happen?"

"Remember you left, and even when you're here, you're not really here." She shrugged and tapped her head. "Just be nice to her, okay?"

"Why does everyone keep telling me that?"

"Because you use all this," she dragged her finger in the air up my body, "to your advantage. It's always worked for you. I'm just sayin' it won't work on her." She looked away.

"I've only dated twice since Jenelle."

"First, don't mention that twat's name, and second, I wasn't referring to the women you've dated. It's more the ones you play with. You're not that much of a man whore, Grim. You're not Rail." She laughed out loud then looked up at me and seemed to consider her words. "You've got some scary clients who come around when you're in town. Male and female." Her gaze narrowed in on me. "I've always been straight with you, so just be careful not to get too comfortable now you're back. Everyone has been working really hard since you've been gone. Relationships with clients are hard won in this town, remember, and you can lose 'em like that." She snapped her fingers.

I licked my lips and tried not to lash out at her words. Minnie and I had been close because Trigger and Brick and I were close. Minnie was good people and always spoke straight to me like she did everyone else. No bullshit. I looked away.

"Look, Grim," she put a hand on my arm, "Kenna's the best thing that's happened to Indulge. She's smart, quick, and sexy as hell. She wins over the worst of them. Not to mention what she has to deal with at the top." *Yeah, her father.* "Just know," she leaned in close, "if she quits, I'll be first in line to steal her and take her to my club full time."

"You lookin' for a hostess at your club?" I mused.

"No," she chuckled, "but she's got some skills that she keeps to herself. I'm this close to convincing her to let me use them." She laughed playfully.

"Skills?" My darker side tuned in. I wanted to hear more.

"Mhm, the girl has a lot to offer, and I don't just mean her tits." She fanned herself. "I might be straight, but I'd switch teams for one night with her."

Her tits were great, perky, real, and begged to be played with.

I chuckled. "I've missed you, Min."

"Well, babe, the feeling's mutual. But I have to ask."

"Yeah?"

"Please don't tell me you're dating Jenelle again."

"Fuck, no."

"Come on," she made a face like I was stupid, "one slice of Chef Dale's chocolate cake and Leo'd tell you his deepest darkest secrets while he sucked it back like a cheerleader on prom night." I smirked, and she leaned closer. "She's had her eye on you forever, and if you open that door, she's going to expect more than just some casual dating. You being back permanently will have her wanting to set her claws in."

"Yeah." I heard her warning. "But I'll be fine."

"Denial looks ugly on you, Grim, and you're far from ugly." Her attention was pulled away as someone called her name. "Sorry, I gotta go. But we're doing drinks soon. Remember, be nice to my girl!"

"Yeah, sounds good." I walked slowly back to my table as I fantasized about what skills Kenna kept hidden. I was sure they'd require some kind of gag.

It felt good to enjoy dinner with my family, and the meal was superb. Vegas restaurants were highly competitive, and Indulge prided itself on its world-class chefs. I was already on the hunt to source the best of the best in LA for Secrets. I wished I could clone Chef Dale, but he was well rooted here at Indulge, and we were lucky to have him.

After dinner, my parents were called away and they excused themselves with hugs all round. I was left with my brothers and Cameron.

"Secrets is shaping up to be quite the hotel." My brother, Knox, leaned back as our dessert plates were removed. "I, for one, am so glad you're home." He chuckled. "My inbox could use a break from your ninety-nine e-mails a day about Secrets' progress."

"A good businessman hates to leave a project." I shrugged.

"I'm just glad I'm not your bitch anymore."

"You'll always be my bitch, Knox." I grinned and he flipped me the finger.

"I love the vibe at Desires, and I'm sure you will too. It's lush, fresh, and private." Kenna's voice found me. I turned to watch her as she pointed out things to a well-dressed man.

"Is it wrong to fantasize about both sisters at once?" Knox whispered to Leo, who shook his head and waved at him to shut up. Cameron was only a foot away from us.

Obviously, a potential client. "Under the glass flooring is an exceptional array of lily pads and flowers," she continued. "See how the crystal blue water sets it all off so beautifully. The best part is how all the greenery around the tables creates little hidden pockets for you to dine in. The Gateses fell in love on a boat on a stunning little lake in Georgia. Mrs. Gates hated to leave the lake behind, so Mr. Gates brought the memory to her here at Desires. It's romantic, if you ask me."

I studied how she worked and noticed Cameron watched them closely as well. It pleased me that she had taken the time to learn my parents' history and had incorporated it into her sales pitch.

"This is exactly what I'm looking for." The man smiled. "I love the design of the place. What are the odds I can get a table for tomorrow night around six?"

"We're normally booked six months in advance, but if you bring that brother-in-law of yours with you from the Bellagio, I'll work you in. And I'll make sure our chef does something special just to show you how much we appreciate your business." She winked, and I glanced at my brother. Leo watched her as closely as Cameron and I were. The kid was learning.

"You're very good at your job, Ms. Lodge. I'll be sure to bring him." He shook her hand then pulled out his phone as he left and put it to his ear.

"Kenna." Cameron waved her over. She checked her watch before she approached like she didn't have time to chat or maybe it was because I was there.

"Yes, Cameron." I noticed she didn't say Dad; perhaps it was a work thing. I figured Cameron liked to keep his personal life and connections separate from his work life, given the nature of his job. His type of lawyering wasn't for the faint of heart. His brand was *helping those misunderstood by today's society.* Whatever. I hated to admit it, but he was a big asset to our family and crucial to our business. My father and Cameron had a working wheel that found us clients and signed them to both the hotel and Cameron's legal roster. They brought in heaps of money and kept everyone happy. Kenna brushed her long, shiny hair back over her shoulder. "What's up?"

"Who was that?"

"Mr. Crane from San Francisco."

"I didn't hear Mr. Crane from San Francisco guarantee he'd show up. I also have never heard of him. He's certainly not a client of mine." His unimpressed sarcastic tone made me look over at him.

"No, he's not, he's one of –"

"So, why are you wasting your time on him, and not Mr. Salazar, who I saw glance at you more than once?"

"Need I remind you Kenna isn't just a host for your clients," I cut in and her eyes went wide. "She's a host for Indulge first, then your clients."

"That's true," he smiled, but his eyes said so much more, "and she's on the clock for Salazar, and he's looking for her to escort him from his table to the bar."

"Just like the other clients who are here in town, I'm sure he can wait a few minutes." I stood and buttoned my jacket. "But if you feel he can't, perhaps I could smooth things over with him myself."

"No, no," he shook his head, "that won't be necessary."

"Do I need to be here for this?" Kenna rolled her eyes, and I shot her a look.

"Don't be smart," her father hissed, his face red. I tilted my head as I watched her lick her lips like she swallowed back a comment.

He caught my expression as I took my seat again. "Let's leave the Gates to their drinks." He wrapped an arm around Kenna's shoulders and steered her out of the restaurant.

"He can be a real asshole when he wants to be." Knox tipped the last of his drink down his throat. "And now they're gone, I'll use this moment to escape."

"We have a meeting at ten tomorrow morning," I reminded him. "At Secrets, and don't be late. The designer is coming in to look at the lobby."

"Sure, sure." He waved me off, and I threw an exasperated look to Leo, who nursed a beer.

"What?" I caught his expression.

"Dad said you pissed Kenna off this morning." He chuckled.

"I friggin' barely remember the chick, and she's in the office telling me I screwed her out of a client years back." I shook my head.

"I'm sorry I missed the lashing." He laughed, and I rolled my eyes. "I've seen her shut clients down, but I'd have paid good money to see her do it to you."

"She's got a mouth." I pulled at my sleeve as my skin heated with the memory of her speaking to me that way. "I won't tolerate it or her fucking father's."

"Mm," he grinned over the lip of the bottle, "Kenna can get away with a lot here, brother. You'll see."

Not anymore, because I'm home.

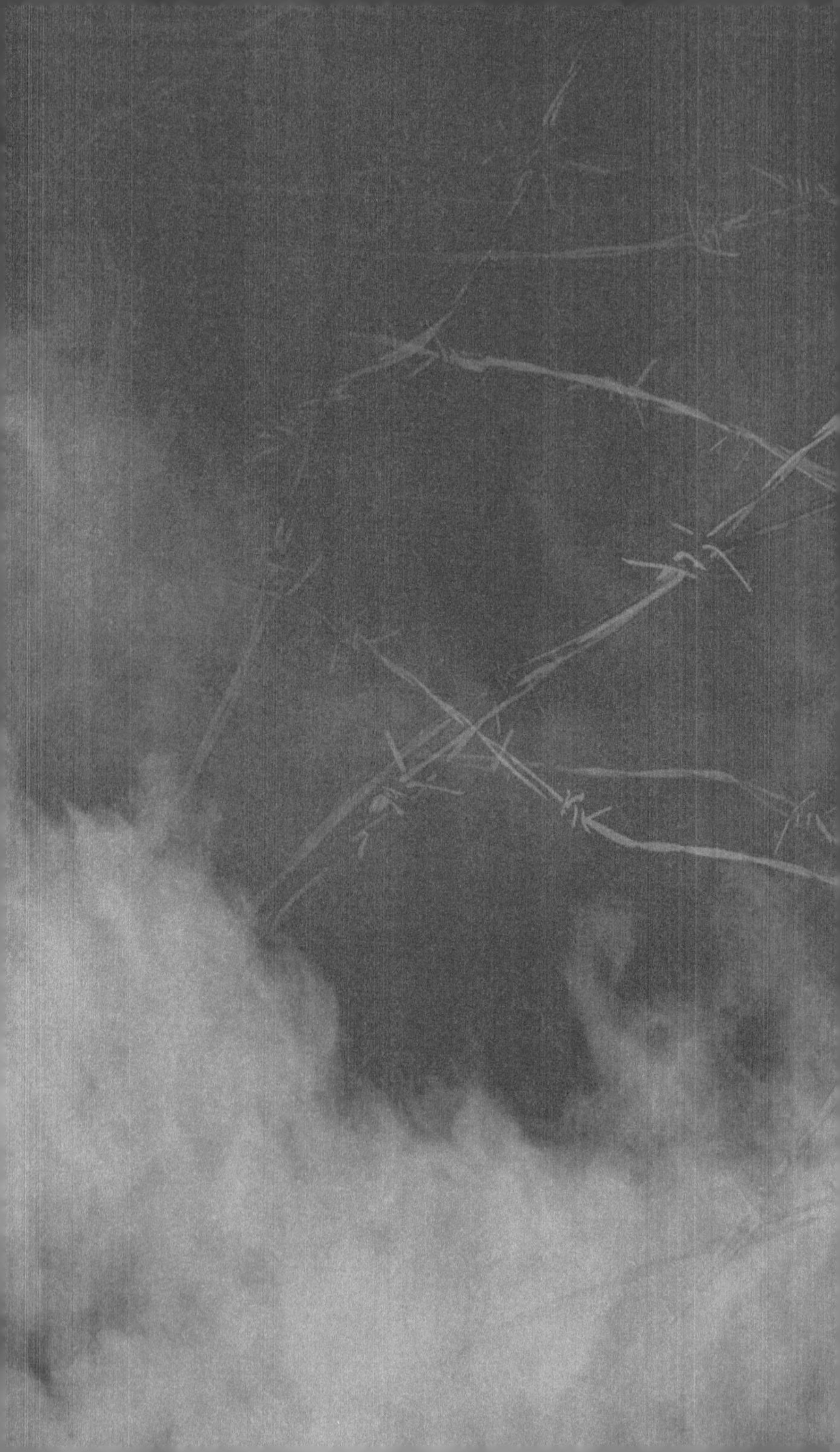

FOUR

SIMON GABLE

"Fuck." I tossed a file on my desk. I'd spent the last two days reading it front to back, forward and backward. "There's nothing."

"There's always something." Calli frowned at me from across the room. "You're just stubborn and won't take a break."

"I don't need a break. What I need is more evidence to prove he was actually there at the same time as the victims." I stood and paced while my frustration mounted. Thanks to Cameron, I'd become a private investigator years back and had worked for his practice ever since. We had similar interests and goals. I was good with computers and finding people. I was also particularly good at manipulating people to be in places they shouldn't be. My job had become a giant game of chess, and each move I made helped Cameron's clients and, in turn, helped me with my plan. I helped his clients when they needed an alibi, or someone to take the fall.

I'd proven time and again to Cameron that I was an asset, and I intended to keep it that way. The trouble was, at that moment I was completely at a loss to see what my next move should be, and that worried me.

"I still can't believe you and Dad even found a witness who was willing to testify." She crossed her legs and inched her glasses farther up her nose. "No one ever comes forward when it comes to assholes like these."

"Until now." I smirked, pleased what money could buy when the stakes were high enough. Calli didn't need to know the witness was bought and paid for. No one did. She was doing enough as it was.

I glanced at a text message that popped up on my Mac computer.

CM: Done.

I erased the message and went back to the file.

"You need to eat." She dropped the red pen in the center of her reference book and dared me to decline. "Come on." She held out a hand, but when I didn't make a move, she pouted. I rolled my eyes, locked my computer, and grabbed my jacket.

We skipped a cab and walked the three blocks to Indulge despite my complaint about her choice of venue. I wanted to eat anywhere but there. I just wasn't in the mood, as the place was always crowded. I had to work on saying no to her.

The moment we stepped into Desires, Cameron came up behind us.

"Finally decided to join the living?" He slapped my shoulder as he pushed by us to sit next to Leo and his brother Grim.

"It's been a while, Mr. Gates." Calli reached over and shook Grim's hand. "Happy to be back?"

"I am."

"Calli." She pointed to herself, and he nodded, disinterested. "Cameron's youngest daughter," she muttered with a pissed look as she looked at the seat next to her father. He grinned at her lovingly as he patted the seat next to him.

I wasn't happy with how crowded the place was but reluctantly took the seat between Calli and Leo.

"How's work going?" Leo asked. I was sure to break the uncomfortable silence Grim created. Grim wasn't like his other siblings. The only time I'd ever witnessed him in any kind of friendly conversation was when he was with a client. Usually, he was ripping someone a new asshole or throwing orders about, and most of the time he ignored people altogether—at least, he ignored me. I didn't mind. I was just as pleased not to have to interact with him. Calli, who'd known the Gates family much longer than I had, always described Grim as dark, brooding, and unpredictable.

"Work's good." I paused to order the crispy roast duck with honey balsamic sauce and mashed potatoes. I might not like the crowds here, but the food was exceptional. "Right now, I'm following a lead that seems to be a dead end."

"What's it like being a PI for him?" one of the waiters I knew asked quietly. He nodded toward Cameron, who was in conversation with his daughter.

"Not as bad as you'd think." I smiled. I knew almost everyone thought Cameron was an asshole, and he was, but he was a criminal defense lawyer and that seemed to come with the territory. The ones I met, anyway. The waiter chuckled and leaned forward to clear a plate. I'd worked for Cameron for several years but only recently started to get to know the Gates family. I had purposely kept my distance as I knew what they were capable of, but now I realized it was time I acquainted myself more with the people in this city, and that included the owners of this hotel. The Gates were a powerful family with a lot of connections.

I'd met Leo maybe a handful of times but never in such a social setting. I heard from Calli he was going to take over Grim's position in Mexico to close out the accounts. Something about it being a learning opportunity. I couldn't help but wonder if that was true or not. Grim gave me the impression he was the type of guy who liked to handle everything himself. I knew Knox pretty well, but that was because Calli casually saw him on the side.

"Dad," Calli put her hand on her father's, "any chance I can get tickets for the show tomorrow night at the Mac? Imagine Dragons is my favorite band."

Cameron looked over at Leo, who shrugged. "Last I heard, they were sold out. Kenna would be the one to ask."

"Dad, you know she won't give them to me." Calli pouted. "Will you ask her for me?"

"All right, all right, I'll call her," he huffed but smiled at her as he pulled out his phone. He got up and stepped away from the table. Cameron played favorites, and it was no secret that Calli was his little angel. At twenty-four, there were times she looked and acted about sixteen.

The moment her father turned his back, she reached under the table and slid her hand over my leg. I covered her hand then froze as I caught Grim's look. I wasn't sure if he'd caught her action or not, and I purposely turned to Leo.

"Did you hear that Mac's thinking of expanding the hotel? They're looking at the new property next to Palms."

"I had." Leo glanced at Grim, who was now distracted.

"What the fuck is he doing here?" Grim murmured as he strummed his fingers on the table. An image of a lion about to pounce on a kill came to me as his eyes gleamed gold then narrowed to a sliver. His reputation of being almost inhuman at times suddenly made sense. He lived up to his name; he certainly looked grim.

I looked at Leo with pinched eyebrows as I wondered who he referred to. Leo shook his head, and I knew I shouldn't ask anything further.

"He's probably just passing through." Leo shrugged as they watched three men stroll by. I noticed they all seemed to smirk as they turned their heads toward the Gates' table. I felt the mood shift to a cold, eerie feel as Grim slowly stood and slid a hand under his jacket. His security team all pulled their weapons.

"Jesse," he rasped, and he seemed to transform into the demon I'd heard about, "time to move."

His right-hand man nodded and was beside him in a flash. Grim muttered for Leo to stay put, then they left.

"Jesus." I swallowed past the lump in my throat. I felt like I had just become a witness to a murder about to happen.

"They're lowlifes from Chicago." Leo checked his watch, completely unfazed by his brother's abrupt change in personality. "They know better than to come to our hotel."

"Sure." I shook my head and tried to get my head around what it might be like to have such money and power. The rules of the outside world didn't seem to apply to the rich.

"Best to not think of it too much." He gave me a quick smile, and I returned it. I understood what he was saying. When you were close to a family like the Gateses, you didn't want to be seen to watch too closely or you just might find yourself the focus of their attention.

Our food came, and Leo left to deal with something. That left just Calli, Cameron, and me to chat. I kept watch on the restaurant entrance to see if Grim would come back, but he didn't.

"Kenna will look into the tickets," Cameron assured her as he sat back down.

"I'm sure she will." Calli rolled her eyes. "The day my sister actually does something nice for me will be the day I sprout wings." Cameron spotted someone and excused himself.

The sisters had opposite personalities and zero interest in being in each other's lives. I couldn't blame either of them for that, Cameron always pitted them against one another and loved to see them fight for his approval. He was odd that way. Kenna was older by three years and apparently got all the looks from her mother, but I knew she had her father's work ethic and desire to win. Calli was cute rather than sexy, and the most obvious talent she got from her father was her love to fight in and out of the courtroom. She might be cute, but she was a scrappy little thing, given the opportunity.

"What do you say we grab a room here?" she purred in my ear. "I can show you that new trick you wanted me to learn."

Calli and I had casually dated for the past six months, but we didn't publicize it. Besides, she was also supposed to be with Knox. We worked together at her father's law firm, and we both knew her father wouldn't approve. The fact that I had a good ten years plus on her didn't help. It was never my plan to date Calli, but she was sweet and available and kept my mind occupied.

"I could use a break." I glanced around then leaned in and kissed her lips quickly. She blushed but giggled in the cute way she did whenever I pushed the line of getting caught. Calli wasn't as wild as Kenna's reputation, but there were times when she'd let loose in bed, and we'd had some fun.

"Hey," Cameron was back and sat next to me as Calli pulled away to give us a moment to chat, "Simon, have you found anything at all yet?"

"No."

"Well, I'm confident that witness should be enough."

"I disagree." I shook my head slightly.

"Why?" He studied my face. "You know, I really think you should consider making that call."

"It's too soon." We can't risk it. "We're close, but I…"

"Okay, but you know I'm not a patient man, and I've been very, very patient. So," he cleared his throat, and I knew he was as anxious as I was to move this case forward, "keep digging, but move it along faster."

"I will," I assured him. I wouldn't stop until I found something. I also didn't totally trust what we had so far. Although I trusted our witness, I wanted a backup. I'd seen too many cases go sideways because people made a move too quickly. I wanted a slam dunk on this one as much as he did. "Everything takes time, Cameron. We'll get there."

"That's the problem, Simon. My time's running out."

FIVE

KENNA

"Jesus, Zara, he even made me run a scanner around his room to check for recording devices."

I sagged my tired body into the elevator wall and rested my arm as I held the phone. "The man is paranoid. I think the only reason I wasn't patted down is my dress leaves nothing to the imagination." I huffed a laugh.

"Well, it would make sense." She lowered her voice. I knew she must have found something after her dig through Dad's files. "He and Yen Hong made a deal at the start of the year, but something happened, 'cause it fell through."

"Yen Hong, as in one of our biggest whales?"

"That would be him." A whale was a high roller,

basically a gambler who placed very large bets. They were our most important clients. "I'll keep digging, but according to the phone logs, Salazar's suddenly getting way more calls from Hong."

"Shit, let's make sure they don't book on the same days." I brushed my hair back over my shoulder.

"About that…" Her voice trailed off. "Salazar extended his stay, and Hong just booked for this Friday morning."

"Damn." I dropped my hand. "I appreciate the info." I glanced at the numbers on the screen above the doors and saw the damn thing had skipped my floor. *Odd.* "Lemme call you back."

The elevator door opened, and there stood Grim, legs apart. One hand was tucked in his pants pocket, the other behind his back. His head was tilted back ever so slightly. If he was anyone else, I might have felt an immediate attraction, but I was wise to his sexual postures. At least to some degree, I admitted, and forced my anger up.

"A word?" His voice was like velvet, and his gold eyes challenged.

"Since you overrode the elevator, I get the feeling I don't have a choice?"

His mouth stretched into a know-it-all smirk, and I stayed put. He pulled out his black key card and reached inside the elevator door to slip it into a small slot meant for only a select few. The elevator would instantly go to that floor. As an owner, I knew he had one.

"Last night—"

"Was careless on my part." I didn't want to have this conversation.

"So, you knew it was me."

"Kind of hard to miss the cold eyes and cross." I pointed under my eye.

"How's the cheek?"

"It's fine." I hated the attention and broke eye contact at the memory. The last time he'd stared at me like that, he'd had his hands on me. "Anything else?"

"Are you always this rude?" I didn't say anything, just raised my shoulders instead. He made a show of running his tongue along his teeth like I irritated him. I wasn't sure why, but I enjoyed that I got under his skin. Maybe it was because most couldn't or wouldn't dare. "How do I know you won't spill our little secret?"

"Why would I say anything?"

"I'm not sure. Maybe to get me out of the way?"

"Wow." He was something else. "No, Grim, I won't say anything because the bastard deserved it."

"Agreed."

"Great," I muttered.

"Did you know him?"

"Who?"

"The man who attacked you last night?"

"No." He studied me for a moment and watched to see if my lie would surface.

"You've a major chip on your shoulder, don't you?"

"And you don't?" I tossed back as I wondered why he'd bother to attempt to figure me out.

"I do, but I can, because I own this place."

"Wait, you own this place?" Sarcasm oozed out of me. "Why didn't you say anything?"

"I figured I'd wait for your smart mouth to take off again before I reminded you."

"Consider me reminded."

"Fantastic." We glared at one another. "Well, if you're quite finished, I thought you might like this back." He pulled my sketch book out from behind his back, and I reached for it and pressed it close to my chest.

"Thanks," I pushed past my lips. I had hoped to go back tonight and find it. I'd planned to take Dale with me this time. It had slipped my mind when I couldn't break free after my father's reprimand earlier. It still smarted that he'd done that in front of Grim and his brother.

"I like your idea on the last page."

"You looked at my drawings?"

"Of course, I did," he drawled.

"Wow, okay." He didn't see how incredibly invasive that was.

"Why are you just a hostess when you can draw like that?"

His comment sucked the wind right out of me. The fucking nerve.

"Not all of us have the luxury of daddy's hotel to pave the way for us," I fumed.

He ran his fingers along his lips, and I could see I may have gone too far, but he had, too.

"This is your first warning, Kenna." His tone made my mouth run dry but also made my legs clench unexpectedly. "The second warning won't be so kind."

"You insulted me."

"No," he shook his head slowly, "I didn't."

A blush ran across my chest and up my neck as I became uncomfortable with his stare. "Anything else?" When he didn't answer, I stepped forward and pulled his card out of the slot. I held it out to him, but he didn't make a move for it as the doors closed between us.

What the hell?

I shook him off and stabbed the number for my floor as I tucked his card in my purse. I needed a good orgasm and some friggin' sleep.

"Well?" Dale asked as I savored his seared scallops with brown butter and lemon pan sauce.

"It's perfect," I purred, not wanting it to end. I closed my eyes and tried to pull out each flavor as I slowly swallowed.

"Yeah." I sighed and opened my eyes to find his grin close to my face. There was a time when those blue eyes made me melt with pleasure. But I could only see the boy behind the smile now, and the knowledge he couldn't handle a mature relationship no longer upset me. We'd become good friends instead, and I knew that was what we were always meant to be. Dale was gorgeous, with short, dirty-blond hair, a lean build, and magical hands. *Damn.* Those hands were useful for a lot of things; they could make magic in the kitchen as well as the bedroom. The sad thing was that I knew Dale needed a woman's affection to feel whole, and that was a damn shame because he'd let me, a pretty amazing woman, go. Someday, he'd grow up, but I wondered how many women he'd leave in his wake. It had been eight months since we'd broken up, but sometimes it felt like yesterday.

"I think I might just need one more taste to be sure." I pretended to look serious.

"Mm," he chuckled as he placed two more plump scallops on a little white plate, drizzled sauce over it, and handed it to me. "I like this." He ran his fingertips over my pink silk skirt. He was as flirty as ever, but I knew it was harmless.

"I thought it was cute." I cut a scallop in half and moaned at the taste. "You really are an amazing cook."

His eyes went to my tight white tank top. It plunged deep and put my girls on display. Though, when were they not? The three of us worked together to nail down clients. My girls and I made a great team. No shame in that.

"You see that new dealer?" I gently stabbed the other half and nibbled on the end as I shooed his fingers away from my chest.

"I did, and again this morning." He beamed as he pulled his hand back. He turned away with a deep, dramatic breath and opened the fridge. I rolled my eyes and laughed, but that was who Dale was. It was no surprise he'd already vetted the new dealer. He made it his personal challenge to vet any new staff member who let him.

"Did you hear Grimson Gates is back?" I used his full name to drive my point home. The spawn had returned to the lair. "Guess you'll have some competition."

"I always love a little competition." He grinned and fingered the edge of my top as he looked at me like I missed something. "That being said, Grim Gates and I have very different tastes. He likes—"

"Chef Dale," Grim's voice made me go still, and Dale's face drained of color, "I was hoping to have a word with you this afternoon before the dinner rush." His cold eyes moved to mine, then dragged down my front, to my crossed legs, and back up again.

"Yes, of course, Mr. Gates," Dale nodded, "whenever you like. I'm free."

"Three o'clock, then. I'll meet you at my usual table." Grim nodded. "Kenna," he addressed me in an emotionless tone, "I believe Mr. Salazar is looking for you."

"He's at his golf game." I stayed perched at the counter. "He isn't due back for another two hours."

"I believe he was looking for you." His tone sharpened.

"He hasn't called," I held his gaze, "so he doesn't need me."

"Kenna," Dale whispered and gave me a side-eye to be careful.

Grim cleared his throat and stepped forward. "Chef Dale, give us a moment."

"Yes, sir." He turned to leave and gave me an *are you crazy* look as he removed his apron and hung it on a hook. He eased past Grim and left us alone with a swinging door. I leaned over and snatched a strawberry from a silver bowl. I nipped off the end and was pleased how well it paired with the taste of brown butter that still lingered on my tongue.

Grim moved toward me, annoyance written all over his face.

"Shouldn't you be entertaining your clients?" His pissed-off face when he entered had already let me know he'd had a shitty morning. After last night, I was ready to fight. "I don't remember entertaining the staff in your job description."

"I'm not on the clock for another forty." I shrugged and finished off the berry. "My clients know that if they ever need me, I'm only a text or call away."

"And Dale?"

"What about Dale?" I dried my fingers with a napkin.

"I don't need you distracting him."

"How was I distracting him, exactly?"

"You tell me, his hands were on you." His gaze burned into mine.

"A lot of men put their hands on me." I shook my head. "It's a job hazard."

"He should be focusing on dinner tonight."

"Not that it's any of your business…" I smirked at my choice of words because really it was. Besides, I knew it would piss him off greatly if I said it. "But I was helping him with tonight's menu. Like I have done for the past year."

He stepped closer, and his jaw visibly ticked. "You don't get paid for that."

"No, I don't." I hopped down and caught his gaze move to my breasts as they bounced. "There's a lot I do that's not my job, but I do it because I love it."

He snagged my arm as I went to leave and towered over me with a look that could kill.

"Stay in your lane, Kenna."

"Or what?" I challenged, but when his eyes went

cold, I decided to ease up. "I'm not trying to step over a line here, Grim. I do my job and I do it well—"

He cut me off. "Then go do it. Get me clients, fill my hotel, entertain their wants, repeat."

I saw red.

"Sure thing." I looked down at his grip on me, and he waited a beat before he let go. "If you'll excuse me."

I burst out of the kitchen and right into Minnie.

"Whoa, girl, where's the fire?" She steadied me on my feet.

"I knew he was an ass," I spat, "but I had no idea he was such a prick." I swiped a hand over my forehead. I was so wound up and irritated.

"Let me guess, you had a Grim encounter?"

"That be it."

"Yeah," she laughed lightly, "I know you, Kenna, and Grim won't tolerate his staff not listening to him. I wondered how the two of you were going to be."

"A warning would have been nice," I fumed as my blood pressure fought to return to normal.

"I figured it could go two ways." She waved at someone then turned her attention back to me. "You'd either be bent over the couch on day one, or you'd kill one another. I had money on the first." She smirked, and I glared at her. "What? Me and the boys all had our bets in."

"Real nice, Min," I muttered as we both caught sight of Grim as he left the kitchen with his phone to his ear. When he caught me looking, he made a motion with his hands to get to work.

"At least he's sexy."

"I hate that he is," I hissed under my breath.

"It's not like you to let someone get under your skin like that," Minnie mumbled next to me.

"You know what?" I stood a little straighter, feeling better by the second. "You're right. It's not."

"Oh, shit," she moved to stand in front of me, "I'm so ready for some fun, so this is what I know." She looked around as she fussed with her hair. "He's got a big client coming in for Indulge."

"Who?" I felt my interest grow.

"DJ Clay."

"He sounds like a child's toy."

"Yeah, well, he's some bigshot in entertainment. Grim wants to land him himself for Secrets. It'd be huge. Don't think Clay's not being approached by the Wynn, Bellagio, Taro, and the Mac. So, Grim needs to come in hard."

"Is that so?" I looked down at myself. "How do I look?"

"Like someone who is about to start a ton of shit."

"Perfect." I turned on my heel and made my way toward the lobby bar where I soon spotted Grim with whom I could only hope was DJ Clay. He reminded me of the singer Teddy Swims.

I kept them in sight as I made a call to Zara and had

her pull some information on him. She prattled off some details, and I sent a quick text to my father asking a question I knew only Grim could answer. I hoped he'd call and distract Grim for a moment so I could slip in.

"Comical as it is, he's a huge country fan." Zara chuckled. "I don't know many DJs who love old school country."

"Examples?" I listened, and when I saw Grim look at his phone and excuse himself, I hung up.

I ran my hands through my wavy hair to pump up the volume and hoped the smell of my vanilla coconut shampoo would escape into the air. Two scents that attracted and relaxed the mind.

I walked straight up to DJ Clay's table and smiled warmly. I knew better than to come on too strong.

"DJ Clay, right?" I extended my hand. "Kenna Lodge. I'm a huge fan."

"Are you, now…" He shook my hand politely, but I could tell he was skeptical.

"I've seen you play at least four times. My all-time favorite was at the Topples Center in LA."

"You saw that show?"

"I did, but I was sorry to hear about what happened when the show wrapped up."

"I appreciate that." He appeared to relax a little. "Seems to come with the job."

"Seems to me, if you had somewhere to play that

managed their security better, you wouldn't have to think about people coming up on you like that." I shrugged.

"Somewhere like Secrets Hotel?" He gave me a knowing look, but I also knew better than to show my cards just yet.

"Or the Wynn or the Mac. Hell, I'd even suggest the Taro at this point."

"Yeah?"

"Yes. Vegas has thousands of people who run through the Strip on any given day or night, and tourists are our livelihood. We invest in only the best of the best to make sure our guests stay safe. I don't know about you, but I wouldn't want to be working at a hotel that lacked proper security and have something wild happen. We'd lose all we worked so hard to achieve." I used all the words the media had printed about the Taro massacre a few years back.

"Didn't the Taro have some kind of a murder?" He leaned forward in his chair, and I tried not to look satisfied he'd taken the bait.

"Not a murder, murders," I made a worried face, "but that was a mafia hit, and I'm sure since then they've changed things up." Thanks to Trigger and the Devil's Reach, the mafia never got far before they were dragged to the desert and slaughtered. That was a big moment for Trigger. He certainly had made his presence known and that he was taking over Vegas as his territory.

"Maybe, but after Topples, my head's still pretty messed up." He waved his hand. His fingers were decorated with several obnoxious gold rings.

"Understandable."

"Tell me, Kenna, what do you do here?"

"I'm a host for an array of clients. I also run interference with them and our hotel lawyer."

"So, you work with some pretty high rollers."

"High rollers who will pay good money to hear amazing music." I winked.

"I like you." He laughed and tipped his beer up to finish off the rest. I felt a sudden warmth behind me. Like heat from the Grim Reaper.

"Miss Lodge." Grim moved up to my side and looked down at me, stone-faced. I could only image what he was screaming behind that mask. "I see you've met DJ Clay."

"Yes, I was keeping him company while you took your phone call."

"Well," Grim rolled his watch over and looked at the time, "shall we move on to the hotel?"

"You'll love the hotel." I leaned forward with a dazzling smile. "It's going to be spectacular. The color scheme is wonderful. There're even some shades of red that the painters are playing with that will set the tone of the hotel to a T." I gave Grim a huge smile. He knew

I referred to the blood pool from the other night that had no doubt seeped into the concrete. A stab to the aorta would do that.

"Actually, Kenna, why don't you come along?" DJ Clay asked as he held out his arm.

"Kenna has a client she needs to see. He should be back from his golf game by now."

"Good news, Mr. Gates." I batted my eyelashes at him. "He just called and told me he'll be a few more hours. I guess he met up with some friends who've joined him on the green." I silently thanked Zara for sending some of our best escorts to keep Mr. Salazar busy. "I'd be honored to join." I took his extended elbow.

"Excellent." He nodded at Grim, who forced a smile. One that faded when he moved his murderous gaze to me.

Two can play at this game.

DJ Clay and I led the way. I caught Minnie's wide eyes as I passed by her with Grim hard on our heels.

Once outside, the stretch Hummer pulled up, and I stepped back to wait for DJ and his entourage to pile in. My skirt was short, and I wanted to wait to sit on an end so I could hop out first and not flash anyone.

"I don't know what you're up to, Kenna," Grim snarled quietly behind me, "but this is a huge deal for my hotel. Don't fuck this up on me." He waved for me to step in.

"See, that's the problem. You don't know me at all." I ignored him then and bent to climb into the Hummer. I was sure I gave Grim a good show. To my surprise, he waited until I was settled then slid in next to me.

Thankfully, it was a short drive to Secrets.

Grim stayed on his phone while I read a few more facts that Zara sent me.

When we parked, Grim got out as the driver opened the door. He turned as I carefully swung my legs to get out and held out his hand. I took it, and he lifted me out with little effort on his part.

"You're welcome." He tapped at my skirt as he moved aside to let the others out. That was the first decent thing I'd seen him do yet.

"Welcome to Secrets." Grim slipped into work mode as he directed the group up the stairs of the new hotel entrance. He kept close to DJ Clay as he gave them a tour and tried to imprint a vision of the lobby and casino on their imaginations. I kept pace with Grim as DJ addressed a few questions directly to me. I was sure he just wanted to see how much I really knew.

"And this would be the club. You'd be up there." Grim pointed to the stage. He must have pulled double time to get the walls up and the skeleton of the stage built. It might have already been done, I reminded myself, as I hadn't come into this area when I was here that night. I hated to admit I was impressed. The club was huge, and the massive blueprints he'd blown up on a touch screen to one side gave a 3D view of what was to come. "The acoustics will be perfect." Grim began a technical description of just how that was planned.

"This is pretty sick." DJ Clay stroked his chin as he thought.

I moved around the room to envision it in full swing. I tuned out the others and brought the scene to life in my mind.

"What do you think, Miss Lodge?" DJ Clay's voice broke through my thoughts. I turned around and knew my eyes were lit with excitement. If I was this enchanted, I knew he'd be able to feed off it.

"I think this is the place any DJ would dream of entertaining in. How could you not bring them in by the thousands just to see this place?"

As I hoped, his eyes went wide as he looked around.

I moved around the room, ready to paint a story. "A new hotel opens on the Strip, a trusted name behind the owner. Every room in the place screams with a promise of sinful pleasure." I lowered my voice to make it husky. "A hot new DJ spins from Friday to Monday but disappears off the radar the rest of the week." I added that last bit, as I knew DJ Clay needed his alone time to reboot before the next show.

I pointed at Grim. "And Mr. Gates is the perfect

person to market this place. Just look at him. He's everything you know you shouldn't want." Grim's cold eyes held mine and one eyebrow lifted. "His very presence screams dark desire. Men want to be his friend, and women want more than just those dark, sexy eyes on them." All eyes were on me, so I used my final hook. "My opinion. If you're going to break out as a headliner show, you do it here, where everyone is excited to experience something new. Something daring. Something," I paused for dramatic effect, "sinful." Grim licked his lips then tore his gaze away from my fingers that stroked down the front of my shirt.

"You'll have the penthouse on the sixteenth floor, with a fully stocked bar," Grim started. "Of course, all meals comped on the nights you perform. I'll come in twenty percent above the going rate. That's more than the Taro or Mac would offer, but my offer only stands until midnight."

I tried to hide my shock. Everyone wanted DJ Clay, so why would Grim give him half a day to decide?

DJ Clay moved his gaze from Grim, to his guys, then to me.

"Okay, Mr. Gates, no need to wait. You got a deal."

"Excellent." Grim snapped his fingers, and his right-hand man Jesse came out of nowhere. "Jesse has the paperwork ready to go. He can email a copy to your lawyer immediately. So, if you'd like to give him a call, we can have this settled within the hour."

I watched as Grim answered every question with ease and expertise. He obviously knew the contract front to back. When they were done, we all piled back into the stretch Hummer, and they cracked a bottle of Fireball whiskey to seal the deal. I felt the want to complement Grim on his business skills, but his stoney face was stuck in his phone again and the moment passed.

Once we were dropped off back at the hotel, I spotted Minnie and waved. I started to head toward her to tell her my good story, but Grim's hand suddenly gripped my elbow and pulled me aside.

"I should have you fired for the way you over-stepped—"

"I didn't overstep."

"And you have a nasty habit of cutting me off," he steamed.

"Have you met you?" I shot back. "Admit it or not, I helped you get that deal." His eyes flashed with anger, and he backed me up against the wall. His fingertips dragged down my arms, sending electricity to my nerve endings. Just as I thought he was going to lose it completely, his face changed, and he smiled. A darkness came over him, and his eyes drew me into their depths like nothing I'd ever felt before. Sounds dissipated and colors muted. It was almost frightening.

"Well, sweetheart, if you want to play with me," he licked his lips slowly, and his voice came from somewhere deep down inside, "game on." His thumb brushed along my jaw as his fingers circled my throat, then he backed off and headed for the elevator.

"Fuck," Minnie mouthed from across the lobby as she fanned herself. I moved and tried to gather myself. I wasn't sure if I should be intrigued that he didn't fire me or be terrified that I'd just started a war with Grim Gates.

SIX

GRIM

Istrummed my fingers on the black velvet armrest of the medieval-style chair. I had it placed so it sat slightly higher than the rest at the table. It was a tad dramatic, but I wanted to make a statement. I wasn't the type to sit in the background. Establishing dominance was key in my world and something I always planned carefully in my everyday dealings. Besides, I always lived up to my name.

My two Doberman Pinschers sat at my feet, Leal on my right and Zhen at my left. They were protective, well trained, and never left my side unless instructed to.

"So, you're telling me that Yen Hong plans to make a move on Salazar while he's staying at Indulge." I eyed Darryl, and he nodded. Darryl was one of the trusted few I'd planted around the various hotels in Vegas. If shit went down, Darryl knew about it.

"Yes, sir." He nodded and handed me a phone with a recording on it. I handed it to Jesse, who stepped away to confirm what Darryl had told us.

Darryl worked the Taro hotel, as a bus boy. He kept his eyes and ears open. He was nothing on the totem pole, merely a blur of color that passed by unseen. Little did they know he was an ex-mercenary and had quite the past in his native Singapore. I'd helped his brother get out of the middle east when he ran into trouble a few years back. I knew he was loyal, and he'd brought me many tidbits of useful information over his years here.

"It's legit," Jesse confirmed and handed the phone back to Darryl.

I crossed my ankle over my knee as I thought. "Anything else?" I didn't need to say any more. Darryl knew even the smallest detail was something.

"Ridder." Darryl waved and another of my men stepped forward and handed me a file with a photo inside. It was proof that Harris, a tech billionaire, was coming to town. I scanned the details and handed it back.

"Mr. Thomas Harris from London arrives tomorrow night." Ridder nodded. Another of my trusted spies,

Ridder's official position was a window cleaner at the Venetian. The second son of an infamous drug lord from El Salvador, I'd hired him on Darryl's recommendation. I never asked what their connection was to each other. It didn't matter. I handed Jesse the file. "He's arriving with his typical entourage and some of his chosen staff." Ridder tilted his head at me, alluding that Harris needed a good time for his male company. "There's talk he's unhappy with his treatment, and after doing a little more digging," he couldn't hide his smirk, "I'd say it's time to show Mr. Harris what we can do for him."

"Excellent." I'd waited six years for this green light. "Jesse, let's get the jet on stand-by and make sure we have the yacht fully staffed at Laguna." If we were doing this, we were doing it right.

"Will do. I've got his itinerary, and we can decide when the best time is to make our move."

"Good."

"Also, sir," Ridder spoke up, "there's a container sitting behind Aria that will need to be taken care of." Ridder glanced at Jesse. Jesse immediately pulled out his cell phone to arrange for the disposal of whoever had gotten in Ridder's way. Ridder didn't have much patience, which was why the Mac had a reputation for staff members going MIA.

"Patrick," I paused, "Lawson, is there anything you'd like to add?" The two other men at the table were both bellmen for the Wynn and Crockfords, and both were ex-law enforcement.

"All quiet," Patrick added.

Nothing is ever quiet in Vegas.

"Which means something's coming." Lawson read my mind.

I looked at my watch and saw it was time to head back up. I waved and dismissed my men while Jesse finished up a phone call.

"Grim," Jesse held up a finger, "someone wants to see you."

"Oh?" I raised an eyebrow and shifted my gaze from him to the door that had just opened. A hard looking Vanilla Ice gangster wannabe came in with a hooker I recognized. He had her arm in a tight hold. She worked a street just off the Strip, but the guy was new to me. I knew a lot of pimps, but nothing about him was familiar.

"Why are you here? Make it fast and don't waste my time." I ran my fingers over Leal's head and up his ears. He held his position, but I felt the tenseness in his lean body.

"Name's Big Cat." The guy scrunched up his nose and tried to act tough. I threw Jesse a humorous smirk. "My bitch Glory here has something to tell you."

"Hi, Grim." Glory sniffed and stood a little straighter then pushed her boobs in my direction.

"Thought you might want to know that people are talking."

"Elaborate." I waited, but she looked at me, confused. "Explain what you mean."

"Tell him." Big Cat shook her, and she struggled to balance on her ridiculously high heels.

"It's about your hotel. People are saying someone's paying off the workers, so they don't work for you."

This wasn't new information, but the fact that it was now knowledge among the locals concerned me.

"And just who are these people you heard this from?"

"Well, I've heard whisperin', you know from here and there, mostly from my girls." I eyed her hard, and she hurried on.

"Okay, so, biggest thing is Cherry Boom, at Clipper's Strip Joint, she told Benny Bunny who told me that Cherry Boom was doin' a lap dance for some big tipper." My head hurt just trying to follow. "Anyways, he was on the phone talkin' about you and how it was time to make a big move. Starting with fuckin' up your grand opening."

I saw red and felt my blood boil. Zhen turned his head and looked up at me. I saw the tremble that went through his body as he begged to be ordered to take them out. Both dogs stood, ready to pounce if I so much as whispered the right word.

"When was this?"

"Last night," Big Cat answered.

"Do you have a name? A photo of this guy? Anything?"

"One of my girls took this." He pulled out his phone and stepped toward me. Both Leal and Zhen growled a warning. I waved at Jesse to hand it to me.

"Back," I ordered the dogs as Big Cat eyed them nervously. They eased back and settled in place. Leal complained loudly. I knew how they felt; the urge to hurt someone had taken a grip on my own gut.

"That's him getting into his car." He moved back and grabbed Glory's arm again. "I know the guy who runs the place and checked. The name on the guy's credit card is Kurt Kyle. Drives a BMW 5 Series."

"I see." I stroked my lip as I studied the man. He was in his late twenties and wore a designer suit and a flashy watch. I couldn't help but wonder if he purposely wanted to be overheard or if he was just stupid enough to talk in front of the dancers. Jesse handed him back his phone then passed me a bottle of hand sanitizer. Who the hell knew where the phone had been.

"I figured your guy might want to give me his number, in case I heard anything else."

"And why, exactly, are you so willing to help me out?"

"I'm new in town, got myself some girls, and Glory told me it's better to be on your good side than not. So, when she told me what she heard, I figured I'd better come down here and tell you right away." He shrugged. "Don't need any more problems." I waved at Jesse, and he handed Vanilla Ice a card. "So, we're good?"

"We'll see."

"On?"

I pulled out my gun and sat it on the armrest and watched as his brows went up and he shifted his weight on his feet.

"On what else you bring me."

"That's all we got," Glory whined with an annoyed look at me.

"Then you better start digging." I pointed the gun at them then rolled my arm to look at my watch. "Leave." I flicked my wrist for them to go. He wasted no time as he yanked Glory out the door.

"Grim." Jesse turned to me as he lowered his phone. I could tell something had happened. "You need to head up to the twentieth."

I cursed and stepped down from my chair.

"With Jesse." I ordered the dogs to stay so I could deal with whatever the hell had happened up there. Of course, Leal growled some backtalk, but when I raised a brow at him, he looked away.

I moved quickly across the marble floor and down the hall. The walls and floor were covered with sound-proof material to prevent anyone listening. I wore many hats in my profession. The legit business at Indulge was handled above ground and anything else was handled below. Once Secrets was completed and my office finished, I would handle everything from up there. My new office would be much more advanced and offer me a good deal more protection than this one.

I tapped my keycard to the black pad, and the door swung open to the elevators. Once on the ground floor, I hurried through the traffic in the lobby and toward our private elevators. The casino was full this evening, and the lineup for the restaurants spilled over into the side bars that were always ready to sell a drink to waiting customers. You could smell the money that poured off them and, in turn, onto me.

"Can we chat?" Minnie appeared at my side as I approached the elevator. She matched my stride.

"Not a good time."

"Even if it has to do with Kenna?" I hated that my pace slowed just slightly. Kenna was a pain in my ass, and if she wasn't so damn important to the hotel, she'd be gone.

"What'd she do now?"

"I really love this whole enemies-to-lovers thing you got going on."

"What?" She was clawing her way into my head like she always did when something was up.

"You asked me to keep tabs on your clients when they're off your property, remember?"

"I did." Minnie was everywhere and had a sharp eye. She also had her own spies, I was sure.

"Mr. Salazar had dinner at Smith Wollensky last night."

"He's allowed to eat elsewhere, Min."

"I understand that, but it was *who* he was with that concerns me."

I pulled out my keycard and held it to the black pad on the wall, then stabbed the elevator button.

"Who?" I had so many things running through my head that I fought to keep up with her.

"Sonny Conti."

I swung around and faced her dead on. Sonny wasn't supposed to be anywhere near Vegas right now. My sources said he was still in Chicago, handling business. Since my conversation with Dad, I'd put people in place to keep me informed of his whereabouts. How the hell was his visit not reported to me?

"Yeah." She read my face. The doors opened, and I stepped inside, but she didn't follow, and something hit me.

"Wait." She turned to face me. "What does that have to do with Kenna?"

"Oh, now you want to know?" The corners of her mouth rose, but I knew if Minnie brought this to me, it was for a reason.

"I won't ask twice," I warned.

"Well, not that I usually eavesdrop," she leaned her

hip into the door and stopped it mid-close, "but I over-heard Sonny going on about some date he has tonight. He made a comment about how he was going to make sure it was wild. Sonny's date is Kenna, though I'd be willing to bet she doesn't know it's a *date*." Minnie finger quoted. "I know my girl can handle herself, but Sonny has a spotty background, to say the least. We don't really know him, do we...?" She trailed off. "I know you have history with Sonny, and I know Kenna hopes to bring him on as a client, but this dinner smells worse than Rail's ass after a lap dance."

"Fuck." I didn't need this right now.

"Brick's is town. You want me to get him to step in?"

"No." I waved her off, but at the last minute gave a nod as a thank you. Minnie was only looking out.

"Jesse," I barked into the phone, "why's Sonny in town and I didn't know?"

"What?" He sounded just as confused as I was.

"Figure it out." I hung up and rubbed my head, feeling the stress of my job once again weigh heavily on my shoulders. I really missed the Cartel life sometimes.

As I exited on the twentieth floor, I could hear yelling and something smashing. I reached for my weapon.

"Mr. Gates," one of the security guards greeted as I approached, "perhaps we should give him a moment."

"Where's my father?"

"Caught in a meeting." He cringed when something was thrown against the wall.

Who the hell? My temper rose.

I slid my weapon back behind my waistband, though I itched to use it. I held up a hand at the security guard, and he hesitated but stepped aside. These men were paid good money to watch over us, but I could handle the asshole temperamental lawyer who presently seemed to be wrecking our main office.

"I said no interruptions!" Cameron seethed, but when he saw it was me, he shook his head. "Jesus, Grim, what the hell do you want?"

"That fuck you say to me, old man?" I dug my heels into the floor as I struggled not to rip his throat out. I wasn't my father and didn't have the history they had. I wasn't about to tolerate his disrespect.

"Sorry," he gritted through his teeth. "I thought you were one of the guards."

I looked around at the mangled furniture and tried to hold back my anger. It wasn't his place to destroy. "What the hell is going on here, Cameron?"

"My reputation is everything." He stormed over and picked up a brass ornament, then put it down again when he thought better of it. "Reputation is everything in this industry," he repeated. When he saw my expression, he tried to get a grip on his temper. "Someone's out to get me." He pressed his lips together until they turned white and slammed his hand against a table.

"Maybe it's the same guy from before doing a victory lap?" I couldn't resist reminding him of the case he'd lost about ten years before. He'd never gotten over it. Cameron Tame's ego was about the size of Texas, and it had nearly destroyed him.

He opened his mouth to speak, but I lifted an eyebrow and tilted my head, and he visibly swallowed back his comment.

"No," he turned away from me and clenched his fists, "I don't believe it is."

"When you work with criminals, you bring out the monsters in this world." I turned a chair right side up as I tried to control myself. Even after all these years, I could see we still weren't safe to be alone in the same room. "I could print an entire list of people who'd like to destroy me, my father, the whole Gates name. Why are you surprised someone would be out to get you?"

"This is different."

"How?" I challenged, staring him straight on.

"Because this is affecting me, my case, my clients, everything." He stomped his foot like a child. "I've only had one minor hiccup in all my years as a lawyer," he snarled.

Minor? It was hardly minor from what I could remember.

"But damn, I had this plan. It was perfect. I made it

a year ago when things went south for my client. I was ahead of the storm; everything was falling into place. This client would bring me," he looked over at me, "*us* unlimited access to something much more than we have now." He rubbed his head. "Now because of—" He pulled back his lips and ground his teeth. "Now, what was supposed to be a smooth trial, a slam dunk, just blew up in my face."

I remained deadpan at his confused speech. I wondered if he was going senile. Cameron might be a good lawyer, but he was a hothead.

"Will whatever you messed up affect business here?" I leaned against the conference table and tucked my hands in my pockets. His twisted face told me I struck another chord.

"I'm sinking, and you're worried about your hotels."

Of course, I am. "It's a logical question to ask. We pay you a great deal of money. Your clients stay here. If they're upset, who's to say they won't cause a problem here?"

"I got your call, Cameron…" Kenna's voice trailed off as she entered and took in the mess in the office. "What happened here?"

"Why don't you tell me?" Cameron's hands clenched into fists and a whole new level of anger showed when he looked at her. "Any of your friends share what they've been up to?"

"I'm not following." She glanced at me, but I gave her nothing mainly because I was still in the dark as to what was going on.

"Martin Castillo." He pronounced the name carefully as he glared at his daughter.

I went still.

What on Earth did this have to do with Castillo, the Mexican drug lord I'd killed? What possible connection did he have to Cameron or Kenna? My mind spun.

"Who's that?" Kenna drew back her chin.

"Don't," he made her jump, "play stupid with me, girl!"

"Dad," she raised her hands, "I swear I don't know who that is."

"You know a lot more than you let on."

"What does that mean?" Again, she looked utterly confused at what he was hinting at.

"So help me God, Kenna, if you know something, if you didn't warn me, I'll—" He pointed at her, and I took a step toward him. The anger burned through my eyes, and he saw it and backed up a step. "What?" he challenged.

"What?" I used my size to tower over him, my spine locked into place, and my fists itched to feel his cheekbones crack. "Watch your tone, Cameron. Unlike my father, I have no loyalty to you."

"I'm merely saying this doesn't concern you."

"It doesn't concern her either."

"How would you know?" He toned it down a bit but didn't waver.

I wasn't about to let anyone know I was the one who took down Castillo. I didn't have a death wish. I'd have one half of Mexico after me and the other praising me. That secret was known by only a select few, and it sure as shit wasn't for Cameron-fucking-Tame.

"It's pretty damn obvious she doesn't know anything. I get that you're upset," I lowered my voice but kept it sharp, "but you need to pull yourself together, straighten up our office, and figure out how to fix whatever it is that's screwed up. If it's a messed-up case you're involved in, just be sure you clean it up fast because if something blows back onto our family's business, you'll have to deal with me." His face turned beet red, but he kept his mouth shut. "Also, if I see you come at your daughter like that again, the next thing you'll see is my fist in your fucking face." I turned to look at Kenna. She bit her lip as she stared at her father. When she caught my expression, she spun around and left.

"You owe me a lamp," I called to Cameron as I firmly shut the door.

I followed Kenna and stood behind her as she hit the down button for the elevator. Neither of us spoke. I took the opportunity to eye her outfit as she stared at the stainless steel door. Her skintight black dress and sparkly heels looked elegant with her dark hair pinned up on one side. Spicy perfume smothered my senses, and I found myself drawing it in to savor it. It was a heavier scent than her daytime perfume. It reminded me of the next morning after a hot night of sex.

"Fuck." I shook the thought right out of my head, but when I opened my eyes, I found she'd turned and was watching me. "What?"

"He has a temper, but he means well." She seemed to struggle with her words like she wanted to believe them herself.

"Does he often come at you like that?"

"He's all bark, no bite." She waved me off, but there was a sense of sadness behind her words.

"Why don't you call him Dad?" I took the opportunity, as I'd often wondered about it.

"Because he's not my dad." She closed her eyes for a second. "I mean, he was, but he's not anymore." I eyed her, confused. "Let's just say he was kind of there when I was younger, but as I matured," she pointed to her breasts, "his clients paid more attention to me than him. He changed. I soon became an asset and then a full-time employee. I guess the daughter part kind of dissolved with me anyway. My little sister fills the gap, plays up to *Daddy* in all the ways I refuse to."

"That's fucked up."

"I don't want your pity." She stiffened.

"I wasn't giving it to you," I shot back as we stepped between the doors.

"Do you have any idea who this Castillo guy is?"

"No one you need to concern yourself with."

"I beg to differ."

"Nice to know you beg." I smirked trying to get under her skin. I enjoyed it.

"You really haven't changed, have you?" We locked eyes as we silently glared at each other. She thought I was a pig, and I was too proud to give her an inch. I didn't owe her anything.

Then I remembered what Minnie told me.

"You're working tonight?" I eyed her open cleavage.

"Yes." She pulled out her lipstick and mirror.

"Cancel it."

"Pardon me?" Her face twisted. "Who are you to tell me what I can and cannot do?"

"I'm your boss." I turned to face her as I pulled out my phone and sent off a quick text. "I make the rules."

"It's a client dinner." She looked confused. "I'm doing my job."

"It's not a request, Kenna. Cancel it." The doors opened, and I stepped out on the floor above the lobby.

My phone rang, and I held it to my ear as the doors closed behind me.

"Mr. Gates, are you sure?"

"Do it."

SEVEN

KENNA

I kissed my middle finger then held it straight up in his direction as the doors closed.

"Such an asshole," I muttered but stared at the number that was stuck on level two. I used my keycard and hit the button for the lobby again, but nothing happened.

"Seriously?" I yanked open the emergency phone and waited for Gavin to pick up.

"Hi, Miss Lodge." He cleared his throat in an odd way. "How can I help you?"

"Gavin, the elevator is stuck."

"Is it?"

"Yes." I looked up at the camera. "Any chance you can unstick it?"

"That will take some time."

"This is a Gates hotel." I chuckled. "Things like this aren't supposed to happen."

There was a pause, and I heard him cover the phone mic.

"Don't worry, I'm doing everything I can to get you out of there."

"Thanks." I sighed and looked at the time. I was already late. "Any idea what happened?"

"Ah, not sure." I heard some buttons click, and I leaned against the cool wall and listened as he worked away.

"How are your kids?" I figured I should make small talk since he was just listening to me breathe.

"Big and bad," he laughed, "but they're good."

"Summer's here. You should take them to the pool. Beat the heat here when you can."

"I'm not so sure they'll be as welcome this year."

"Why?" Jim Gates always seemed pretty cool about the staff bringing their family by to enjoy the pool.

"The new boss likes to run a tighter ship." He referred to Grim, and I rolled my eyes at the camera, making him chuckle again. "I don't need to piss him off, and neither do you."

"Asshole behavior brings out asshole behavior, I guess."

"You've got some balls, girl."

"Mm." I checked the time again, and something

suddenly hit me as his words repeated in my head. *I don't need to piss him off, and neither do you.* "Gavin," I drew out his name.

"Come on, Kenna, don't ask me." He caved like a house of cards.

"Son of a bitch." I closed my eyes and wanted to scream.

"Orders are orders."

"I know." I would never ask him to go against his boss. He had a family to provide for. Then I remembered something. "I gotta go." I knew the camera recorded everything, so Gavin wouldn't get in trouble. I opened my purse and plucked out the pretty little black master keycard and tapped it to the pad. Like magic, the door opened.

"Ha!" I was positively gleeful.

I flew out of the steel cage and ran straight into Rail. I didn't have to see his face; the smell of weed, leather, and bleach told me it was him. Well, that and the words that flew out of his mouth.

"Fine, if you want me to grab your boobs, just ask." He steadied me on my feet and smirked down at me. "Hey, doll."

"Have you seen Grim?"

"If I did?" He pointed to his cheek, and I rolled my eyes and gave him a quick kiss. Rail was my weakness. He was crude, crazy, and completely unpredictable. I was only one of those things, so I lived vicariously through him.

"Sorry. It's been a day, and I'm insanely late for a business dinner."

"He left saying just about the same thing, like twenty minutes ago."

"Unbelievable." I glared around the lobby.

"You need a ride?" He grinned, and I shook my head.

"Once was enough." I shuddered at the memory of Rail's driving skills. Plus, Trig's wife Tess told me that once you accepted a ride on a guy's bike it meant you belonged to them. I loved Rail, but it was strictly platonic. "I'll see you tomorrow."

My phone rang, and I quickly fished it out in case it was Sonny trying to contact me.

Hanna? My mind spun with the things I needed to do, and I knew if I answered her call at that moment, it would take away some precious time. Hanna and I had met in Morocco when we were both doing an internship abroad. She became close with my family, and I loved her like a sister. If she was calling, I had to answer, if only to let her know I couldn't talk.

"Shit, hello?" I answered as I spotted one of the drivers for the hotel heading my way with a phone to his ear.

"Kenna!" She sounded as stressed as I felt. "I need to talk to you."

"I'm so sorry, Hanna. I'd love to talk, but now's not a good time."

"Kenna, please."

"Hey!" I waved and grabbed the driver's attention, so I didn't need to chase down a cab or find parking.

"Come on." He didn't even ask what I wanted, and I didn't have time to explain.

"Hanna, I'll have to call you later, okay?"

"Okay, but soon. Promise me you will."

"I will." I dodged around a bunch of tourists. "Can you text me whatever it is?"

"No. Just call me back tonight." The line went dead as I slid into the back of the car and tried to catch my breath.

To say I was furious was a total understatement, but Grim thrived on getting under my skin, so I needed to calm down and gather myself.

Deep breaths.

"Under the armrest." The driver's voice reached me. I looked up to meet his eyes in the rearview mirror then swung open the lid to find a good bottle of bourbon nestled inside. "Mr. Gates takes this car sometimes when he wants to be a little more discrete." He winked.

"How devious of him." I chuckled and unscrewed the cap then took a deep swig. I really needed a little liquid courage. "Yikes, that's strong," I breathed out as I felt the heat seep down my throat like honey. I grinned at the lipstick mark on the rim as I replaced the bottle. I didn't wipe it off and turned a satisfied look at the back of the driver's head. "Your name is Shore, right?"

"It has been for the past fifty-one years." He switched lanes, and I realized I never told him where I was going.

"Did Gavin call you to help me out?"

"That, he did." He checked the mirrors. "You've been good to my cousin over the years you've been coming here, and I was on my way here to pick up a guest anyway. How else am I supposed to keep up on what's going on." He shrugged and smiled, and I matched it. He pulled around the big circular drive-way, and the door was immediately opened for me.

For a brief moment Hanna filtered her way into my thoughts. She'd had her fair share of man problems. I only hoped the last loser wasn't back, as he'd been a hard one to get rid of. I figured I'd better crack a bottle of wine and put my feet up when I called her back. But Hanna would have to wait. I had to focus.

"Thanks, Shore." I handed him a tip, which he gladly took, and shimmied out of the car. Feeling much better about everything, I hurried into the hotel, through the sea of gamblers, down a very long hall-way, and finally slowed my walk and straightened my shoulders as I got close. I stopped for a moment and pulled out the tiny perfume bottle from my clutch and dabbed a little oil on my wrists then massaged a little into my neck. I let the delicious scent settle my head.

Here we go.

Feeling like I'd won, I smoothed my hands down my tight black dress, checked if the girls were ready, which they were, and put a swing in my hips which immediately caught the eye of a guest. I gave him a glance as his eyes dragged down my body. I smiled but kept my momentum toward their table.

To my surprise, I saw Salazar was at their table. When he saw me, his smile wavered as he glanced over at Sonny. What was my number eight doing here with Sonny Conti, of all people?

I wasn't a fan of Sonny at all. I knew what he was capable of, but I'd been told to go after him by both Jim Gates and my father. I hadn't earned the reputation I had by backing down from a challenge. This was what I did, and I was damn good at it.

"There she is!" Sonny beamed as Grim turned around and shot me a baffled look. It turned angry then morphed into something wicked. I almost hesitated, suddenly a bit rattled, but refused to let it show and pushed on. This was my deal, not his.

"My apologies for arriving late." I smiled around the table but swallowed hard as Grim continued to stare at me. "Thank you, Mr. Gates, for keeping my guest company." I kept my voice cool.

"Kenna," Salazar rose and leaned in, "I only just

learned from Mr. Gates that you were to meet with Mr. Conti this evening. My apologies if I'm intruding. I was under the impression this was to be a business dinner between Mr. Conti and me."

"Perhaps he was trying to fit us both in at the same time." I force a smile at Sonny. "Why don't we have dinner another time, Mr. Conti, so you two can finish up?"

"Not to worry." Sonny pulled out a chair for me. "I'm pleased you're here, though I don't think Mr. Gates is, and he was just telling us you weren't feeling well."

"I'm sure it's just a misunderstanding." I chuckled as we both took our seats.

"Yes, Mr. Gates told us you couldn't make it. Are you sick?" Salazar eyed Grim, who just shrugged and leaned back in his chair. I appreciated his lack of comment as I tried to quickly fill in the blanks as to what was going on.

"Nothing a little food couldn't fix." I turned to Sonny. "It's a pleasure to meet you again, Mr. Conti. I hope you've thought more about what we discussed?"

"Oh, please," he poured me a glass of wine, "no need to be so formal. Call me Sonny." He ignored my question.

"As long as you call me Kenna." Sonny leaned in close, and I felt Grim tense next to me.

"It's a deal." He gave Salazar a quick look, then

Grim. "Kenna, I assume by the way Mr. Salazar greeted you, you've met before?"

"Yes, we have a few times." I kept my answer vague. I was good at keeping my clients' information to myself. Being discreet was what Vegas was all about.

"That's great. Maybe you can tell Mr. Salazar a bit about me and vouch that I'd be a good person to work with."

"Hmm," Grim muttered annoyed, and Sonny gave him a pissed look and licked his teeth.

"So, Gates, now that Kenna has arrived, don't let us keep you from your business. Surely, you have better things to do with your time than hang out with the likes of us." He chuckled lightly.

"I cleared my schedule for the evening. It's fine." Grim tapped his fingers on the table, and I could feel him vibrate with anger. "Shall we order?" He handed me a menu, and when I went to take it, he caught my gaze, and I felt my entire body run cold. He was positively petrifying, but there was a strangeness behind his dark look that seemed to pull. I was suddenly intrigued instead of frightened. Any rational human being would run for the hills, but I sat there and held his gaze. I could hear the other men talking while I had my moment with Grim.

"I thought you might like to know the elevator's fixed now." I kept my voice even and watched as his pupils dilated and his jaw twitched. "That makes us what?" I couldn't help but egg him on. "Two to zero?" His lips thinned into a hard line as he leaned in, and I was engulfed by his scent.

"Watch yourself, sweetheart." He let out a warm breath that brushed my collarbone and brought out a few goosebumps. "You don't want to bring out the beast in me. I normally keep it tightly caged."

I arched an eyebrow but didn't respond, and his gaze dropped down to my lips.

"Or maybe I do," I whispered, and his eyes shot up to mine.

"What can I get you?" The waiter arrived, and it broke our connection. We pulled apart to order, but I felt as though I'd been seared with the heat that came from his eyes.

Dinner came, and with it the small talk that was all part of winning over a client. You needed to put the time in to show you were all about them and their interests ahead of anything else and anyone else. I waited for Sonny to include Salazar or bring up whatever they'd been discussing before I arrived, but he didn't. He just focused on me.

"Sonny, you and I have gotten to know one another over the last several months."

"We have." He purred at me, and I fought not to roll my eyes.

"I think it's time we delved into things a little deeper."

"The door is open. I love deep." He chuckled, and I ignored his obvious inuendo.

"You've been a guest at the Bellagio, the Wynn, the Taro, but not at Indulge. Why is that?" I cocked my head to the side and brushed my hair back away from the girls as I asked the question.

"I guess I just didn't know *you* were at Indulge." He gave me a sleezy grin.

"And now that you know I'm there?" I challenged.

"I think that leaves me disappointed."

"Oh?" I squinted, trying to follow.

"You see, I'm more tempted to see what Grim's new hotel Secrets has to offer, but if you're not going to be working there and only at Indulge, maybe I..." He leaned back and raised his hands as if to say what was he to do.

"She'll be there," Grim bit out before I could tell Sonny that Jim had offered me the chance to work at both hotels if I wanted. Just as long as I funneled the older clients toward Indulge and the younger ones to Secrets. Vegas needed something for the older, more established guests, but there had to be something more fast-paced and wild for the younger generation.

"Excellent." He grinned at me. "Now you have my full attention."

"And on that note," Salazar stood and buttoned his jacket, "I need to get going." He tossed his napkin on his plate. "Kenna, it was an unexpected pleasure. I'll leave you to your meeting with Mr. Conti." He turned to Grim. "Mr. Gates, I'm very glad you were able to join us tonight." I knew there was more to that comment; Salazar was an intelligent man.

"Me too." Grim stood to shake his hand.

"I'll be in touch." Sonny smiled and waved at Salazar from where he sat. I'd put good money that Salazar saw Sonny for what he was. Not someone to get too wrapped up with.

"Miss Lodge's schedule with her clients is quite full right now." Grim jumped right back into the conversation.

"Of course, I always find time for my regulars," I added. I wasn't sure what Grim was doing, but if I had to sell myself right now to get Sonny to sign on for either hotel, I would.

"And just what does a regular need to do to get your attention?" Sonny draped his arm along the back of my chair and leaned closer. My shoulders tensed, but I played it cool. I was used to men like this.

"The more money you play, the more of me you get to see." I finished off my wine, but as I set my glass on the table, he filled it up again.

"Just how much do I get to see?" He wiggled his eyebrows, and I looked away and popped open my purse and pulled out the contract. He plucked it from my fingers and held it up.

"Let's move this party to my room."

"Don't misunderstand me, Mr. Conti. I handle all my business professionally–"

"I promise you I'll make it worth your—"

A sudden darkness blocked my view of Sonny as Grim leaned between us.

"If you want an escort sent to your room, I'm sure your host here would be more than pleased to get you one." He pulled me out of the chair as Sonny rose.

"Don't overreact, Grim. I don't want an escort. I just want Kenna to come have some fun." Sonny laughed and held up his hand. "Seems to me there was a time you liked to have some fun yourself."

"Kenna's still on the clock," Grim kept his grip on my arm, "and a client just arrived at the hotel that she needs to get situated."

Sonny moved in front of us, but Grim had at least a foot and half on him.

"Think wisely, here, Sonny," Grim growled. "I can make or break your time in Vegas."

Sonny's mouth twisted with anger, but he thought better of taking Grim on.

"I'll be in touch with my decision, Kenna." Sonny held up the contract, and I was surprised Grim didn't snatch it from his hand. I nodded when Grim looked over at me but didn't dare speak. There was playing Grim at this game, and there was just being stupid. The added level of violence that had suddenly been tacked on to the game warned me to stay quiet.

"The next time you want a meeting with Miss Lodge, expect me to be there." Grim moved his hand to my lower back and urged me forward.

He rushed us out of the restaurant, through a sea of people looking to party at the nearby casino, and out into the lobby. I caught Jesse, his right-hand man, and a few of Grim's other security behind us in the reflection of the shop windows. I hadn't even known they were there, but it didn't surprise me.

A limo waited at the bottom of the steps, and the driver opened the door as Grim ushered me inside. He said something to Jesse then ducked inside and sat across from me. I took a moment to collect myself and admire the limo. It was insanely gorgeous, and I had been in my fair share of limos before. The seats were made of the softest leather, a fully stocked top-shelf bar was behind glass doors, and the under-glow lighting was low and sexy. I wasn't sure why he had chosen his limo and not a town car, but it was spectacular. The only thing that disconcerted me was the horseshoe-style seats made us face one another, and his steel cold eyes were locked on mine. He seemed to vibrate with anger. I remained quiet for a few minutes while my mind spun. I was embarrassed, pissed, and confused all at the same time.

"You embarrassed me back there," I muttered. "I had it under control."

"Did you?" He didn't miss a beat as he fired back at me.

"You know, all the time you've been gone," I crossed my legs as we eased onto the main road, "I've been doing this job, here, there, abroad. This isn't new to me. Sonny is just like every other asshole out there. Men are driven by sex, so I use my assets to get what I want. I know how to conduct myself."

"That's not how you should be conducting business."

"Really?" I scoffed. "First, I always conduct my business professionally, like I reminded Sonny a few moments ago. Second," I sat straighter, "it's Vegas, Grim, land of money, power, and sex. I didn't hear you or your father complain when I brought in Yen Hong, Ahmed Adil, or Dylan Benjamin."

"That's different." He yanked at his tie.

"How is it?"

"He slipped a drug into your wine."

"What?" I hadn't seen him slip anything in my drink, and I was usually quite observant.

"As he poured your wine, he dropped a drug into your drink." He shook his head, frustrated with me.

I pulled out my phone and saw a message from Hanna, but he snatched it from my hands.

"Grim!" I hated how he was treating me. "I can protect myself." I pressed my hands against the seat, afraid of my actions. "As I said, I'm used to men like that. They are scumbags, yes. But they're scumbags with fat wallets, and I bring them to you. It's my job, remember. He's not the first to try to get me to his room. I know how to get myself out of situations like that."

He rubbed his mouth as he thought then leaned forward with a heavy scowl. He tossed my phone on the seat next to him.

"Okay, prove it."

"Prove what?"

"Overpower me." He swung himself to sit next to me. One hand ran along the back of the seat, and his free hand landed hot on the inside of my thigh. Instantly, I felt flushed as my body shamelessly reacted to him being so close.

He started to slide his hand upward as he leaned into my ear. "You said you can defend yourself against men who want you." His words were heavy and laced with a needy undertone, it almost made me moan. I grabbed his wrist and tried to push it backward, but he didn't budge. He leaned over me and pressed his hard body against the side of mine. "Come on, sweetheart," he purred, taunting me, "show me what you got." I tried again, but my strength gave out as his fingers discovered I was going commando. "Jesus." His lips pressed to my neck and sucked gently.

"Grim," my head clouded, "it's—"

"Say I'm right." He licked a spot on my neck, and I

felt a little fight arise inside. I twisted and tried with all my might to push his chest back, but somehow, he grabbed both wrists in one hand and lifted me to straddle his waist. The moment gravity kicked in, I let out a small cry at how hard he was.

It had been twenty-eight days, not that I had counted, since I'd last been with a man, I was so wound up inside that I could have burst. I was sure dust and cobwebs would have shot across the limo.

"You're tiny, Kenna." His hands took my wrists and held them behind my back. My breasts arched up toward his face. "They could manhandle you for hours, and you'd be at their mercy."

My hair was wild, so I flicked it back to tumble off to one side. "I wouldn't have gone to their room. I know better than that!" I leaned my weight to one side to attempt to punch his balls, but his free hand latched on to my arm to hold me in place.

"You're not going anywhere until I make my point," he huffed.

I hated that he *may be* a bit right in his concern, but it wasn't anger that ran through my veins right then. It was pure lust. Lust and anger were two totally different things. Grim Gates had a body like a god, and it wasn't fair to be put in this position. His body was so damn perfect it was hard to deny. Everything about Grim's body was designed to distract a female. The way his tattoos lined his jaw begged me to lean down and lick the seam. The cross under his eye called for all things sinful, and I hated that I was tempted to know just how sinful he could be.

He leaned in and kissed my collarbone, then inched downward to the top of my breast, then licked between them, until he found my nipple through the fabric of my dress. He sucked gently, and I was furious when my body reacted so shamelessly. My thighs flinched and my head tilted back to allow him more access. My hair cascaded down my back as I arched toward him.

"I'll give you an advantage." He chuckled and let my hands go. They moved to his shoulders, up his neck, and into his hair as I ground on his lap, in need of the friction. His hands slid up my dress and over my bare ass. "Say I'm right," he muttered, which pissed me off further.

I felt the opportunity and seized it. I reached down with both hands and grabbed his erection and gave it a good squeeze. His head rolled back with a groan, and when he looked up at me, his eyes weren't steel anymore, they were honey yellow.

Oh, shit.

One moment I was on his lap, and the next I was bent over the other seat, his body covered mine, and his fingers found their way to my soaked entrance.

"You disobeyed a direct order from your boss tonight," he growled in my ear as he pressed his fingers gently inside my slick folds.

"Oh!" I nearly lost it. I was used to regular sex and the odd time with Dale when he couldn't keep it in his pants. He was good. I let that memory quickly die. No one, besides maybe him, could feed my sexual appetite. I was drawn to the darker side of sex. I was no delicate flower. Show me you want me by taking whatever you want. It was my need. It was why Minnie and Tess were my soul sisters—they got me. I knew I needed this; I just hated that it was with Grim.

The game we'd been playing had taken a dark turn, and it was a dangerous one for so many reasons. The fact that he was my boss was only one thing, and this would most likely end badly. My brain whirled with so many thoughts. But oh, my God, I shuddered when he dragged the pads of his fingers back and forth and any bad ideas were kicked out of the way.

"You escaped the elevator. You knew I didn't want you to go, yet you still attended the dinner. What if I wasn't there tonight? Huh?" He rubbed over my sensitive spot again but differently. His erection pressed into my backside, and I leaned back, seeking contact. "What happens if they took you to his room and it was their fingers inside you right now?" He was right. Tonight could have ruined me. "I nearly shot him under the fucking table." He licked the shell of my ear as I built higher and higher. My arms bore my weight as my hands flexed over the soft seat fabric. I was so wound, so deliciously close to what I wanted.

"Grim!" I cried. I needed any kind of release. His huge hard body covered mine, and I swore I could feel his heartbeat through my back.

"Would you be this wet right now if I'd drilled a bullet into Sonny's skull?" He moved his hand to cup between my legs, massaging his palm in delicious circles. I moaned, and my head went back to hit his shoulder. His other hand slid up over my strained breasts to my neck and gave it a light squeeze. It was as if he could read my wants. He turned my head to look up at him.

"Answer me."

"I'd be soaked," I barely whispered as his thumb tugged at my bottom lip. His eyes widened, and I saw something dark and exciting flicker through them. I could feel the draw. It was evident that Grim Gates had a wild side, too, and I thought I just showed him mine.

"I want to ruin you so I'm the only person you see."

"Many have tried," I moved my gaze to his lips, "and many have failed."

His groan vibrated through me, then his fingers were back inside me as he pressed upward and caused me to come. His lips smashed into mine and muffled my cries. He tasted sweet, and his aftershave overloaded my senses and overwhelmed me. His tongue was just like the rest of him—it demanded. I just clung on for the ride. Deep down, I knew in a moment we'd be right back to where we were, but so many colors flooded my vision, my hearing went out for a moment, my skin heated, and my body coiled and burst all at once. It was amazing. It was exactly what I needed. His hungry pants matched mine; he was right alongside me for the ride. It was raw, animalistic, and primal. Grim was relentless. He didn't stop until he knew I was finished.

I vaguely felt him wipe between my legs as I lay limp over the seat in an effort to gather myself.

"Will you listen now?" His voice was rough, but there was a hint of humor to it.

"I don't tame that easily. You settled a need I had, that's all." I shot him what I hoped was an angry glare but noticed he was still incredibly aroused. I guessed he didn't finish. I moved to another seat and fixed my hair and dress.

A moment later, his phone rang, and he cursed like he didn't want to answer it.

"What?" He listened. "No, keep him there. I'm just dropping Kenna off at the hotel. Give me ten."

I leaned over and snagged my phone. I tapped the screen to see Hanna and Minnie had texted.

Hanna: Don't forget. Tonight.

I tapped to Minnie's message.

> Minnie: I'm thinking thigh boots, and
> maybe a white t-shirt? Every man's
> wet dream.

I smirked and had to agree. It was time to ramp up my skills at her club.

> Kenna: Count me in. See you soon.

Grim buttoned his jacket as the limo stopped in front of Indulge. I ran my hands through my hair and stepped out as the driver opened the door. I suddenly wondered if he'd noticed what happened, and I didn't look up at him. My legs were like rubber as I got out.

"The deal with Sonny is off," Grim muttered as I made a show to go through my purse then pulled out my keycard. His eyes were back to cold steel.

"That's not your decision to make." I started to walk away.

"Hey," he snagged my arm and pulled me close, "I'm serious, Kenna."

"I know, but you need to run this by Cameron and Jim. My orders came from them both."

"My order is the only one that counts." He pushed my hair back and looked at my neck with sudden interest. "Don't get yourself alone with Sonny—"

"Kenna." Jayden, the manager of the hosts at

Indulge, came out and looked fit to kill as he stared up from his phone. "Good evening, Mr. Gates."

"Jayden," Grim addressed him, slowly letting me go.

"Kenna, I need you to work tonight."

"I'm only off now," I looked at the time on my phone, "and I need to be at Minnie's in twenty."

Jayden gave me a look, and I knew he was unhappy I wouldn't work. It looked like he wanted to say more but didn't because of Grim. I really didn't want to give up my night off. After what just happened, I needed time to relive it all in my head.

"Oh, I see. Of course." He nodded.

"I agree that Kenna needs her night off." Grim smiled at him. "You can find someone else for tonight, Jayden."

"I'm sure I can. I'll work it out. How was your evening with Jenelle, Mr. Gates?"

Huh? I turned to look at Grim. Now the limo made sense. He had a date. I didn't wait for the answer; I just started up the stairs.

"Well, I need to go find Rail," I threw back over my shoulder.

"Remember what I said, Kenna." Grim's bossy tone found me. "Orders are orders."

Yeah, yeah. I called Hanna, but it went straight to voicemail.

EIGHT

GRIM

Ileaned back in the limo where only moments ago I
had lost it with Kenna. She wasn't like any other
woman I'd been with. Most thought they liked to be
manhandled, until they didn't. Kenna had a fire in her
that pissed me off to no end but drew me to her at the
same time. It was maddening. I fucking hated it.

I strummed the fingers that had just been in her
against the seat and closed my eyes, remembering how
she felt, how she smelled. And the fact she got off on
the idea of me shooting Sonny. You had to be a jacked-
up individual to be turned on by those things. I knew
because I was one of them.

My mind bounced from being sexually charged to
incredibly pissed. I thought about what could have

happened with that idiot. How could she be so fucking blind! Then the memory of my tongue on Kenna's slender neck made my insides twitch. My mouth nearly watered at how she tasted. Her breasts in my face took all my control not to lose it. Christ, they were sexy.

I adjusted my pants. My erection was on full alert as it wondered why in the hell it hadn't gotten the attention it deserved.

I ran a hand through my hair, patted my erection in sympathy, and took a deep breath. I closed my eyes and circled my shoulders as I tried to shake it off.

The limo pulled up to the curb in front of Secrets, and Cartwright let out a hiss between his teeth. He looked around then got out and came around to my door.

"What's wrong?" I could feel his nerves. "Do you see something?"

"No, just the opposite." His eyes narrowed. "Not enough movement."

I pushed Kenna out of my head and focused on my surroundings. I hired people for a reason and knew better than to ignore Cartwright. "If you see anything."

"Understood, boss." He closed the door behind me and waited for Jesse to join me, then he got back into the driver's seat.

"Where are they?"

"That's the problem, boss." Jesse waved for me to head inside. "They aren't here."

As soon as we stepped into the unfinished lobby, the foreman rushed over as he ended a phone call.

"Good evening, Mr. Gates." He extended his hand, but I gave him a hard look, and he tucked it behind his back. "I have no idea why my men aren't here, but I just located them. They're at the Venetian on a different job. I don't understand how this happened." He looked like he might pass out.

"Call them. Get them here. Now!" Jesse's face went red as he yelled at the guy. My temper flared along with his. This was unacceptable.

"I did. I called my boss, then my boss's boss, but it seems someone overrode your instructions." His voice cracked at the end. I tucked one hand in my pants pocket to keep from strangling him and rubbed my chin instead as I stepped forward. The gap between me and the man who was now costing me thousands of dollars by the minute closed.

"Who?"

"I don't know. I just got off the phone with the engineer," his face gleamed with sweat, "and he had no idea either. No one can tell me."

"Grim," Jesse pulled my attention and whispered in my ear, "any chance this could be Sonny?"

I saw red.

"Give me the names of the men you spoke to." The

guy prattled off the information as I nodded at Jesse. He knew what to do.

"Potatoes?" Laura handed me the dish of mashed potatoes.

"Don't mind if I do." I smiled at the oldest boy who was eyeing my Audemars Piguet watch.

"There's no numbers." He scrunched up his nose. "How do you tell the time?"

"You know how a watch looks with the numbers one to twelve around in a circle?" I pointed to the face of the watch. "Well, each one of those little lines represents those numbers. Everything is the same. It's just with lines in place of the numbers."

"Dad says watches are only for old people."

"Zackery!" Laura scowled at him.

"You're correct. It's a dying fashion that I hope will come back around sometime. I much prefer a watch than looking at my phone." The door opened, and we could hear footsteps and their dog's excitement. Laura stood quickly.

"Something smells amazing." Rich, one of my contractors, came around the corner, but his face fell the moment he looked at me.

"Rich," Laura pointed at me, "I wish you'd told me you had a friend coming over. I could have made

something better than pork tenderloin and potatoes."
She gave him a hard look as I cut into the dry pork.

"Mr. Gates, what a surprise."

"Is it?" I dipped the overdone meat in the relish
and hoped the moisture would help me choke it down.
"Seems to me you might've been expecting me to come
by, considering what's been happening with my
hotel."

"Laura, take the boys to their room," he ordered.

"No," I dabbed the corners of my mouth, "Laura,
stay right where you are." I set my gun on my lap. I
kept it just out of view of the children but where Rich
and Laura could see it. "Why don't you have a seat?"

"Do as he says," Rich warned his wife, whose face
had drained of color. He slowly set his bag down and
made his way over to the chair at the end of the table.

"Wise choice." I smiled at him then at his wife, who
had eased back into her chair. She drew her boys close.
I smiled at them to put them at ease. "Now," I took a
long draw from the water glass and kept my voice
conversational, "I want a name."

"Mr. Gates, I don't know who it is."

I looked away and studied the photos on the wall
as I wondered why no one at this point ever told the
truth.

"Your youngest here was telling me about his
hockey game this weekend. At the T-Mobile Arena,
wasn't it?" I looked at the child.

"I play defense." He piped up, and I smiled warmly at him as his mother told him to keep quiet.

"I see your father is playing the same position." I gave Rich an accusing expression.

"Mr. Gates, I get my orders from above, then tell my men where to be and when."

"I understand how the construction world works, Rich." I cleared my throat, annoyed. I wasn't getting anywhere. "Perhaps, Laura, you should take the boys next door. It would be a pity for them to overhear something that could threaten their mental health in the future."

"No." Laura looked torn. "You've got the wrong man. You—"

"Laura." Rich cut her off, and I raised my hand to shut him up.

"Go on." I waved.

"You want Mr. Tupot. He's the snake at the top that makes all the underhanded deals." Tears flowed down her cheeks, and the boys began to grow nervous.

"Very good, Laura." I smiled at Rich, who looked sick. "But now you need to do as I asked and take the boys next door."

"No, you can't hurt him." She started to panic while Rich yelled at her to leave. "You can't! We need him, the boys need their father. They—"

Bang!

I fired a shot at the ceiling, and they all went still with wild eyes and gaping mouths.

"I won't repeat myself again."

She grabbed both boys by the arm and hurried them out of the room. I moved my attention over to Rich, who had his hand over his mouth. His eyes were red and wild.

"If you're going to play in the dark, you need to be prepared for what that brings, Rich."

"I was only doing what I was told."

"And now I'm here to tell you that you better fill me in on what you know, or I'll involve your family in this shit you're playing with."

"I don't kn—"

I grabbed his hand and jammed the steak knife through it. When he screamed, I pressed my napkin over his mouth and held his head back. I took the water pitcher and poured slowly over his napkin, waterboarding him into a manic state. He squirmed and choked, his eyes wide and fearful, but he needed to know I meant business. I wasn't one for showing weakness, especially with so much at stake.

"Now," I tossed the glass pitcher against the wall where it shattered into a million pieces, "I'm asking you this one last time. Tell me what you know, or your wife is next."

"Mr. Gates," he heaved, "please—"

"Maybe I'll start with the hands. Lord knows she can't cook. I'll start with her pinkie and then work my way up to the important fingers."

"Fine," he moaned as he held his bloody hand to his chest, his breath coming in heaves. "Tupot said he made a deal with someone." He fought to catch his breath. "He's a slimy bastard who does work with all kinds of shit. There was one name mentioned..." He struggled and squeezed his eyes shut. "Alina Li."

I froze then swung around to sit in front of him. "Are you absolutely sure the name was Alina Li?"

"Positive." He stared at me, his face the picture of pain, "Mr. Gates, at the risk of overstepping, I think whatever's happening is far bigger than you realize."

"Why?"

"Because Tupot is a cocky son of a bitch. He even bragged when he won your bid, saying he'd got you by the balls." He shook his head as though he couldn't believe what he'd just said. "Sorry," he huffed. "What's strange is that he got a call, and whoever it was scared the shit out of him so badly he didn't show up the rest of the week. Tupot never ever misses his daily visit to the worksite. He makes our lives a living hell."

"I see." I slowly let everything process. Rarely was a developer at a worksite every day. That in itself rang a bell in my head. I had to admit, I'd been pleased to accept that bid. It was lower than the others. Not at the bottom, but comfortably mid-range. Leo had given me the particulars, and the firm checked out as being a very competent company.

"My-my phone," he painfully nodded at his phone on the floor, "his address is inside."

"I have it." I tapped my fingers on the table then stood and buttoned my jacket. "Kids are chatty and share more than they should. Remember that if you find yourself in a position to share tonight's events with anyone else. I got in once. It'll be much easier a second time."

"I won't say a word, and neither will my family." The sweat rolled down his face as he spoke, and I nodded.

"If you remember, see, or hear anything, I'm the first person you call. Understood?" I leaned down in his face. "Anything at all."

"Understood."

I pushed my chair in and looked around the house. Then I took my time and left via the front door.

"Jesse." I waved him over from where he kept watch in the bushes. "We have a problem."

The next day came and went, and though we got another crew in to work, countless manhours and money had been wasted, and I was still in the dark on what happened with very little to go on. Sonny had been with an escort all night, and my men confirmed Salazar—not that he was our main focus—was at

Indulge for drinks with friends almost all evening. We couldn't rule anyone out at that point in time, so we kept a close eye on them anyway.

I rested my forearms on the railing and peered down at the busy life below. The sun was hot and heated my shoulders through my dress shirt. The rooftop of Indulge was one of my go-to places when I needed to get away. You had to have VIP access, so it weeded out the general public and anyone under the age of twenty-one.

We had tables at the far end, so you never had to stop gambling. One pool was designed to lounge in, not splash or play games. Part of it was covered, one part had chairs so you could soak and tan, and the other had a fully stocked swim-up bar. Servers catered to the select customers' every need from a water massage to something to eat, to a lap dance. Indulge had it all. It catered to a more sophisticated crowd, which was why my father wasn't concerned that I wanted to build Secrets. It would scoop up the younger clients on the other side of the market without hurting what we had here.

"Only a few days home and you look more stressed than a church boy in a titty bar." Rail chuckled from behind his cigarette. I just huffed and continued to watch the people below. Rail was one of Trigger's closest men, and I trusted him with my life. Rail, Brick, Morgan, and of course Trigger were welcome at

Indulge anytime. Trigger's uncle Gus and my father became close after Trigger and I met back in the day, and we welcomed the Devil's Reach bikers whenever they were in Vegas. The guys always had our backs, as we did them.

Once Trigger's wife Tess took over her mother's burlesque house, the Devil's Reach fully took over Vegas as their territory. Trigger was fiercely protective of Tess and his club, which worked in my favor, given how close I'd become with both Trigger and Elio Capri, the mafia boss in Italy.

There were a lot of people who weren't pleased to have an active bike club in Vegas, but I didn't give a shit. My family's companies were booming, and so were Trigger's. Well, most of our business was. Secrets was my baby, and I planned to get her built as soon as I could. My anger flared with that thought. I was determined to get to the bottom of what was happening sooner rather than later.

"Shit's going on, and I can't figure it the fuck out," I confessed to Rail as he stood smoking quietly next to me. I knew whatever I said to Rail would stay private.

"Shit always takes figurin' out. Makes life interesting." He coughed then dragged more smoke into his lungs. "But I guess it also comes with people always wantin' ya dead."

"Mm." I nodded.

"Heard Sonny's in town." He eyed me. "Son of a bitch got some balls."

"Yeah, well, new money will do that." I glanced around. "Dad wants his business, but I think he's a ticking time bomb. It's only a matter of time before he fucks up again and causes more trouble."

"I'm with ya. That fucker is a loose cannon. I heard he tried to fuck with Kenna." I squinted at him. "Yeah, Kenna." He decided to elaborate. "A few drinks in at Minnie's, and she told the story. Tess has a knack for pulling shit out of people, too. I hear it was a good thing you were there." He eyed me, and I wondered what else she'd shared.

"If she'd followed my orders in the first place and stayed put, she wouldn't have been in that situation."

"Have you ever wondered why Minnie, Tess, and Kenna are such great friends?" he asked and looked at me with a wry look. "It's 'cause they're all the same, man. Fuckin' feisty, fearless as hell, and damn sexy. It's where wet dreams come from." He shook his head. "It's a scientific fact, Grim, trust me." He grinned and rubbed his crotch.

"The shit you share." I laughed and felt some of the tension ease in my neck.

"Nah, it's the shit I don't share that's really good, like what Kenna's really up to at Minnie's."

"Meaning?" That caught my attention.

"Grim," Leo was behind us holding some papers, "a quick word?" He nodded at Brick.

"I'll be back."

"Yeah, sure." Rail inhaled deeply and waved me off.

"First, the crew didn't show up at the hotel, and now the electricians are sayin' there's an unexpected problem with supplies." Leo showed me an email he had printed off. "What the hell's going on?"

I snatched the paperwork from him and read the bullshit excuse.

"Someone's fucking with me, and I don't think it's Alina Li." I ripped open the door and headed for the elevator with the paperwork jammed in my fist. I slapped my keycard to the panel and cursed every second it took to reach the twentieth floor. The moment the doors opened I heard the cheering. "What the hell!"

The security guards gave me a nod as I rushed down the hall and flew into the office. Cameron and my father held up their drinks.

"Grim!" my father called. "Come, son, and toast with us."

"What's going on?"

"Kenna landed Sonny Conti!"

The air was sucked out of the room as I stood and stared at them. Anger flowed down through me like thick molasses, and I could feel my adrenaline rush to mix with it.

"And why are you so happy?" I glanced at Cameron. He looked as excited as Dad.

"Because he signed me on as his lawyer."

This was a fucking nightmare.

"And when did this happen?"

"Sonny just left." Cameron threw back his drink.

"Fuck." I was about to say more when Dad handed me the contract.

"Look who else she brought on."

Son of a bitch.

"Victor? Sonny's father signed on, too?" I tried to keep my cool, but it was slipping fast. "Are you fucking kidding me?"

"Both!" Dad cupped his mouth as he grinned. "I know how you feel about them, son, but this is huge. Victor can keep an eye on his son, and they can both spend their money in our casino. They've got a lot of friends with fat wallets."

"Yeah, a lot of friends along with Solly D. We can't sign off on the Chicago Outfit, Dad, no way!" I shook my head. "You know better than to play with those guys. They ran Chicago the way John Gotti ran New York. I trust Elio Capri, and he told us long ago to stay the hell away from them."

"Calm down, son." Cameron put his hand on my shoulder.

"Hand! Now!" I barked as I glared at him. It immediately fell away, and he stepped back.

"Just because we landed two crime bosses doesn't mean the rest of them will follow." Cameron tried to smooth shit over. "I mean, who are we to talk?"

"Cameron," I hissed, "I am not your son." I drew the words out slowly then turned to my father. "Dad, I know I said I'd back off, but you did say that if I came home, I'd have a say in everything that happens at Indulge. I thought signing one of them was a terrible idea, but both of them? It's simply insane. We've got twenty-four hours to revoke the contract, and I insist we do it."

"Well, I disagree." My father set his glass down. "But tell you what. I did agree you'd have a say, so if you still feel this way in the morning, we'll discuss it further." My father was always fair and generally had good reasons for what he did, but this went too far.

"My mind won't change."

"This is huge, Grim. Take the win," Cameron chimed in. "These are just stupid folks with a lot of money."

"Well," I checked the time with the knowledge I needed to be elsewhere, "I can promise you one thing, Cameron. Victor and Sonny will not step a foot inside Secrets Hotel. So, be sure to let your *clients* know that." I eyed my father hard and threw the door open. I wanted to be as far away from them both as I could. I needed to think.

> Grim: I could break some bones.

> Trigger: Good timing. You know
> where to go.

> Grim: See you in ten.

The moment the doors opened, the pandemonium of noise and excited people found its way to my wild head. It felt like an electric charge. It was the thing that Trigger, my friend Elio Capri, and I could all relate to. It was what originally brought us together and carried over to handling business together.

"You're up after this round." Trigger tossed me some knuckle tape as he walked by.

"Thanks." I closed the door to the changing room and opened my locker. I stripped down, pulled on my shorts, and taped my hands.

The law might forbid underground fighting, but I never understood why they'd ban something so basic. It dated back to Roman times. It's innate in humans to fight. The need to strike, to break bones, to bring a man to his knees. That need to conquer. Trigger, Elio, me. All of this was part of us, what we needed to ground us. It cemented our friendship.

"Time." Brick knocked on the door.

I took a deep breath and stepped out into the chaotic room. The crowd went nuts, which brought the volume to a deafening roar. Men screamed with the thrill of the idea of one winner left standing, and women screamed all kinds of promises. This was one of the many things that fueled my tainted soul, breaking bones.

"Make a show of it." Brick shouted from beside me. He knew I was a performer in the ring.

I ducked under the rope and slipped my mouth guard in. My opponent was in the opposite corner.

The bell rang, and I was in the zone.

Whack! His fist drilled into the side of my face, and I smiled as I shook off the delicious pain. He stepped back with a grunt and paced the side of the ring as he tried to figure me out.

This fight was all about speed and was a favorite of the spectators. The fastest time won. The first man to hit the floor lost. The winner would fight nine competitors and hold the title of "Rapid Winner."

My plan was not to win. I just wanted to force my opponent to slow down, make a show that he couldn't take me down under the necessary seven minutes. The fight ended at that point, and if I wasn't down, the club won. I intended to savor every single one of those minutes from each opponent who stepped in the ring with me.

I took their hits, no matter how hard they swung. I

only blocked the ones that came at my face. I had a lot of business to handle every day, and I couldn't afford to look beat up while I did it. I was a professional businessman and needed to look the part, and what I did in the ring was far from businesslike. Seven men came, each thinking they had the upper hand, and lost. I played my part, dragged it out, gave them hope, then showed them the mat.

By the eighth, I lost control of my mind and let it slip.

Jab! Jab! He hit my stomach twice. *Jab! Jab! Jab!* Three to the shoulder. I landed a punch on his jaw and knocked him backward as Kenna's face suddenly popped in my head. I shook her off, but she came right back. My own words echoed in my head. "Remember what I said, Kenna. Orders are orders." *Jab!* I felt my back muscles contract.

Did I need to prove to her that I had the final say? Did I need to pin her down again and—the sounds she made when my fingers were inside of her took over, and I struggled to clear my head.

I felt a punch to the stomach again, but I barely registered it. How could she make a deal when she knew I had forbidden it?

I was so pent up that the normal release I got with these fights wasn't happening. Instead of the usual burst of endorphins, it felt like tiny pinpricks designed to irritate, not relieve. I squeezed my eyes shut and tried to force myself to feel the pain. Suddenly, I was shot backward and bounced off the ropes.

"I'm all for the show, Grim, but shit, are you with us?" Morgan yelled from somewhere, and I jolted back to the present just in time to duck when my opponent swung at my jaw.

He grunted as I swung around and kicked him in the back. I punched his calf and he fell to his knees, then I nailed him in the ribs. He fell hard with a yelp, and I knew he was down.

The crowd went insane, the bell could barely be heard, and my arm was tossed in the air as the winner for that round.

A movement in the crowd caught my attention, and I saw Calli Tame making a beeline for someone. Then I saw who it was. Kenna. A fight broke out between them.

"Last up!" The announcer said his name, but I blocked him out. The crowd screamed louder, but I was focused on Kenna's hands that were up as she tried to get her sister to back off. Minnie was by her side in a flash. Calli gave them both the finger and whirled around. She stomped angrily to Simon, who stood by the door. What the hell was that about?

I felt the footsteps as he stepped in the ring and turned to find Melvern Trident, Jr. His name alone made me want to punch in his pretentious face. Melvern was the youngest son to the Mac hotels with an ego the size of Texas. He also had a huge chip on his shoulder when it came to the Devil's Reach. He and I were oil and water in business. In the ring, he was determined to take me. Normally I'd make a show of embarrassing him, but tonight I was finished here.

"Let's go, Reaper," he hissed, and I hit him fast and hard in three places. A hit between the neck and collarbone, another under the armpit, and a kick to his ankle. He crumpled like a piece of paper, knocked out cold. The place went silent then went nuts.

I didn't wait for the bell or the announcement. I knew I'd won the club a shit ton of money tonight. To us, it wasn't just about the money. It was the fact that every tournament the club won drew in that many more people. More people meant more business right across the board.

I jumped down and pushed through the crowd and out to the hallway to my private room. I showered and got dressed in record time.

"That was somethin'." Trigger leaned on the wall as I came out of the bathroom. "Feel better?"

"No." I fastened my watch.

"Need any help?"

"Remember Alina Li?"

"Your crazy ex from Singapore?"

"Yeah."

"How could I forget."

"Well, apparently her name is being connected to Tupot's construction company."

"Shit." He knew all too well what Alina was capable of. "She didn't take your leaving very well."

"I know." I rubbed my head and thought how I attracted the crazies. "I think I need to pay her a visit."

"You want to return home in pieces?" He chucked darkly.

"Anyway, have you heard anything else about the Stripe Backs and Minnie's place?" I asked as I shrugged on my jacket. I caught a glimpse of myself in the mirror. You'd never know I'd just gone nine rounds in the ring other than my battered hands. He shook his head.

"Morgan caught two of 'em headin' this way last night. It's why we're back. Followed them to the Strip then lost 'em."

"I'll mention it to my guys, make sure they watch for them."

"Appreciate it." He nodded. "Tess has some shit to sort out at the house because of the renovations. I ain't leavin' her here with rats around."

"Understood." I checked my phone and saw a call from Leo. He could wait.

"Got Cooper runnin' the club for a bit. We're here a while."

"Good plan." I could feel his eyes on me as I tucked my gun in my waistband.

"Trig," Rail came through the door, his normal cig hanging from his lips, "Minnie's got identical triplets here! Flown in from Brazil." He rubbed his hands and could hardly contain his excitement. "Wanna go up top?" He pointed to the ceiling.

Trigger looked at me and shrugged. I figured, why the hell not. Fighting hadn't relieved anything, but maybe a female could. Well, multiple females.

NINE

KENNA

"**W**hat about this?" Tess held up a man's white dress shirt. "You looked good in it last time."

Minnie smirked. "Like a wet t-shirt contest, but in a man's shirt. They'll love it."

"Who's they?" I gave her a pointed look. I didn't do this for anyone but me.

"I just meant later, if you change your mind."

"Which you should," Tess chimed in. "You're in your prime."

I peeled off my dress and took the shirt from Tess. I noticed she glanced at Minnie. I pretended not to realize that they could tell I was off, as she gathered my clothes to take to Minnie's office. The girls started their shift soon, and I wanted to keep what I did here private.

"You okay, honey?" Minnie handed me a pair of red heels.

"Yeah."

"Was it the other night at my club when you—"

"No." I cut her off. I didn't want that thought in my mind.

"Was it dinner with Sonny?

"No." I slipped my feet into the shoes. She studied me for a moment.

"What did Grim do?"

"It's what Grim's going to do." I sighed.

"Oh, shit," Tess hissed. She knew Grim was as dark as Trigger when you disobeyed. "What'd you do?"

"That's the problem. I mean, I wanted to listen to what he wanted, but then I had a job to do and…" I stopped as I heard my cue.

"Whatever it is can wait." Tess turned me around and studied my outfit. "Go blow off some steam in there. Come out, drink some vodka, dance, and things can only get better."

"That's your answer for everything." I laughed but she was right. I needed this.

I stepped through the door and into the box when the orange light came on. Minnie reserved this private viewing room called Wet and Wild for me when I needed it. It resembled a cage, and no one could enter without the right key card. Perks of being friends with the owner.

The music started, and I shook my head free of all thought and let my body sway to the beat. A slowed down instrumental version of *Summertime* by Sam Cooke flowed through the speakers as the rain started. It was a steady light spray and felt wonderful. Within a minute, I was soaked. As I spun on the pole, drops sprayed from me and spattered over part of the glass ledge which created quite the effect in the lights all around me.

I fell to my knees, slid to my stomach, and with a roll, I turned on my back and extended my legs in the air. I pressed my legs against the wall and tightened my abs then did a sexy roll back onto my stomach. As I did, I flung my wet hair and was back on my knees again. I reached above my head took the pole in my hand and slid straight up then spun around with an arch in my back.

I didn't dance like this for anyone but me. I wasn't on display for my clients, I wasn't looking to make money, nor was it a cry for help. No, this dance was about me feeling confident about myself. It was a place where I could let my body go completely without any inhibitions or restraints. I could empty my mind of everything and just be alone. Being sexy didn't always have to be for someone else, it could be just for yourself.

When the song ended, I let a lazy smile slip across my lips as I stepped from the box. I felt so much better as I got into the small shower. I refused to let any thoughts mess up this good feeling as I dried off then twisted my wet hair into a messy bun.

I slid my midnight blue fringed dress back on. I loved this dress. The fabric was a see-through material with fringes artfully arranged to cover the necessary areas in a unique pattern while the rest of me was on display. It was my feel-good dress because I knew the girls wouldn't always stand at attention like they did now. My twenties would be their best years, and I was going to let them live their best life. I'd had a shitty day, but now that I'd danced and was in my lucky dress, my girls and I were ready for a great night.

"Watch out!" one of the newer girls Minnie had hired barked at me as she rushed by. I stepped back and eyed the room at the end of the hall as someone left and let the door slam loudly behind them. A flashback flickered momentarily in my head.

"What are you doing here?" He stared at me as I came into the room.

"Ready?" Jack, the security guard for the floor, pulled me back to the present. He waited to escort me out to the club.

"Yeah." I shook off the sudden tension of the flashback. I wouldn't let it ruin my night.

The club was packed. When I got upstairs, I was

delighted to spot Dale double-fisting glasses of Very Sexy Martinis. My all-time favorite drink. They were pink, served in a long-stemmed glass, garnished with a raspberry and a leaf of mint.

"Minnie called and told me you needed some cheerin' up." He winked and handed me a glass.

"Where are Minnie and Tess?" I couldn't see the girls up on the platform, as their table was raised up for protection. It was a place for the girls who worked here to party safely. No clients or guests could get too close.

Horseshoe seating with the bar in the center gave the clubbers complete three-sixty-degree access to drinks. It was specifically designed with shelves of booze in a room inside with everything they needed to keep the bar running smoothly. It was a neat design and made the club feel large yet sectioned off. It was so much nicer than one giant mosh pit.

"They're here, but first, drink up." Dale tapped a finger to the stem as I drank. "I wanna dance!" He laughed as I downed the double vodka recipe and plunked the glass down.

We slid together onto the dance floor and moved our bodies to *Night Running* by Cage the Elephant and Beck.

Dale, as always, caught the attention of many of the girls around us. I had to smile because he really was a beautiful human.

I tugged out the elastic and ran my hands through my damp hair as I swung my hips and mouthed the words to the song. I loved that Minnie played all kinds of music. People got a kick out of the fact that her boyfriend was the VP of Devil's Reach who loved all things rock and heavy metal, yet he still hung out at her club.

Minnie appeared out of nowhere with Rail. He balanced a tray of shots. We all did two, then she handed the tray to one of her guys.

"Cheers to tits and clits," Rail yelled.

"Cheers!" We all laughed.

Rail was the only Devil's Reach member who would come out on the dance floor. It just wasn't their thing. I'd heard about Morgan's dance moves, and they could stay at the clubhouse.

The song switched to *Go Fuck Yourself* by Two Feet, and some guy grabbed me by the hips and walked me back into him. Dale stayed close, and Minnie glared until I shook my head to let her know it was all right. I needed to let loose a little tonight.

The heavy bass of the song traveled up my body and pulsed the vodka straight to my head. A fuzzy buzz went through me.

I tilted my head back against the guy's shoulder as his hands grabbed my hips, and we ground to the music. I spotted Trigger and Morgan on the balcony as they scanned the crowd for possible problems. Morgan gave me a wave, and I grinned back. I was close with everyone in Devil's Reach since I'd met them through Minnie. Rail was crazy but loveable in a fucked-up way, Minnie and Tess were my partners in crime, Trigger was like the scary uncle you called when you needed something handled. Mind you, you'd never ask exactly *how* it was handled. Then there was Morgan, my "sweet when no one was looking" Morgan. If I'd been born a twin, I'd want it to be him. I'm not sure why I felt that way about him, but I did. I imagined we shared a soul once, connected as family somewhere in the past. I just wished he was around more than he was.

Morgan suddenly left my thoughts, as a different vibe came over me.

I felt a pull and scanned the room to find Grim's intense expression locked on me. He stood at a high-top table with Jesse, Knox, and to my horror, my sister Calli.

He pointed at me then flicked his finger for me to come.

The fuck? Did he just summon me?

Instead of obeying, I held his gaze and let the man behind me run his hands around my body as we dirty danced to a song I didn't recognize.

He shook his head slowly and I could feel his anger. I knew he wanted to rip a strip off me for what happened with Sonny and the contract. I wasn't in the mood; besides, I wasn't on the clock.

A moment later, I saw Jesse coming toward us.

"I need a water," I shouted at Dale. "Thanks for the dance."

"Anytime." The guy peeled himself off me with a smile then disappeared into the crowd.

I held up a hand to Jesse. I knew he was only following orders, but I knew better than to push it any further. I followed him.

"You summoned, my Lord." I snickered, and Calli rolled her eyes.

Grim set his drink down and stood to tower over me. He fingered my wet hair and threw me a questioning look. I didn't react, and he leaned down and whispered, "I distinctly remember that I gave you an order to leave the contact alone."

"You gave me an orgasm too," I countered.

"Is that what you're looking for, sweetheart? A way to get another?" He pulled back and cocked a brow. His cologne engulfed me, and for a hair of a second, I let myself be lost in it.

"Don't flatter yourself, Grim. It had been almost a month since I came. I was horny, that's all, and you figured out how I like it."

"Yes, you seem to have quite an appetite for all things dark and dangerous."

"I'm not ashamed of my tastes."

"Don't be." His mask slipped for a moment, and I got a flash of interest. I felt as if my taste in sex might be perfect for him, but he blinked and then was angry again. "What the hell happened?"

"With what?" I didn't want to do this. I wanted to let loose.

"With Sonny." His tone was so chilly that I swallowed back a shiver. "You disobeyed me. You knew I didn't want you to have any contact with him again. The next thing I heard, you made a deal not only for him but for his fucking father too." He slammed a fist on the table, and I jumped. Knox looked concerned while Calli just stared.

My own anger flared. *Deep breaths, Kenna.*

"Listen, Grim," I stepped close to him and looked into his eyes, "I worked on getting Sonny to sign on for nearly five months. Under both of our fathers' orders. Just because you're back and everyone is terrified to piss off the great Grim Reaper doesn't mean you can come in and change things. You know working with clients takes time and effort. A lot of it. So, all my hard work with Sonny can't just be dropped. It isn't that easy."

"Yes, it is."

"Besides, you don't know shit about what happened!" My voice rose, and Knox's mouth flew open. I blinked. Had I gone too far?

"See why I'm Dad's favorite." Calli stabbed her cherry with her straw, and I glared at her.

"No, you're Dad's favorite because you lack a backbone to be anything but his yes bitch."

"Raise your hand if you have a degree here." She pushed her fake glasses up her nose and made a face.

"Hey," Grim pulled my attention back to him, "explain it. What the hell happened then?"

"Look, Grim." I took a deep breath. "I didn't come here to get yelled at on my night off." I raised my hands. "I came here to relax and have a bit of fun. Can't we talk about this in the morning?"

"Kenna, come dance!" Rail grinned at me, but when he looked at Grim's furious face, he read the vibe. "You've had a day." He pushed a chair toward Grim. "I'm buying you a lap dance." He snapped his fingers, and a girl in a skimpy bikini came over.

"Yes, that's a good idea." Knox pushed his brother into the chair, and the girl dropped down and started to grind around on his lap. He totally ignored her and kept his angry gaze fixed on me.

"Wow, someone was ready for me." She beamed and pointed down at his erection. "I must be good at my job."

"It wasn't you," he grunted, and I felt a tight pull in the bottom of my stomach.

"Excuse me, any chance you'd be up for another

dance?" The guy I'd dirty danced with earlier held out a hand.

"No," Grim flicked his wrist, dismissing him, "she's busy."

"Actually," I scowled at him, "I'd love to." I took the guy's hand and started to leave.

Jesse stood in our path, and I turned to Grim, outraged.

We were obviously at an impasse. *Play the game, Kenna.*

"Perhaps another time." I let go of the guy's hand and waved at him to carry on with his night. He showed regret in his expression, but a glance at Grim and he knew better than to push it.

"Hey," I gently pulled the girl off Grim as I reached into his coat pocket for his wallet. I was shocked he let me. "Take this." I peeled a hundred off his thick wad of bills. "Consider it a well-earned tip."

"Thanks, doll!" She grinned and moved on to the next table.

I held out his wallet, and when he went to reach for it, I pulled it back and he pushed himself forward toward me. His broad, muscular chest made me want to put my hand on it. I forced myself to put both my hands on the arms of his chair, then I leaned forward and pressed the girls hard against him and stared straight into his eyes. I moved my lips close to his ear.

"You want to be a dick tonight, fine, but you don't own me. And it's high time you learn I'm just as stubborn as you are." I dragged my tongue along his neck and flicked his earlobe. With that, I tucked his wallet back in his pocket and stood. He snagged my wrist.

"You'll learn to take orders from me," he growled inches from my face.

"I think you and I know that will never happen." I ripped my wrist from his hold then snatched his drink off the table and took it with me as I disappeared into the crowd to look for Dale.

I couldn't relax because of Jesse's presence. I knew he felt bad, but Grim was his boss, and he had orders. I knew he didn't have the liberty I had to disobey.

"Hey." A man moved between Dale and me. I attempted to step around him, but Jesse removed him before I could speak.

"Sorry, Kenna." Jesse made a wry face. "You pissed him off big time tonight. Why can't you just tell him what happened?"

"Would he listen even if I tried?"

"Yeah, I think he would," he seemed to think, "but maybe not tonight. You got him all wound up now." He smirked to show he knew it wasn't just his boss that was wound up. I hated how even having Grim in the same room turned me on, but also set my temper on fire.

"Why's Jesse hovering over you?" Minnie asked as she danced close to me.

"Grim's in a mood about what happened, and this is his punishment."

"His punishment is to keep guys away?" She gave me a wry look. "Why don't you two screw, already? I heard he's insane in bed. Just like you." She grinned. I took a casual sip of Grim's drink and tried to avoid eye contact, which, of course, she caught immediately. "You little twat, you've been holding out on me!"

"It was nothing."

"No, it was something." She grabbed my hand and pulled me off the busy dance floor. "Spill it."

Fine. "He wanted to prove a point after the dinner about Sonny, and I ended up on all fours, in his limo, with him over me." I wiggled my fingers.

"And?" Her grin spread, and her eyes widened with excitement.

"So, the rumors are true."

"I knew it! His darkness spills over into his sex life. So?"

"So?" I was confused.

"So, are you guys gonna keep playing?"

"No! It was a moment of weakness."

"A moment of greatness, you mean."

"Minnie," I pointed at her with the glass in my hand, "he drives me insane. He tries to bark orders at me, tells me who I can and can't book as clients even after his father gave me explicit instructions. He's—"

"He's ruthless in business, as well as in bed, and it's what makes him so great." She looked delighted. "I mean, come on, Kenna. The sexual tension positively drips from the two of you."

"Sexual or not..." someone caught my eye, and I went still. The lights bounced off a man's shiny, bald head, and as he turned, I caught his big, bushy mustache.

"What?" Minnie caught my mood swing, and I reached out for her hand. "Kenna, what?"

"That's his guys."

"What guys?" She started to look around, but I stopped her.

"Minnie, I-I need to go."

"No, babe, let me get Brick."

"What if they..." I couldn't finish my sentence. *Shit. Shit. Shit.* I stepped back from her, suddenly over-whelmed by the music.

"Kenna, wait!" Minnie shouted after me, but I couldn't risk it. I had to get away.

I bolted off in the other direction as fast as I could. I pushed my way through the people and didn't stop until I had the door in sight. I cringed at the men who tried to get my attention as I went, hands reaching out to touch my body as I hurried through the pulsing crowd. I pushed them away, as I felt the panic rise. My heart pounded in my chest as faces blurred around me.

A cold prickle raced up my spine as I reached the door. I felt like they were right behind me. Maybe they knew my secret and had come here to find me. I knew there had been more than one of them there that night, though only *he* was in the room alone. I knew a couple of his men saw me leave.

I swung the door open and flew through it in my panic and ran straight into Grim. His eyes narrowed in on me as he exhaled the smoke from his joint. I turned around and faced the door and pressed my hands against it, terrified, they'd spotted me.

"Who do I have to kill this time?" His tone sent a shiver through me.

"No one." I needed to run. "I just need to get out of here."

Grim didn't waste a beat; he ushered me toward his blacked-out Bentley. His driver opened the door, and I dove inside.

"Follow us, Jesse," Grim ordered as he slid in next to me. The driver didn't wait for instructions. He eased out of the parking lot and drove off. My stomach visited my throat and dared the alcohol to come back up.

"What happened back there?" Grim asked calmly as he sucked on his joint, and the smoke filled the space around us.

"Noth—"

He cut me off. "Don't lie to me."

"It was an old client," I lied, trying to curb my panic. "Didn't end the best."

Grim reached behind me and angled his body in my direction.

"You know Trigger and I have been friends for years." He studied the way the paper burned down the joint. "One thing we have in common is the ability to spot a lie." His gaze moved to mine. "I've looked into you, and you don't have bad blood with clients, you don't back down from anything remotely reckless," he tisked with annoyance, "and when something's going on, either Minnie, Rail, or Morgan step in to help you out." He held up the joint as an offering. I took it, as I needed something, anything to calm my nerves. "They know nothing, which means whoever you ran from back there is a big problem."

He watched as I wrapped my lips around the pencil-thick joint and inhaled the drug deep into my lungs. He tipped my jaw up, and I held the smoke in. His eyes burned into mine as he tried to read the last ten minutes of my life.

I gave him nothing. Over the years, I'd become somewhat of an expert at hiding my fears and disappointments. It came with being a member of the Tame family.

I broke eye contact and blew the smoke away from his face.

Lord, that was a strong hit.

I held the joint up to give it back, but he pulled my hand to his mouth and took a drag from between my fingers. The smoke encircled my hand as he inhaled the perfume from my wrist. These were the moments where I felt myself slip with Grim. Everything he did was incredibly sexy, from the way he touched me, smelled me, even the way he tried to order me around. He drew something out of me that I couldn't fathom.

When I tried to define this man to myself, I felt like he might be on the verge of losing himself with me. Though there were times I pushed back for sport, it was also in defense because I could see that if I gave in to Grim Gates, he might totally consume me. I already had that in my father, and I certainly didn't need another man who wanted me under his control.

"Let me help."

"No," I whispered the truth, "you can't."

"Do you know who I am, Kenna?" His hand moved to my shoulder, traced my collarbone, followed my strap down to where my breasts were barely covered by a fringe. "That night I found you in Secrets, I had just taken care of some Stripe Backs. We hunted them down and tortured them for information." With two fingers, he spread the fringe and revealed my nipple.

He rubbed his thumb over it with a hiss. "The man who attacked you that night was a mere inconvenience." *Not to me, he wasn't.* "So, tell me, sweetheart," he kissed my shoulder as we stopped at a light, "who do I need to kill so I never have to see that look on your face again?"

I felt his pull with my whole body. How could you fight someone in your mind while your body turned traitor and screamed for him to tear your dress off and do whatever the hell he wanted?

I squeezed my eyes shut and tried to focus. His lips were soft, and his tongue was hot. I forced my mind back to the reality of the situation I was in and knew I couldn't bring that to him. This was much bigger than he realized, and I was afraid of Grim's reaction if he knew the truth.

"He's an old client," I repeated, and I felt him stiffen with anger. I could almost hear the boxing bell go off in my head.

Round two.

"Jesus, Kenna," he growled, "I've never met someone who turned me on yet pissed me off just as much in my entire life."

"I never asked for your help, Grim."

"I didn't see you deny it either," he shot back. "The panic was all over your face. You needed me to save you. What would you have done if I wasn't there?"

"Ran." I fixed my dress, and he scowled at me.

"Have you learned nothing from the last time you walked back from Minnie's?"

I pulled away from his arm as I realized we were about to enter the hotel parking lot.

"Tell me one thing, Kenna. Does this guy have anything to do with the blood on your sketch book?" My face fell as I blinked at him. "Nothing gets by me." His brows went up.

"That was from the guy you killed." I jumped out the second the car stopped, but Grim was right on my heels. Jesse blocked my path as Grim turned me around.

"Wrong answer. Your sketchbook was too far away at the time to get blood on it."

This entire night had flip-flopped on me, and I fought to think straight.

"Grim, please." I looked around at the people. I didn't want anyone to see us arguing, but he kept his gaze on me. "Let it go."

"I can't."

"Why?"

"Because..." He stopped himself and glared like he wasn't comfortable with his first thought. "Because I think you're reckless and you'll end up dead somewhere."

Wow.

"Well, I'll tell ya what." I stepped back with a

shrug. "I'll spare you the media attention and promise I won't end up dead here."

"Kenna," he snarled, "get back here."

"Goodnight, Mr. Gates." I turned on my heel but wavered in my step when I saw Jayden watching us. I didn't have the headspace to deal with him. It was just my luck as soon as I headed across the lobby, he intercepted me.

"Mr. Hong was looking for you tonight."

When will these people ever realize I know where my clients are at all times? I'd know when and if they ever needed anything.

"Mr. Hong has been settled in his room. I escorted him to and from dinner, and he knew I was off tonight. I also didn't get any calls from him or any of my other clients, so I think you may have me confused with someone else." I side-stepped him and kept walking, but he stayed with me.

"Kenna..." He kept his voice even, but I knew he wanted to push. This was not a time to try to cross a line I wasn't going to cross, especially when we were in front of other clients and guests. "Where were you tonight?"

"Out."

"I can see that, but where?"

"Jayden," I quickly lowered my voice when I saw some guests look over at us, "I don't have to tell you where I've been."

"Were you out with Mr. Gates again?"

"Excuse me?" I punched the button on the elevator. I couldn't believe he felt he had the right to pry. I knew he liked me and wanted to be more than just a friend, but that wasn't going to happen, not now, not ever.

"Kenna," he softened his voice as he often did when he wanted me to hear him out, "you know your father wouldn't approve of you fooling around with your boss. Besides, he's been seeing that Jenelle girl."

"What the hell did you just say to me?"

"Please," he gave a pointed look to remind me we weren't alone, "actions have consequences, Kenna. Be smart about yours," he scolded then walked away. *The nerve!*

Years ago, I'd made the mistake of having dinner with Jayden, and he thought that meant we were more than friends. Though I'd let him down easily, he avoided me for days. When he finally spoke to me, he said I deserved the world and that he wanted to make sure I got it. Jayden said that because my father and his were good friends, he'd made it his duty to watch over me. He explained it was the least he could do, considering the type of clients I often had to deal with. It was sweet, but I told him many times it wasn't necessary. He never listened, and sometimes he made me almost angry with his attempts at "big brothering" me.

I stepped into the elevator, and as the doors closed, I caught Grim's pissed off look from where he stood.

He had a couple women on his arm. *That didn't take long.*

I huffed and called Hanna again, but it went straight to voice message.

"Hey, love, sorry for the phone tag. Call me tomorrow my time if you're free. I'm about to knock out cold." I sagged into the wall and watched the numbers climb.

TEN

SIMON

"Coffee?" The waitress asked as I stared across the hotel lobby.

"Yes, please." I leaned back so she could pour.

"Anything else?

"No, thank you." I briefly smiled up at her then returned my gaze to Kenna, who looked to be avoiding Walter's son, Jayden Wallace.

I knew why. I overheard them the other night as they argued by the elevator. It hadn't taken long once I arrived here to realize Jayden watched out for her, but I also saw him as a spoiled little gym rat who loved to throw around that his and Cameron's family were longtime friends. Walter and Cameron went way back, and Cameron was the one who had gotten Walter the job at Indulge overseeing the super hostesses. Once Jayden was old enough, Walter moved him in as a manager. Jayden never let anyone forget his title.

My phone buzzed.

> CM: Leaving his house now. Fifteen
> minutes.

I turned my phone over when Calli sat down in front of me. She rubbed her shoulder.

"What happened to you?" I sipped my coffee.

"Knox." She rolled her eyes. "He wanted to try rope play."

"Ah." I nodded and twisted my nose at the coffee. It was too strong. "How many rounds did you go?"

"Three." She sighed dramatically. "Thankfully, one of the girls showed up and took over. I swear he'd hire a necrophiliac for when he's dead."

I chuckled. "Thanks for that image. So, you'll be too tired tonight?"

"For you?" She grinned. "Never."

A few women flocked to Grim as he came into the hotel. I saw Kenna slip around a corner before he could see her. She was an exception; the guy drew females like a magnet. Most likely it was because he barely gave them any attention. For some strange reason, there were women who seemed to like that in a man. Not me. I was all romance. Hearts and flowers kind of guy. There was a time I drove two hours just to get a girl her favorite cookies from a mom-and-pop bakery. I remember they were shaped and frosted like daises with a sparkly center. She claimed only that place made them perfectly. I pushed away that memory. That was a different time. I was still a hopeless romantic, just a broken one now.

"Calli?" I pulled her attention from the selfie she was taking with my coffee.

"Mm?"

"What's Jayden Wallace like as manager of the super hosts?"

"He's like any other rich kid in Vegas." She tapped her long fingernails against her phone screen. I reached over and lowered her phone and gave her a pointed look to be with me in this moment and not with her online friends.

"Meaning?"

"Meaning," she tucked her phone away, "he does his job. He just doesn't really do his job."

"I don't speak twenty-four, hun."

"Okay," she closed her eyes like she searched for the right words, "if you work for the Gates family, you have to have an edge." She rolled her eyes. "Someone who can do their job without even thinking about it. Jayden's there to make sure nothing slips through the cracks. You know like that white stuff people put along their tiles in the bathroom."

"Caulking?" I chuckled. "You're saying he's a seal to make sure nothing gets missed."

"Yes, caulking." She rolled her eyes again. "He's good with the little details, but that's about it. The only reason he's got that job is because of his father. That's his edge. And because he keeps his eyes and ears open. He watches people then rats on them."

"Okay," I waited a beat, "how do he and Kenna get along?"

"Have you met my sister?" She made a face.

"She must be great at her job, or she wouldn't be a super host here at Indulge."

"I..." She paused to think. "Kenna's *good* at what she does, but," she held up a finger as my smile widened, "one of these days she's going to get herself into trouble with the kinds of clients she has."

"They're our clients, too," I pointed out.

"Sure, but we're defending them. Keeping them out of jail. She parties with them, fills their every want and need. Probably sleeps with them all." She stuck out her tongue.

I shook my head. I knew Kenna wasn't that kind of hostess. I also knew she was one of the best. She kept her clients in line and fulfilled their desires by handing them off to those who were good at whatever it was they asked for.

"And let's not forget who she hangs around with," Calli continued. "She has friends in low places.

Besides, Kenna's mouth always gets her in trouble. I told you how she spoke to Grim last night. I still can't believe he didn't fire her ass on the spot."

"Yes, that surprised me, too." Grim liked things to go his way.

"As for Jayden, all he sees is that she's better at her job than he is. Plus, he's been in love with her for as long as I can remember. He's all sweet with her, but she just brushes him off. Asshole sister, remember."

I took her story with a grain of salt. Calli often saw any story with her sister in it as being different than it really was.

"Oh!" She leaned over the table as she let her mouth run. "You know I caught him once watching her change in the bathroom." She shuddered. "He claimed it was an emergency and he needed her, but what guy with a job like his would go into the women's room to look for her instead of getting someone to fetch her or call her?"

"Creep." I shook my head in disgust but dismissed the story. More than likely, he was looking for her and Calli walked in. Situations without context are often misunderstood in a negative way.

"Mm, at least it's not me he's after."

"Yes, I'm not ready to go to jail."

"I love how protective you are of me." She grabbed my hand and squeezed it.

"You're too sweet to have anyone hurt you."

She cooed, "Why can't all men be like you?"

"Because we're a rare breed." I quickly kissed her fingers then bumped her leg under the table with a wink. I glanced at my watch and saw I had to leave. "Sorry, Calli, gotta go."

"Where you off to?"

"I promised a friend I'd say hello before he heads home."

"I'll miss you."

"As will I." I dropped a ten on the table for a tip and rushed off. Just as I was leaving the lobby, I caught sight of Grim and his right-hand man, Jesse, discussing something. Grim pulled his gun, and his entire face morphed into that monster expression I'd seen before. I wasted no time slipping through the main doors and out onto the Strip. Christ, he was scary.

The mid-morning heat was on full blast, and I was pleased I'd chosen a t-shirt and shorts versus my normal pants and dress shirt. I didn't make enough money to buy expensive suits like Cameron or the Gates did. I envied them their suits; they were well ventilated and made for the climate here. Vegas sure wouldn't be my number one place to set down roots. I was here because I had a job to do.

I answered my phone. "Gable."

"Calli said you were out this morning?" Cameron questioned.

"I am."

"Who's your friend you are meeting?" He waited, and I didn't answer. "Do I want to know?"

"Probably best not, at least until we're in person." I knew better than to discuss things on the phone.

"Don't be too long. I need you back here."

"I won't." I hung up as I spotted the very man I'd come to see. I waited for him to get close. He looked like any other businessman on the street, cheap suit, crappy briefcase, probably just downed some gas station coffee before he had to meet a client. He was the kind of lawyer who had clients who could barely scratch up enough money to pay his fee, and they'd no doubt wind up in jail because they put their life in the hands of a guy whose own life hung by a thread.

"Morey Ines?" I held out my hand, and he looked up at me as he tried to place my face.

"Yes. You are...?"

"I'm the guy who's got an offer that you're gonna want to hear."

"Not interested." He moved around me.

"WestPoint Industries." I called out the name of the company that had a suit against him for misrepresentation. He'd been out of his league on that case and had pulled some stupid moves. He could lose his practice and probably do jail time. He stopped and slowly turned to face me. "Give me twenty to hear out my offer, and if you're not interested, fine. It'll be the last you'll see of me."

He made a show of looking at his watch, but I knew I had him. He knew he needed a miracle, and I might just hold out some hope.

"Shall we?" I pointed to the diner next to us, and he marched inside.

His face was stone by the time I explained my idea. I knew his pea-sized brain was sifting through the little bit of the law he actually knew as he tried to look at it from all angles.

"I don't even know," he lowered his voice, "who that person is."

"It's best that you don't."

"How?"

"The less you know, the more authentic your testimony will be."

"So, all I have to do is say I saw this man," he pointed to the photo, "and that he was there that night in the parking lot around eleven thirty?"

"Yes."

"Why me?"

"Why not you?"

"Because I'm just a small-time lawyer who just picked up a case my firm doesn't want anything to do with." He tugged on his ill-fitting jacket. "I'm a nobody."

"Exactly. Why would you have a reason to lie? Besides, you were in town that day, and who knows, maybe you did see him and just forgot."

He rubbed his head, and the crow's feet that sprouted around his eyes deepened.

"If he's found guilty, how long will he go away for?" I hid my amusement that this man was a criminal lawyer and couldn't figure out the answer himself.

"If this guy went and shot up a club and your brother was one of the people slaughtered, what would you want him to get?"

"Fuck." He covered his mouth, and his face drained to a pale gray. "I'm not sure I can lie. What if someone finds out?"

"They won't." I didn't miss a beat. "You're on the side of the law. This is what you do. You protect the unprotected, only this time you're doing it in a different way. But it all means the same in the end. The bad guy goes to jail and justice is served."

"Shit." His shaky hand stroked the loose skin under his chin.

"He's getting off easy if he gets death row." I pushed one last time. "He isn't a good person, Morey. The law failed all his victims." I pulled out photos from multiple other homicides, but he couldn't know that. "Why should the families of all these people live the rest of their lives without their loved ones, while he gets to walk free?" He placed his elbows on the table and leaned his chin on his hands. "If you do this for me, I'll make sure WestPoint Industries drop all the charges against you."

"How?"

"Does it really matter how, as long as it goes away?" He closed his eyes and muttered something I didn't care to hear. "I have a meeting in an hour. This is your chance to turn your life around. Take the deal, Morey, or maybe he'll end up your cellmate."

"Fine," he bit out. "Tell me where and when I need to do this, and I'll be there."

Excellent.

"First, learn this script. Meet me here," I handed him a business card with an address on it, "when I say so." I shimmied out of the booth and stood. "Think, Morey, by the time this is over, you'll be free of that demon on your shoulder. You're doing the right thing."

"Wait." He twisted in the booth to see me better. "How do you know so much about me?"

"It's what I do." I pushed my sunglasses on and headed back outside. Two down, three to go. I was determined to make sure that son of a bitch went down for good. I stroked my tattoo like I often did for good luck and fought like hell to curb my grin.

ELEVEN

GRIM

My head pounded as I leaned against the headboard in my bedroom. I loved my suite in the penthouse. I'd had it redecorated a few years back when I was forced home from Singapore for a few months to recover from a business deal that had gone bad.

The designer spent a week with me and decided my bedroom would be an expression of who I was. Dark and powerful with a note of elegance, she said, and I had to agree she'd captured my taste perfectly. The massive bed was custom built, and she had it flown in from Italy. It was magnificent and the main focal point of the room. Leo said it reminded him of a bed from Game of Thrones.

The bed did have a castle-like look to it with its fifteen-foot headboard with black satin cushioning part way up topped with black wood that came to a square with a half-moon on top and a vine carved out in the center. The half-moon had spears sticking out the top and represented a cast iron gate.

To me it was a masterpiece of craftsmanship.

The same wood was used on the wall across from the bed, which ran the entire length of my room. A five-part bookshelf with a backdrop of red velvet held my leather-bound books.

An arm twitched where it lay across my stomach as last night's events came back to me. Three women in the lobby approached me and wanted to party. I was wound so tight from my fight with Kenna that I jumped at the chance to release some of the pent-up anger that consumed me. They weren't quite as exciting as the triplets Rail had suggested, but Jesse would have vetted them, or they'd never have been allowed in. Most of the pool bunnies were regulars, and I recognized the blonde as one who often hung off the high rollers. I knew it would only be a Band-Aid for my problems and not a fix, but at this point, I'd take it.

I only wished I didn't have to hold myself back and could let loose with my required tastes, but I knew these women could never take the wrath I'd unleash.

"Morning." The redhead's eyes popped open, her

hair in disarray. "Gimme me a sec and I'll be ready to go again."

"I need to get to work." I checked the time. "Time to get up, ladies!"

Leal let out a growl as one of the women raised her head from where she was sprawled out on the couch. Zhen looked at me then at his brother before he too started to growl. I sympathized. I knew they never liked it when I brought company up here. It was the one place where the three of us could relax, and if someone else was there, they never settled. They probably hadn't slept at all during the night. I lifted an eyebrow and kept my voice firm.

"Go on," I ordered. They both immediately got up and left, but Leal circled back and popped his head in the room to give me an extra hard look. "Leal," I warned and shook my head at him, and he left, but his point was made.

"Those two are scary as hell," the redhead muttered from beneath her arm.

"That's their job." I rubbed my face and wished they'd get the hell out.

"No," she rolled over and exposed her fake boobs, "dogs are supposed to be cute and cuddly, not nasty and looking like they just came from guarding a junkyard."

"Maybe I should call them back in here and show you just how nasty they can be." I gave her a hard stare, and she hid under her arm again. I hated it when people judged a dog simply by its breed. They were as different as people, and their personalities were formed by their owners. It was all in how they were raised. Of course, there were always exceptions, I had to admit. Humans could be worse; I knew because I was one of them.

"It's cruel, what you did to their ears, too," she murmured. "Plus, it's ugly."

I actually didn't agree with cropping a dog's ears, but I certainly wasn't going to explain to her it wasn't me who had it done.

"No one asked for your opinion." I made a mental note not to engage with this chick again.

"You're mean."

"You have no idea." I smirked, and she rolled over and reached for her shoes. "Now, leave." I had things to do. I peeled the blonde's arms and legs from me and dragged my hungover body to the bathroom and slammed the door.

I turned the water to hot and let it pour over me. Though last night was fun, it was only fun. Nothing particularly excited me these days. If I held myself totally back when I was that pent up, I knew it would be bad for me. I'd burn inside and go so dark even a trip to the desert wouldn't help. I knew I had to get away from these women before I unleashed that side of me. A craving I recognized ached inside.

I showered, changed, and downed some of the coffee Jesse had brought. I'd heard him come in. He sat and sipped his own steamy cup in my comfy reading chair. We both looked into the bedroom through the open door. Jesse pointed at the redhead, who looked quickly up at us then away as she buttoned the top of her dress. She looked frightened. Good. *Get the fuck out.*

"Someone isn't happy." He pointed to Leal, who was now glued to his leg.

"I know." As I walked by, I gave the pup a much-needed pat then shot the chick who had insulted his looks a nasty glare as she hobbled on one shoe. I had no doubt Leal had given Jesse an earful when he came in about the girls being in their space. Zhen moved close to my feet and pushed against me to demand his turn.

"How are the boys settling in?" He looked at Leal, whose ears twitched. He was hyper-focused on the girls in the other room. "Going from a house in Mexico to a penthouse in the sky must be a big adjustment for them."

"They're adjusting." I shrugged. They flew with us everywhere, so it wasn't like they weren't used to new places. Although I knew they'd appreciate a routine when I finally got settled. "They seem to be good with that dog walker, Darcy."

"'Cause she's cute." Jesse gave me a shit-eating grin. "They have an eye for the ladies, you know.

Except when you bring them here," he added. My mind went to Darcy. She certainly was cute, but she was young, and I didn't go there. I liked a mature woman with a strong mindset. Kenna's face flashed in my head, but I shook that right back out. "The girl knows her stuff and gives the boys a good workout." Movement in the bedroom made both dogs sit up and tense.

I was pleased to see rule one was being enforced by one of my security team.

"All right, ladies, you've been warned to get moving, so chop-chop!" Janice, one of my female team members, tossed the rest of their clothes at them. Rule one, when the sun comes up the girls get out.

The blonde thrust her bare boobs toward the ceiling and gave it a last try.

"Sure you don't want to go another round?" she called. She was attractive, but I was no longer interested in her.

"No."

Janice shooed them into the elevator. She gave me a curt nod, but I caught her grin as one of the girls tried to grab her ass.

"Sorry, hun, I'm not into pussy." I had to laugh. Janice was all right.

"I'd ask how your night went, but..." Jesse shrugged and pointed at the bed.

"Just needed to take the edge off."

"And?" he asked, and I didn't respond. I didn't blow through women like Knox did, but right now I'd take twenty just to unleash the hold a certain woman seemed to have on me. She infuriated me, and it drove me to want to hurt someone. "Are you going to change, because we have roughly five minutes." I whirled around, confused as to why we weren't going to the gym. "Your father called a meeting late last night for this morning."

"I didn't see anything come through."

"Maybe that was because Macallan got in your way?" He turned the empty scotch bottle around.

"What's the meeting about?" I ignored his comment.

"I could tell you, but where's the fun in that?" He held up his phone, and I realized I was going to be late.

"Shit." Janice was good. Not a trace remained of last night's company. I pulled on a fresh shirt and pants, and grabbed the first jacket I could spot. Thankfully, I had already showered. I grabbed my cufflinks then headed out to the next room. I waved at Jesse, and he nodded and followed me out the door.

"Ready?" He had his phone out, texting away to someone.

"Yes." I wanted to probe about the meeting, but my hangover had other plans.

"Painkillers?" He rattled a bottle of pills, and I

shook my head. I welcomed the discomfort, as I knew it would help distract me.

"Boys," I said and pointed to the floor in front of the elevator. "Pendiente al área," I commanded them to keep watch, and both obediently dropped to the spot where I'd pointed.

One of the perks of living where you worked was that it was only a short elevator ride down to the meeting. The door was open, and we walked right in. Jesse closed it behind us.

Kenna was there, and I glared at her. *Fuck.*

"You want those pills now?" Jesse chuckled behind me, and I snatched the bottle from his hand. I might need something stronger to deal with this chick today.

Kenna eyed me up and down, and her brows lifted. It was as though she could see right through me.

I forced myself to keep a blank face as I looked around the room. Her father Cameron, my father, and to my absolute surprise, my mother all sat around the conference table.

"Good, Grim, you're here." My father smiled.

"My apologies," I mumbled and looked at my watch and realized I was ten minutes late. I was rarely late for anything, especially a meeting. I looked at Kenna again and realized her merely being in the room rattled me. I shook it off. "I missed the email about this pop-up meeting."

"Scotch will do that to you." Kenna smirked, and I was sure my hangover was written all over my face.

"Kenna, always a pleasure."

"I'm glad you feel that way," she shot back without missing a beat.

"And why are we here, exactly?"

"Well, when Kenna shared her concerns with me last night, I thought it was best to hash everything out this morning," Dad replied and mouthed, "You're late."

"I know," I mouthed back when Kenna looked down. I made my way over to my mother and kissed her cheek. "Mom, wonderful to see you here. To what do we owe this pleasure?" I loved when she joined in on the family business. She had a heart of gold but was ruthless in all things business. I was sure dad married her for that exact reason. They had a balance.

"I figured Kenna could use a little woman empowerment in this meeting." She lifted the same brow I could at me, and I smiled.

"You sure about that?" I tossed an annoyed look at Kenna, who shrugged off my sass.

"Lions need to be tamed sometimes." Mom shot me a look then sat up straight the way only she could. She oozed power. "And who better than two lionesses to take that on?" She winked at Kenna, who smiled sweetly at me.

"And boy, do you need to be tamed," Kenna gritted through her teeth, making Mom chuckle.

"All right, all right, settle down." Dad waved for me to sit in the empty chair next to Kenna.

Mom reached down and pulled up her mini-Doberman to sit on a chair next to her. She thought it hilarious to have what appeared to be a miniature version of my dogs.

The little shit jumped on the table and raced over to stick its wet nose in my face.

"LeeLee, down," Mom gently scolded. I internally groaned at her humor. She'd used a spin-off name taken from Leal. I snagged him and held him up in the air in case he pissed on the paperwork, as he'd been known to pee around me. He whimpered and wiggled, and I put him down.

"Aw, come here, Lee." Kenna scooped him up and cradled him to her chest. *Lucky bugger.* "Don't worry. He only pretends to be scary." She kissed his head. "We can take him." She eyed me and smiled as she took him over to Mom, who apologized to the room.

"Are we going to start?" I cleared my throat and felt my erection grow at Kenna's tight ass as she passed the mini pinscher back to Mom.

"Yes, let's get everything out on the table." Dad jumped in again. "Kenna, you called this meeting, so why don't you start?"

"Thank you, Mr. Gates." She nodded politely.

"Grim," it wasn't lost on me she used my first name, "you and I need to set some ground rules."

"We do?" I nearly laughed, but my mother's expression made me swallow it down. I would never disrespect her, even if Kenna was way out in left field with her comment.

"Yes." When she shifted, the fabric of her blouse pulled down, and I had a clear shot of the curve of her breast. I squeezed the pen I held hard enough to snap it. "I know you're upset with me for signing Sonny and Victor –"

I cut her off. "You're right, I am."

"*But,* as I said to you yesterday, I'd been working hard to set up that deal for nearly five months. That morning when they came into the lobby, they came to find me—"

"It's a good thing they did, too—" Cameron butted in.

"Please." Kenna cut him off in the same way he had her. He shook his head, pissed she'd spoken to him that way.

"They came to find me," she repeated, "because Sonny was excited that his father decided to join him. They'd both signed the contract, the one I'd given Sonny earlier. The same contract your father handed me and asked me to get them to sign. It was business."

"It was a bad business move," I tossed at her.

"No, it wasn't!" Cameron stepped in, and I glared

at the man who I felt had zero business being mixed up in mine.

"Not your place, old man." I banged my fist on the table and looked at Kenna. "It was a bad move to make."

"Says you." Her tone was sharp, and I fought not to snap back. "As far as them being dangerous, know that Morgan and I were already in conversation in the lobby when they approached me. I was ensuring that Morgan knew about the situation with Sonny." A gasp from her father made her put up a hand. "Yes, because we're such good friends, I wanted to share my concerns with him, and—"

"You let one of those bikers in on a business deal!" Cameron shouted at her. "That's private information. What the hell were you thinking? What if he said something to the wrong person? What if—"

"Cameron!" she snapped, and his face went beet red. "This is my meeting. If you want to lose your shit, wait your turn."

"Pardon me?" He stomped his foot and leaned forward in his chair as I rose to my feet. I saw red. "What did you just say to me?"

"Enough." I raised my hand just as my father was about to step in. I also knew Morgan well. He was high up in the Devil's Reach club, and like the rest of them, I knew he could be trusted with anything. I just hadn't put it together how close he might be to Kenna. When I thought about it, though, it made sense. Kenna was close to Minnie and Tess, so of course she'd know most of the club members. They were good people. "I've warned you once before, Cameron. I'll not remind you again."

"You can't speak to me like that!" Cameron said furiously.

"If you want to come at someone, come at me."

"It's okay." Kenna tried to smooth things over, but it wasn't going to work.

"You think you're something else—" Cameron started again like the adolescent child he was.

"One," I drilled my fist into the table and made everyone jump, "more fucking word out of your mouth and you're done, Cameron." I shot him a look of death. His temper was going to meet my fist in his jaw soon. He muttered something I chose to ignore because his phone suddenly rang loudly. How my father had done business with this man for as long as he had was beyond me.

"Maybe we should do this another time." Kenna's voice was low and calm.

"No, you go on." I waved at Kenna, happy I was finally about to hear the truth of how things had gone down. The fact that I now knew she'd had Morgan there calmed my nerves a bit. He had quick hands and would have been discreet about it if he had to step in.

"Thanks for the permission." She shot me a wry

look, but I could see she was pleased her father was preoccupied. "Morgan wasn't more than ten feet from me. I might be weaker than you *physically*," she referenced our limo ride, "but I'm smart enough to have heard what you said."

I tapped my fingers on the table while I mulled over her words. I glanced at Mom, who seemed to be impressed that I even continued to listen to her at this point. Dad had a shit-eating grin on his face as he lowered his phone. No doubt he had just filled Leo in on the meeting. That I was in a room with Kenna and neither of us had ripped each other's throats out. Yet. The room went quiet for a moment.

"When?" Cameron's voice came to us. He was in the far corner of the conference room with his phone to his ear. His body language had changed suddenly, and his voice had a different quality to it. "I guess I don't have a choice, now do, I?" He sounded almost nervous, enough that Kenna glanced at him curiously.

I cleared my throat and went back to the task at hand. I leaned back in my chair and went with my gut.

"Like I expressed to you both," I glanced at Dad then Kenna, "I don't like this deal. My gut tells me they're going to be nothing but trouble. I've seen enough to know what kind of element they attract. They aren't the kind of people we want."

"Maybe so, but my part in this isn't for you to have

a say in." Kenna straightened in her chair, and I flexed my jaw at her consistent need to push back.

"I disagree, Grim," my father said calmly. "They have a lot of money and are reckless with it." He pulled out a file and slid it across the table to me. I flipped it open and scanned the numbers. "That's how much he lost at the Venetian, on that one visit alone. One-point-two million at the blackjack table. That's also when Kenna distracted him with the business deal." He chuckled, and she smiled at him.

I knew my father saw a lot in Kenna when it came to what she did here, but I didn't like the fact she seemed so close with them. It seems I'd missed a lot over the years about how close she was with Devil's Reach and now my family.

"Let's not forget how this deal brings me business, too." Cameron rudely tossed his phone on the table.

"That part doesn't interest me." I dismissed him and tried a different angle. Maybe they'd listen to it since *they all seemed so close.* "Did I mention Sonny slipped a drug into Kenna's drink at dinner?"

"What! I never heard that." Mom sat up and looked at Kenna.

"Grim." Kenna looked uneasy. I knew she wouldn't like that little detail being revealed. "I'm fine," she assured my mom, who had a look of concern on her face. "I didn't drink any of it. I had it handled."

"Handled?" I lifted a brow. *Seriously?*

Kenna mouthed, "Fuck you," and I fought back a satisfied smirk.

"Did he really do that?" Cameron's face showed no concern for Kenna. He wore a smug look. "And who was your source for that?"

"Me." I held his gaze until he shifted in his seat.

"It's Vegas," he chuckled, "and who are you to talk? Didn't you spend the better part of a decade making sure your hotels had the best drugs in town?" I hated that he knew our family business as well as he did.

"There's a difference between willingly taking a drug and having one slipped into you without your knowledge, Cameron," Mom explained. "The intent of which is usually rape. Jim, now I'm nervous of this guy." Dad laid a hand over hers and gave it a pat.

"It's Vegas, darling. We've seen worse."

"Surely, somewhere in law school they taught you that, Cameron?" I turned to him. I couldn't believe this guy. We were talking about his own daughter. "And I'm confused. Why are you even here for this meeting?"

"I'm usually at all the meetings. You'd know this if you were actually here."

"Well, lucky for you, I'm back, so there's the door."

"All right." Dad rubbed his forehead, and Mom placed her hand on his arm. He gently pushed her hand away and shook his head. "Kenna, I'm glad you're okay. We'll keep a close eye on Sonny. Lord knows we don't want a reputation for that sort of thing. It was probably Rohypnol. It's been used at several hotels lately and seems to be becoming popular again. Sadly, it's very hard to police. That being said, Grim, I'm sorry, son, but I'm overriding you on this. Sonny's a real catch for us. You know how many hotels are after his business. The fact that we beat them all out and got him as well as his father is just too good to pass up."

A vein ticked in my neck, and I knew it was a warning to leave.

"I disagree." I tapped my fingers and tried to calm myself. Then my phone vibrated, and I saw that Jesse, who had stepped outside the door when the meeting started, sent me a text. I stood as the rage that had started when this meeting began now shifted to the text. "I need a moment."

"Something more important than this?" Cameron muttered as I yanked open the door.

"What the fuck?" I motioned for Jesse to follow me into my mother's office. She had one right next to my father.

"I got in contact with our window guy, and he said the shipment never left the warehouse." Jesse held up his hands, as he knew I was about to lose it over my fucking hotel.

"Well, that's a fucking lie because we got the paper-work saying it did." I rubbed my head and tried to think through the rage. Someone who had knowledge of my business dealings was fucking me at every turn.

"Let me call Deborah and see what she knows. She's due to arrive tomorrow, anyway."

"Good." I eased down onto the couch and jabbed a thumb above my eyes to relieve the pain that stabbed. "Also find out where Tupot is."

"Another dinner?" He winced.

"Let's hope his wife can cook."

"I actually felt bad for Rich. His wife needs major lessons. Okay, I'll be in touch." He left me alone, but the door didn't close, and I looked up and saw my mother come in.

"Everything okay, Grimson?"

"No." I let out a long sigh. I knew it was pointless to lie to the one person who knew me the best. "But I'll get through it."

"Of course, you will. You're my son." She moved over to her desk and picked up a photo of her and Dad in Egypt. "Kenna sure gets under your skin." She chuckled, amused.

"If it was up to me, I'd fire her ass."

"Why? Because she won't take your shit?"

"Because she doesn't take orders at all."

"Reminds me of someone else I know." She eyed me.

"She's reckless, mouthy, defies me at every corner."

"Beautiful too."

"Looks don't mean she's a good employee." I was smarter than to pull at that thread. I knew my mother would love nothing more than for me to meet someone and start a family.

"Son, she's not only beautiful but a force to be reckoned with."

"Maybe." I heard a door slam and saw Simon appear in the hallway. Mom spotted him, too. "Seriously, Mom, this deal with Sonny isn't sitting right. It never has. Sonny's dangerous, and the shit with the drug was done right in front of me. Like he thought I'd be all right with it."

"Maybe it was a test?"

"And if it was?" I shook my head, frustrated. "I know how people view the Devil's Reach or the Capri family or whatever crime family we deal with, but they aren't like the Contis. They're a whole different breed."

"I know." She placed the picture down and ran a finger across the frame. "I'll admit these people were never someone we thought we'd bring in. But they have a lot of money and are willing to spend it here."

"So?"

"Grimson," she lowered her head and took a deep breath, "I need you to let your dad have this one."

"Why?"

"Your dad needs this win."

"Meaning?"

"Meaning," she sat down next to me and threaded

her hand through mine, "I'm asking you to let this one go."

"Is there something I should know?" I held her gaze, then I glanced at Simon again, who seemed to be reading something on his phone.

"No, son, I just think your dad needs a win right now, and this is it."

A million thoughts ran through my mind before I gave her a small nod.

"Good boy." She squeezed my arm. "Now, will you ease up a little on Kenna?"

"No. That's asking too much. Speaking of which," I shook my head, "how are you guys still doing business with Cameron?"

"I know," she shrugged, obviously exasperated, "but you know your father. Loyalty runs deep with him."

"I get that, but he's getting progressively worse as the years go on."

"Why do you think I skip most of the meetings?" She chuckled lightly. "I've learned to tune him out. He means well and is good for the hotel, but I agree he oversteps a lot."

"Understatement."

"Imagine how poor Kenna feels." She gave me a look. "She's got such a good head on her shoulders and has proved she can bring a lot of business to the hotel.

So, if dealing with Cameron's little outbursts is what it takes to keep Kenna around, we can deal."

"I won't."

"I know you will." She laughed. "You'll do it for your father because we all love him."

"Yeah." I gave her a smile. I'd do it as long as I could, but I was back for good, and things were going to change. I knew there'd be a lot of people who wouldn't like it. Kenna's face flickered.

I got up and offered my arm as Simon retreated to Cameron's office. Mom and I walked together back into the conference room. I sat down, crossed my ankle over my knee, and took a moment before I looked at them.

"If Sonny and Victor are staying, then you need to find a different host, because Kenna isn't going to be theirs." I glanced at Mom, and she gave me a nod of approval. I wasn't a total monster; I didn't trust Sonny not to pull something else on her.

"The hell she's not." Cameron laughed like I was crazy. "She signed them, and that's the agreement. That makes her their host."

"Have you been in this meeting at all, old man?" I licked my dry mouth. "Do you have any awareness of your daughter?"

"This is a business meeting, not a family dinner." Cameron pressed a finger into the table.

"And if it was up to me, you wouldn't be at either

one." A bullet wedged in his skull would look mighty fine right now.

"Maybe it should be up to Kenna?" Mom's smooth voice took command of the room, and I backed down. He was like fighting with a five-year-old. "What are your thoughts, Kenna?"

"Yes," I gritted my teeth as I dared her to defy me on this too, "what are your thoughts?"

"Truth," she folded her arms at my tone, "I'm not interested in wasting my energy on them. Sonny has other intentions for me. He's made that clear. I'd be fine stepping aside for someone else to play *dodge the creep*." I felt a sense of relief that she didn't fight me on this, because I would have won this battle whether she liked it or not. "I like the clients I have right now. I love the chase to land the clients. It's a challenge. But if there's an option to give the Contis to someone else, I'm all for that."

"And what if Sonny disagrees?" Cameron countered, and my blood pressure went up.

"Then Sonny can fuck right off. It's not his decision," I grunted.

"Then we cross the bridge when we need to." Kenna sighed. It must be exhausting to have a father like hers.

"Good," Dad hit the table with his fist like a judge, "that's settled. Sonny and Victor Conti will stay on, but with a new host. Now, it's time for lunch."

"Actually," Kenna glanced at my mother, who gave her a nod to go on, "I have one more thing to discuss."

Here we go. I rolled my eyes.

"Mr. Tame?" Zara, Cameron's secretary, popped her head in the door. "Forgive the interruption, but Mr. Griple is here to see you."

"Shit." He glared at her, and she blushed and disappeared. "Go on without me." He pushed to his feet and marched out like the cocky son of bitch he was.

"I'm going to kill him," I growled at Dad and pointed at the door Cameron had just closed behind him.

"Kenna?" Mom prompted her to go on.

"I believe I've proven myself to all of you here at Indulge. I think I've shown I've got what it takes to land a magnitude of clients."

"Agreed." Dad nodded.

"I think I've earned the right to have more of a say on who we bring on, and if I represent them or not."

"A say would mean you'd need to be able to compromise." I stepped in. "I sure haven't seen much of that from you so far. Is it something you think you can strive for?"

"Given it's handled the right way, yes." She glared at me.

"I think that's fair." Mom looked at Dad. "She has a knack when it comes to reading people. She's proved that. She should have a say, especially if someone makes her feel uncomfortable."

"Fine." I had to agree if we looked at it from that angle. I'd just gone to bat for her not being the Contis' host, and this went hand in hand with that. Mom's face showed surprise. Probably she was shocked, as I had a reputation for not being easy to compromise with either. But I felt this made sense.

"Thank you." Kenna managed a small smile. I thought maybe she'd fight me less now that I'd agreed to her request. I doubted it, but one could dream. Her smile immediately returned to a scowl, and I glared at her. The moment was certainly over. I made a mental note to try to find a way to work with her better so I wouldn't be constantly planning her death.

"I think that's a smart request, Kenna." Dad stood. "I'll get your contract revised this afternoon."

"Thank you." She smiled at my mother and shook Dad's hand. I was awarded a nod.

"Mom and Dad, I'll meet you at the restaurant. I need a moment alone with Kenna."

"I have to meet Mr. Hong," she complained.

"He can wait."

"Of course, dear." Mom kissed my cheek. "Remember we're witnesses, so return her in one piece."

No promises.

Once they left, I swung around to face her. She stood with her arms folded and her knees locked. She looked ready for battle. I sighed and huffed out a breath. Her white sleeveless blouse that crisscrossed in the front was tucked into her tight red skirt. I knew if she was about to go meet Yen Hong, she'd want to change into something more casual. Yen loved the pool.

"I don't have the energy to go head-to-head with you, Grim. My father wears me out."

"Out of respect to my parents, I didn't slam my fist into his head. He certainly deserved it."

"I'm glad you didn't." She always let her father off the hook. I couldn't figure out why.

"One day it'll happen. I've been known to have a temper."

"Never guessed." She dripped with sarcasm.

I walked over to the folder on the table and flipped open the file on Sonny. "You and my mother seem close."

"Does that threaten you?" She pulled her hair to one side, and it drew my attention to her throat. My hand twitched to wrap around it.

"Not much threatens me."

"Sonny seems to."

I swung my gaze over to hers, and she matched my glare.

"Be careful, Kenna. Just because you're close with

my mother doesn't mean you can speak so freely to me."

"I really get under your skin, don't I?"

"You're like a parasite that's crawled your way into my brain, pissing me off at every thought."

"Wow," she looked away, "I had no idea I pissed you off that much."

"Well, you do now." Between her and the fact that I was once again being screwed up with my hotel being built, I wanted to snap something in two, and it wasn't a pen. Something popped into my head. "What was going on last night?"

"Well, since I have you alone, and apparently extremely pissed off at me," she huffed, "I might as well say this now." I hated that my temper sent my blood in all directions, but mostly to my erection. "We will not discuss why I left Minnie's club the way I did. Not now, not ever."

"Oh, really? Well, we will discuss what the hell rattled you because something did. Do I need to go ask Minnie?"

"Grim," she looked me square in the eye, "it was something personal and something I very much wish to keep private. Let it go." I smirked at that. She really didn't know me very well. I wanted to know every-thing that happened in my city.

"Why were you and Calli fighting at fight club last night?" I asked, and her brows pitched.

"Dad sent her to do his errands, and I sent her away."

"How close are you and Morgan?"

"Why would you ask that?"

"Why was your hair wet?"

"Now, that's really none of your business."

"You dodge a lot of my questions."

"You ask a lot of questions." She flipped her hair off her face. "Also, you'll never set your watch dog, Jesse, on me again. It wasn't right, and it put him in an uncomfortable situation."

That will happen again.

"And three."

"Oh, there's more?"

"Us."

"What about us?" I closed the file and gave her my full attention.

"You're my boss."

"Nice that you finally accept that fact."

"One who thinks he can control me."

"I know I can control you."

"We already crossed a line in the limo."

"You didn't seem to mind."

"In that moment, I didn't." She raised a hand to stop any comeback. "Problem is the scoreboard is uneven."

"Is that so?"

She leaned against the table, then, to my surprise

and total delight, lowered to her knees. I reached back and removed my gun and set it on the table next to her head. She eyed it for a second, and though I was curious to know what went through her mind, I wasn't about to break the moment.

"Always good to even the scoreboard." I groaned when she tugged on my belt and popped the button on my pants. Everything inside me coiled. I fought hard not to wind my hands in her hair and make her take me to the base the moment she touched me with her tongue. She was going to be the reason I'd get a good night's sleep tonight. I could already feel the tension ebb. She slid her hand over my pants, and the heat from her palm made me twitch with need. "That's it," I purred, savoring the moment. "Wrap that pretty little mouth around it."

"Grim!" Knox burst through the door with the three girls who had left my bedroom earlier. I grabbed my gun out of instinct. "I found your three-course meal from last night." He had been day drinking and didn't notice Kenna right away. "What ya say? Wanna do round two, or would it be round three?"

"Are you replacing me, baby?" The horny blonde from earlier pouted at Kenna. "Maybe we can have a competition on who's better?"

Kenna had stayed still up to his point and dropped her hands away as she stood. "That wouldn't be much of a competition." She casually wiped her mouth with her sleeve.

"Kenna! You want to play, too?" Knox grinned, and I pointed at the door.

"Leave!" I said through gritted teeth.

"No, I'm the one leaving." Kenna stopped as she passed the girls. "He's in a foul mood, but maybe you can help him out," she turned to look at me, "*again.*"

She left the room. I cocked my gun, and Knox's eyes widened.

"Shit, let's go find someone else to play with." The blonde girl pouted, and I ran a frustrated hand over the back of my neck as I tucked my gun away. I sank into a chair and felt the uncontrollable ache between my stomach and legs that was impossible to shake. Never had I had a woman do this to my head. I fucking hated it. I needed to do something, or I was going to lose my mind completely. I grabbed my phone.

Grim: I need one of Tess's best.

I stood, fixed my belt, and popped my button back in place.

Minnie: Setting something up for you
now. I'll be in touch.

Good.

I pushed the chair back against the table and left. I

slowed my pace as I heard someone yelling down the other hall.

"Who's in there?" I asked one of the guards.

"Mr. Tame has a client meeting." He paused and grabbed a tablet that had a record of who was where and when. "Mr. Griple."

I knew it wouldn't be wise to be around Cameron at that point. I couldn't be trusted with how pent-up I was. But I needed to channel my rage somewhere and could use a good fight. As I got close to the door, I could hear his client's anger. Nice to hear Cameron was getting it from somewhere else. Lord knew the asshole deserved it.

"You promised you had this handled, Cameron! I trusted you."

"I can fix this."

"Fix this how? He's dead, and last I checked, you can't bring people back from the dead."

"I can find someone to take his place."

"We go to trial soon!" the man screamed louder. "So help me God, you have no idea what kind of shit I have coming your way if we don't win this. If we don't win—"

He stopped when I opened the door, and I stared down at the man in the high-priced Italian suit.

"Can I help you?" he snapped but did a double take when he looked at me.

"Yeah, by getting the hell out of my hotel."

He swallowed and reined himself in. "Mr. Grim Gates," he nodded tightly, "I didn't recognize you." That, I doubted. Not many were tattooed from head to foot. "I was just leaving."

"Good idea."

"Mr. Tame," he turned to Cameron, "watch your back." He stormed out, and I crossed my arms at Cameron.

"Mind your business, Grim. I have it covered."

"The fuck you say to me, old man?"

"I can't do this right now." He waved for me to leave, and I felt my need to kill someone course through my body. I slammed the door shut and turned to him.

"I think you need a reminder of who the hell I am and that one day I'll own the hotel you work for."

TWELVE

KENNA

I slid my purse farther up my arm as I hurried through the back hallways and opened the door to where Dale was putting the final touches on a lunch plate.

"Hey," I sidestepped a girl with a tray, "here's Yen's request for his meal."

"You could've sent it to me like always." He ground some fresh pepper over a salad then wiped the side of the plate clean to ensure it looked perfect. "What's up?"

"Nothing."

He looked over his shoulder. "Out with it."

"You know that blonde who's always hanging out

with that Ron look-alike from *Jersey Shore*, down by the cabanas?"

"Blonde? Oh, you mean Starbi."

"I guess, yeah. Did her mother purposely pick a stripper name, or did she change it?" I rolled my eyes and hated her even more.

"Didn't care to ask." He winked. "What about her?"

"How far did you get with her?" He glanced at me again, and I got it. "She any good?"

He chuckled. "Solid six, I guess."

"Why a six?"

"Why do you want to know?"

"A client spotted her in the pool yesterday, and before I recommend her, I figured I'd do my homework." That was a lie, but it was a white one.

"Smart." He shrugged. "She's cute and all, but she's a talker, doesn't have much suction, but biggest complaint, one that might actually work in your favor, is she's also a stage six clinger. So, if you're looking to get some free time away from a client, she's your chick."

"Good to know."

"Yeah, it took me a while to point her in Danny's direction."

"Yeah, thanks a lot, man." His line chef grimaced.

"Anything else?"

"She's looking for someone to take care of her,"

Danny snickered as he flipped a piece of salmon over on the grill, "so flash some money around and she'll come running."

"Appreciate the insight." I waved and headed out of the kitchen.

"Just the chick I wanted to find." Minnie snagged my arm and pulled me away from the kitchen. "You want to tell me about last night?"

"I'm not following."

"I mean about how you said Grim was going to be upset with you. What happened?"

"It was a misunderstanding with a client being an asshole. Grim doesn't want me working on his contract anymore We got it cleared up." I felt like an ass giving her the CliffsNotes version, but I was just too done with it to discuss the whole thing with her.

"Oh, you mean Sonny Conti." She waved her hand.

"Minnie," I decided to share this part, "be careful, okay? Sonny's dangerous."

"Girl, please." She folded her arms over her ripped Metallica t-shirt. "Who do you think tipped Grim off that Sonny was going to try something with you?" My mouth dropped open, but then I realized who I was talking to and closed it. "Morgan had a run-in with Sonny in Arizona a way back. Then when he heard about what he was up to he told me to go to Grim or he'd do it himself. I figured you'd appreciate me telling. I mean if you weigh the options of being locked in the elevator versus what Morgan suggested Grim would do." She shrugged. "Seemed a slam dunk."

"You heard about that, did you?" I dropped my head. I loved that Morgan was always looking out for me. The fact that he was also a good friend of Grim's didn't factor in a whole lot. I tried not to hold it against him, anyway. Minnie told me once that Grim and Morgan had taken out a small MC in Phoenix that tried to mess with Trigger's half-brother Zay. They'd roughed up Zay's girlfriend and all hell broke loose. The result was quite impressive.

"Listen, Grim will get over the Sonny thing or he'll kill him. Either, or." She shrugged. "So now that I know that, tell me why you took off like a jackrabbit last night."

"No." I started to walk away, but she stepped in front of me.

"Kenna, we need to talk about that."

"You said you handled it all, right?"

"Yes, of course I did. You know I'd never let anything happen to you."

"Thank you." I swallowed past the lump in my throat. "See. There, we talked about it, and it's over with."

"Kenna, I need a little more than that. You told me to call you from the club when—"

"I know what I said, Minnie." I looked around in case anyone watched us. "And I know I put us in a bad situation, and that was never my intent, but it's over with now, and things need to go back to normal."

"I don't think that's possible, Kenna."

"Why?" It was so terrifying to even think about, I wanted to shed a layer of skin.

"Because whoever the hell that was at the club last night, that scared you enough to run, had some questions for *me*."

"What-what did you say to them?" The walls around us tilted.

"What I had to," her gaze narrowed in on me, "but babe, I don't think this is going to go away that easily."

"Well, it has to." I smiled when Brick approached. He squinted at me like he could read our body language but was smart enough to stand back and give us some space.

"Hey," she took my hand, "you know I'm always here for you. You usually tell me everything. We don't have secrets, so why can't you tell me this one?"

"Because." It slipped from my mouth as I broke with a quiet sob. "It's bad, Minnie."

"Jesus." She let out a long breath, and we both pulled it together. "Would it help if I got Trigger to talk—"

"No," I cut her off, "no one, Minnie. It's bad enough I got you involved."

"Min?" Brick took a step toward us, and I looked away, feeling raw.

"It's all good. I'll meet you at the pool." She smiled at him, and he studied us for a moment with a doubtful expression, then left.

"Great, now I'm on Brick's radar." I used the back of my hand to dry a tear that slipped out.

"I'll just mention your vagina and he'll forget everything he saw." She grinned and reached out to play with the twist of hair on my shoulder. "I'm letting this go for now," she gave me a pointed look, "but if anything else happens, and I mean anything, you need to spill it."

"Yeah." I agreed. "You can't even tell Brick about this, Min. I'm serious."

"Tits and ass until under the grass." She smiled, and I knew she'd always have my back. "Now," she wrapped an arm around me and started to walk with me, "I heard Grim had some company over last night and his brother let it spill over into your meeting this morning."

"Knox was day drinking again." I rolled my eyes.

"Mhm," she pressed her lips together, "did that bother your little bean?" She pointed to my crotch. "Because if I was as wound as you've been lately, and Mr. Tall Dark and Angry was playing on me with his fingers, I might be inclined to feel a little jelly."

"You're right I am jealous." I turned to look at her.

"Jealous that he's getting some and I'm not." Her face fell a little, like it wasn't the reaction she'd wanted. "Minnie, we live in Sin City, where zillions of penises are walkin' around looking for their next snack. I happen to have a very lovely snack box that's just waiting to be eaten. I even come with toys." I huffed, and she laughed.

"I think I may have just the answer for you." She pulled her phone from her purse and started to tap the screen. I was glad we were off the earlier topic. I wanted to bury it deep and move on. I needed to get my head on straight.

"Well, there you are, Kenna. You look as great as ever." Yen Hong joined us. He looked stylish in his navy blue and white striped button-down, salmon-colored short shorts, and a pair of Brunello Cucinelli white sneakers. Not a look I particularly found attractive, but I also wasn't his type. "Shall we?"

"Wait, I need to know one thing." Minnie had her hands on her hips. "How did you get out of that elevator?" A slow, lazy grin spread across my lips, and I knew my eyes twinkled with mischief.

"I got my hands on one of the black and golds." She knew I meant an exclusive card, and I could see she wanted to ask how I'd gotten it, but she wouldn't risk it in front of a client.

"I've taught you so well." She belly-laughed.

"Indeed." I nodded in lieu of a bow. "I'll text you

later." Yen looked curious but was too polite to ask. Minnie waved me off, and I followed Yen through the hotel to one of our best sushi restaurants. Of course, we skipped the line and were escorted to one of the best seats in the house. It looked out over a Zen Garden in keeping with the theme of total relaxation. It told the guests to relax and indulge then go back out and gamble. It was the perfect place to eat before a relaxing visit to the pool.

Yen pulled out my chair, and I thanked him as I draped my napkin over my lap.

He smiled at me from across the table, and I wondered what he was thinking.

"Did you get my notes on my friends?"

"Of course." I smiled.

"Memorized who does what?"

"You've never questioned me before, so why are you now?" I gave him a pointed look and his smile grew.

"I just want this to go well."

"You have my word, I'm on task." I winked as his gaze shifted over my shoulder. He stood and I mirrored him.

He made introductions and everyone sat. Yen looked to be on cloud nine. It had to be rare to be excited over something when you have everything in life.

I made sure to cover all the points that Yen had

requested of me. Everything flowed naturally because that was what I did, and I did it well. When dinner came Yen gave me a nod that I had done my part well. The first course was placed on our table, and we began to eat.

"Ms. Lodge," one of the men studied me, "Yen says you're the best of the best of the super hosts."

"When has Yen ever been wrong?" I made the table laugh.

"He says you know all about the city that never sleeps."

"You heard correctly." I placed my chopsticks down and dabbed my mouth. "In order to be the best, you must be the best at everything."

"May I pick your brain?"

"I insist."

"Best club in town?"

"Well, here at Indulge, of course." I winked. "But aside from Club Sinful Sweets, it depends on who you ask," I twisted the wine glass in front of me. "In my opinion, it's Delilah at the Wynn. It has live entertainment, and celebrities often jump up on stage to perform."

"It's hard to get a table."

"Well, if you were to stay at Indulge you wouldn't have to worry about wait times at all. I'd personally escort you to your table and have your drink of choice served." I leaned forward. "El Alto," I remembered his drink, "would be waiting for you. We do, after all, have the best entertainment in Vegas." I winked. "However, regarding the Wynn hotel, you just stay at their hotel, book directly through their concierge or, of course, let me know and I can get you a table. But barring that, if someone wanted to book it, be sure to tell them to book at least two to four weeks in advance. Always ask for a reservation for four, then call and adjust down."

"Okay," he nodded, "what about brunch? Besides here, of course." He laughed.

"Spago, inside the Bellagio, behind the fountain. The food is amazing, and the service is even better. The La Neta has the best avocado toast in the city. It's off the strip. I highly recommend you get the drink Roses are Red. And if pancakes are more what you crave, you must try their espresso pancakes." I didn't have to think; all that information was catalogued in my head. "Then there's the Jardin at the Wynn. Their lobster bennies are out of this world. If you crave something sweet, try their Red Velvet Cotton Candy pancakes. They're heavenly." I looked around the table. "Last, but certainly not least, the Pepper Club's gold glittery drinks are really great, and if your son takes too long in the bathroom, it's because of the wallpaper." I winked.

"So, you know your food." The other man seemed to like this game. "What about the don'ts of Vegas?"

"Common sense is number one. Keep your wits about you and never walk alone." I hated that I shifted at my own advice. "Stay away from street performers. They work in groups to shake you down for money then split it afterward. Booths in the hotels are meant to look like customer service but they're not. Snappers hand you a card with a picture of a naked lady on it in hopes you'll want to hire her, but the person who shows up won't be the one pictured on the card."

One of the younger men laughed. "I found that out a few years ago. Lesson learned. Then we used it to play a joke on a friend." He made a face as Yen shook his head, unimpressed. "Okay, what about bands? Where do I go for the best?"

"At the moment, I would suggest Brooklyn Bowl, very intimate, and you can get right up close to the band."

"Why at the moment?"

"Because the best place to see a band is being built as we speak."

"I'm impressed," the first guy who started the game grinned, "even more so because you didn't totally push Indulge. Though, of course, I know that's your job." He inclined his head.

"I really don't need to. The facts speak for themselves. That's why Mr. Hong chose to stay here, and it's why you should too."

"She's good." He nodded to Yen.

"She really is."

"And you know all of this for only working here a year?" the younger one asked.

"I was raised in Los Angeles, but Vegas is my back yard." I smiled.

"Which makes her wealth of knowledge that much more impressive," Yen complimented me.

"Thank you, Yen."

Yen's company said their goodbyes and left for a meeting. That left Yen and me. He ordered us another drink.

"I have a confession." He smiled as he sipped his Manhattan. "The men you were just speaking with aren't just old friends of mine. They are my soon-to-be associates."

"Oh?"

"We're merging companies."

"Congratulations."

"I think you just signed them to stay here as well." He chuckled. "You have something, Kenna. You're not just smart, you have finesse. There's a line between schmoozing someone and winning someone over because you're genuine."

"I'm flattered, thank you."

"Kenna, I think you're amazing at what you do, and I think you'd be perfect for the new hotel I'm building in Hong Kong. I'd like to have you come work for me."

"Oh." I didn't see that coming.

"I know you have a good thing going on here, and there's no hurry to answer me, but it's something I'd like you to consider. I'll certainly make it worth your while." At a nod, one of his men approached and leaned over to hand Yen a file. "Look this over, see if there's anything you'd like to change or add, and I'll make it happen."

"I will." I slid the folder close and rested my hand on it. I couldn't think of anything else to say.

"Now, I want to go swim off the extra pounds I likely just consumed. Instead of accompanying me, why don't you take the evening off, and if anyone is looking for you, I'll cover." He patted my arm. "You're young, pretty, and single, so go live it up tonight, and tell me all about it tomorrow."

"Thank you, Yen." I was lost for words. "That's very thoughtful. I'll certainly think about your generous offer." Also, his very considerate suggestion that I take the evening for myself.

I felt my phone vibrate in my purse and pulled it free.

> Minnie: Room six, second floor, you
> know where. Be relaxed and wear
> pink.

I opened the calendar for the spa and booked myself a spot. *Why not?*

Kenna: Count me in.

Two hours in, and my muscles were relaxed, my skin was soft as silk, and now I was draped in a thick layer of aloe while I soaked in a river of warm water. This treatment was meant to soothe not only your skin but your mind. The room looked like something from Star Trek, and when you closed your eyes you felt you were transported somewhere else. That was until I heard someone come in and sit down.

"Question." I lifted the cucumber peel and found Knox with his arms folded and a knowing smirk on his face. "What, exactly, did I walk in on this morning?"

"Fought off that hangover, did you?"

"Hair of the dog, always does the trick."

"I'm sure your liver loves you."

"So," he grinned again, "about how you were on your knees."

"Maybe that's a question for Grim."

"Or maybe it's for you. Because last I heard, you drive him to the brink of murder, and the next I see you —with my own eyes, by the way—on your knees about to pleasure my dear older brother. What about this situation did I miss?"

"Maybe we should talk about how you're screwing my little sister?"

"That's a casual thing, and I'd be more than willing to share the details of what your sister likes."

"Out." I pointed and dropped the cucumber back in place.

"I know what I saw, Kenna." His voice disappeared as he left the room.

Grim's hooded eyes flashed in front of me, and I moaned with the knowledge that relaxation time was now over.

Damn you, Knox.

THIRTEEN

GRIM

"I wondered when you'd come visit." Tess, Trigger's wife, peeled off his lap and handed me a drink from a waiter's tray. I took in their newly redone back yard. Tess owned a prestigious burlesque house here in Vegas and had just finished major renovations to both the house and property. Business was back in full swing, and everyone and their mother panted to buy a membership. She had the best women, and men, in town and held some very interesting parties often incorporating the newest sex fad.

"I'd have come sooner, but—"

"It wasn't until now you needed to blow off some steam?" Tess knew me well.

"Something like that." I sipped my bourbon.

"Rail mentioned you were havin' a night," Brick cracked a beer, "but something tells me it got worse?"

"Yeah." I recognized a ratty old chair next to the bar with a cheap beer in the holder. "That's Gus's, isn't it?" I pointed to it.

"I couldn't part with it." Tess looked back at Trigger, who heard my comment but didn't say anything. Trigger's Uncle Gus was a favorite, and what happened to him weighed heavy on everyone, including my father. "Shall we do a tour?"

"Sure." I followed her inside while Rail trailed behind.

"Check-in is where you entered." Tess pointed to the front desk. "Fingerprinting is over there, and no one comes in without provin' they're clean. Through here are our sex rooms." She scanned a card, and we entered a viewing room. "You can watch or participate." Two men and a woman were in some kind of sextangle, and all seemed happy.

"Impressive."

"Thanks. We offer lots of stuff." She proudly grinned. "We have tease rooms, oral rooms, full-blown sex rooms like this one, then we get into the kink." As we stepped out of the room, a man dressed as a bunny came out and looked me up and down. I slit my eyes at him as a warning, and he nodded and passed me by. "That's our furry room. People get off dressin' like animals and do whatever." She shrugged and made a face as if to say *who knew.*

"It's an oddly satisfying room." Rail winked and lifted one shoulder.

"Like I always say," Tess chuckled, "if there's sex in the air, Rail is there."

"It's true."

I'd seen enough in my travels around the world to know there was something for everyone on this planet.

"Moving on." Tess laughed and led us to a different part of the house. I couldn't believe how many furries walked around the place. They were in and out of the rooms.

"They seem to be traveling in packs these days." I made a wry face at Tess. *To each their own, I guess.*

"We've had quite an influx of," she paused, "animals this week. There's a convention going on at Taro Hotel. Well, a couple of hotels, actually." A woman dressed as a fox dragged her puffy tail across my cheek as she walked by. I didn't miss the wink she gave me behind her mask, and it left no doubt in my mind she'd like to feed on me. I'd tried a lot of things, but that wouldn't be one of them.

"Hey, Tess." A well-built man stepped out of a room dressed in leather chaps. He held up a pair of handcuffs.

"Hey, Garrett, what can I do for you?"

"These broke." He held them up. "I have the real

thing if the house permits it." I looked at Tess, and she mouthed the word *cop*.

"No need," she radioed to someone, "I'll have a fresh pair brought to your room."

"Thanks." He turned to leave and gave a little bare-ass wiggle as he walked away.

"Rail would be a horse for that cowboy any day." Brick snickered behind us, and Rail tried to punch him in the nuts. Suddenly, Minnie appeared and gave Tess a grin.

"You're just in time," I heard her murmur.

"You should see the ecstasy room." Tess smiled and pulled open a door. Minnie happily joined us and took over from Tess.

"You take a little Ecstasy, or a little pot. You pick your own poison and indulge." She gracefully waved as she pulled back a curtain, and there on the other side of the glass, in a velvet-draped room full of fancy pillows and low red lighting, was Kenna. She was in a pink silk teddy and was being kissed all over her breasts by a man in dress pants and a shirt.

I immediately forced my mind back to the fact that she, my fucking employee, had just signed two known criminals to my hotel against my damn orders.

"What'd she take?" I growled.

"This time, weed," Rail answered. "Gotta love this place, right?" He slapped me on the back. I kept my eyes fixed on Kenna.

This time? How often did she come here? Apparently, I had a lot to learn about Kenna Lodge.

"This is also a viewing playroom." Tess moved next to me. "Highest bidder takes over." She pointed to the card reader. "This right here is for volume. There's mics everywhere so every little moan can be heard." She raised her brows at me.

"Everyone out." I took a deep breath as they all quickly filed out the door. I turned the volume up and listened. The music was low enough that I could hear her breathe. It was fascinating.

The guy planted kisses all over her, then tenderly caressed her stomach. He slowly moved to her bare thigh and drew circles above her knee.

She took his hand and slapped it to her ass, and he smiled but went right back to his kisses.

"God, you're sexy," he murmured, and her eyes squeezed shut. I could see her frustration. "I want to…"

"To?" She tried to coach him.

"I want to pamper you all night long."

"Look," she sat up, "I don't want to be pampered here. I'm just trying to get off."

"This isn't a sex room, though," he complained.

"I'm not looking for sex from you. I just want a need filled. You just have to get a little more aggressive with me."

"I'm not good at that." He looked doubtful.

"Well, let's try this." She blindfolded herself and lifted her arms over her head as she balanced on her knees. "Now, I can't see you. You can do whatever you want to me. Just come at me with a little authority."

"Okay." He awkwardly took her hands and held them down then slapped her ass.

"Yes, that's a start." She grinned behind her blindfold. "Turn the music up. It'll help." He leaned back and turned up the song. I recognized it. *Twisted* by Missio poured through the speakers, and I watched in fascination.

He sat her down and moved between her legs. He hiked her legs up onto his shoulders then sprawled his hands over her stomach. He looked completely lost. His face was flushed as he tried to figure out what to do next.

How can a guy like that be at a sex house and have no idea what the hell he was doing? I closed my eyes and realized Tess and Minnie had planned this entire thing. I would have caught on if I wasn't walking around with a massive erection and a one-track mind.

I should have left, but I was rooted in place. My hands gripped the windowsill as my erection begged me to go inside.

Fuck it.

I tapped my card to the reader and typed in a thousand. I set my max price ridiculously high. The light above the door went from red to green and I heard a soft click. I tossed my coat on a leather couch and headed inside.

The guy moved back and looked over at me as he realized what had happened. He looked almost relieved when he saw that I'd undone my shirt, and it draped open. I put a finger to my mouth to tell him to stay quiet then waved a hand at a different door to tell him to get the hell out. He tried to look pissed, but I knew it was just for show. He was completely out of his league here. He didn't argue. Besides, that was the rule of the room he'd chosen.

I placed my hand against her blindfold and applied a soft pressure then plucked a silk tie from the box of toys behind me and tapped her legs to open. I sat between them and then tugged her arms toward me. She obeyed, and a slow, lazy smile spread across her pretty pink lips as I tied her wrists together.

Moving my legs under hers I waited for her to relax then gripped her waist and swung her up to staddle my hips.

"Nice," she breathed.

I leaned in and kissed the spot where I just was yesterday. She jerked back, and she frowned. I tried again, and she reacted the same way.

"Not there," she warned. I wanted to ask why, but I didn't want to give myself away.

I pumped her plump breasts and rolled her nipples with the pads of my thumbs. She seemed to like this, so

I moved on to find out what else she liked. I slid my hands around her waist and fingered the lacey thong she had on. I knew the playrooms required underwear and some kind of teddy or t-shirt. I wrapped the scrap of lace around my thumb once and gave it a good tug while I pinched her nipple. A shot of hot breath slipped from her lips. I was curious if she'd catch that move since I did it in the limo too, but she didn't. She moved her bound hands over my head to stabilize herself. Her perfume made my head swim.

"Again," she moaned. I did what she asked, only this time I leaned down and nipped her nipple, making her yelp. As she did, I ground my erection into her and buried my face into her cleavage. She smelled fresh and woke up every part of me. A shaky breath traveled through my body as it hummed to be closer. Her slender neck taunted me, and my mouth started to water at the need to taste her there.

With all my willpower not to give in and just take that spot, I lifted her in the air as I stood.

"Oh!" She was startled by the sudden movement but wrapped her legs around me. "You learn fast."

I pushed her to the padded wall and lowered her to her feet as I moved her hands above her head. I used my thigh to hold her up as I ran my hands down her arms then cupped her breasts for a moment. I hated her teddy; it was just another struggle not to rip the fabric away. Then I flattened my palm on her stomach and slipped into her wet panties. Holding her arms with one hand, I slipped a finger inside her. Christ, she was so hot.

A hungry moan dropped from her lips and strained her head to one side.

I couldn't take it anymore.

The moment she felt my lips on her neck, she froze. She tried to wiggle free, but I pressed another finger inside her.

"You feel…" She trailed off into a throaty cry as I rubbed circles. I got high from just the feel of her falling apart in my arms. She was vulnerable and submissive, but I sensed the fight that was inside her wanted to be unleashed. I sucked harder on her neck, and she fought to break free of my hold. "Not the neck." She managed to find the words.

"Why?" I grunted.

"Not your place."

I smirked. I liked that. I was conceited enough to accept that she had a place on her body that was now reserved only for me.

"Whose?" I couldn't resist.

"The Reaper's." She chuckled darkly, and I lost it. I grabbed her hips, swung her around, and laid her back down on the pillows. I caught myself with my arms and flattened my body over hers. I hiked her leg up and slipped a finger back inside her.

"Yes!" She panted. I fed my fingers into her and

gave her probably the best job I'd ever given to a woman. She felt amazing under me. I gave it to her as if we were having sex. My insides pleaded with me to give in and take all of her, but this room had rules, and I wouldn't attempt to break them.

It was torture, but there was a twisted part of me that enjoyed it. The knowledge that I'd had this with Kenna without her knowing it was me was heady stuff. I wanted that. Only I would know that when she saw me during the day, she'd remember what I could do with just a few fingers. I thrusted in and out, rocking my body against hers, kissing and sucking wherever I could. I ravished her body, soaked up her noises, and watched as everything strained to ignite.

"I'm about to come!"

"Give it to me, sweetheart," I purred in her ear, and her masked face flipped to mine as she recognized my voice.

"Grim!" My fingers changed direction. "Oh!" Her cheeks pinked, her breathing hitched, and just as she fell off the ledge, I moved to her neck and sucked in her sweet skin at the spot reserved for me. I wanted to mark her, remind her that this happened, that I could make her submit to me in the best way possible. She trembled beneath me, and her hands squeezed my forearm as an anchor. It was one of the most erotic experiences I ever had with anyone. Maybe it was the setting, or maybe it was the knowledge that she'd tried to get it from someone else and I turned the table on her plans. Whatever it was, I needed it.

She ripped off her blindfold before her body had even finished its ride, but she couldn't do anything but let it take her. When she came back down and I knew she could hear me properly, I moved my lips to her ear, "Two to zero, sweetheart."

"Grim! What the hell?" Her eyes flared but wavered when I gave her one last flick of the fingers. "How did you even know I was here?"

"Seems our friends played us." I smirked, and she pushed against my shoulder so she could sit up. I leaned back and crossed my arms behind my head. "Feel better?"

"I did." She flipped her hair out of her face as she stumbled to stand. "I'm going to kill Minnie!" She stormed toward the door.

"So, you have a spot on your body, reserved just for me?"

She flipped me the finger as the door slammed shut behind her. I laughed and got to my feet. My pants strained and my erection felt worse than ever, but at least my head felt clear. I snagged the blindfold and tucked it in my pocket as a souvenir as I whistled my way back into the viewing room for my jacket.

My jacket had been moved. I stood there a moment and studied the small room. I wondered who had been in here and how long they might have watched us. The guy from before had exited through a different door. I'd allowed myself to be led by my dick and not my head. It should have occurred to me anyone could just walk in and watch us the very way I had her. It was how these rooms worked.

A movement behind me made me duck in time to miss the bat that came for my head, but not quick enough to stop the punch to my jaw. It took me a moment to realize there were two of them.

The whoosh of air from the bat as it swung again made me dodge to the side. I quickly assessed the situation as they circled me. The man who held the bat seemed nervous and his gaze flicked around the room. He would be the weaker one, so I homed in on the other guy. He seemed more confident as he took another swing at my jaw.

"Like the show?" I asked as I dodged his fist and, for a split second, he looked confused. The bat came at me again, and I grabbed it and pulled it out of his grip. I smoked the side of his knee, and he dropped to the floor with a shriek.

Whack! I got a fist to the side and hit the wall.

"That's two." I flipped the bat in my hand and caught it by the handle then snapped it in half over my thigh before I tossed it aside. I preferred to use my hands to fight; I liked to feel the damage I caused.

Fire surged through me, and my anger spiked up a level. I grinned as I plowed my balled fist into the side of his skull and sent him into the wall. I was on him the moment he fell. I yanked him to his feet by his jacket and slammed his head against the doorframe.

"Okay! Stop!" he cried and squeezed his eyes shut when I raised my fist again. "I was paid!"

"Paid?" I questioned. "Speak while you can."

"We were paid four hundred to rough you up." I gave him a pathetic look. "I didn't know you could fight." He whined.

"You call that a fight?" I scoffed. "Tell me everything," I warned, "or I'll show you just how well I can fight."

"I don't know!" He fought to speak while the wimp on the floor still sobbed in pain. What a pathetic pair to send after me. It was an amateur move on someone's part. I snapped one of his fingers, and his mouth dropped open with a scream. "Okay!" His scream turned into a hiss. "Shit, me and my buddy Joseph," he nodded to the shit on the floor, "were just enjoying lookin' at all the titties and ass around the place when a guy came out of that room," he nodded at the room I'd been in. "He offered us money to beat you up when you came out."

"Why?" I slammed his back into the wall.

"He just said you were some dirty business guy!" He coughed from the impact. "Look, man, I moved mountains to get a membership here, but that doesn't include anything except to look. Four hundred could have gotten us into a pleasure room or at least a lap dance!"

"What the hell?" Tess was suddenly behind me with Trigger on her heels.

I dropped the shit to the floor next to his buddy and used my thumb to feel along my jaw. Trigger pulled out his gun and moved Tess behind him.

"Someone paid these guys to jump me." I chuckled darkly, but Trigger could see there was more to it. Tess had her bouncers in the room within seconds and they peeled them off the floor.

"Kiss your wildest dreams goodbye boys because you'll never set foot in here again." Tess gave them the same finger Kenna had given me.

"Where's Kenna?"

"I'm not sure." Tess left in a hurry, and that left Trigger and me to talk. I nodded at him to follow me into the room.

"What do you know?" He sat on the arm of the couch. I filled him in on the little information I had. Brick rushed in with a laptop.

"Here." He pressed play on the surveillance video, and we watched as someone dressed in a wolf costume entered the viewing room shortly after I had gained entrance to the pleasure room. As we watched, I did the math; he would have left just after I'd made Kenna come. We saw him as he stopped the two guys in the hall, pulled out some money, and they talked. Then he left, and the two men came into the room and muttered something about how they were going to attack me.

"There's no cameras in the rooms." Trigger pointed to the glass. "We have security measures for anyone inside, but they need to trip the alarm."

"Let me see." Kenna, who was now dressed in a loose skirt and halter top, slipped by Tess and squinted at the laptop as Brick replayed the video. "I can't believe this." She looked over at me. "Are you okay?"

"Yeah."

"Someone you've pissed off lately?" Tess asked with a wry look.

"You mean right now? Or in general?" I shrugged with sarcasm. "I have a few ideas but not one that would include this kind of thing. This feels more personal than business."

"Agreed." Trigger nodded. "This points more toward you, Kenna."

"Me? Why?"

"Seemed he watched you two goin' at it, then went after Grim." He studied her.

"What about you, Kenna?" Tess asked softly. "Have you pissed anyone off lately." I noticed Kenna looked down as she shook her head. "Has anyone been bothering you lately?"

"No."

"What about the men at Minnie's club?" Brick cut in, and Kenna looked quickly at Minnie. "No, she never said anything, Kenna. I'm just trying to put some pieces together here."

"Ken—"

"No, Minnie!" Kenna cut her off while she avoided eye contact. "Like I said, that was just an old client pissed I'd dropped him."

"Kenna," Trigger rubbed his chin, "you and Grim are family. Years of friendship and loyalty are what seals that. You need my help, you got it. We got your back."

"And I'll always have yours." She straightened her spine. "I appreciate the offer, Trigger, but I've got everything handled."

"Babe," Minnie pleaded again, and I got she knew more than she let on.

"Okay, Trigger, I do need your help." Kenna cleared her throat. "I need you, all of you, to let this go, for," she swallowed hard, "for me."

"Okay." Morgan, who must have slipped in the room, raised his hands and glanced at Kenna. She looked relieved to see him. "I think we all could use some fuckin' space. I, for one, am sweatin' my balls off and could really use a drink and a lap dance."

"Well, we don't have a ton to go on anyway, Grim." Tess switched gears. "You don't need a key card to open the viewing door. You'd only need one to open that one." She pointed to the door that led into the pleasure room. "He obviously didn't swipe his card to make a bid. He just watched. Me and Brick can scan the footage again to see if we can see him anywhere else. Try to pinpoint the prick."

"I'll go talk to the hostess." Brick rushed out.

"I'll call you later." Kenna squeezed Minnie's arm as she left the room.

"Minnie?" Trigger had waited till Kenna was gone. "The fuck you know?"

"Nope," she raised her hands to show she wouldn't talk about it, "I won't lose her over this."

"How bad is it?" I hoped she'd at least share something.

"From the part I do know, bad enough. Kenna tells me everything, but this, whatever it is, she wants me far from it. Lips sealed and all that."

"Fuck." I rubbed my jaw and wished I could just beat it out of her.

"Grim," she stepped close, "please be careful with Kenna on this one. I've never seen her so closed-mouthed. She disconnects whenever I try to bring it up. She's never done that before."

"Yeah." I looked away and tried to tell myself I would be.

FOURTEEN

KENNA

"You seem off, Kenna." My mother reached for my arm. Her gold bangles clinked as she attempted to soothe me. "What's going on?"

"Did you ever do something for the right reason but knew the consequences of anyone finding out could crumble your entire world and those around you?" Mom looked a little taken back but thought for a moment.

"That's a heavy question."

"It is."

"You know who deals with heavy all day long?" She gave me a shrug, and I shook my head.

"Dad has a lot going on."

"He always has time for you girls."

"No, he always has time for Calli." I dropped my head into my hands. I didn't care I'd probably smudge the lenses of my new sunglasses.

"You know he loves you both, Kenna. It's all in your delivery." She tossed her long, gorgeous hair over her slim shoulder. "You and your father are just too alike. You're both stubborn and don't back down. If he knew you were struggling with something and wanted advice, he'd be there for you. Just leave your defenses at the door and let him in."

Maybe there was a time we'd been close, now there were times I hardly recognized him. Besides, I needed my father far away from this situation. Things were fucked up enough as it was.

"Easier said than done," I scoffed. My father wasn't an easy man to deal with at the best of times. I guessed that was why he was one of the best lawyers around. I only wished I agreed with Mom, but the truth was he wouldn't be there for me, especially on this. No, this would send my father off the deep end. I had to take this secret to the grave.

"I ran into Laurel Gates this morning, and she told me you were impressive in the meeting. Held your own and got what you wanted."

"I did." I smiled and remembered how good it felt.

"I also heard that Grim is back for good."

"Yup, he came in like a bull in a china shop."

"What does that mean?"

"It means as soon as he got his toe in the door he tried to meddle with our well-oiled machine. Swinging his balls around, thinking he holds all kinds of power over me and others."

She smiled at my words. "He's quite attractive too. Got that whole biker, billionaire, dark knight thing going on."

"You forgot bossy and demanding."

"You mean alpha and sexy?" She knew me too well.

"Oh, you mean arrogant and spoiled." That last one wasn't true, Grim worked his ass off, but I needed another word.

"Sounds like he's your perfect match."

"Perfect match in a ring, maybe." I sipped my lemon water and checked my phone. I waited for Salazar to let me know when he was ready to gamble. "Whatever, I'm glad you're back, Mom. I hate it when you leave."

"I'm back until after summer then I'm off to Hong Kong." She ran a painted fingertip down the length of her fancy drink then delicately licked the condensation from her finger. "You can come with me if you like." My mother is an archaeologist and often travels to far away sites to share her expert knowledge. As a child, I often was schooled on the road and experienced life in person instead of textbooks. We'd had our adventures, she and I, and a lifetime of experiences people only dreamt of having. There was a part of me that wondered if Mom had tried to keep me away from the crime side of life my father brought home, but as I got older, the trips became less frequent. Maybe she just thought I was a young adult and needed to deal with what life brought me, or maybe it was something else. I never asked because I didn't think I wanted to know the answer.

Mom was a force to be reckoned with, as untamable as she was beautiful, and would never let anyone get in her way when it came to her passion. She often commented that I got my drive from my father, but I knew I really got it from her.

"Maybe." I shrugged. It might be a good idea to investigate the place where Yen offered me a job. Who knew? If my world did implode, I might need to run away.

"Want to talk about why Minnie's watching you like a hawk right now?" I looked across the club and saw Minnie as she pretended to just notice me. She waved.

"She's just being a good friend. I brought on two clients that make me uneasy." I shared half the truth.

"Would these clients be Sonny and Victor Conti?"

"Yes, how do you know?"

"Your father filled me in."

"Oh. Did he say anything else?"

"Not really, he's just excited. Is there more to it? I'm sure he's proud of your accomplishment." I pushed aside the little hurt that came with the fact that my father clearly hadn't shared the roofie mishap with her. Dad truly did put business before family.

"Enough about me, Mom. How was India? Did you and Claudine have a good time at your conference?"

"It was wonderful." She grinned and made me feel instantly better. As she told me all about her adventures, I felt some of my tension drain away. My mother and I were very close, and she was the only one who saw Dad for who he was sometimes. Difficult and scary. I never understood how he landed someone as amazing as her, but as the saying goes, opposites attract. He worshipped her, and their love was real. It was just hard, as I often felt like an outsider looking in.

> Salazar: Meet me in the blackjack room.

> Kenna: On my way.

"Mom, I'm sorry, but I have to go. Duty calls." I slid off the chair as she laughed.

"I understand that one. Don't forget dinner tonight at six. You know it's tradition." She squeezed my hand. "Promise me you'll come."

"I promise." It was tradition to have dinner together whenever Mom returned from her trips. The idea of being in the same room as my sister didn't appeal to me, but I wasn't one to miss an opportunity to spend time with my mother. I kissed her cheek and hurried off toward the blackjack tables.

As I whisked through the noisy room, I waved at a few guests who were regulars at the casino. I loved my relationship with the locals and felt at home whenever they came to play. A group of showgirls fluffed their feathers at me playfully as they handed out advertisements to the gawking men.

"Hey, Kenna," one waved a sparkly hand at me, "love your shoes."

"You too." I beamed at her hooker heels that flashed red lights as she walked.

Vegas was all smoke and mirrors, a constant distraction to have you look one way when you should look the other. Money, sex, booze, drugs, and fantasy were what this city was about. The shear indulgence of it all made people delirious with excitement, and I thrived on it. The chase to provide it all for my guests brought me the fix I needed, and I wanted to be the best.

Suddenly, a chill spread through me and my attention was moved to a man at the bar. He stared directly at me. When we locked eyes, he waited for a beat. He seemed to want me to know he was watching. Then he slowly turned around and paid his bill. I second guessed myself. Perhaps I'd misread the situation? Then I shivered at the thought that this man might be connected to *him*.

That was the problem with Vegas. When you stopped and squinted, when you really looked hard at it, behind all the glint and glamour, you'd see there was a darkness that hovered, ready to snatch you up.

I looked at the man's back again, but he never turned around. I shook it off and forced my head back on straight.

I gave a nod to the bartender, and he immediately caught my pointed look at Salazar and began to mix his favorite drink. I tipped the bartenders good money to make sure my clients were their priority.

"How much?" I asked the girl in the cage. I knew she'd just spent the night with Dale. I'd overheard him when he bragged to his line chef about how wild she was.

"He's bet a hundred thousand." She waved her hand, unimpressed. "His card limit today is two million."

"Yes, I know." I tapped my finger on the ledge. "He's either nervous to play because Yen Hong was here yesterday, or he's using the table as a way to watch for him."

"What did Yen do?"

"I'm not entirely sure." I thought for a second then made a phone call.

"Leo," I turned to look at the camera where I knew he was watching, he always watched the blackjack tables at this time of day, "I need the Lion Den's for a client."

"Salazar?"

"Yes."

"He's barely playing."

"I know. I think it has to do with Yen."

"The room's free, what else do you need?"

"I can ask—"

"I'm here, Kenna. What do you need?" I loved that Leo trusted me enough to help me out in these situations.

"He's a Lee Fields fan, low orange lighting, don't fill the table, less is more, or he'll get spooked, and no Yen Hong."

"Got it."

Fifteen minutes later, Salazar was seated at a table of six, his double-shot drink rested on a gold-plated coaster, and a magnitude of playing chips sat in front of him just waiting to be lost to the house.

Normally, I'd sit close to a wall when I wanted to give a special client moral support, but Salazar liked me next to him. I sat slightly back so I could look over his shoulder.

Every player had their own style when they played. Salazar was a risktaker, loved to look like he had the best hand even when he didn't. It was well known he bluffed constantly so the other players studied everyone else but him. I noted Salazar currently held a flush.

I didn't care who won; I only cared how much they lost. Though I'd always be there for my client, the hotel was who I rooted for. Whenever I was in the room with a client, it was my job to be their biggest supporter. And how I did that was to make sure everything was to their liking. I'd never once glance at the time, and never once show any emotion when any kind of move was played.

Three and half hours later, the pot was just over six million. It was down to Salazar and one other man named Mr. Pin.

"Call." Pin tossed his last chip in the pot.

Salazar dropped his cards, and Pin cursed as he tossed his cards in the center.

"Whatever." Pin pushed to his feet, signed some paperwork, and left the room with a scowl.

I smiled and sat forward now the game had ended. I knew the casino just got a small percentage of that six million. It might not be a ton, but it was good enough for a single game of poker.

"How do you feel?" I put my hand on Salazar's arm and spoke softly as the players left the room.

"Much better." He slid a black chip toward me as a tip. "Thanks for making this happen."

"That's what I'm here for." I motioned for one of the guys to clear the chips away.

"May I ask you something?"

"Of course." I smiled.

"How did the rest of your evening go with Sonny Conti the other night?" I was caught off guard because my mind was on Yen Hong.

"It didn't last much longer after you left." I sighed as I remembered how tense everything had been. "I must say I'm surprised. I didn't expect a man like you would entertain the idea of doing business with a person like Mr. Conti."

"One must never pass up an opportunity that's presented until you feel things out." He thought for a moment. "Sonny had a few business deals that sounded interesting, but it didn't take long to see he was all talk. He seems to be a man who lives in the moment."

"He's not someone I would normally work with either, but it wasn't my choice."

"I think you handled yourself very well." He smiled politely.

"Thanks." I smiled despite my discomfort with the topic and decided to dive right into Yen. "You know I only want what's best for my clients."

"I do." He seemed sincere. "Thank you," he said to the cute little waitress who held out a tray with a warm smile.

"Are you and Yen Hong all right?"

He looked away, and I noted his fingers flexed. "It's

just business. We were both going for the same thing, I won, and he wasn't happy about it. Then the contract fell through, but by the time Hong found out, someone else stepped in and snatched the deal. It's created some animosity, but nothing time can't fix."

"All right, because you're both my clients, and it's my job to ensure the two of you are happy. I need to know I'm not going to be caught in any crossfire."

"You have my word, Kenna, you won't be." He took a drink and downed about a quarter of it. My stomach hurt at the thought.

"Well, I'll see you later." I gathered my purse that hung off my chair.

"Thank you for today."

"Sure thing." I checked my watch and knew I needed to get ready for dinner. "If you need me, you know how to reach me." I patted his arm and quickly left. I knew I was going to be late if I didn't get a move on.

"You're Kenna, aren't you?" The cute little waitress who had served Salazar stopped me in the lobby.

"Yes?"

"I know you don't know me. I work here, of course, but I also pick up shifts at the Venetian. I wanted to tell you something."

"Okay. What is it?" I gave her an encouraging smile.

"Well, I was working the tables next to you when

you were having dinner the other night. I overheard Sonny Conti talking to a friend after you left. I can't be sure, but I think this friend was waiting to join you guys upstairs after." I swallowed past the lump in my throat. *This wasn't going to be good.*

"I see."

"You should know you're on his radar."

"What do you mean?"

"Well, he told his friend he was angry that Mr. Gates had embarrassed him and messed up their evening with you. He said he was going to get his time with you. It didn't sound very nice, if you know what I mean."

I was shocked. Sonny was flirty, but he'd never made a move on me. He usually ignored me when there were other women around. It was why I'd agreed to try to get him to sign on with Indulge. I would have thought I was far from that man's radar even more now that Grim stepped in.

"Thanks for that. Is there anything else?"

"There's one more thing. Sonny caught me when I walked by his table and asked where you went on your time off. Of course, I said I didn't know."

Shit, like I wasn't looking over my shoulder enough already.

"All right," I dropped my head and tried to process what she'd told me. "I hang out at Distill, a local bar off the Strip."

"Really?" she seemed confused why I'd tell her that.

"No, but that's where you'll tell him I go if he ever asks again."

"Got it." She nodded with a tight smile.

"Thanks…" I paused for her name.

"Cynthia."

"Thanks, Cynthia."

I hurried through the back employee hallways and took the stairs to the third floor to avoid the shift change. I used Grim's black card to override the elevator and shot straight to my floor without any stops. I smiled as I removed the card from the slot and thought how he'd have to pry it from my fingers now because the thing was gold for getting around this massive hotel.

A quick body shower, a makeup touchup, a new outfit, and I felt better. I was pleased at how my white T-shirt clung to my body. It was tied above my belly button and paired with a cute flowy pink skirt that hit about mid-thigh. I tugged on a pair of ankle boots and glanced once more in the mirror. The gold jewelry lifted my casual look, and some light gloss sealed the outfit.

I felt the familiar knot in my throat that came whenever a family dinner was in play. Nothing for it, I headed out.

The Lure Restaurant boasted a high-end menu and

an even higher-end clientele. Of course, my father would reserve a room there on one of the busiest nights of the month. He loved playing the *lawyer to the owners* card. There were five exclusive rooms with glass walls, so you'd be on display. The rooms had their own private access to a shared balcony. The idea was you'd eat, drink, and mingle, then eventually migrate your way down the stairs to another private balcony used for an even more exclusive playing room. This was one of those places you had to know about and have enough money to get into.

"Kenna?" A voice oozed moist breath next to my ear, and I spun around. *Yikes.* Sasha, an ex from my late teens pulled me in for a hug. "How are you?"

"Good." I stepped back with a shudder and managed not to wipe my ear. I clenched my purse in front of me with both hands to create a small shield between us. My father had introduced us when he and his friends had appeared in Vegas and then again at our home in LA. Dad said they were doing some work for him. I knew my father had been very stressed at the time over one of his cases. He was genuinely nice, and at eighteen, I was more easily impressed. It still hadn't taken long to wonder what kind of work they did for my father. When I asked, my father would just say they were helping with his case. The creep factor began to show with his buddies, but my heart was invested in him. Things got physical, and he was my first. But after six months, I started to pull away when I found out that I wasn't the only one in bed with him. That was over a decade ago, yet Sasha is standing in front of me. *Aren't I lucky?*

"You look nice." His eyes went down my body. "I haven't seen you in a while. Maybe we could do dinner sometime."

Sasha often spent time in the casino, and I'd seen him off and on. He'd watch me, but not in a way that showed he wanted anything more. He just watched.

"Yeah, maybe." I looked away. "Are you staying for dinner?" *Please say no.*

"No, I just need to touch base with Cameron." He began to walk with me.

"Everything okay?"

"Of course." I repeated. With him in my head, it was always the same answer. "I just need a minute with Cameron, then he's all yours." He raced ahead.

I watched him lean down and whisper something to Dad. Then he looked over and waved at me from where I stood in the doorway.

Something felt off, but I pushed it aside. I needed to focus on one shitty moment at a time.

Everyone was already at the table. I noticed Simon Gable, my father's PI and personal ass kisser, at our table. I liked him, but it bothered me that my father seemed to view him the same way he did Calli. With pride.

"My apologies for being late. Salazar won at the blackjack table, and we celebrated." I beamed at how well he'd done.

"Good for you." Dad nudged a napkin at me as I took a seat. I placed it on my lap with an inward sigh that he never gave me the chance to show my manners. "What will you do for him tomorrow?"

"Nothing."

"You don't have a plan?" His face had a shocked look.

"He's leaving for LA for two days, so I don't need a plan. Yen Hong has requested my presence." He nodded at that and seemed satisfied. He began to scan the room behind me in hopes someone watched us. He did love to be on display. I tried not to take it personally; I wasn't going to let him ruin my evening.

"Darling, be happy for Kenna. She did well for the hotel tonight." Mom smiled at me. "I'm so glad you're here, dear."

"Now that we're all finally here, can we please order?" Calli glanced at her menu then dropped it back down with a bored look. We all knew what she would order—a kale salad with the dressing on the side. Whereas I ate whatever I wanted whenever I had the chance. I rarely had time for anything but work most days. Besides, I worked out religiously and had no need to worry about my figure.

"Mom," I leaned toward her, "Dale was telling me

the chef here just got in a shipment of Prince Edward Island scallops, and they're to die for."

"I heard the Nova Scotia ones are better." Calli shrugged.

"Well, then, scallops it is." Mom smiled and tilted her head at Dad. I knew she wanted me to talk to him, but I wasn't interested in discussing it now, especially in front of everyone. I shook my head at her, but she ignored me. "Cameron, Kenna has something that's bothering her. Maybe she could run it by you?" I inwardly cringed.

He looked over at me, and I knew I had about thirty seconds to get my words out.

I needed to be vague.

"Hypothetically speaking, if someone did a bad thing for—"

"What bad thing?" He cut me off.

"I don't know," I stumbled. "Say someone assaulted someone. That isn't a good thing to do, but say the victim wasn't a good person and then—"

"I won't give out free legal advice to your loser friend Rail." I could see his temper rise. He hated Rail.

"I never said it was Rail." I tried to curb my annoyance. None of us were saints, after all.

"You didn't have to." He had to have the last word.

"See, Kenna," Calli jumped in, and it took all my willpower not to tell her off, "if you went to law school, you'd know the answer."

"Calli..." Mom scowled, but it did nothing, like always.

"Were there any witnesses to this hypothetical assault?" Simon spoke up. I was shocked. I knew he had eyes for Calli, and normally he'd never take a chance of irritating her.

"I don't think so."

"Any evidence left behind?"

"No."

"If a tree falls in the forest and no one hears it, does it make a sound?" He gave me a tiny smile, and I let my chest relax.

"Thanks, Simon." I felt mildly better despite Calli's rude snort.

"Do any of these hypotheticals need representation?" Dad asked, and I glared at him. It was always business with him.

"Hypothetical, Dad." I shook my head.

"Hypotheticals are normally based off something." He got his last word in, and I swallowed back a comment.

When dinner was served, I let my mind wander as I tuned out Calli and Dad's conversation. Thankfully, Mom made small talk with Simon and occasionally attempted to draw me in. I wasn't up for it, so the moment I could, I slipped out to the balcony.

It was nicer out there despite the noise below. Anything was better than the sound of my sister's high voice whenever dad was around. I leaned against the railing and drew in a deep, controlled breath. I watched the people below and saw Grim. He stood with a woman on the players' balcony. The woman smiled at him and ran her hand down his arm. I got it, he was sexy as hell and a primal wildness oozed off his hard body, but with that came his need to boss the shit out of me, and that wasn't going to happen.

"Jim was saying he was impressed with your meeting." Dad leaned on the railing. *Wow, he came to be with me.* I licked my lips and was all ears. "He said you asked for the meeting yourself."

"Does that really surprise you? I've called for a few meetings, and it's helped to advance my career."

"No," he paused, "it's just nice to hear."

"Thank you, Dad." I wasn't sure where this came from, but I'd take it. "It's nice to hear when someone is impressed or proud of you." He glanced at me. "Words can make a difference."

"I'm impressed, Kenna." He turned his back to the balcony and looked at me. "You brought a situation to Jim and won."

I felt a warmth spread through me. I forgot what it felt like to have him say things like that to me. I batted away the instinct to show emotion.

"I'm glad." I knew better than to make eye contact and break the moment.

"I have a situation of my own," Dad said quietly

as someone came outside from another one of the special rooms. He waited until they went down the stairs.

"Kenna," his tone made me hyperaware, and I saw he looked stressed—more stressed than normal, "I need a meeting with Trigger."

"What?" I nearly choked on my own saliva. That sure wasn't where I thought this conversation would go.

"I'm in trouble, Kenna."

So am I. I knew I could never talk to him about it.

"I need you to set up a meeting for me."

"With Trigger?" I couldn't keep the shock from my voice.

"Yes, and it can't come from me. I need to keep it quiet." He sniffed and rubbed his nose. I knew he always did that when he was hiding something.

"I'm really not comfortable with asking him, Dad."

"Sometimes we all have to do things that make us uncomfortable, Kenna. You'll do this for me."

"No, Dad, you don't get it." I stood straight. "In all these years of knowing the Devil's Reach, I've never asked for a favor."

"Aren't they your friends?"

"Yes, and I intend to keep it that way."

"Friends help out friends in a time of need." He looked at his watch. "Nine a.m. tomorrow." He took a firm grip on the top of my arm as he leaned down so his face was close to mine. "I need this, Kenna, so don't disappoint me." Anger shot from his eyes.

My mouth opened, but nothing came out. *Shit.*

I watched him go back into the restaurant then whirled around to take a deep breath. My mind spun as I contemplated a hundred different ways around this. Immediately, my head thought of Morgan. Maybe I could ask him instead?

"Kenna?" I turned to see Simon with his hands in his front pockets looking uncomfortable. "I'm sure I'm the last person you want to see right now."

"That's not true." I sighed, feeling bad for the guy. I was sure my father wasn't easy to work so closely with. "Are you here to tell me to speak with Trigger? Dad already scooped you on that."

"He told you?" He visibly relaxed and came closer.

"Yes, he *told* me all right."

"Oh, yes," he scrunched his nose, "the famous Tame temper."

"That'd be it." I tucked my hair behind my ear. "Am I to guess it has something to do with a client?"

"Yeah." He nodded then looked over. "It's ugly, Kenna. Not sure how he's going to get out of this one." He let out a long breath. "I know it's a big deal, and it's on super short notice, but he could really use Trigger's help."

"It's unusual for Dad. He doesn't even give Trigger or his people the time of day. Why now? What good is it to get Trigger involved?" Suddenly, I knew why, Trigger knew almost everything going on in this town, at least on the darker side of things, and when he wanted to find out something, he'd find it.

"I see you know why, because you just thought it." He smiled, and I smiled back as I realized he was good at reading people. We stood in silence and watched the people in the restaurant eat and chat.

"Look. Kenna, I know you don't know much about me, only that I'm the guy in the background at some of your family gatherings. I appreciate being included because I don't have any family to do that stuff with, and your dad knows that. It's nice of him to think of it."

"I appreciate the buffer you bring." I chuckled darkly.

"Glad to be of service," he snorted slightly as he leaned toward the railing and looked over at the other balcony. Grim, the woman he was with, and Leo all laughed as someone must have made a joke.

"I'm sure it can't be easy working for a man like my father."

"It has its challenges," he grimaced, "but he's good at what he does."

"Mm," I mumbled.

"Maybe I'm stepping over a line here, but I see some things Cameron does that I don't agree with, especially when it comes to you and Calli." I dipped my head in embarrassment at his words. "Why do you think he's so hard on you?"

"Is this a bonding moment?" I shifted uncomfortably.

"Maybe Cameron just doesn't want you to get involved in his work. He deals with some pretty nasty people. Could be his way of protecting you."

"And all along I thought it was because *I* didn't want to get involved. Guess his asking me to contact Trigger is an exception?" I lifted a brow, calling bullshit on him. "You're smart, Simon, but you're wrong on this one, and trust me when I say, my father has involved me in his work on many occasions." I blinked away the worst of the memories. "There's a reason Calli's his favorite and not me. I won't bend to whatever game he wants me to play. He's tried in the past, but I won't steamroll over other people for personal gain."

"Maybe you're right," he rubbed his chin, "but has he ever asked you to do something like this before?" *No. He hasn't.* "All I'm saying is he's in trouble and has asked you for help. He's involving you because he doesn't have a choice."

I could feel Grim's eyes on me from across the way, so I met his gaze. The woman and his brother had left, and he stared as he sucked on a joint. Two men next to him were in conversation, but he only seemed to have eyes for me. I fell into his gaze for a moment, seeking the comfort of his protection, then I purposely turned toward Simon.

"I didn't mean to make you upset," Simon mistook my silence for something else.

"Simon?" Calli was in the doorway and looked less than impressed he was out there with me.

"I should get back." He smiled at her, and I internally rolled my eyes. Great. He was under her hold, too. "Have a good night, Kenna."

"You too." I forced a smile, and when I looked back at Grim, he was gone.

I summoned a pair of balls then went in search of Minnie.

As I walked through the lobby, I chuckled at Rail. He had a smile from ear to ear as he hit on some girl at least ten years younger.

"Hey, have you seen Trigger?" I asked as I got closer.

"Maybe." He grinned and tapped his cheek. I gave him a quick kiss, and he beamed. "Yeah, he's over there."

"Thanks." I heard the girl ask who I was, and he replied I was his ex. I laughed; he was something sometimes.

Trigger was at the bar in the lobby. He stood next to Morgan as he nursed a glass of whiskey. I felt better the moment I saw Morgan.

"Hey, stranger," Morgan leaned in for a hug, "if I

didn't know any better, I'd say you've been avoidin' me."

I was, kind of. I hated that I felt like a target and anyone around me could be in the crosshairs. The situation made me wary.

"Sorry," I held on to the hug for an extra minute, "things are crazy. I miss you, though."

"No worries. It's good to see ya." He leaned back, and I looked at Trigger. My hands went cold.

"I hate to interrupt, but, Trigger, do you have a sec?" His green eyes turned to me, and my stomach dropped into my toes. Grim's eyes had the same effect on me at times. But with Grim, it was something that fanned a fire inside me. One I couldn't seem to help but fire back. These eyes just seemed to see through to my soul. I swallowed.

"Yeah." He was a man of few words, and I knew I needed to choose mine carefully. I looked at Morgan and eyed him to stay. He got my intent and sat on a barstool.

"I have a situation, and I was hoping you could help me."

"You have my attention."

"My father asked me for your help." He slowly tapped his fingers on the bar top. "I wouldn't ask if I didn't think it was important." I swallowed hard.

"What kinda help?"

"I'm not sure, but I think it involves one of his clients."

"You got something going on." He studied me a bit. "If I do it, I wanna know what you're hiding." I lowered my head and felt the weight of what I held inside twine its tentacles deep into my soul. A further promise that I was screwed no matter which way things went.

"No," I squeaked, and my face went hot. "Trigger, I'm so sorry, but I can't tell you about it. I just can't. If that means no, so be it." He studied my face with those green eyes, and I felt like I was on trial or maybe his next hit.

"Gimme a reason, then."

"Because my father came to me for help. He's never done that before, so I want to come through for him. I know something big must be up for him to ask for my help."

Something strange passed over his face.

"When?"

"Tomorrow in his office. It's on the twentieth floor. Nine a.m."

"Fine." He turned back toward the bartender and took a sip of his drink before I dared look at Morgan. He looked just as shocked as I did that Trigger agreed to meet with my father.

"Grim know you came to me?" Trigger said without turning around. *What? No.*

"No. Why would Grim be involved in this?"

"Just askin'."

"I really appreciate it, Trigger."

I mouthed a quick thanks to Morgan and motioned I'd call him. As I turned to leave, I heard Trigger's voice.

"Kenna," Trigger's gaze found mine in the mirror in front of him, "tell Grim you came to me."

"Why?" I felt my anger kick in, but I pushed it down.

"His hotel. If I'm fuckin' doing something for one of his, he needs to know."

"All right."

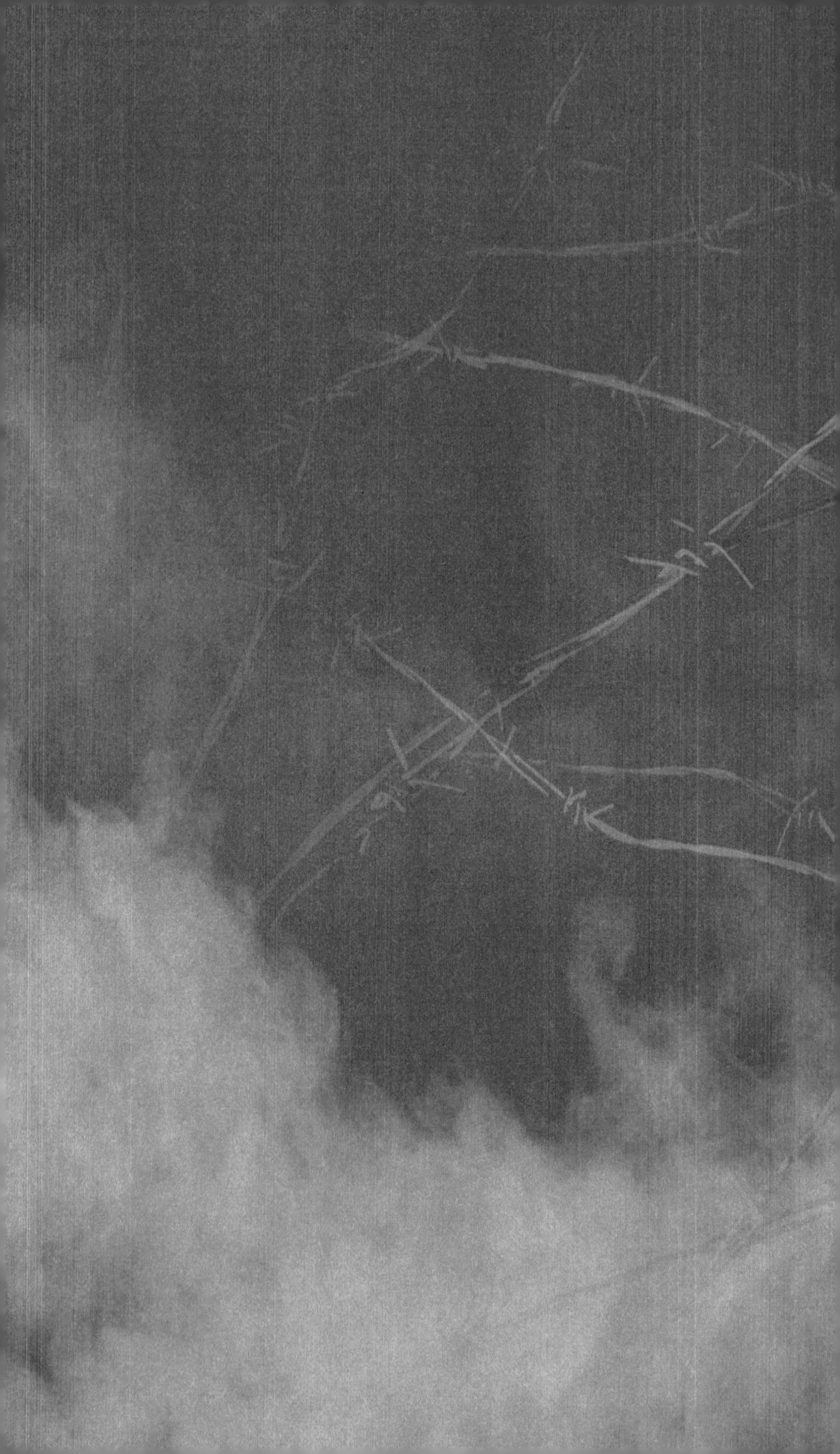

FIFTEEN

SIMON

Tap! *Tap! Tap! Tap! Tap!* One of Cameron's security guards gave me a hard side eye, and I realized my pen wildly tapped against the rail. I willed my fingers to still, and the silence crept back in. I'd been up against criminals like Trigger before, but this was different, this was coming at him from a whole different angle, and it made me second guess this meeting. My gut told me it wasn't wise, but my mind argued we needed answers, fast. It didn't help that I was Cameron's private investigator, and I'd come up emptyhanded.

My phone vibrated, and I jumped at the sudden intrusion into my thoughts.

"Excuse me." I held a finger up to the armed guards

and slipped around the corner. "Simon Gable," I offered as a greeting even though I knew exactly who it was.

"We have a problem."

When do we not?

"Which is?"

"He's sniffin' around."

"Who?"

"You know who," the voice on the other end snapped. I pinched the bridge of my nose. "He's getting too close. He's following some fucking lead that took him to someone's house where he almost discovered—"

"Got it." I cut him off. I didn't need to know what he almost discovered. "Let me see what I can do."

"You better think of something fast because you put me in a bad situation here. You know I never liked this idea in the first place. We should've killed him in Mexico when we had the chance. I'm not sure how much longer I can keep things at bay."

"Give me a few days."

"You've got one." The line ended.

"Shit." I heard a door open and knew Cameron would wonder where I was. I stepped around the corner and came face to face with Trigger. He stared down at me, and for a moment I wondered if he'd overheard the phone call. I forgot how huge he was in person, over six feet, well over two hundred, but it was all muscle. His tattoos showed under his leather cut, and when he rubbed his beard, I saw his knuckles were raw. He was a cage fighter, just like Grim. I swallowed hard and tried not to back up.

"Thanks for coming." I tried not to trip over my words when I saw he'd brought Brick along. "Right this way." I awkwardly moved around Trigger and pointed back down the hallway. The chains that swung from their belt loops made an eerie sound as we walked. Maybe it was because I'd seen what those were actually for, and it wasn't to protect their wallets. "Can I get you anything?"

"No," Brick grunted.

I was good at my job, but over the years I'd learned when to show confidence and when to keep my head down and just get the job done. It didn't help that when we stepped into Cameron's office there were four more armed men inside. I tried not to think of a video I'd seen of Trigger as he took down a bunch of guards in the blink of an eye outside Minnie's club. In fact, I feared Grim even more because he was younger and was Trigger's prodigy. Even the thought that Grim knew what Trigger knew was somehow terrifying.

"Trigger." Cameron stood and offered a hand, but Trigger just looked at him. "Right." He must have remembered Trigger didn't like to be touched. "How are you, Brick?"

"Standin'." Brick shrugged slightly.

"Good. Please take a seat." Cameron pointed to the conference table, and they sat. I moved to the opposite side of the table to sit across from them. Not that the distance or the table between us would do much if they wanted to kill me. "I'm sure you're wondering why I wanted to see you."

"Kenna said you got trouble." Trigger's voice was low and harsh.

"I do." Cameron cleared his throat uncomfortably. "It's no secret that when I'm hired, I get the job done. It's why I'm one of the best criminal defense lawyers in Arizona, California—"

"Don't need your fuckin' resume." Trigger cut him off. "Out with it."

"What I mean to say is," Cameron's temper idled, and I prayed he'd keep calm, "I don't lose. Which brings me to you. I had all my ducks in a row for a client looking to face life without parole for murder. Suddenly, the guy who I was setting up to take the fall for my client ends up dead before trial. To make matters worse, *I* only find out three days before trial."

"Shit happens." Brick spoke up.

"Not when you have people hired to protect him," I tossed back.

"The fuck you need me for?" Trigger seemed annoyed.

"I," Cameron leaned forward, his face red, "need to know who killed my fall guy."

"Why don't you ask your hired men?" Brick asked.

"They're dead, too," I answered to try to keep Cameron calm.

"Who was your fall guy?" Trigger looked at me.

"Martin Castillo."

"Guy like Castillo's got a lot of enemies." He rubbed his chin. "Why would you care who took him out?"

"Why don't you just find him for me and let me worry about that." Cameron eased back into his chair, and I held my breath. Christ, he was stupid sometimes. Silence ticked.

"What's in it for me?" Trigger shot a look at Brick. Brick smirked, and I felt a sudden shift in their mood. The hair on the back of my neck rose.

"My services for free." Cameron waved a hand at himself like he was some kind of prize.

"Try again." Trigger scrunched his nose like he wasn't impressed.

"Vegas immunity."

"Already got that." Trigger leaned back and pulled a joint from somewhere and lit the tip.

Seriously, Cameron, that's all you have to offer?

"I got a guy in Mexico with the best cocaine."

"Better than Grim's?" Trigger glared at him through slit eyes.

Jesus. I shot Cameron a look not to answer that.

"Better." He gave him a cocky grin, and Trigger's face was like stone.

Fuck! I raced to think of something to smooth the situation over.

"Whoa. Let me get this straight." Brick suddenly leaned over the table. "I understand Jim Gates hired you to be his lawyer years back when he faced some serious charges. Since then, he's taken care of you and kept you on retainer. He lets you and your family live here, work here, gives you unlimited access to his hotel and all it offers, and now you sit here in front of us and say you're willing to undercut his son's *business?*"

"Grim has many businesses."

"You didn't answer my question." Brick held his gaze.

"Yes," Cameron said through clenched teeth, "I guess if you're going to word it that way, I am."

"You know Grim is a member of the Devil's Reach, right?" Brick looked at him like he was insane, which I now realized was incredibly accurate. "Meaning our alliance falls with Grim. Meaning that you offerin' us something over Grim's head really isn't a smart choice."

Cameron waited a beat then squeezed out the word, "Yes."

"Just making sure." Brick shook his head, obviously unimpressed, at Trigger. I looked at Cameron whose face had gone white. I hoped he wouldn't race out of the room after that error in judgement.

"Still waiting to hear what's in this for me." Smoke rose from Trigger's lips, and I felt my own head lighten from the drug. I started to panic. This conversation was tanking, and we needed a name to point the blame at for our client. Cameron might not live to see next week.

"Money?" Cameron blurted, and I dropped my head.

"We're done here." Trigger got up.

"Simon once worked a job with your brother, Brick." Cameron swung the attention of the entire room to me. I felt like the floor had just been ripped out beneath me.

"What did you say?" Brick went for his weapon, but Trigger already had his pulled.

"Hold on. Hold on. What?" I glared at Cameron and fought to keep upright at the rush of blood that flooded my head. My face burned.

"This here is Matt Montgomery," Cameron pointed at Brick, and my eyes widened.

"Holy shit," I sucked in a gulp of air trying to get my brain to unstick from the gun he held. "Matt Montgomery? That's you? I worked a job in Nashville with your brother years back. He told me a bit about your club. I just figured you'd left. I didn't know you went by a different name."

"Prove it." Brick's gun didn't waver, and I second

guessed if this was worth my life or not. I sent Cameron a look of frustration. I was furious at him for his lack of warning.

"Let's see," I pushed my glasses up my nose, buying a second to think, "your dad left when you were a baby, joined the DR, and died before you got to meet him. You guys have a sister named Jilly." I swallowed and looked at Cameron who now had two guards by his side. Where the hell was *my* protection! "Please, lower your weapons!" I pulled at my tie as the oxygen strained to get down to my lungs.

"If I'd known how touchy this topic would be, I wouldn't have said anything." Cameron looked innocent as he tried to smooth the tension. It was too late; my heart was jammed in my throat, seeking escape.

After a beat, Trigger nodded at Brick, and he lowered his gun. I noticed he didn't put it away.

"Where's he now?" Trigger growled as he sat back down and drilled me with his eyes.

"Not sure. Shit went sideways after that job, and we got separated." I fought through the fear and struggled to think. "Last I heard, he took a job in Mexico."

"When was that?" Trigger's voice was low and frightening. Brick sat like stone.

"Ah," I rubbed my head and did the math, "ten – eleven years ago, give or take a year."

Brick moved then and glanced at Trigger, and something passed between them. I fumbled to fucking breathe. I wasn't prepared to discuss this today or any day or I would have thought harder about the facts. It was only desperation that drew the words from my lips. "Ahh," I tried to get my head on straight, "I have a friend who's really good at finding people."

Cameron suddenly spoke up. "Yeah, he's got someone good. He's a DEA agent."

My jaw dropped. Who was Cameron to give that information away?

"Something like that." I glared at Cameron. "Anyway, if you help us, I'm sure I could find something."

"What name did he use?" Brick said as he licked his lips, and I could tell I had caught his attention.

"David, I mean Dave Wilson."

I saw Trigger eye up Brick as the room went silent. My heart pounded in my chest, and I thought I might pass out.

"If you have his real name, it would be a starting point for me." I figured if they were going to shoot me, they would by now.

"Figure it out yourself." Brick looked like stone.

Trigger suddenly spoke. "Luis Aguilar."

"Sorry, who's that?" I looked at him, confused.

"The guy who killed Castillo." He shrugged and took another pull on his joint. "You and I have a deal." Trigger ignored Cameron and looked at me, and I felt the full weight of his power. "But if you don't hold up your end and get some info on Brick's brother, I'll fuckin' kill you."

"Understood," Cameron blurted as he jumped to his feet. "Thank you." He reached to shake Trigger's hand again then yanked his arm back as he and Brick brushed past him and left the office. I sank back into my chair and ripped off my tie as I fought for breath. Coming so close to death rattled me, but even worse was what could come from the deal I'd made.

"Are you fucking insane?" I blurted at Cameron, not caring at that moment that I worked for him. "A little warning might have been nice."

"We needed a hail Mary, and we got it." He watched them leave through the glass. "Wait for a few weeks, then gather the information and hand it over."

"Cameron, I'm—"

"Going to do your job." He cut me off and I knew we were finished with the discussion. "Nick," he yelled to one of his guards, "follow them." He nodded at the elevator.

SIXTEEN

GRIM

I swirled my spoon around my mug as I watched the sunrise spread across the city below. I hadn't slept more than a few hours over the past couple of nights; the delays at my new hotel played on me. Jesse and I had spent the previous day locked in my office under the hotel with Darryl and Ridder trying to follow a lead to do with the local Las Vegas contractors. Christ, if Melvern Trident Jr., whose very name pissed me off, was able to add on to the Mac hotel without any evidence of issues, why the hell was I constantly plagued with problems? There'd been no work stoppage on their site that my guys could see, and no one even liked Melvern.

I had to agree with Darryl; I was being targeted

personally. I knew I was going to have to go elsewhere and probably have to pay a lot more to hire someone from out of state or Secrets would never get finished. The timeline for the grand opening had already been shot to hell.

I glanced at my watch as the elevator dinged. Zhen ripped by me and stood at the elevator door while Leal stayed put near me. I heard him growl as he waited for the door to open. I ignored them; I knew who it was.

"Whatever it is, Leo, it can fucking wait," I hissed. I needed time to think.

"And I'm the one with the mouth?" Kenna's wry voice made me spin around. Her tight top and loose skirt with its waist-high slit instantly clouded my head. "I tried to call, but," her voice broke as Zhen sat in front of her, "you weren't answering."

"So, you just decided to come up to my floor?" I hated to admit it, but I was glad it was her and not Leo. I wasn't ready to prep for today's meeting just yet. "Stand down." I ordered, and Zhen immediately turned and went into the kitchen with his brother close behind.

"When Trigger tells you to do something, it's kind of scary not to follow through."

Trigger?

"I see, so you'll follow his instructions but not mine." I gave her a narrow look and finished off the rest of my coffee.

"It's different." She looked away, and I wondered what ran through that devious head of hers. "He's," she visibly fumbled, which amused me, "scary." I knew that wasn't the word she wanted to use.

"And I don't scare you?" I set my mug down and rubbed my chin as I stepped toward her.

"Maybe, sometimes," she admitted as I got close. "Other times you're just an ass." She smirked.

"Maybe, sometimes," I repeated and chuckled, and she lightly joined in. My eyes raked down her body, and that crackle that always seemed to be between us spiked. She broke eye contact with me after a second and looked around.

"Your place is nice."

"Thank you," I said quietly and licked my lips with a sudden urge to taste her skin.

"It lives up to your name." She leaned to see past me. The gothic-style living room, much like my bedroom, was quite dramatic. "It's got a very dark, medieval kind of feel. I half expect to see Bill Compton walk out with a set of fangs."

"I do love my spot on your neck," I couldn't help but say, and her gaze moved back to mine. I closed the gap between us.

"Grim," her hand landed on my chest, and my body heated, "I need to tell you something." I brushed her hair off her neck and thumbed my spot. It had turned a beautiful shade of light purple. I was pleased she hadn't covered it with makeup.

"So, talk." I leaned down, and just as I grazed her neck, she stepped back. Instantly, my temper flared.

"This," she flipped her hair with a huff, "every time you're near me you get this hold on me. You lure me in like…" She stopped herself mid-sentence. "It's all adding up now." She pointed around my place with a chuckle. "Cue the coffin and toss me a stake."

"No, I much prefer my Boll and Branch sheets and Tempur-Probreeze mattress, though I do love the night." I pretended to think.

"I'm serious. You cast your spell, and I become something I'm not used to being." Her smile slipped. "It's not fair."

"Fair?" I nearly growled and hauled her to me, my hands flexed against her lower back. "I've been walkin' around this hotel with a hard-on since I returned, thanks to you." I ran my hand up her spine and enjoyed the feel of her.

"I was going to fix that until I found out you already looked after it yourself the night before," she snapped.

"Hardly. If you must know, it didn't help much." I grabbed her ass and pressed her into my hungry erection.

"Why not?" Her sweet breath brushed my cheek.

"It just didn't work. I guess it wasn't what I really

needed." I tried to sound in control, but with this annoying little vixen here alone, in my place, it made me wild. I let my hands run up and down her back. I craved her tight little body.

She pushed back then her hands fumbled with my belt, popped the button, and unzipped my pants. Then, before I could react, her hand slipped inside my briefs, and I jolted forward.

"Maybe this'll work," she whispered, and I squeezed my eyes shut.

"I have an important meeting in twenty. Leo will be here any moment." My mouth ran.

"Then I guess I'll have to be fast." With that, she dropped to her knees, and I twisted my fingers through her hair with a gulp as she pulled me free and pumped the length of me. Her hands were soft and warm as she handled me, then her tight lips formed an 'O' and she took me to the base.

"Shit." I blew in and out several times and fought to stay upright. Her mouth superseded my expletives as she sucked from the root to the tip then popped it out like a lollipop, licked the end then slid me back in. Her hot mouth and silky tongue drove me to a height I'd never experienced before. She twisted her hands and bobbed her head. Then she moaned, and my head clouded as the vibration made my stomach tighten. I might not like that mouth of hers at work, but I sure wasn't going to complain about what she did with it behind closed doors.

My hands gripped her hair as I directed the speed. "Jesus, Kenna," I groaned as she increased her suction. Fantasies of her against the wall in the hallway, over the counter in my kitchen, in Tess's club, came rushing to me. I tried to control myself, as I wanted to have her every possible way.

When she changed the pressure once again, my vision went spotty, and I thrust myself past her lips. She gripped my hip with one hand and held the base with the other. She wasn't backing down from what I'd given her. She'd risen to the challenge; she friggin' raised the bar.

"More," she huffed from around me, and I nearly lost my shit. Both my hands held her head still as I took what I wanted from her infuriating mouth. I lost all sense of awareness and felt everything inside me coiled tight. We locked eyes, and I let her know I was about to come. She didn't break rhythm or eye contact as weeks' worth of pent-up aggression burst from me and flooded into her.

The monster within crawled its way through my chest and broke free as I took what I needed.

Sweat broke out across my back, my knees locked, and my hearing went in and out as I rode the glorious wave. Her shampoo smothered my senses, and her throaty moans made me thrust one more time as I savored every-fucking-second.

I was an animal at best, and my needs were nearly impossible to meet, but this woman fed the beast. A heavy, dark smile ran across my lips as I welcomed the calm that settled over me.

She didn't move when I finally came back down. My chest heaved as I gently pulled free and wordlessly handed her a cloth napkin from the side table.

I held out a hand and tugged her to her feet then wiped myself and tucked my semi-erection back into my pants.

I knew at that moment, I wanted more. Much more.
Behave.

"Drink?" I asked. She nodded and gave me a smile, and I hurried to grab a bottle of sparkling water from the bar. Other than her pink cheeks, you'd never guess she'd just given me an insane blowjob.

"Thank you." She nodded politely.

"You do have a death wish, don't you?" I shook my head at her. She took the drink from my outstretched hand and ran her finger along her bottom lip.

"When it comes to you, maybe." She popped her finger in her mouth then sucked the tip.

"Don't do that," I warned. "I've been known to go multiple rounds." I removed her finger from her mouth and popped it into mine. Her pupils dilated and her neck strained as her breath picked up. I kissed her fingers and squeezed her hand. "If I didn't have this meeting, I'd have you tied to my bedpost so fast you wouldn't know what hit you."

"You'd have to catch me first." She shrugged playfully. "Look, Grim, I hate to break this moment, but—"

"You didn't come here to be on your knees."

"No." She ran her hands down her skirt as she shifted herself back to work mode, an asset I admired about her. "My father came to me for help." I raised an eyebrow at that. We both knew it wasn't something her father would normally do. She shrugged to show she got my point. "He asked me to get Trigger to meet with him. Said he had some sort of trouble but didn't explain. I said no, but he insisted I do it."

"I see." I didn't like that.

"Anyway, given that he's never asked me for a favor like that before, I really want to give him this."

"Any idea at all what it's about?"

"I'm guessing something to do with a client."

"So, you asked Trigger?"

"I did."

"And?" I fiddled with my cufflinks as I tried to fathom what sort of trouble Cameron had gotten himself in that he needed help from Trigger.

"He said he'd do it as long as I let you know. He said because I was your employee."

"And when is this meeting happening?" Fuck, something else to push into my calendar.

"It was yesterday morning."

"Yesterday?" I dropped my arms and stared at her. "As in yester-the-fuck-day?"

"Yes." She nodded.

"Why didn't I know about this the moment Trigger knew?"

"Because after I asked him, I was coming to tell you, but I ran into Minnie—"

"And?"

"*And* she needed me for a moment, and that's when Salazar found me with one of his business friends and asked me to join them for a nightcap."

"Is your phone broken? Did you go home with these men and spend all of yesterday with them too?" Her face went angry.

"Look, I called you twice, you didn't pick up. I figured anything to do with Trigger shouldn't be left in a voicemail." I remembered she'd called. Yesterday's meeting was too important to be interrupted. "Yesterday got away from me. Minnie needed me to ID someone and—"

"You don't work for Minnie, Kenna," I stood closer, "you work for me."

"I know that." She fisted her hands and took a deep breath. "Check your damn cameras. I spent a lot of time looking for you. I even spoke to your father." She was angry now, and I tried to curb my own temper.

"I don't like that Cameron asked Trigger for a favor."

"Trigger's a big boy. He could have said no." Her eyes flashed, and I looked at my watch and wondered why my brother was late. "Are you done flipping out on me now?"

The elevator dinged, and Leo strolled in, completely missing the mood in the room.

"Hey, Kenna, what are you doing here?"

"Getting my ass handed to me like always," she growled at him then seemed to gather herself. "How are you, Leo?"

"Stressed. We need to prepare for today's meeting."

"Well, I won't keep you." She turned to look at me. "It's always a pleasure to even out the scoreboard, Grim. Fun as always."

"It is," I agreed and watched her ass as she headed toward the elevator. Leal stepped into my line of vision and her perky ass was replaced with his judgy glare.

Jesus.

"Do I even want to know?" Leo dropped into a seat and patted Leal, who immediately relaxed. He might be on edge with strangers, but he knew and loved Leo.

"Did you know that Cameron met up with Trigger yesterday?" I wondered if he knew anything about it.

"Why?"

"That's what I need to know."

"Well, that can wait, because this can't." He tossed a

file on the table, and I tried to get my head in the right place as I joined him for a quick rundown.

The conference room smelled of fresh pastries and coffee as we took our seats at the boardroom table.

"Okay let's get right into this." Dad was all business.

"Right here," Deborah pointed to the large screen on the wall, "across from the Encore, it's now up for grabs, and they'll start accepting offers first thing tomorrow morning."

"Current asking price?" my father asked, and Deborah handed him a folded piece of paper with the amount on it.

"I'm not sure why we're not jumping on this now. It's a great investment." Cameron added his usual two cents' worth.

Jesse, who stood against the wall, shook his head, just as irritated with the man as I was.

I reached for my phone then cursed quietly. It had been a while since I had been in one of those meetings where we frosted the windows and mirrored the walls. No electronic devices but a laptop and a TV for streaming information were allowed inside the room. The guards outside were instructed to stand watch, and only a select few would ever be let through. Now more than ever, given the bullshit I'd been having with Secret's build, we needed to be extra careful. Which made me wonder why Dad felt his criminal defense lawyer should be in this meeting. We had our other lawyers here, so I couldn't see the need.

I leaned over toward Leo and whispered, "Why, exactly, is Cameron here?"

"When I asked Dad, he said Cameron needed to know everything that was happening in order to represent Knox in this new case that's come up on him."

"The fuck has Knox done now?"

"Nothing a little money won't clear up." He waved it off. Clearly, it wasn't anything too important.

I closed my eyes and wondered once again why my father, who was always so careful with people, let this hot-tempered, moody lawyer slither his way so deeply into our lives. I knew they had history, but if Knox's case wasn't that big of a deal, why was Cameron here? I stopped my spinning. I knew why. Because Cameron insisted. My level of irritation rose.

Cameron reached for the piece of paper with the price of the property on it, but I slammed my hand down on top of it before he could.

"Well, gentlemen..." Deborah stumbled and shot me a look, but when I didn't say a word, she continued to give details on the property.

Cameron backed down but gave me a pissed-off look.

"So, any questions?" Deborah looked around. A few questions came from our lawyers and from several investors. Dad and I covered a few things as well.

Suddenly, a commotion started on the other side of the door. Dad quickly turned the screen off and most of us quickly closed our file folders and pulled our guns. The door flew open.

"Grim!" Kenna's voice called, and I jumped to my feet as she flung herself through the door. Her wild eyes caught mine. "Your hotel. Secrets is on fire!"

Fire! It was a dreaded word anywhere, but especially here in Vegas, as the desert heat made everything so dry. Leo jumped to un-frost the windows as we raced to look outside. Secrets was covered in a ball of flames. A cone of heavy, dark smoke went up to the sky. It seemed to blow away from the street.

After a quick glance, I whirled around and ran toward the elevator. Even with my card it seemed to take forever to arrive. I felt the darkness that I'd just managed to keep at bay fester then burst through the surface of my mind. I jumped inside as the doors opened, and Jesse leapt past my brother and father as I jabbed the button and the doors slammed shut on them. I caught sight of Kenna's red face behind them. They could get the next one.

My driver, Cartwright, was ready for us as we stormed out of the private entrance and straight into the car. He didn't say a word, just jumped in and sped toward the fire. A police barricade was being set up as we approached.

"Grim." Jesse handed me a loaded gun and I swapped out my normal one for it. He tucked his in his waistband, and we both jumped out. The police recognized me right away and waved us under the taped barrier.

"Mr. Gates," the chief of police squinted at the smoke, "we've got nothing for you yet. Only that some passersby smelled gas then a few moments later the flames were visible." I ran my tongue along my teeth and tried desperately to contain my temper.

"Gas?" I pumped my fists, and he stepped back carefully.

"Apparently, but let us get it under control, and I'll get a complete report from the fire chief. We'll get to the bottom of it, sir."

I watched in horror as my hotel seemed to be eaten up by a starving monster. Everything I'd worked so hard for over the past year was going up in smoke. A heat built inside my body that rivaled the flames that greedily fed.

Minnie caught my attention when she reached my side. She held hands with Kenna. Then I saw Trigger and Brick as they scanned the crowd. Trigger locked eyes with me then chin-pointed at someone.

I drew in a deep breath as I saw the fucker. He stood next to a truck. A wild expression that resembled a grin was spread over his face as he studied the flames. Then he spotted me, and his face dropped. Everything in that moment told me he was responsible. In a split second, he disappeared into the crowd. The sound of a bike as it sped away found us, and Trigger smacked my shoulder for me to follow him.

"Back to the hotel," I ordered Minnie and Kenna. I didn't want them involved.

A few minutes later, we arrived at the spot where Trigger and Brick left their bikes. A familiar whistle, and Louis jumped from my bike and tugged off my helmet to toss it to me.

"Jesse called. He thought you might need her. Your bag's ready to go too." He threw me the keys, and I nodded my thanks at Jesse who had just appeared.

"Stay here, make sure the chief knows you're my ears." He nodded as I took off my jacket and dress shirt and changed into a white t-shirt. I couldn't ride well in dress pants and designer shoes, so I made quick work of stripping down. If I was going to do this right, I couldn't run the risk of being recognized.

"Hey," Trigger called and pointed in the direction the shit must have gone. I grabbed my Devil's Reach cut from the back of the bike and felt the thrill I always felt when it settled on my back. I pushed a pair of sunglasses under my helmet and fired up the bike. The roar of the engine made people jump. I kicked her into gear and blew past the chief of police. I wasted no time catching up with the others. This fucker was mine.

We split traffic and ran two reds with the knowledge the police were preoccupied with the fire. Switching the bike to fourth gear, I sped up to ride behind Trigger and Brick. Morgan and Rail popped out of nowhere and filed in on either side of me.

"If there's blood to be had," Morgan chuckled over the radio, "I'm not missin' it." I was glad he was there.

"Cooper said Niccola Capri's in town," Brick piped in a moment later. "Guess he came by the clubhouse then came here when he heard we were in Vegas." Niccola and Vinni Capri were cousins to Elio Capri, who was the mafia king to most of Italy. "Word from their end is some Stripe Backs bragged about a job they got. Your name came up, so they figured it had to do with you. Not hard to figure what it was now." I saw his bike swerve as he avoided a pile of sand on the road.

"That's a start," I grunted. My mind spun as we rode. The faces of anyone who might have been bold enough to burn down my hotel flashed before my eyes. The risk to the rest of the Strip was huge. I thought about then discarded a lot of people as I ran their names through my mind. They'd have too much to lose if the fire spread. A job like that would be a big risk.

"Up ahead." Rail pointed. We gained on the guy,

and he looked over his shoulder as we picked up speed.

"Where there's one Stripe Back..." I didn't need to say the rest. They traveled in packs, so we all knew this was a lure to take us down. With the pace Trigger set, I knew he didn't care. No one touched what was his, and as a friend he'd feel the same way about what was mine. If either of us showed weakness or mercy, we wouldn't be where we were today.

An eighteen-wheeler headed toward us in the distance, but still no sign of other bikers.

As we got closer to the biker, we formed a horseshoe around him. It was a scare tactic, but it also meant if anyone wanted to kill us, they'd risk him too. I pulled ahead, and Trigger allowed me to lead.

"Slow your bike or lose your head," I shouted at him with my gun aimed at his face. I had a steady hold on my bike and was sure he couldn't hear my words at this speed, but he'd get my meaning. We were close to seventy miles an hour and going higher. Morgan moved up and wove closer to his other side and tried to push him over to my lane as the truck came closer. The guy wavered but went right back to the center line.

The trucker started to blow his horn and began to brake. The guy on the bike looked at me then at Morgan, no doubt trying to weigh his options.

The horn got louder, and I kept my gun on him. Trigger shot a bullet over the guy's shoulder as the horn blew again, and suddenly, he stepped on the gas and propelled his bike straight into the truck's grill. In a blur, we flew past the truck then as a group circled back around. The brakes on the truck were all we could hear as we got off our bikes. Burnt tires and the smell of brakes forced their way into my senses.

Blood spattered the road along with bits and pieces of his body and bike. I saw part of his torso and searched for his wallet among its remains. I pulled out his ID, wiped it dry on my leg, glanced at it, then tucked it in my pocket.

Trigger and Brick were on their phones calling it in to their contacts here in Vegas. Rail lit a cigarette as he straddled his bike and admired the carnage around us.

"Hey." I walked to the truck and circled it to check for body parts. I climbed up to pull on the handle of the trucker's door, but it was locked. "Open the door!" The man stared straight ahead. He was in shock and probably terrified of what I'd do to him. He refused to look at me at first then seemed to zone in and began to desperately punch numbers into his phone. I pulled my gun and pointed it at him as I banged on his window. "Open or join him."

"Okay, okay," he stuttered and dropped his phone as he opened the door. He held his hands up.

"This is what you're going to do." I leaned into his cab and snapped a photo of his trucker's ID. "Call 911, tell them you were driving, and a biker swerved into you. No one else was here." I held up my phone to show him I had his information. "You say anything else, and I'll come find you. Ben Anderson."

"Yeah," he nodded a bunch of times, "not a word." I jumped down.

"We got company, boys." Rail pointed back from the direction we'd come.

"They're not here for you," I assured the terrified man. "Make the call."

"Lure them to Devil's Breath?" Brick asked as he looked at Trigger. "Not a whole lot of other options."

"Yeah." Trigger nodded, and I jumped on my bike. We headed off toward the bar that only local bikers knew about.

I tilted my mirror to avoid the sun behind me to keep the other bikes in view.

"Here we go."

SEVENTEEN

GRIM

I felt my heart pound in my chest at the thought of breaking some bones. The sheer disappointment I'd felt when the biker chose death by truck was slowly replaced by pure adrenaline at the chance of a fight. The flames that rose above my hotel now burned in my memory, and it fueled my anger.

We peeled into the parking lot, hopped off our bikes, and prepared to shed some blood.

I flicked my gun at a delivery driver when he came back outside for another box of chips. His eyes went wide, then he disappeared back inside.

We all knew Slade, the owner of the bar, and we knew he was in with everyone as it served his business, and that meant we couldn't count on his help.

He'd protect his place at all costs, so the odds wouldn't necessarily go in our favor. The fact that we'd obviously been lured here didn't sit right either.

"Rail." Trigger pointed to a particular spot. I knew he wanted him out of sight. "Just fucking start shooting when I say so."

"You had me at *just fucking start.*" He chuckled darkly and pulled two compact rifles from his bike.

I cracked my knuckles at a look from Trigger and nodded at him. None of us knew the direction of the threat; there were multiple options. Nor did we know how many we'd face. Then we heard them. Trigger popped his neck, and Brick's eyes flicked to mine as the bikers traveled toward us. Trigger gave a soft whistle and held up a hand to Rail to be ready. The motors shifted down. I squared my shoulders as we all raised our weapons and prepared to fire.

They turned off the road, revved their engines, and some jumped off their bikes and pulled their weapons.

"We need to talk!" one of the men called with his hands out to his sides. He slowly got off his bike and began to walk toward us. He held a gun, so I stood up and aimed between his eyes.

"No." I shot him in the head then ducked as they began to fire their weapons.

A bullet zipped by my shoulder, and I couldn't believe I hadn't been hit. The guy had shitty aim.

"If you're gonna shoot, don't fucking miss!" I shot

him in the throat when his head peeked up from behind the vehicle again. Meanwhile, all hell had broken loose around us. I dove behind a truck where Trigger had taken cover. He grinned at me then took aim and continued to fire. We were sick fuckers and lived for moments like this. The dirt kicked up around us. Rail sprayed bullets, taking out two men. More bike engines could be heard, and soon came pouring into the parking lot. We were wildly outnumbered, but the rush of madness that ran through me made it all worth it. I ducked under the truck and shot a guy in the ankle, then when he stumbled out into the open, I shot him in the chest. Another bullet zipped by my head, and I laughed as I sent the shooter to meet his maker.

Morgan and Rail were across the way firing rounds at anyone who shot back. It was a bloodbath.

"Wait, wait!" A guy waved a shirt, and Trigger yelled at us to hold off.

"What the fuck!" I yelled in frustration as I reloaded.

"Easy, Grim," Trigger warned.

"Don't shoot. We have orders to talk to you!" The guy stood slowly, then turned, and warned the men to hold up. He tossed his weapon to the ground, and Trigger and I did the same.

"Go ahead, Grim, this one's yours." I nodded at Trigger and stood and began to walk toward the guy. When I was close enough, I drilled my fist into the side of his head. He stumbled and fell but stood back up with a head shake. The men behind him seemed to waver, and a few took a step forward.

"Rail!" Trigger called, and a shot hit the ground in front of them. They stopped.

"Like I said," the guy rubbed his jaw and glanced at the dead men around him, "we've got orders to talk to you." He turned to the men around him. "If any of you fire, I'll kill you myself."

"Since when do we talk?" I drove my fist into his stomach, and he doubled over but still managed to stay on his feet.

Trigger often spoke about how he slipped into the black when he fought. I'd never been forced to fight the way he had. I fucking fed off the pain like an addict. I ran into a fight like it was my next fix.

The asshole muttered something in Spanish then launched at me.

I needed this. I elbowed him in the cheek, and as his head went down, I drove the heel of my palm into his nose. The sound gave me a delicious shiver. I spun on my heel, and as I turned, I grabbed his neck and pulled him back over my bent knee about to snap his spine.

"Don't touch me!" Her voice broke through my murderous rage, and I held the man mid-kill as I tried to process it. My chest heaved as I felt a new kind of venom course through me. Kenna stumbled out of the bar with a gun to her head. The Stripe Back grabbed her hair and yanked her backward. When her wild gaze found mine, I could see the terror in her eyes. I blinked slowly as my own lids heated and shifted my brain into a different mode. I could feel my pupils shrink.

"Like he said," a man with a full black beard and a scar running the length of his neck stepped out behind them, "we just wanna talk."

"New Pres," Trigger grunted behind me. "Grim." His voice held a warning.

"Fuck!" I dropped the piece of shit on the ground and stood. My fists clenched, and the rest of me stood ready to move the moment I had the chance. The frustration inside me grew.

"Give her to me," I ordered, but the man yanked her backward as their President stepped forward.

"Not until we talk." The two men behind him opened the door to the bar and shoved Kenna back inside and out of my view.

"Morgan," Trigger kept his voice low, "offer what you need to."

"Got it." He nodded. Then Trigger headed inside the bar with Morgan, Brick, and me close behind. I sent off a quick text to Jesse to head this way, I needed to get Kenna out of here before she got any more involved.

While Morgan paid off the bartender to have our

backs, and with Rail as our eyes outside, we took a seat at the huge wooden table in the far back of the bar. Kenna was pushed into a chair next to the asshole with a death wish. She was far enough away I couldn't reach her.

"She'll be okay." The guy winked at me with a grin, and Brick eyed me. He knew I was close to my boiling point.

"We haven't met yet." The President of the Stripe Backs looked at Trigger. "Caleb. You knew my old man, Big D. His brother, my uncle, was the club's old Pres before you killed him."

"I did the world a favor," Trigger grunted.

"That you did," he agreed, then looked over at me. "You got no reason to trust me, Grim. Shit, I have one of yours." His teeth showed as white as the streak in the beard of the guy next to him when I pulled out my switchblade. He grinned at my audacity. "I needed your attention." He shrugged, and I moved my gaze to Kenna, whose eyes were wide with fright, but she seemed to have it together. I saw her mascara was smudged, so I knew she'd shed some tears at some point.

"Sorry," she mouthed, and I shook my head, trying to process that she was even here.

"You have it," I leaned back in my chair and did my best to suppress my need to break every bone in his body, "but it won't be for long."

"Someone's been hiring my men to come after you." His lips twisted like he was uneasy. "I don't need more enemies than I got. My uncle left me plenty, and I'm no fucking saint, but as Trigger can tell you as President of the DR, I'm up against it. I wanna keep my promise to the old man and keep the Stripes alive and movin', but I can't do that if I'm pissin' off the DR. I know you ride with them, but I know who you are, and I know your family. I don't need that kind of heat."

"Don't." Kenna pushed the man's hand off her chest. He lowered his arm and, in that split second, I whipped my switchblade at him. It sliced through his bicep and into the wooden chair behind. He screamed and Kenna jumped up, but the guy on her other side grabbed her and pressed a gun to her temple.

"Touch her again, and your dick's next," I seethed at the whimpering fool as I pulled out another knife and turned my eyes toward the man who held the gun. "Lower it."

"Lower it," Caleb snarled, and the man did.

"Did you burn down my hotel?" My voice was hardly recognizable as I addressed this new Pres.

"Yes, one of my men did but as I said, it wasn't on my order."

"Who?" I could barely speak.

"The one you followed here, and—" Caleb pulled his gun and casually shot the man next to him in the head. A couple of his guys stepped up, but Caleb raised a hand, and they backed off.

"Don't know who's doing the hiring, but they pay real good. Seems they get a call, do the job, and the cash is left for them. Guess it's too much to pass up." He shook his head.

I gritted my teeth in frustration. He'd just killed the one man I itched to torture since the other chose to kill himself.

"Your guys at Minnie's club a few weeks back?" Trigger's eyes burned as he spoke. I wanted the answer to that as much as he did.

"Yeah, they were paid to find out everything they could on your girl here because of her friend." He nodded toward Kenna. Her eyes shot over to mine then around the room.

"Me?" She looked panicked. "Why me and what friend?"

"Don't know." He shrugged.

"Did you know this was happening?" Trigger asked.

"No." He looked at his Vice President, who also shrugged. "You'd have to ask him." He pointed to the guy that bled out on the floor.

"Thanks to you, we can't," I growled. It wasn't lost on me that he'd killed him before we could question him.

"A lot's been going on," Caleb continued. "I only

just stepped into this role a short time ago. As things are coming to light, I'm dealin' with them."

"You're trying to do right by us, but you're keeping my girl over there." I rubbed my lips in an effort to stop myself from ripping his throat out.

"I needed insurance you'd listen." He shifted in his seat.

"And I'm listening, so give me what's mine."

"I will, but listen, whoever it is that's got it in for you, he's targeting your hotel. He hired some of my guys to rough up some of your foremen and probably some of their guys. Now that I know this, I've pulled them back, but I don't know how long I can keep 'em reined in. My club was left with a lot of debt, and I got hungry mouths to feed. We got families, too. Not all the guys who are wearing stripes are ours anymore. Some of them left when my uncle was killed, so they aren't under my command." Caleb looked at the man on the floor. "They'll be dealt with in time."

"How are they contacting them?" Trigger asked.

"Cale." He signaled one of his men to start talking.

"They're targeting our cuts." It was clear he wasn't pleased to share this information. He wouldn't make eye contact. "They approach us after a few drinks outside that strip joint that *his* bitch owns." He nodded at Trigger, who just smirked. *That man just sealed his death.* "They give us a card, with a number, and twenty-five percent down. There's a time on it, you call at that time, a man gives you the details, you do the job, he calls back and tells you where you find the money."

"Nothing's traceable." Caleb answered my next question. "That's all we know."

"Is it the same man who answers every time?" Brick asked.

"Don't know." Cale shrugged.

I cut in. "You got a copy of this card?"

"Nope, burned it." The guy named Cale shrugged. The guy who held Kenna chuckled from under his beard as he lifted his chin at me. Caleb turned in his seat and eyed him. "Wouldn't matter anyway. Don't know if it's the same guy, but it's a different time and number."

"That's what we got." Caleb stood, and we mirrored his movement. "I hope this counts for something." He nodded at me and then at Trigger. "Mong," he pointed to Kenna, "let her go."

The man who held Kenna shoved her forward, but when I reached for her, he yanked her back.

"You better watch this pretty young thing." He sniffed her hair as Kenna struggled to pull away. "She's unmarked and up for the takin'."

"I'd rather skin myself alive," she hissed at him and tried to rip her arm away.

"Mong," Caleb barked as I stepped forward and sliced him across the face and down his arm. I grabbed

Kenna and put her behind me as he digested what I had done.

"She may not be marked, but you are." Blood pooled down his face and body, and the pain started to kick in.

"You want him to live?" Trigger snarled at Caleb. "I'd suggest you get movin'."

"Watch your back, Grim," Caleb warned. "Hers too, because you guys pissed someone off real bad, and they're coming for you both." As they filed out, I felt Kenna grab my shirt from behind. I turned around and she pressed her face into my chest. Her entire body shook.

"Watch yours, too," I tossed back.

"He's got an interesting way of gettin' someone's attention," Brick snarled to Trigger.

"You okay?" I held her away from me and brushed her hair off her face. She nodded a few times. "How did they get you?"

"I was grabbed after I left Minnie, and it just happened so fast. Just—" She hesitated. "Just give me a sec, okay?" she whispered as she stepped into me again. I pulled her to my chest to give her a moment.

"She okay?" Morgan asked, and I nodded as Rail flew in the door.

"We lettin' them go?" He threw a questioning look at Trigger, who nodded. I knew Rail must have a lot of questions as to what happened here. He whirled around with a huff and made a beeline for the bar.

"Do we head back?" Brick looked at Trigger, who rubbed his face. I knew he wondered about the same thing we did. Was it safe to return on the side roads, or would they be lying in wait somewhere along the way? None of us trusted the Stripe Backs before, and now we knew some had gone rogue, it just made things a whole lot worse.

"Jesse's on his way." I knew he'd be here soon.

"We head to Dirt's." Brick's face lit up at Trigger's words. "Get Jesse to meet us there, Grim, it'll be safer than here."

"Yeah, okay."

Kenna took a deep breath and then looked up at me for a moment. Her normal hard shell was gone, and she looked stressed and vulnerable. It was refreshing to see that side of her, if only for a second. Then she seemed to realize she'd let her guard down with me and stepped away.

"You should let Jesse know." She let out a shaky breath as I sent off another text.

"Let's ride." Trigger headed for the door.

Dirt was a wild, unhinged member of the Las Vegas division of Devil's Reach. He'd hit the jackpot at Treasure Island Casino years back and built himself a little paradise outside the city. I knew Trigger rarely went there because Dirt was unpredictable and often partied with the wrong company at the wrong times. But his ten-foot concrete walls, unlimited supply of weapons, and the fact that he was loyal as the day was long to the DR made his place exactly where we needed to go to wait.

"You ever rode on a bike before?" I asked Kenna as we headed out into the hot night air.

"Better fucking not have," Morgan grunted. "She knows the rules."

"Yeah, trust me, I've tried. She lasted five minutes." Rail winked at me and moved my attention back to her.

She laughed. "Depends on what you mean by ride." She took the helmet, and I lifted a brow at her, my interest piqued by her comment.

She shimmied up her skirt so she could swing her leg over the seat. The slit that helped her get on her knees that morning gave me a shot of her smooth, toned thigh. I eased in front of her and tried to control myself as I slid between her legs.

"Tuck your dress in tight," I ordered. "I don't need anything else to distract me."

"Shouldn't I be in the front?" she huffed behind me, and I flicked her an evil look in the mirror. "All right." She huffed and wrapped her hands around my stomach. "Let's get the hell out of here."

She put up a good front, and I admired that about her, but I wondered what kind of toll the night had taken on Kenna. From what I knew of her, from the moments she'd let me in, she could take a lot. She could hang fine with Minnie, Tess, and the rest of them, but it didn't mean she was comfortable with their lifestyle. Though God fucking knew what Cameron had exposed her to over the years.

This woman both drove me nuts and intrigued me; I just couldn't figure out what I wanted from her. Or didn't want. I felt her legs tense around me and reached back to rub her thigh. She relaxed again, and I found myself wishing she was indeed sitting in front of me.

EIGHTEEN

KENNA

Grim pulled the bike over next to Trigger's near some parked vehicles. I licked my dry lips and thought about a drink. My nerves were shot, and during the ride, a lot of things I'd tried to push down for the past month had come creeping back into my head. I didn't want to let the guys see how upset I was, or they'd start to ask a lot of questions. The fact that I couldn't share the truth with them about what I had going on really made things hard. But I knew I couldn't. Not ever.

I hopped off the bike and let my skirt fall back in place. I clipped the helmet to the back of the bike and drew my fingers roughly through my hair. I was too exhausted to care much about what I looked like. I glanced at Grim. He hadn't moved off the bike. He watched me with that intense gaze he often wore. I wish I knew what he thought about when he studied me like that.

"Well, well, well, who do we have here?" A man who I guessed was Dirt approached us. He was dressed in skinny jeans, and a t-shirt with a DR cut over top. His long, curly hair was swept straight back over his head and hung down his back. He looked me up and down before his eyes went to Grim.

"This here's Kenna," Trigger drawled as he swung a leg up over his bike to sit sidesaddle.

Dirt held a massive bong that swung around as he turned back to me. Fire flickered from the big concrete bowls set around the walls. Their light played over his face. "You're a tight little package." He squinted at me, and I raised my chin at him. His lips curved up in his drug weathered face. "Oh, you got some fire in you too."

"That she does," Grim grunted, and I turned my head to glare at him.

"She yours?" Dirt asked him. "Because if she's not—"

"I am." I didn't need another man with his hands on me tonight. Dirt stepped closer and looked into my eyes.

"Pity."

"Not for me." Grim slipped an arm around my waist and pulled me to him.

"Well, come-come. Your guys should be here soon, but until then, get behind the walls." He seemed to snap out of his trance and waved us to follow him through the steel gates.

"Be careful with him," Grim whispered into my hair then urged me forward. "He's used to getting what he wants."

"Like you?" I looked up at him, and his gaze moved to my lips.

"Exactly like me." He tapped my ass to get me to move faster.

Dirt's place was impressive with its open-concept, huge, raised pool, hot tub, and lounge chairs. Full outside kitchen and bar all set behind solid concrete walls.

"Can I offer you a drink?" He waved around. "Please get comfortable and help yourself to something to eat."

"First, we need a minute," Grim ordered, and he steered me by the hip away from the others.

He found a quiet place and rubbed his chin as he thought. He grabbed a glass and filled it with water from a jug and handed it to me. I nodded my thanks and gulped down the cool water. Instantly, I felt my body come alive again. I held the glass to my lips a little longer than necessary to take a moment to study his toned body. It looked damn fine under his tee. The sleeves were rolled up some, belying what was underneath. His colorful arms were finally on display for me, and it took a considerable amount of effort not to reach up and trace the lines to see where they led. He sat on the ledge and allowed me time to gather myself. I was pretty amped up, and I knew it showed.

Grim pulled a joint from the pocket of his cut and lit the tip then drew the smoke into his lungs. His throat contracted then relaxed as he blew it away from me.

"Take some. It'll help." He held it up but kept it close to him, so I had to step between his long legs to reach it.

He tilted his head as I slowly pulled the joint from his fingers then pressed it between my lips and drew in a much-needed hit. The drug seeped its way into my system and masked some of my rattled nerves.

His hands moved to the backs of my thighs and slid up under my skirt. I ran my hand over his shoulders and noted they were as hard as the steel gates outside. I let my hand continue up through his hair with the joint between my fingers. He hissed as his fingers slipped between my legs and brushed over my sudden arousal. We weren't alone, but this was how things seemed to need to be with Grim and me when we were fired up.

"I want to know what happened at—"

"Any word on the hotel?" I didn't want to talk about me yet.

"Jesse said some of it's still standing. It's bad, but we can salvage a fair bit." He shook his head as his hands roamed.

"I'm sorry, Grim." I sincerely meant it; I knew how important Secrets was to him. "I can't believe what's going on."

"Kenna, what the hell happen—" He stopped himself and looked over my head. "Jesse's here. We'll talk later. We need to go." He gave me one last stroke over my thong then stood slowly and dragged the length of his body all the way up mine.

"I got booze and bitches!" someone yelled as they came through the side gate with a trail of people behind.

"Come meet my friends." Dirt called them over, and I saw about six guys with a girl on each arm. I recognized two of them as locals who often hung out at Treasure Island, and the girls with them were paid escorts that had caused me no end of trouble in the past with a few of my old clients. They were the last people I had the mind space for today.

"Fuck this place." Grim took the joint I held up to him and rested it in his mouth before he grabbed my hand. "We need to leave." The moment we stepped into the light of the lounge area, I heard her ear-piercing voice.

"Oh, look, Charles, it's the princess from the Indulge tower." Katherine, who went by Glory on the streets, snapped her gum at me.

"Glory hole," I wasn't in the mood to curb my tone, "how's the clap treating you?"

"Better than your daddy treats you." She grinned at me.

"At least my dad came back with the milk," I tossed at her, knowing her daddy had left years ago.

"Oh, shit." Brick hit Trigger's arm. "Minnie's gonna be pissed she missed this."

"You wanna fight me?" Glory stuck out her mini chest as Grim hissed at me to stop. He pulled me to his other side.

"Deal with the ho, Keller," Grim growled as Jesse came close and whispered something to him. "Stay here with the others for a sec, then we're leaving," he ordered and pressed me against the wall. He waved at Morgan to watch me.

I slowly edged my way to stand next to the door and hoped he wouldn't be long.

"Hey, gorgeous," Keller purred like the creep he was, "I see you're looking better than ever."

"And I see you're still hanging out with the STDs of the world." I shot Glory a look. Charles Keller wasn't someone I'd ever wanted to see again.

"You miss me?" I looked away, not wanting to play his stupid games. "Because we're here in this big house, and it's got plenty of mattresses." He grabbed my arm, and Morgan was next to me in a flash. "I could—" He stopped and eyed Morgan, who looked at him like a bug that needed to be crushed. He let go of my arm and held up his hands as he backed away then stopped hard as he hit something solid.

"You have a reason you're touchin' something that's not yours?" Grim growled above him.

"Well, fuck me, it is Grim Gates. What in hell brought you out here tonight, anyway? Run out of jet fuel, or did your Mexican supply dry up?" He made the motion of snorting cocaine.

"Keller." Grim moved quickly between us then pushed me behind him and raised his fist to take a swing, but I grabbed his arm and held up a hand to Keller. Grim shot me a look.

"It's not the night to fuck around." I couldn't take any more. "Back off."

Keller stuck his chest out and shrugged. "Letting pussy call the shots now?" Keller drawled, and I felt Grim's body go rigid. I moved in front of Grim and turned to face him and begged him to stand down with my eyes. His body vibrated, but I saw he got it. I turned toward Keller, and he dropped his gaze to me. "I'll swing by the hotel sometime, and we'll finish what we started years ago, little girl." He tried to hit my ass as he moved by me, but I shifted out of the way. I hated that I knew he meant it. Keller didn't back down easily;

it was one of the reasons I stayed clear of him. The only reason he did back down was because Grim looked ready to snap him in two and Morgan's eyes hadn't left his face.

"Christ, I can't leave you alone for two fucking seconds," Grim gritted at me as we watched Keller take a seat next to Glory at the bar.

"I don't need protecting." Before he could answer we heard a laugh.

"Damn, tempers are high tonight," Dirt called with a grin on his face.

"Yeah, and I can't decide if it's 'cause Grim's hotel went up in flames that's got him all riled up or," Keller pretended to pump his crotch, "that his girl is making all of us stiff in the pants."

"The only sex you probably get has a tip at the end." Grim shook his head as Keller's buddies laughed.

"Charles gets plenty of action, Grim. You jealous?" Glory batted her eyelashes in our direction. "I mean, are you two even screwin'? I know you were with Jenelle the other night." She put her finger in her mouth and made a sucking sound.

I didn't like that it bothered me a little that Grim was with someone else. Or maybe what bothered me was that I hadn't been with anyone lately. *Except Grim.* Or maybe it was because every time I did hear he was out with someone it was that Jenelle woman.

"We're not exclusive." I shrugged, not wanting this tramp stamp to get the better of us. "Though his fingers drive me mad." I wiggled them before I gave her the finger.

"Whatever," she held up a hand, and I saw Jesse head toward us, "you know where to find me."

"Bare assed in the back of a dumpster, no doubt." I snickered, and she stood, and I took a step toward her. I was incredibly hyped up and looking for an outlet.

"Seriously?" Grim hooked my waist and pulled me to him. "Weren't you just tellin' me to back down?" He tilted my chin to look at him. "Are you always this wild?" He smirked, and I shrugged, feeling that hunger I had for him. "I know that look." His thumb swiped my jawbone. "I feel it, too." Jesse moved into our line of vision, and I pulled away.

"Let's go." Jesse waved us over, and Grim whistled at the guys. It was time to leave. They all hopped on their bikes while Grim and I ducked into the town car. Jesse took the front with the driver and wasted no time giving Grim an update on the status of his hotel. Though the fire did a lot of damage, they were able to save over half of it. Jesse's voice was low as he spoke, and when he went into detail, I let my mind go and took a moment for myself.

I couldn't believe how the night turned into such a shit show. One moment I was with a client, and the next Secrets was on fire and I'm running like crazy to tell Grim, then I went from watching the flames with Minnie to being shoved in a car with some fucking Stripe Backs. How I ended up back in a car with Grim made my head spin. I could handle crazy situations. I'd learned that trait from being around my father, but shit, I needed a moment to catch up with this one. I thought I was also coming down from the adrenaline rush.

"I got the owner's address." Jesse's words found their way to me. "We can visit there tonight or tomorrow." I could feel Grim's gaze move to me.

"Not tonight," he answered in a raspy voice that found its way low in my belly.

"Understood." Jesse turned around then held up his phone. "Ah, probably not the time, but Jenelle called. Wants to know if you're free tonight." His voice filtered away, and he looked back as though he remembered I was in the car. "I'll let her know you're busy and you'll be around tomorrow."

"That's fine," Grim answered curtly.

There was Jenelle's name again. I tuned them out and listened to the roar of the bikes behind us. Maybe I should have ridden home with Morgan. It would have been physically uncomfortable, but easier on the head.

Focus on anything else, Kenna. The moon hung heavy in the sky, and the stars twinkled brightly out here away from the Vegas lights. I didn't get out of the city often. I sometimes forgot how quiet life could be away from all the bells, whistles, and flashy lights of Sin City. I breathed in and out and relaxed my mind until I heard the bikes suddenly fade away.

I was instantly alert as something caught my attention in the distance.

"Grim," I whispered as I studied it harder. "Grim." I turned to look at him. He looked out his own window, and I saw something else. "What is that?" I barely registered what was happening as Grim shoved me to the floor and threw his body over mine to shield me from the rain of bullets that struck the doors and windows of the vehicle. It sounded like rocks hitting steel as I squeezed my eyes shut.

"Stay low," Grim yelled, and I opened my eyes as he sat up. He had his gun in his hand. I heard Jesse scream at the driver to speed up.

"Jesse!" Grim's voice found me.

"On it," he yelled. "We're taking fire, Trigger!" Jesse shouted. "Okay, we'll head there." There was a pause as more bullets struck the armored doors. "Yeah, there."

"Stay down," Grim yelled in my ear again as more bullets slammed into the car. I jumped as each one hit and prayed the car could hold up to it all. I'd lost count of how many times we'd been struck. How bulletproof was bulletproof? The way my heart pounded in my chest hurt like hell.

"I can see them," Jesse yelled. I didn't know if he

meant help was here, or he meant he saw who was shooting at us.

"Lights off," Grim ordered the driver, and I squeezed my eyes shut again thinking the worst. "No, Trigger, we got this. Keep going the other way!" Grim shouted, and it took me a moment to realize he had his earpiece in.

I screamed and buried my face under my arm as another rain of shots found us. Then what I feared the most happened. The car suddenly dropped down on one side, and I heard a loud pop. We were thrown about as the driver tried to get control.

"Shit, shit!" the driver yelled, and I felt the car swerve. Pure fear forced me to look up, and I saw Jesse reach over to help him. Grim had one hand against the window frame and opened the window about an inch. *Was he insane?* Then he desperately tried to aim his weapon at the swirling world outside. We made a massive turn, and the car felt as though it would roll over, but somehow it righted itself. I wondered whose screams I heard until I realized they came from my own throat, and I forced myself to stop.

Tires screeched, not ours, but from somewhere else, and the sound sent more fear through me. I grabbed Grim's leg and held tight.

"He turned around," the driver yelled with a laugh. "Whoever it was knew better than to follow us."

Suddenly, I felt Grim's muscles relax, and he sat

back a bit on the seat. His gun stopped its racket and went still in his hand. I dared to look at him. His face was grinning. It was a psychopathic grin. I'd seen it before, and it threw me now as I couldn't imagine he wasn't scared to death at what we'd just gone through.

"Dodged another death wish." Jesse laughed as he blew out a long breath.

"That, we did," Grim laughed. Then he looked down at me as a calm expression replaced that frightening smile. "Come here." He lifted me off the floor and sat me next to him. "They're gone. They won't dare come into the city limits."

"Who's they?"

"I don't know, actually."

"Then how do you know they're finished shooting at us?"

"Gut."

"Wanna know where my gut is right now?" That made him smirk, whereas my hands shook as I tried to find my center. It didn't work. I was a rattled mess, and I could only imagine how I looked on the outside.

The car came to a stop, and Jesse got out and began to tug at the door next to me. I jumped as the metal scraped and squealed as he pulled it open. I was shocked to find we were at the private entrance of Indulge. I could barely process how we got there. As I exited the car, I gasped at the mangled mess that undoubtably had saved our lives.

"Your poor car." I covered my mouth and knew it was a write-off.

"It can be replaced." Grim shrugged and took my arm. He guided me toward the elevator without another word.

Once inside, I leaned against the wall and shivered in spite being in a ball of sweat. Grim and Jesse spoke quietly in front of me.

Jesus. I rubbed my head and thought about how much I had to deal with when it came to my clients or my father, but the thought that Grim dealt with stuff like what we'd just gone through blew my mind. His line of work brought him a whole other side of awful. When the doors opened again, I stood with my knees locked, unable to move or form another thought.

"Go downstairs and see what you can find out," Grim ordered Jesse.

"Kenna," Grim said sharply, and I snapped out of it. He had stepped out on his private floor. I noticed Jesse used one of the black and gold cards as he pushed lobby and floor fifteen at the same time. *Odd.*

"I want to go to my own room." I wanted nothing more than to crawl under the covers of my own bed and shut out the world. Maybe sleep for a week.

"No." He stepped forward and hauled me out of the steel box. He led me into the living room. His two Dobermans glared at me as he left me to stand next to a chair. I looked around as he removed his jacket and tossed it on a side table. Yesterday seemed so long ago. "Drink?"

"Yes," I took a step farther into his lair, "please."

"Leal," his voice made me jump as he addressed one of the dogs who had edged close to me, "go."

The dog growled some backtalk to him but moved away immediately while his brother simply watched me from where he sat near Grim. His face seemed a little sweeter than the other dog's.

"Here." Grim handed me a glass. The contents had a gold tone to it, and I took a sniff. It was whiskey. "It'll take the edge off."

"Thanks." I downed the drink quickly and regretted it instantly. Second degree burns lined my throat and stomach, and my eyes watered. After a moment, the burn turned into a warmth that spread through me. My shoulders slowly relaxed, and I walked over to his floor to ceiling windows. Zhen, the dog near Grim, stood. I turned and saw his eyes were glued on me. I turned away to look out the window.

"I get the impression your dogs don't like sharing your company," I whispered as I watched the cars move along the Strip. I loved how they looked like Hot Wheels toys.

"That's how they were trained." I watched him through the reflection of the glass, as he settled into a seat behind me and rubbed the dog's tall ears. "They're very loving, but they're also very protective of me."

"That must be nice." I folded an arm around my middle as a vulnerable feeling came over me. I thought of my father and how his work always came first. Protection wasn't something I was used to. After the trips with my mother slowed down, I was home a lot more, and if I ever shared a concern about one of his clients while they were in our house, Dad just told me to deal with it. Maybe that's why I loved the Devil's Reach so much. They were protective of one another even if they weren't actually blood family. I guess I hadn't thought of it before, but I craved that safe feeling.

On the outside, I knew I seemed to have everything together, but inside I knew I was often a mess. Alone, frightened at times and often insecure about whether I could really handle the things I got myself into. Not that I'd ever admit that to anyone.

"Don't you feel safe here?" He hit the nail on the head, and I kept my back to him.

"Safe is an overused and yet underrated word." I sighed. I was suddenly tired of the topic.

"That doesn't answer my question."

"Ask a different one, then," I pushed back. His face went hard at my unwillingness to play by his rules.

"Fine," he muttered, "tell me exactly what happened yesterday."

I glanced at the time on his mantel in the realization

it was after one thirty in the morning, I guessed the fire was yesterday, too.

"I was helping Yen Hong with something, when Dale came running over and said his friend who worked at Mac was out for a smoke break and saw flames at Secrets. He called Dale, and Dale found me to go tell you."

"And?" He waited.

"And after you left the hotel, I caught a ride with Jayden, who was heading over there too and then found Minnie."

"Kenna," his tone was sharp, "move the story along." He was right, I was stalling.

"And once I saw you leave with Trigger, I told Minnie we should go back, like you said. I wanted to find Jim to make sure he knew about what happened with the biker and all that. Anyway, she wanted to stay, so I said I'd meet her back at the hotel." He nodded, and I turned to the window and went on. "Well, one minute I was walking back, and the next I was grabbed around the waist, and someone covered my mouth. I was pushed into a car." I cleared my throat uncomfortably and heard him get out of the chair to stand next to me. He turned me to face him.

"Then?" His gaze pierced into mine.

"Then I struggled, I fought back." A wave of anger went over me. "Damn it, the more I fought, the more they seemed to enjoy it. I could hear them laughing." I could feel their hands on me.

"What happened then?" His eyes blazed.

"Then I stopped." I looked down. "I knew they enjoyed it. The one you cut he was the worst. I'm glad you got him for me."

"I'm glad, too," he nodded, "but now I know cutting him isn't enough, I'll find him again and take him to the mines."

Mines? I wanted to ask but at the same time knew my head couldn't take any more at that moment.

"Anyway, once that Caleb guy showed up at the bar, he kept them in check for the most part."

"Did they hurt you?"

"Just," I closed my eyes and willed my own anger back, "Grim, I'm fine. You guys showed up, and things are good."

"Things are far from good," he snarled. "And who the hell is this friend they're talking about?"

"I have no idea." I really didn't.

"Think."

"I have," I growled at him, and Leal matched my growl.

"They could have killed you, Kenna."

"You don't think I know that?" My voice broke at the end. "You don't think that wasn't going through my head when that asshole had his hands all over me."

I shuddered at the memory. "All I could think about was—"

His phone rang and Jesse's name popped up. I could see he struggled if he should answer it or not.

"Was, what?"

I pointed to his phone. "You should get that."

"What?" He growled as a greeting. "Bring them to the office. I'll deal with them later." He hung up and his murderous gaze moved to mine, and I swore they flickered between honey and silver. "Was what?"

"Grim, let it go." I turned to leave, but he snagged my arm and pushed me up against the window.

"Finish your sentence."

"Why?"

"Because I said so."

"No."

"Kenna," his face twitched like he tried hard to hold back a part of himself that he couldn't control, "I swear to Lucifer, you push me to a point that I don't know I can come back from." I searched his eyes and saw the truth.

"Was, could they be connected to what happened before?" The moment the words slid past my lips, I knew I'd made a huge mistake. I couldn't tell anyone what had happened.

"Meaning." His chest slowly seemed to grow larger as his eyes narrowed in on me. It was as though he tried to see inside my head to read the rest of the story from my thoughts. "Tell me what you're hiding from me."

I knew it was stupid to flirt with his dark side, and I seemed to at the very worst of times. It was reckless, but something in Grim just pushed me to a place I never went before. I loved how much his darkness brought out a thrill I'd never experienced. It was heady.

I lifted a brow and stuck out my chin as something seedy and delicious went through me. I leaned in, pressed my lips to the shell of his ear, and whispered, "No."

His hand wrapped around my throat, and he pushed me back against the window. He towered over me and hissed his fury as he fought for control. Suddenly, his face changed, and he smiled. He was dangerously close to my lips. The smile was almost frightening.

"You sure you want to push me on this?" His voice was dark and threatening.

I could almost feel my eyes dilate. The excitement at what darkness he might bring left me breathless.

"You don't own me, Grim," I added for good measure. I wanted to push any buttons he had left because I was maxed out. I pressed my hands against his and squeezed his fingers into my throat.

He let out a slow chuckle then spun me around and pushed my chest against the glass pane. He pulled my hair to one side and began to kiss the side of my neck.

"Do you have any idea how hard you make me, walkin' around in those tight little dresses?" I heard the zipper of my skirt as he ripped it down over my backside then his fingers tore at the fabric, it dropped to the floor, and I kicked it aside. "You drive me mad because I know what's underneath." His hands were all over the back of my shirt as he undid the buttons. I felt the cool air as it fell open. He chuckled as it followed my skirt and fell at my feet. I was left in my thong, bra, and heels. He tore off his own shirt, and his hand slid around my stomach, and he turned me to him. My head fell back as I bared my throat to him. He leaned in and hissed in my ear.

"I see the way men look at you. They're hungry for a taste." His lips dragged across my neck, then clamped down as he drew my skin into his mouth. His hands slid back to my hips, and he pressed me against him. "I'm craving a taste of you." He sucked hard, and I felt the pull from deep inside. I arched my back and pressed my hips hard against him and felt his arousal. "Then," he breathed, sending shivers through my body. His lips tugged on my earlobe, and his fingers flexed around my waist. "I find you in a sex house looking for anyone to get you off." He turned me again, and I felt my heavy head hit his shoulder.

"I was," I whispered, caught up in his story. One

hand moved slowly across my belly, then finally dipped into my panties, but just above the spot that ached for his touch.

"Why?"

"Because…" I trailed off.

"Because you have a certain kind of taste in sex."

"I do." He spun me back around and grabbed my chin roughly while the other hand moved to cover my throat, giving it a gentle squeeze. His eyes flared and his throat contracted with excitement. We both knew with one practiced snap, he could kill me.

"Wreck me," I whispered. His fingers moved around my chin and into my hair, and with a swift jab he smashed his lips to mine. His tongue commanded, and I lost all rational thought. I jumped up and wrapped my legs around him as I matched his intensity. I ran my fingers through his hair and pulled hard, and he clamped a hand at the base of my neck and pressed me even closer.

He walked back a few steps and, without a break in our frantic kisses, he slammed me back against the cool wall and unclipped my bra with one hand. When my breasts burst free of their lacy cages, he licked his lips and dove at one nipple. Exquisite pain went through me as he used his teeth. I gasped and drove the heel of my shoe into his ass to let him know what that did to me.

"Fucking perfect," he purred as he moved over to the other and gave it the same attention.

Suddenly, he flung me over his shoulder and slapped my ass then grabbed it with one hand. The other held my ankle, and he moved quickly with me to the bedroom and threw me onto his huge bed. For a fleeting moment, I was aware of soft velvet, but then his hands were on my hips as he ripped off my thong. When I reached for him, he grabbed one wrist then the other, and bound them together with a silky tie. He looked into my eyes as he secured me to one side of the bed. I was on my back, arms outstretched above my head that hung just slightly over the edge. My breasts were plump, and my nipples were hard nubs. Every inch of me craved his touch, I desperately clamped my thighs tightly together to seek some relief. The room was dark except for a tiny gleam of light that fell across my heaving chest.

"Grim?" I huffed, suddenly nervous as I lay there in the silent room. "Where are you?"

"You don't think I can own you?" His voice came from somewhere close, and I searched the darkness for him. I felt his fingers tightly grip my hair, then he pressed his mouth over mine and kissed me deeply. Then just as quickly he pulled away, then slid his erection into my mouth.

I didn't hesitate and took him right to the base. I swallowed around him, and he hissed his pleasure. He thrust himself against my lips a few times then pulled out and with both hands pressed my boobs together and slid his huge erection between them. He moved at a good speed for a moment, then slid back in my mouth again. This time I held him there and sucked hard. I flexed my tongue and gave him my all. I gave Grim everything I had because I wanted to. I wanted him to crave me, to think of me, to lust after me. The same way I knew he wanted me. I wanted to consume his every thought.

This was part of our game, and I was determined to win.

He pinched my nipples, and I bowed my back, wanting more. His hips picked up speed, and I fought against my bonds even as I used them for leverage. The sound that echoed through the bedroom was erotic and intoxicating.

"Jesus," he moaned. He slowed and fought to hold back. I could feel his leg muscles clench as he tried to control himself. The only warning I got that he was about to come was the hitch in his breathing. I took it all without so much as a moan. It was all I had, and I flexed my back with how hard it was not to scream. Grim Gates was a different breed, and I wouldn't let him best me.

"I need more," he growled as he yanked the tie and my hands were released. He tossed me like a doll, so my head was on the pillow, then yanked off my shoes and threw them. He bound my wrists above me once again, and he left me there in the dark, panting and full of pent-up frustration.

A strange sound filled the air, like a low hiss from a snake, and my heart thumped as I wondered what was next. I was wildly intrigued and desperate for more. Flames appeared on the walls on either side of my head, then two by two around the huge room torches came on. Each flame flickered on long black holders. The walls were matte black in contrast to the deep red bedding. A massive bookshelf lined one wall, and several gothic chandeliers also flickered with fire and cast shadows overhead. I knew I'd probably wish I'd focused more on the room but at that moment all I could see was Grim. He stood at the end of the bed, his pants now off as he watched me like a wild animal ready to feed…on me.

His toned, thick muscles, and perfectly carved stomach were intensified by the dark tattoos that covered every single inch of him. Well, nearly every inch. His chin was high as he stared down at me with hooded eyes. I lay there and smiled at him as I shamelessly admired the view.

"I won't be gentle," he said quietly as his mouth twisted in what looked like a smile. His eyes were black, and I saw flames reflected there.

"I won't let you." I flopped my legs open.

He moved quickly up along the bed, climbed

between my legs, and plunged deeply inside me. I cried out, not in pain, but at the sheer power of it. Nothing could have prepared me for how wonderful it felt. He swallowed my scream with his lips as he began to thrust hard. His arms were steel by my head, his stomach locked, his hips like a motor, but those eyes. They were locked on mine. Suddenly, I was lost in that frame of time. I was blind, out of control as I enjoyed the most intense sex of my life. My orgasm built and built; my body begged me to let go, but I held on. I was hiked up by my legs, now over his shoulders as he lifted me off the bed to an even more intense angle. He was deeper, and if it was possible, he had swollen even thicker. A cold heat broke over my skin as I fought against the power the orgasm brought. My head screamed wait, but my body overruled it.

"Grim!" I let it all go. I broke the silence with my screams as I exploded into a million pieces and felt as helpless as a bit of foam in a storm. I clamped down around him and moaned as a wave of euphoria flowed through me. I was barely off my high when he started to kiss across my chest and squeezed my breast with a hungry groan.

My hands hit the pillow as they were released from their hold and Grim scooped me up and flipped me onto my stomach.

"More," he grunted and hauled my hips to him.

"What?" I panted as I tried to move but he pulled

me back and my mouth opened in an 'O' of surprise as he slipped into a whole different opening. I went still, and his arm tightened on me as he held me down. He struggled to catch his breath. It wasn't the first time I'd had sex like that. It wasn't new, but with Grim's size, the burn was real. Thank God, I was slick with pleasure which helped him glide in easier. I rocked a little and pressed my face into the pillow as I adjusted to the invasion. His grip still didn't soften, and I knew he fought not to come.

I covered his hands with mine and pushed up on my knees and started to move a bit to slick the opening better. Up and down, I moved, and with every stroke I heated with need again. Grim rocked back on his heels and began to squeeze my breasts. It gave me a moment to take control, but it didn't last long. As I lifted, he did too, and he pushed me forward with his hips as we moved up to the headboard.

"See that bar?" he grunted in my ear. "Grab it." I didn't waste a beat and grabbed it as he stood, with his hands holding my hips. I was bent from the waist down as he continued to thrust from behind. I was glad I did yoga four times a week. It brought a whole different level to my already hungry sexual appetite.

I let out a throaty moan, completely consumed by this man. I needed this more than I realized. Sex was something I certainly needed, but what Grim brought was something I craved.

Slap! He hit my ass, and I flinched around him, making his grip on me tighten. Some women might find this appalling, but I grew more turned on.

We were relentless, over and over and over, we both took what we wanted. Neither of us wanted to fold first. He'd slap, caress, rub, you name it, he was doing it, while I held on and did my best from whatever angle I was at.

I reached back and gave his balls a tug, and he broke.

"Dammit!" Grim roared as he came, and with a violent shake I finally gave in, and my orgasm chased after his.

I collapsed on the bed, limp and well used. Grim flopped down next to me as we both tried to catch our breath.

Fights and sexual tension were how Grim and I co-existed to this point, so now lying in bed with him, after such an event, I wasn't sure how to navigate us.

"Give me two—"

He stood and disappeared across the room to where I guessed was the bathroom. The water started to run, and I looked around. The room was dramatic and dark like the rest of his place, and it suited his personality perfectly. The door opened, and he stared at me wordlessly for a moment, then he stepped back into the bathroom. *An invitation?*

I moved across the gray shag rug and into the bathroom where he stood under a ceiling-high rainfall shower. The water poured down his muscular body, but it was his now honey-colored eyes that made my heart skip a beat. How could someone be so sexy but terrifying all at one time? I swallowed and stepped through the spray to face him. Water poured down our faces as he swiped his hand over the curve of my ass. I noted that his erection was back and that he was partly tattooed up the base. I had noticed it before but hadn't had time to admire his artwork up until now. As painful as it must have been to have done, it was beautiful the way the pattern swirled around and drew the eye.

"Good?" he asked, and I forced my eyes away.

"Yeah," I replied then moved to the other side of the huge shower and grabbed the soap. He did the same, but I finished before him. With a towel wrapped around me, I gathered my things and headed for the elevator. I didn't bother to change; the keycard ensured I'd arrive on my floor without company. Both dogs watched me leave and, as the doors closed, I heard the water turn off. Thus ended our night.

NINETEEN

KENNA

"**W**hy do you look like you rode a horse?" Minnie eyed me as I slid into the chair with a wince.

"Because I was ridin' one last night."

"Someone got to snack on your lunch box?"

"Yeah, my pie hole, my sushi, and," I wiggled my butt, "he even tossed my salad." Minnie loved colorful sex conversation, and I gave her the whole enchilada; it was just how we rolled.

"Sweet orgasm in a fuckin' clutch purse, that just made my toes curl," she hooted. "What about the girls?" She pointed to my boobs.

"Oh, please, like they'd be left behind."

"Okay," she took a deep breath and closed her eyes,

"make all my dreams come true and tell me it was Grim."

"That be the one."

"God damn, that's a good visual!" She shouted and put her hand to her heart. Everyone in the coffee shop looked at us. "My girl just got clam slammed."

"Wow," I laughed behind my cup.

"So, tell me, then, are the rumors true? Does he play for the big leagues? Louisville slugger? Bauer goalie stick?" She beamed her joy at me.

"Why do you think I want a rubber donut to sit on?" I smirked, and she flopped her head into her hands.

"So," she jammed a cinnamon roll into her mouth, "what does this mean?"

"What do you mean?"

"Are you guys dating?"

"Ha!" I laughed loudly at the sheer idea of it. "No, it means we were both running off no sleep, adrenaline, and weed. We finally both got pissed enough at each other we gave in to take the edge off. You must know that feeling."

"I mean, I do, but it ended with me dating Brick."

"And I'm very happy for the two of you, but Grim and I are like light and dark. We can't co-exist in the same place."

"But the sex is good?"

"The sex is great." I nodded.

"And you'll do it again?"

"I won't say I won't, but from what I understand, there's another girl in the picture. So, I'll tread carefully."

"Who?"

"Her name's Jenelle."

"That twat-waffle!" Minnie rolled her eyes.

"You know her?"

"Not really, but Brick does, and he told me she's been after Grim forever. I thought she gave up hope when he first left for Mexico, but clearly, she's still circling."

"So, they have a history?"

"Yes," she popped another piece of pastry in her mouth then looked up at me, "but that doesn't mean shit, Kenna. No ring means game on. So, if you like a good munch-a-lunch, you don't back down."

"There are plenty of ladies who have their eye on him—"

"Just like there are plenty of men who have their eye on you," she reminded me. "If you're having fun with Grim, then have fun, but hey, maybe that big heart of yours will finally let someone in."

"That thing is locked up so tight, I'm not even sure if it beats anymore."

"Raymond really did a number on you."

I looked away as I forced myself to block the memory.

"He left a couple scars, not that he can ever know."

"You know I wouldn't." She patted my hand and pretended to lock her lips and throw away a key. "I'm sorry he cheated on you, in your bed, on your birthday, with a friend." She shrugged.

"Again, all things no one needs to know." I swallowed the uncomfortable lump that the truth about Raymond brought me. We had dated before Dale, and before I moved back here. I let him in, and I got burned. Then I jumped into a relationship with Dale because I was hurting and missed the warning signs that he wasn't ready for anything serious. Truth was, I'd had a few bad relationships since Dale. I mean, what did I have to go by? I knew my parents were far from the norm. Mom left every chance she got for parts of the world few people could even pronounce, and Dad, well, he was who he was, and it was far from the storybook father.

"I just don't want to get hurt again," I admitted and let her in a little. "The best way for that to happen is sex with no strings. Anyway, that's the best kind of sex, right?"

"Sex with love can be lonely too." She sighed.

"I know, hon. Brick's not around enough these days, is he?"

She just lifted her shoulder and looked away. "And when he is, he's distant."

"I'm sorry." I decided to keep things light. "How

can we be lonely when we're surrounded by the best friends in the world?"

"You want me to put a hit out on Raymond?" She grinned at me.

"Not yet." I winked and tucked my own hurt feelings back inside. Minnie was the perfect example of why I kept myself so guarded. She loved Brick with everything she had, and her heart still hurt.

I stood and pressed on the top of my to-go cup, careful not to slosh my coffee. My phone bounced around on the table, and I snatched it up.

"Oh, shit, Min, I have to take this."

"Everything okay?

"Yeah, I just need to take it." I threaded my purse over my arm, waved, and threw a kiss at her as I raced out of the café.

"Hanna?"

"Kenna!"

"I'm so sorry we've been playing phone tag, but I have a few moments—"

"Kenna," she cut me off. She sounded out of breath. "I need to ask you something." I heard a car horn. "Do you remember Sa…"

"Wait, you cut out, Hanna." I moved through a restaurant with a wave at the waitress to let her know I needed a moment. Still no response, so I moved through the door out onto the patio.

"...Sasha Landry," she yelled into the phone. "Do you remember him?"

"Of course," I yelled then lowered my voice. Why would she bring him up? "You know we dated. Why?"

"Is he still around?"

"I saw him just a bit ago."

"Kenna," her voice sounded a warning as she loudly whispered, and a cold chill replaced the Vegas heat, "you need to stay away from him, from all of—" Her phone cut out again, and I couldn't make out her words.

"What? What do you mean?" I repeated myself until I could hear her. I might not be a fan of Sasha, of any of them, really. They were creeps at best, but they certainly didn't scare me enough to be concerned.

"Listen," she used that haunted tone again, "I saw something the other night. You need to listen to me, Kenna. I think you might be in real trouble."

"Hanna, I need more to go on than that. What did you see?"

"You just—" I heard her suddenly suck in a breath. "I need to call you back. I just sent you something. Watch for it, okay?"

"No, Hanna, you can't just leave me like that. Wait!" The call disconnected, and I stared at the screen and hoped it would magically reconnect again. What the hell was that? Hanna was never one for dramatics, and she'd never been cryptic before. She'd always been wonderfully blunt and real. Suddenly, my mind went to the conversation with the Stripe Backs. Could Hanna possibly be the friend they referred to?

"Hey," Leo was behind me, "everything okay?"

"I honestly don't know." I tried to gather myself as he studied me. I forced myself to shake off the strange call. I needed to think that through. "It was just a girl-friend. Everything's fine. I'm sure she'll explain later. What can I do for you, Leo?"

"There's a new client in town, and Grim really wants to tap him for Secrets. I told him I'd help, but I've got stuff going on myself where I really need to be. I can't interrupt him right now to talk to him about it, but he'll kill me if I mess this up. Any chance you could help?"

"Of course. Who's the client?"

"Tom Harris. He's a tech billionaire, and word is he isn't happy at the Venetian anymore."

"Sure. It's basically what I do, anyway. I'm not sure why he didn't ask me."

"It was something he wanted me to handle myself since he can't." He looked a bit guilty. "I kind of have this date."

"You don't need to explain. I'm more than happy to help. That's what I'm here for." I was pleased to hear Leo was going out. He needed to have some fun. I heard a few rumors that his first run down to Mexico to close Grim's accounts hadn't gone so well. I knew, like me, he spent a lot of time trying to prove to his father, not to mention his older brother, that he could handle the business. An attractive young man like him should take the time to have fun with the ladies.

"Thanks, I could really use a night out."

"I hope you're not working too hard."

"Just a lot going on." He shrugged, and I saw something heavy cross his face.

"I hope everything's okay with you." I sent his earlier comment back to him.

"It'll be okay." He smiled. "Anyway, I was just speaking to Knox, and he's doing up a new version of our contract. Since the fire, there've been a few changes. I'll get him to email a copy to you within the hour."

"Perfect. I got this." I grinned. "Go have some fun."

"Thanks! I will." He grinned and rubbed the back of his neck. As he left, I called Zara, and she filled me in on everything I needed to know about Tom Harris.

I wined, dined, and partied on a rooftop with Tom Harris until the sun came up. The Weekend's mysterious, dark music and Harry Styles' soul set the mood for a great time. I really was living my best life. It turned out, Tom was a pretty fun guy and had equally fun friends. They were respectful and made sure I was well taken care of. To say they'd make excellent guests at Secrets was an understatement. They were full-time gamblers, and money flowed like water from their wallets.

Apparently, Grim had a whole thing planned for them in Laguna, but they wanted to party here in town instead. The only issue I had was that Knox was supposed to send over the contracts, and that never happened. I figured he got hooked up at Minnie's with his pals soaking his liver in tequila with his face stuck in some stripper's breasts or he was with Calli. Both were equally as bad. He certainly wasn't Leo, and I wondered what his brother would say if he found out he hadn't sent the contract over.

Thankfully, I had the frame of mind to record us when we discussed the contract and how he'd wanted to sign that night. I assured him I'd get the contract asap because nothing was ever certain without a signature. I texted and called well into the next morning.

By four-thirty in the morning, I still hadn't gotten hold of Knox. I'd called several times and left messages. I had called one of his friends, then called his father, but even Jim never called me back. I even went so low as to call my own father, who I knew would give me the world's biggest lecture about going to meet a potential client without a contract at hand, but even his phone went straight to voicemail. This was Vegas and no one ever cared what time it was. If it was anyone but Leo who asked me to handle this situation, I would have thought I was being played, but Leo was too kindhearted for that. I wished I had Jesse's number. I needed to make a note of that.

"I think I need sleep." Tom leaned his head back on the couch from where we sat next to the pool. Shit, my guests were winding down. It didn't help that they'd told me Melvern Trident Jr. from the Mac Hotel had entertained them the night before so now they were running on fumes. Thankfully, like most people who met Melvern, they didn't like him, so I wasn't overly concerned about that. But shit could happen, and I needed that damn contract.

"Let me get you some rooms at Indulge." I tried not to beg.

"Don't trouble yourself, Kenna, just a car back to the Venetian would be fine."

"Of course." I cursed inwardly.

With no other moves to make, I called Grim; this was, after all, what he wanted.

The line rang three times, and just as I was about to hang up, I heard a female's voice.

"Grim Gates' phone," she yawned.

"Hi. This is Kenna Lodge. Is Grim there?"

"He's in the shower. Can it wait?"

"No, it can't, actually." I felt uncomfortable as I pictured her on the same sheets as me.

"Well, Jenna, he's had a long night." I rolled my

eyes when she said my name wrong. I knew for a fact Grim had it programmed correctly in his phone. "Once he's out, I'll be sure to let him know you called."

"Right," I glanced at Tom, who fought to keep his eyes open, "this really is time sensitive, though." I couldn't let all the work I had done go to waste.

"Maybe you should try his secretary, or his younger brother Knox. I know he's been helping Grim with his business."

"I know he has." I tried to curb my annoyance that some woman was informing me on information I was well aware of. "It's just this has to do with a contract and—"

"Well, try the secretary, then, perhaps during business hours." She cleared her throat, and it was clear she wasn't going to get Grim. We both knew Vegas didn't have any such thing as normal business hours. "Like I said, I'll pass along that you called."

"Who am I speaking to?" I needed to know.

"Jenelle Borrows." At her name, my stomach plummeted. "He'll touch base soon, Jenna. Have a good night." She hung up, and I licked around my dry mouth. On a normal day, I'd have access to all contracts, and I knew it would look unprofessional for me to have him sign an old one then have to get him to resign another.

With defeat heavy in my chest, I called us a car.

"Kenna, tonight was so much fun. The music, the

talent, the food, all of it was top shelf." Tom nudged his friend on the seat next to him to open the door, and I stepped out of the car to say goodbye to them.

"I'm pleased to hear you enjoyed yourselves." I gave him a firm handshake.

"Let me get some sleep, get my head on straight, and I'll be in touch."

I cringed with the knowledge that I'd failed to do my job. I should've had his signature by now. I'd have up to eight new clients for Secrets instead of just a receipt to submit for over fifteen thousand dollars.

"I look forward to that, Tom. Let me know when you want to see the blueprints for Secrets. She's pretty spectacular."

"I'm sure she is." He yawed and waved for his buddies to follow him inside. I shook hands and watched them go like zombies. Then I sagged against the car while my frustration built. My driver, Shore, patiently stood outside his door and watched the surroundings. It was reassuring, as I was exhausted.

"Heads up, Ms. Lodge," he whispered across the top of the car.

"Kenna?" I didn't have to turn and see who it was. It was just the fucking cherry on top of this shit-filled morning.

"Hello, Jayden."

"I was just doing my eight-mile morning run and felt a cramp in my side, and when I stopped to hydrate,

I asked myself, now, who's that little hottie." He'd packed a lot into that sentence.

"That's nice."

"Yeah, it's all about getting fresh air, while beating the heat. It's a great way to stay in shape." I filtered out every other word he said. My frustration consumed me. "Okay?" he asked and pulled my attention back to him.

"Yeah, sure," I muttered and opened the car door. He got in next to me. "What are you doing?"

"Cramp," he pointed to his stomach, "remember?"

"Right." I moved closer to the opposite door as Shore got in, then he eyed me in the rearview mirror. I shrugged, and he glared at Jayden but started the car and headed back to the hotel. I noticed he ran two yellow lights. Bless his heart for trying to hurry us back.

My phone rang, and I saw it was Grim, but given my temper, lack of sleep, and the fact that there was nothing I could do now, I sent it to voicemail. A moment later a text popped up.

Grim: You called.

Grim: Why aren't you answering?

Grim: I don't appreciate being ignored.

I cleared them from my home screen as I caught Jayden reading them.

"Your father invited me over to dinner Friday night."

"That's nice." *And I will not be attending that one.*

"He's a pretty impressive man, your father."

"That's nice." I felt another text come through, but I didn't look.

"Are you going to the charity ball tomorrow night?" That caught my attention.

"It's part of the job." *Damn, I'd forgotten the ball was tomorrow.*

"Well, I was going to ask if you wanted to go with me."

I would rather poke my own eyes out. "I have a date, actually."

"Don't tell me it's Grim Gates."

I shot him a look but remembered who I was sitting next to, the snitch of the hotel, my own daddy's favorite, the man who followed me into a restroom and demanded I tell him who I was having dinner with. Of course, Calli had walked in right at that moment. I was too exhausted to think.

"She's going with my son, Randell," Shore said as he pulled into the hotel's driveway.

"I didn't know you had a son," Jayden muttered.

"You never asked." He winked at me in the mirror, and I gave a slight nod as a thank you.

"Well, if your plans change, I'll be dateless."

"Why don't you go with Chantelle, the cute little one who started at the tables last week?" *Anyone but me.*

"She's going with Dale."

Of course, she was.

"You know your father would like to see us together."

"My father would like me to do a lot of things, but this time I'm going with Randy."

"Randell," Shore corrected me with a grin. He only had daughters, which Jayden would know if he actually took the time for people.

"Randell," I repeated, "but thanks for the offer." I hopped out and raced inside before he could say another word. I showered and changed into a silk tank and panties as quickly as I could manage and was finally able to flop into bed with the comforter up to my chin when my phone lit up by my bedside.

"No." I groaned but tilted the phone so I could read it.

Grim: Answer me.

Kenna: It's over now. Going to bed. I'll touch base later.

TWENTY

GRIM

The gym was fairly empty in the early morning, just a few of the high roller dealers blowing off steam after their night shift. Though, one nod from me and they scurried away. I guessed they were worried they might piss me off and lose their job. They weren't entirely wrong; I liked the silence, anyway.

After five miles on the treadmill, I tossed my soaked t-shirt on the floor and ran my hands through my hair to slick it back. I needed more, so I moved to the weight section and dropped to the floor and began some push-ups. I lost count after eighty-two. I was in the zone, and as my body burned, my mind drifted back to hours earlier.

"Can I come in?" Jenelle batted her eyes at me from the elevator.

I held back a curse and waved her in. It wasn't a good time, but I knew her, and she wouldn't give up that easily.

"Drink?" I walked to the bar and began to make her favorite gin and tonic with a twist of lemon.

"Yes, thank you." She dropped her purse on the table and made herself comfortable on the couch. "I heard you had company last night."

My brows pinched as I wondered who had fed her that tidbit. My eyes went to the window where I'd pressed Kenna up against it, an image I savored for a few beats. I enjoyed the idea that she was at my mercy, pliable and willing to go wherever I led.

"I did." I forced myself back to the conversation.

"Was it work related or something else?"

"You want to ask that question again?" I warned and held up her drink. "Just because we've slept together doesn't mean you can pry into my life."

"Of course." She was wise enough to back off. "I was just curious." She pretended to flick a bit of lint off her knee as she took a sip of her drink. Then she got up and moved to where I sat on the couch and slid onto my lap.

Her weight felt good on my erection.

"I was just thinking," she rubbed her hand under my open dress shirt, "that now you're back and I'm

setting down roots in this city, maybe we could set some together?" I went still and covered her hand to stop its movement.

"Jenelle..."

"I know you're scared of commitment, Grim," she interrupted and placed a finger against my lips. "It's a lot, I know, and we can take it slow. I just wonder when you're going to see we'd be perfect together."

She removed her finger and nodded at me as if to say I could now speak.

The fuck? I removed the hand she's placed on my chest, and she scowled.

"I don't do relationships." I stood, and she slid off my lap and had to catch herself from stumbling.

"You're thirty, Grim. Life doesn't go backward."

"I'm not looking for a wife right now, Jenelle. I have too much going on."

"All I'm saying is, I'm already in your world, I know how the business works, you wouldn't have to worry about explanations when you disappear occasionally. I'd get it." She moved in front of me. "If you'd just let me in a little, I can be there for you."

Like a leech on your skin, I could hear Leo snicker as if he were here.

She reached up to kiss me, but I grabbed her hands and stopped her.

"Okay, fine, moving on." She smiled and stepped back. I was glad she didn't push further.

"So, what color tie are you wearing so I can match?"

"Match? What are you talking about?"

"The charity fundraiser, silly." She rolled her eyes when I didn't follow. "If you're wearing purple and I show up in yellow, I would die. So, what color?"

"Fuck," slipped through my lips. There was no way I could say I wasn't going. I'd asked her ages ago, and it was my family's organization that always hosted it. "Red," I grunted.

"Perfect. I have a gorgeous yellow dress that would pair perfectly."

"Great," I'd cringed at the color she chose and forced myself not to kick her out the door.

I blinked away the memory and dropped to the floor as my arms burned and my lungs heaved. I rolled onto my stomach and wondered if I'd passed two hundred push-ups. I glanced at the time on the wall and hopped to my feet.

I'd been patient enough.

I wasn't normally a fan of white furniture. It was too bright for my liking, but this chair wasn't too bad. It matched the white and gold of the rest of the place. The polar opposite of mine, which wasn't lost on me. It was very clean, classy, and modern, but also lacked personality. Why wasn't I surprised?

I checked my emails then looked up when I heard footsteps from the other room. I went back to my emails until I heard her jump.

"Fuck, Grim!" Kenna's hand flew to her chest. "What if I had a gun?" I lifted an amused eyebrow and studied her choice of sleepwear. A tiny black silk tank clung to her curves with matching cheeky panties.

Down, boy, I whispered internally to my erection.

"What are you doing here, in my living room?"

"You wouldn't answer my calls." I gave a light shrug.

"Do you do this to all your employees when they don't answer you right away?"

"No, because they know better." I hit send on my email and looked over. "You, on the other hand, insist on pushing all my buttons, so rather than chase you around the hotel today, I thought I'd come here."

"Where was this ambition five hours ago?"

"I was busy."

"Ahuh." She shook her head as she headed for her kitchenette. I followed her and stopped at the island. "So, I take it Jenelle passed along my message."

"She did." I felt my phone ring.

"Did you correct her on my name?" She glared over her shoulder.

"I did." I'd known what game Jenelle had been

playing, and so did Kenna, apparently. "So, what's this about a contract?"

"Seriously?" She slammed the mug down on the counter and her eyes flashed with that fire that never seemed far away. "You didn't speak to Leo, your father, Cameron, or, I don't know, fucking Knox?"

"No." I heated at her tone. "Tell me what's going on," I demanded.

"Leo asked me to entertain Tom Harris last night. For you, apparently."

"What?" This was the first time I'd heard of it.

"So, I did. We had a great night, by the way, and he would have signed up for Secrets."

"What?" *All this happened last night?* "What do you mean, *would* have? Where's the contract?"

"All business now, aren't you? And that should be *my* question." Those eyes flashed fire again then she poured herself some coffee, grabbed another mug, and poured me one.

"Leo would never ask you to try to hook a client without the paperwork in hand."

"No, he wouldn't." She tapped my hip, and I moved so she could open the fridge for some cream. "Knox dropped the ball." I felt a harsh blast of heat run up by back. "After countless calls to him, I gave up and called everyone else I could think of to find him. I finally called Jim. Shit, I even called Cameron but got nothing." She rubbed her face. "That's when I called you and got her."

"I'd stepped out to speak with Jesse privately. That's when she answered my phone."

"So, not in the shower like she claimed." It wasn't a question, and she twisted her lips, annoyed. "Grim, not one person picked up. I may have lost that deal, and I don't lose deals." I could hear the raw anger in her voice. "Fucking Knox was probably at Minnie's again."

"Does he go to Minnie's a lot?" I knew Knox was young and wild, but he had a job to do, and it should always come first. I was going to fucking tie his nuts in a bow when I saw him next.

"Almost every damn day," she huffed.

"Seems I have a lot to learn about my little brother's comings and goings."

"Harris met with Melvern Trident the night before," she added as she handed me a mug.

"How'd that go?"

"How you'd expect, but still I had my shot and let him walk away."

"I'll deal with Knox."

"Maybe he just shouldn't be put in charge of that stuff." She wrinkled her nose at the coffee and reached to lift the cover on the sugar bowl, but it was empty.

"Don't tell me how to run my business, Kenna," I warned, and she slammed her mug down on the counter.

Her anger flared again. "Fuck you."

I grabbed her around the waist and slammed my lips over hers. Her skin was warm and smooth, and her body vibrated with anger. I lost all self-control. My hand grabbed her breast through her silky top, and I sucked hard on my favorite spot on her neck. She bit my shoulder then drew her head back to look up at me.

"Did you sleep with her last night?" She leaned in and licked the side of my jaw.

"No." I rolled her nipple between my fingers, and she huffed in my ear, driving me wild.

"She said you were in the shower."

"She lied." I'd deal with Jenelle later.

"How pissed were you that I didn't return your calls?" she purred.

"I saw red."

"Good." She pushed down her panties, leaned forward against the wall, and spread her legs then looked over her shoulder at me. "Show me."

"Death wish." I smirked. I opened my pants to free myself, cracked her across the ass, and made her jump. Palming the red area, I did it again. I rested the tip of my erection at her opening and nudged forward the slightest bit.

"Yes." She wiggled for me to move inside her, but I didn't. I teased her with the possibility of pleasure with my need to drive her as crazy as she'd made me last night.

"It's so close," I pushed in a little more, "but yet it's so far away." I pulled back and wondered just who was being tortured the most.

She suddenly stood straight and turned to look up at me. "And now you know how I felt." She took a step around me, but I grabbed her and sat her on the counter. I tilted her chin, so she'd look at me. She held my gaze, but I broke it to look at her lips.

I pulled her close and devoured her mouth. She wrapped her legs around me, and her hands were in my hair, tugging at the roots. I pulled back from the counter then slammed inside her. She yelped into my mouth. I was so turned on I couldn't help myself, and I continued to thrust hard, lifting her off the counter. We were both so hungry for release, and she met me with equal madness. We attacked each other like caged savages, wild things. She scratched my back and bit my neck as we pummeled each other. My head clouded with her slurps and moans. The fury of it had my knees almost buckle.

"Damn, girl." I grabbed her hair and held her to my neck then pressed her against the wall for support as we took everything we needed from each other. The intensity was almost too much. I held on as I wanted her to lose it before I did. There was something primal about taking Kenna; it was how it needed to be.

Finally, I felt her clench around me, and she screamed, and I let go with her. Our bodies slick with sweat, we both slid to the floor and lay together in a sodden heap. When had I removed my clothes?

Our chests finally slowed as we lay there.

"You should go deal with Knox." She pulled back and slipped me out of her. I shivered and wondered if I could go another round. "I need to be able to walk today." She got up and headed for the bathroom.

That was Kenna, and I liked it. She always slipped back into work mode without any of the awkward expectations that came after sex.

"Wait." Something hit me.

"Mm?" She turned with one hand on her hip.

"Is your house decorated the same way as this?"

"How do you know I own a house?" I cocked a brow at her. "Of course, you know everything." She waved me off. "No, it's not. Why?"

"Just curious." Now I wanted to see her house.

"Right," she smirked. "Bye, Grim." She disappeared, and I got dressed and washed my cup and put it away before I left. I felt lighter somehow. Sex with Jenelle was good, but sex with Kenna fed something inside me that I desperately needed.

As I entered the lobby, Leo found me.

"A word?" He pushed through one of the doors that was hidden next to a pillar and waited for me. When it closed behind me, he spoke. "Don't kill me, but I sent Kenna—"

"To sign Tom Harris, and she couldn't because fucking Knox screwed off. Yeah, I heard."

"Did Kenna call you?"

"Yeah." I skirted around the topic.

"It was the one night I'd turned off my fucking phone in almost a year."

"No one's faulting you, Leo. Where is he?"

"No idea. His phone's off."

"Fuck." I pulled out my phone and called Minnie, and before she could answer, I spoke. "Minnie, I heard Knox might have been at your club last night. Can you confirm that?"

"Morning, sunshine," she mocked me. "No, he wasn't."

"Well, I had heard he's there often, so I thought I'd check."

"That's right, your little brother has an addiction to my strippers, and yeah, he's normally here most nights pissing away the good Gates' money. But he wasn't last night."

"I didn't know that. I'll put a stop to it."

"Hey, I'm not complainin', sugar pie. I mean, it's not like I'm not putting the money right back into your pocket, but he does tie up my rooms. Him and his pals can kinda put the kibosh on any new clientele getting in to have some fun."

"Understood. Thank you for telling me."

"Grim."

"Yeah."

"If he isn't here, maybe he's with Calli. Lord knows you Gates men like your Tame women." She laughed at her inside joke, and I licked my teeth. I hated that more and more people were privy to my personal life.

"I'll check there. Thanks."

"Anytime."

As the phone disconnected, I turned to my brother. "He wasn't at Minnie's, but she thinks he was at Calli's instead."

"Of course, he was." Leo held up a hand. "This is my mess. Let me deal with it."

We walked back out into the lobby, and at that moment Jesse saw us and rushed toward us. I knew something was up. I could feel something shift inside; something dark was circling.

"You go deal with Knox, but keep me in the loop." I pointed with my head, and he hurried off as Jesse reached me. "What's going on?"

"I got in touch with Tupot's people, found out where he's staying, and paid him a visit. Turns out the guy has a lot to say, especially when he thought I had his daughter in my truck."

"Makes it easier when they've got kids."

"It really is." Jesse grinned. "So, while Tupot's daughter enjoyed an ice cream with Tess, he sang like a bird and gave us some names. Also says he can tell us what's happenin' with your hotel. Let's just say you have an invite to join Trig at your usual spot in the desert."

"Excellent." We slipped into the town car and got to work on a plan.

By the time we arrived at the rendezvous, Trigger had our vision created. Officers and pilots were paid good money to look the other way, so we had no fear of prying eyes.

"He really is resourceful, isn't he?" Jesse admired the Devil's Reach handiwork.

Rail gave me a breakdown of how it all worked. Impressed, I nodded at him, and tucked away the knowledge never to underestimate his creativity in all things wicked.

"All you need to do is light this."

"Impressive."

"Oh, I know." He puffed on a cigarette. "It's fuckin' awesome." He urged me to take the lighter as he waved at Trigger to join us.

"You ready to do this?" Trig asked with a grin.

"More than ready." I grinned back.

"Do we want just midnight black or midnight black with blood red stitching?" Cartwright held up two pressed jackets. He understood my theatrical side and encouraged it.

"Let's do blood red stitching." I switched jackets and ran two hands through my hair as excitement built.

I nodded at Brick and Morgan, who opened up the back of their van and dragged out the three bound men. They grunted and fought as they were dumped in the center of the circle.

Once they were in place, I nodded at Jesse, who pulled a blindfolded Tupot out of a second car driven by Brick.

"Where the hell am I? What's going on?" he yelled and tried to figure things out.

"Let's call it an unofficial welcome gift." Rail chuckled behind me.

I flicked my hand, and Jesse tore off his blindfold and he squinted to clear his vision.

"Holy shit. Grim?" He looked up at me in confusion then lost his balance and fell backward on his ass. Jesse pulled him back up onto his knees. "Where the hell are we?" He looked around and paled when he saw the men. The very ones he'd outed to Jesse. They were bound and gagged in the center of some sort of contraption in what looked like the middle of Ass-fuck, Nowhere. We were actually an hour northwest of Vegas, just below my beloved Mines.

If the bottoms of those mines could speak…the stories could put a man away for eons.

"This is how we'll start." I ignored his question and pulled out my phone to let him know we still had his daughter. The photo of his twelve-year-old had been taken at the movies. Of course, a photo is subject to context, so this one had been taken next to Rail, who smiled widely for the camera.

"It was the Barbie movie," Rail chimed in. "Have you seen it yet?" Of all the movies he could have taken her to, he'd chosen that one. "Wear pink." He puffed smoke out his nose. "Big mistake not wearing pink," he muttered to Morgan, who just made a face at him to shut up.

"Right now, she's okay, but you'll determine what her fate will be." I swiped to the next photo. "Then there's your wife." I watched his face twist again. "Now, she's a pretty little thing."

"Dibs on her." Morgan smirked at him. That was comical because Morgan wouldn't hurt a woman for anything. He had hard lines drawn, and we all respected him for it.

"Please," he started to beg like the piece of shit he was, "please don't hurt them."

"Let me get this straight. You can fuck with my life, but I can't fuck with yours?" My rage built quickly.

"Mr. Gates, please, I didn't have a choice. You don't say no when the Cartel gives you orders." *What. What was that?* I glanced at Trigger and saw he'd picked up on it. "They came to me, told me what they wanted, and I did what they said."

"Explain fast, or your daughter loses her tongue."

"No, no, no." He held up his bound hands as he panicked. "Okay, okay, ahh," his eyes went round, and the sweat on his forehead ran into his skin creases. "About a week before you came back to the city, I got a call." He stopped to think, and I grew impatient. "Yes, then this Hispanic guy came and said that—"

"What guy?"

"The one in the center with the long mustache." He pointed at one of the men, and I ripped my gaze from him to the man who sat between the two others. "I remember him because he had on one of those cowboy hats, and a fancy belt, and, and…"

"Move it along."

"He showed up at my office and handed me a photo of you, said you'd killed someone important and that you weren't going to get away with it. He wanted me to mess up the work so's to make sure you'd miss the deadline for the grand opening."

"I see." I ignored the fact that it was his own company that would look bad if the hotel missed its deadline. I allowed the anger to burn inside me as I stared at him. "And who did I supposedly kill?"

"Oh, God, I can't remember. He didn't say!" His eyes closed as he began to beg.

"Three," I started a countdown, "two, your daughter really does have pretty eyes. It would be a shame to see the light in them go out."

"Martin Castillo!" he cried, and I went still. "Martin Castillo!" He repeated through a sob. "That's who they said you killed." His mouth shaped into a sad clown face as he sobbed uncontrollably. "Please don't hurt my baby."

I tried not to look shocked. I'd known there might be some kind of blowback to Martin's death, but I certainly hadn't connected it to what was going on. My mind spun. Everyone had made their kill that day, and there shouldn't have been any witnesses except those who were directly involved. Something nagged at the back of my mind, but it would have to wait. Right now, I had to find out exactly what this man knew, no matter what it took.

"Did this guy," I pointed with my chin, "order the fire at my hotel?"

"I don't know. Honestly. He used burner phones and business cards to hire people to screw with you." His mouth foamed in the corners, and I grew tired of his whining.

"Tupot, I need you to pull yourself together and listen to me."

He stopped his insufferable wailing while I bent down to his eye level.

"I want you to watch what I'm capable of, so that the next time someone comes to you and pulls this kind of bullshit, you need to ask yourself who is worse. Me or them?"

I pushed to my feet, snapped my knuckles, and walked toward the men in the contraption. Some music would be perfect right now, but I wanted to drill my point home. I wanted Tupot to hear every single snap of human bone, every cry this grown man would make while being disfigured. I wanted him to experience the silence as shock took over then the screams as I pulled him back to my hell. He needed to know what would happen if he ever crossed me again.

I grabbed the one with the mustache and pulled him to his feet and away from the contraption. I tugged him a short distance then let him stand there alone for a moment, then with all my might I drilled my fist straight into his chest directly over his heart. The man staggered back as his heart fought to absorb the blow and his lungs emptied of air. As he struggled to breathe, I steadied him then drove my knee into his face. I heard his nose break, along with his cheek. More than likely, he was now blind in the right eye. Not that it would matter. I let him lie in the sand where he landed.

I pulled back a moment and let his pain wash over me, fuel me, drive me into what I needed to do next.

Fuck, I loved a good killing, but I loved it even more when it was a means to an end.

I quickly moved to the other two men and pulled out one of them and drilled the heel of my shoe into his ankle. His screams made me grin. I danced around to the music in my head as the rush of endorphins filled me with each bone I broke.

I grabbed Mr. Mustache as he'd dared to sit up and

took him by the arm. I held it up and kicked his back and sent another blow to his heart. When he gasped, I shoved his head into the fine dust and listened to him suck in the tiny particles. His lungs rejected the invasion, and he started to cough uncontrollably.

I focused on the last fellow and broke his bones as if I were creating an artistic masterpiece.

"This is my favorite right here," I looked over at Tupot's horrified expression, "I call this the rag doll." I broke the man's shoulders and reconfigured his arm positions.

"Dear Lord!" he shouted, and I relished his mental trauma.

Big and small bones snapped and echoed in the quiet of the night. Crickets and beetles didn't dare give up their location in case they were next. The men were soon past the ability to scream and were now in a state of shock.

The man in the middle had vomited, and his blindfold was soaked with sweat and tears. I ripped it off and let him take in his mangled buddies, now part of my artwork. I slowly removed all their eye coverings as I prepared for the grand finale.

I shook my hands to bring the feeling back into my battered knuckles as I walked toward a sick looking Tupot.

"The trick," I bent down over him to bring more impact to my words, "is to bring them to the brink of death, let them feel the pain, then let them get a taste of the sweet bliss the afterlife offers. No pain exists there, just endless sleep. Then when the Reaper is circling, you yank them back."

I waved at Rail and Brick, and they hauled the three men back into the middle of the contraption. Then I caught Tupot's eye and dramatically pressed a button. Spray came out from misters and covered the men in a light dusting of gasoline.

"What is that?" He blinked at the display in front of him, then the breeze carried the smell to his nose. "Is that?"

"Yes, Tupot, just enough to coat the skin, a little jolt to bring them back to life before the burn kicks in."

I turned off the misters, lit the lighter, and watched the three lines of flame from the gasoline poured earlier travel toward them.

One by one by one, the three men were jolted from their coma-like state to the pain of their flesh as it burned.

Rail pulled out a bag of marshmallows and started to eat one.

"You ruin every childhood memory for me," Brick grunted, and Trigger chuckled as we watched and listened to the men's screams as they barbequed. Tupot's cries of horror blended in like music to my hardened soul as I caught the bag of squishy treats Rail tossed my way and we stood together until the flames died.

"You have thirty days to rebuild what the fire took," I looked hard at Tupot, who stood quiet and pale. "My hotel will be complete in time for the grand opening. Do I need to make it any clearer?"

"No, Mr. Gates, that's impossible."

"No, Tupot, nothing's impossible, and because of the trouble you caused me, you'll do it for free."

His eyes bulged, but he nodded. "Yes, for free."

"Good." I turned to Trigger, who looked at me with pride. He nodded at me, impressed. He'd been my mentor since I was nineteen and had filled an empty space inside me that no one else could. He slapped me on the shoulder and nodded toward my car, to let me know I had to go. My other life waited for me.

Jesse and I slipped into the car, and for the first time since the fire, I could take a deep breath. There were still unanswered questions, and the Cartel being behind things almost made sense. At least it was a devil I knew. Not knowing what I was dealing with was worse. At least it was a start.

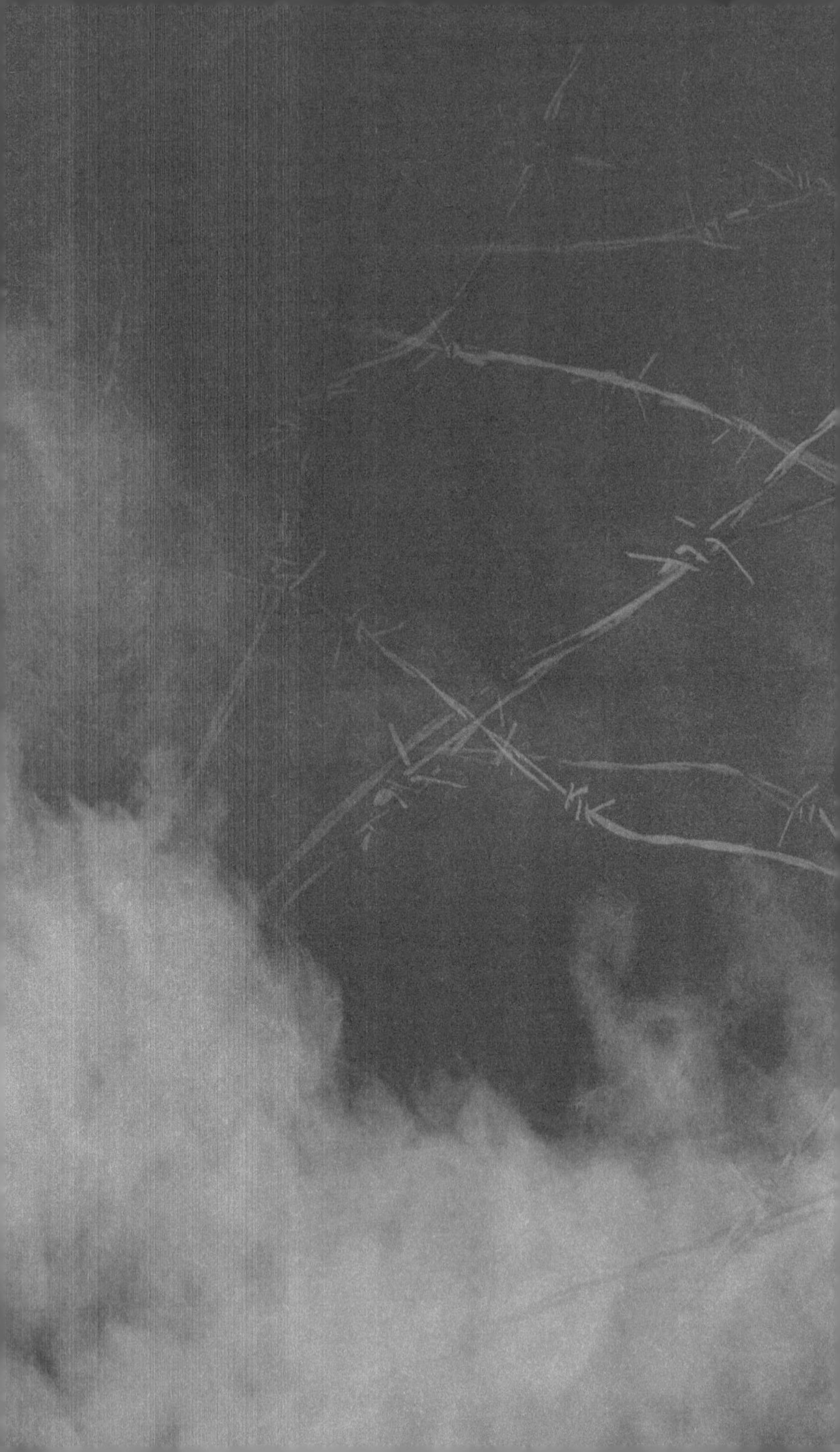

TWENTY-ONE

SIMON

I enjoyed dinner by myself. It gave me time to think things over without the need for forced conversation. Plus, everyone was getting ready for the fundraiser, so I knew I would be left alone for the most part.

My wagyu steak was, of course, cooked to perfection. Chef Dale never disappointed. It was the only reason I'd decided to eat here in the first place. I'd considered several options, but the thought of that steak made my mouth water, and everything else paled in comparison.

I dipped the medium rare meat into the gooseberry chutney and savored the warm flavors of cinnamon and cloves. Dale had paired the steak with fresh carrots and a few baby potatoes with a creamy, buttery sauce.

"Should I interrupt?" Kenna smirked at me. "Because you look like you might want to take that home tonight."

"If it was socially acceptable, I would." I matched her humor.

"May I?" She pointed to the chair across from me, and I nodded as I dabbed the corners of my mouth with the napkin. I noticed she had her hair and makeup freshly done. She must have caught me as she walked back from the hotel's salon.

"To what do I owe the pleasure of your time on what I would assume to be a busy evening?"

"I saw you come in earlier, and since I had everything done," she waved her hands at herself with a smile, "I slipped over to pick your brain on something. I waited until it looked like you'd finished." She smiled.

"Color me intrigued." I waved the waiter over. "Another glass, please." I pointed at my red wine, as I knew she also enjoyed J. Lohr.

"Thank you." She smiled at me then pressed her lips together in thought. I studied her and waited. Kenna was a gorgeous woman, more mature looking than Calli. She had a reputation for having a strong backbone in both her personal life and in business. She was in a predominantly male world with the life her father subjected her to, and she'd shown countless times that she could hold her own in it. It was rather attractive.

"Are you hungry?" I felt the need to offer.

"No, I'm just stalling." She chuckled, and although her eyes lit up, her face told me something was up. "At the risk of stepping over a line, I'm going to ask you something. I know we aren't close, and a huge part of that is because your interests lay with two people I try to avoid." She shrugged and smiled as her hand unconsciously rubbed her throat. It drew my gaze, and I noticed a faint marking on her neck. *Is that a hickey?* "Look, is my father going to be okay?" She blurted this as her eyes went to my face.

"Okay?" I repeated, my mind still on the hickey. I wondered who she'd been with.

"Yes, okay." She paused, and I could feel her study me. "The situation with Trigger." Her brows went up.

Oh! I finally got what she'd been worried about. "Yes, he's willing to help him out." My mind went immediately to the deal I made, and it made my stomach drop.

"That's good." She seemed to relax some, and I honed back in on her slender neck. I found myself picturing someone kissing her from her jaw down to that very spot... "What did he want?"

"Who killed Martin Castillo." I paused and blinked at my own admission. *What the hell!* My eyes flew to her face and her surprised expression at my answer. *Oh, shit.*

"Who on earth *is* that?"

"My apologies, Kenna. That shouldn't have slipped out of my mouth." Cameron might actually kill me.

The waiter set the glass of wine down on the table, and she picked it up and took a long sip. The way her lips formed around the rim of the glass drew me in and hypnotized me. I had to force myself to look away. I hadn't had a one on one with her before and now understood the magnetism many felt around her.

"Was he a client of my father's?"

"No." I shook my head then popped a potato in my mouth needing something to keep it busy.

"Then why would his death be so important that he'd needed to talk to Trigger?"

"I'm sorry, Kenna, I can't."

"Well, Simon, this can go two ways." She dug her heels in. "I can start digging and pull my many resources to find out who this guy is, or I can ask my father. You can save a call from Cameron once he finds out you dropped the ball and told me."

"I don't do well with threats, Kenna." I leaned back and tossed my napkin on my plate. I searched my brain for how to fix this.

"And I don't do well when I only get part of a story. My father asked me for help, I gave it to him, and now I want to know exactly why my help was needed."

Fuck.

"If I tell you, that means you're getting involved in your father's business." I tried a different tact.

"What makes you think I'm not already in it?" She put her elbows on the table and leaned toward me. Something dark ran over her face, and I wondered exactly what Kenna Lodge knew about what her father had going on. I couldn't imagine her being all right with it if she really knew the truth.

I tapped a nail on my wine glass and chose my words carefully. I hoped I wasn't about to crack the lid on Pandora's box.

"Martin Castillo was a Mexican drug lord in Rosarito. He was very dangerous, unpredictable, and dumb as a post. Trouble is he was getting tangled up in some business of Cameron's—"

"What kind of business?"

"Client stuff." I kept it vague, but she gave me a look, and I went on. "He was supposed to take the fall for one of Cameron's clients but wound up dead instead." I skirted around some major details.

"And what, Dad thought Trigger killed him?"

"No, but we think Trigger knows who did."

"And does he?"

"He gave us a name."

"And?" She waited, and I cleared my throat. "Simon come on."

"We're waiting to see if the information matches."

"If Trigger told you who it was, then that's who it was. He doesn't fuck around like that."

"Let's hope."

"And if this information doesn't match up? And match up with what?" She scrunched up her face.

"That's not for me to answer, Kenna. That's up to your father."

"So, this Castillo drug guy is dead, and you can't find the man who did it." She chewed her lip. "So now dad has no way to protect his client? Is this client someone big?"

"Let's not go there."

"No, let's." She held my gaze, and I felt a crackle of electricity and knew she wasn't going to let it go. "I can handle it, Simon."

"I believe you, but it's more that your father wouldn't want you to know."

"Don't underestimate me. I'm more his daughter than you know."

"Perhaps you are," I huffed. I decided I'd already let her in, and it would be better to have Kenna on my side, as I'd begun to realize she might make a formidable enemy. "Let's just say, if a guy named Luis Aguilar killed Martin Castillo, then your father can point the focus there. If he can't, retaliation could sting."

"Sting or kill?"

"We won't let anything happen to Cameron," I assured her.

"The one and only time he lost a case, we had a few visitors and they never left," she muttered. "I hate to think who might visit this time."

"It'll be okay. We just need some answers and quick." I hoped maybe she would keep her eyes open and see what she could dig up from her people.

"Just keep this between us, please."

"Of course." She tipped the glass to her pink lips again and downed more than half of the ruby liquid. She sat back and mulled over what I'd told her. While she was deep in thought, I watched her and found myself curious where her mind took her.

"May I offer you a little advice?" I figured I'd step over a line again since that's what we'd already done.

"I'm listening."

"Be careful who you surround yourself with. Not all around you are trustworthy."

"I know you guys don't trust the Devil's Reach—"

"I'm not referring to the motorcycle club, Kenna."

"Then who?"

I swung my gaze toward Leo and Grim, who were on the edge of the room talking. They both looked fit to kill. I studied her as she watched them as well and wondered if it was Grim's handiwork on her neck. I doubted it, though. They seemed like oil and vinegar.

"Grim Gates is the least of my worries." She seemed a million miles away.

"Is he? Maybe he knows something." I planted the seed that Cameron would kill me for. "Something that can maybe help?"

"Maybe." Her phone rang, and she glanced at the ID. "Thank you for the information." She reached for her purse. "I hope you enjoy the rest of your day."

"Did I miss the dinner invite?" Calli's high-pitched voice made Kenna's face flinch. Calli wore an all-red pantsuit with matching red glasses. I knew they weren't prescription.

"Nope." Kenna smiled at me as she got up. "Thanks for the chat, Simon. I hope to see you later tonight." She nodded at her sister.

"Have a good evening." I smiled and watched Calli's face as she glared at her sister.

"Run along to the pool. I'm sure a wet t-shirt contest is happening." She sounded like a child.

"At least I'd have a chance to win." Kenna grinned, and Calli's face fell. She did have smaller breasts than Kenna.

"Enjoy your date?" Calli pushed Kenna's glass away and signaled to the waiter. "Another, please."

"Of course." He rushed away.

"Are you jealous?" I reached under the table and gave her leg a pat.

"Of that? No. I just don't trust she'll bring you to the dark side."

"The only side I'm on is yours," I assured her, and she rolled her eyes. "Tell me something, is Kenna dating anyone?"

"Why, you on the market?" She studied the menu, but when I didn't answer, she looked up. "How should I know? Minnie'd be the one to ask. She's the fiery redhead who's dating Brick. Why?"

"I wondered if she might be dating Grim Gates."

Calli dropped her head back and laughed so loudly she drew attention from others around us.

"Grim?" She laughed again. "The only way Grim would give her the time of day was if she was on his hit list. She drives him crazy, and he isn't happy if he can't control you. If you said Leo, maybe I could see it, but not Grim."

"Understood." I dropped the topic and slipped into easier conversation.

Later that evening, when Calli was in the shower prepping for the fundraiser she was to attend with Knox, I slipped out to the living room to answer a call.

"Gable." I used the same greeting whether I knew who it was or not.

"I've called three times."

"Well, I'm not alone, so that makes it difficult to answer," I growled.

"You're flirting with a dangerous line, sleeping with his daughter."

"Maybe, but it helps me keep tabs on everything." I leaned back and glanced toward the bedroom door to make sure Calli hadn't come out yet.

He obviously disagreed but didn't say anything else about it. "Well, I have some news."

"And?" I slipped on my glasses and pulled the sheer curtain back a little to look outside.

"Luis Aguilar, born June twenty-fifth, nineteen-seventy-seven, in Yuma, California, died eleven months ago in a shootout at a nightclub in El Salvador."

"Wait, what?" I pressed my hand to the wall. "That's impossible. Castillo was killed only weeks ago."

"Yup." He made a sound with his tongue.

"How reliable is your info?" This was bad.

"I trust it. I did a job last year with Tommy Tide, and when I heard he was hustling in that area, I called him. Turns out Tommy's the one who pulled the trigger on Luis. So, either there was some confusion, and your source was misinformed, or your source lied."

"Shit." I felt the blood drain from my face.

"I have something else for ya."

"Yeah?"

"Yeah, I'm sending you a photo now."

I pulled my phone back out when I felt it come through. It was of Martin Castillo's house in flames, and in the background by a tree, I could make out a Devil's Reach vest.

"You can thank me later." The line went dead, and I sank into a chair wondering how I was going to navigate this one. Was Trigger behind Castillo's death?

TWENTY-TWO

KENNA

My head swam after my conversation with Simon. I hoped like hell that Trigger knew what he was doing.

"This is impressive." Salazar looked around the grand room and admired the red, silver, and black décor. It screamed Gates Family like nothing else. "I'll be sure to make a sizable donation."

"That's very kind of you." I sipped my champagne and tried to focus on the party. "So, you're leaving?"

"Yes, I must get back to handle some business. I won't lie, I'll miss your company."

"You know where to find me," I assured him.

"I do." He spotted Yen Hong the same time I did.

"That's my cue to go write a check. I'll see you when I'm back in town."

"I'm looking forward to it." I gave him a handshake, and he slipped into the crowd.

"Well, well, look at you." Yen took my hand and spun me around. "Kenna, you must break hearts everywhere you go."

"Only when I'm standing next to you." I waved a hand at his jacket. "What is this, Sebastian Cruz?" He beamed, pleased I knew his designer.

"It is. You certainly know your fashion."

"But of course." I caught my own reflection in a window. I was so pleased with my dress. It was a blood red silk gown, and the skirt had been cut into seven panels, which created such elegance when I moved. There were seven slits, one at each seam that went straight up and connected with the lace halter-top bodice. It was sexy and gorgeous all at once. Of course, Minnie was the one who found the dress for me and insisted I wore it.

I'd kept my dark hair in long waves, so it tumbled down my bare back. My eye makeup was very dramatic to match the mood the Gates had gone for. Much like Grim's penthouse, the décor at the ball was done in a sort of chic-goth theme.

"Oh my God, you wore it," Minnie cooed as she swept me up in a hug. She looked equally as sexy in her silver pin-up outfit. She stepped back to admire me. "He's going to lose his shit."

"Who?" Yen stepped closer, loving the drama Minnie was dying to spill.

"No one." I laughed and shot her a look. I tried hard to keep my private life away from my clients. Even if Yen was different, I had boundaries.

"As long as it's not Grim, Leo, or Knox, I approve." He chuckled, and Minnie gave him a strange expression. "I just mean because I offered Kenna a job in Hong Kong, and if the Gates get a tight hold on her, she'll never leave."

"Oh, really?" Minnie's eyes were in slits as she studied me.

"I haven't made any firm decisions. I've only been full time in Vegas for just over a year. Things are still new."

"Yes, well, I wasn't kidding about what I said about the contract. You write whatever you want in there, and I'll make it happen." He leaned in and kissed my cheek. "Have a great time and go flash that dress around." He left, and Minnie shook her head.

"Look at you, Miss Popular. Remember, though, you can't leave us. You know I can hide bodies, so they'll never be found. So don't do me no wrong."

"Ha! You're funny." I gave her a wry look. "His offer was kind, and one I would have considered a year ago, but I really love this city and all of you, threats or no threats, so don't worry."

"Okay." She huffed, then looked thoughtful. "Although a backup job far away might be good if you needed to hide. Wouldn't be a bad thing." She eyed me.

"Trust me, that thought passed through my mind already." I waved at my mother who had just spotted me.

"You look amazing, by the way." She gave me a dirty grin. "Lift up one of those panels and show me what you got."

"And give away the goods so early?" I tisked playfully. "You look pretty gorgeous yourself."

"If only Brick was here to see it."

"Where are they, anyway?" I looked around.

"Business in the desert." She shrugged. "They should be back anytime now."

"Min, can I ask you something?"

"Shoot."

"Trigger knows what he's doing, right?"

"What do you mean?"

"Like, when dealing with my father. He'd be careful, right?"

"I've never known Trigger to be reckless when it comes to business or shady shit. Something bothering you?"

"I don't know. This whole thing with my father

asking Trigger for help. Something feels…Oh, shit," I muttered when I saw Knox heading in my direction, "this should be good."

"Mm."

"Kenna, I'm so sorry. Leo told me to get the contracts, and I had every intention of doing it. I just got pulled in a different direction and totally forgot."

"And I suppose my zillion calls and texts didn't help jog your memory?" I still fumed but tried to keep it in. "You cost me that deal. A deal that would have been great for Grim's hotel."

"I know, it's just that Calli needed me, and—"

"Wait, you flaked on me because of my sister?"

"We just became exclusive last night. That's a big step for me."

"Yeah, it is," Minnie snorted.

"Don't you have a dive bar to run?" He made a face at her.

"Yes, and you've paid for more than half of it," she shot back, and he flushed. He knew she was right.

"Look, make it up to me by never doing that again." I touched his arm and tried to look like I forgave him.

"I won't. Trust me, Grim already tore me a new asshole for it."

"Okay, then, it's over." That wasn't quite true because it would take me a long time to get past his reckless behavior, but a scene wasn't going to change anything. "Just be careful with Calli, okay? That side of the family is slightly off."

"Spoken like a true sister." He laughed. "I can handle myself." He snatched a drink off a waiter's tray and slipped right back into being Knox. "I'll see ya around."

"I hate that he's dating the *see you next Tuesday* of Vegas," Minnie grumbled. "I thought she was all up on Simon Says."

"Just say cunt, Min, because that's what she is." I sipped my drink. "And that's what I think too, but I'm staying out of it."

"Cunt," Minnie repeated under her breath.

"There you are." Jayden was in front of me with a drink.

I shot Minnie a quick look, but Brick had arrived and wrapped an arm around her shoulder and was whispering something into her ear. She was so in love with Brick that it made my heart full. I knew he loved her, too, but he seemed to be having a midlife crisis or something. He didn't seem to realize how much he was hurting her. Minnie leaned back with a smile and kissed him. I wondered if I'd ever find love like that.

"You look like you just stepped off a runway, Kenna. Wow."

I took the drink Jayden handed me and forced a smile. "Thank you."

"I see the Gates spent a pile of money on this event.

They could have just donated it all to the charity instead."

"That's unkind, Jayden. A lot of this stuff is donated, and they do match whatever is made on the event. I think that's quite impressive for one family to do."

"When you're rich as fuck, I guess it pays to look humble."

Wow.

Suddenly, I felt eyes on me, and scanned the faces and found Grim. He was in a jet-black tux, with gray velvet swirls, and red stitching. His hair was slicked back, and his eyes that burned into me were a cold gray. He couldn't look any more like a villain if he tried. He said something and stepped away from the man he was with. As he made his way toward me, I felt as though I was being stalked like prey. His eyes never left me.

"So, where's your date, Shore's son? Whatever his name was. I thought I should meet him," I vaguely heard Jayden ask.

A jolt ran through me as I thought back to the morning when I found Grim in my living room. We'd been like savages. He'd claimed me as his, at least in those moments of intimacy. Was that intimacy? I was his and he was mine, and no one else existed then. It was unlike anything I'd ever experienced, and nothing I'd ever imagine I'd let someone do.

"Good evening, Miss Lodge." Grim stopped inches from me and drank me in as he kissed my cheek. His hand slipped discreetly inside one of the silk panels on my skirt, and he let out a small, carnal moan only I could hear.

"Shore's son?" Minnie asked as Jayden repeated his question. She looked at Jayden funny, and I suddenly tuned in to them. "Shore has four girls. No penis made its way into that family."

Minnie, no!

"But he said his son was your date tonight." Jayden looked at me then at Grim. He then seemed to make the connection that we were together. We weren't; I'd come alone.

"I'm sorry, Jayden, I didn't want to be rude." I tried to be kind but truthful. "I just wanted to attend alone."

"Right," he chuckled like he couldn't believe I would lie to him, "alone." He threw a look at Grim, who didn't react. "Well, I guess I'll leave you to be *alone.*"

He stepped into the crowd and made his way out of sight.

"Shit, girl, I'm sorry." Minnie looked contrite. "Me and my big mouth."

"No, it's okay, Min. He's been trying to get my attention lately, and he's not getting my hints. It needed to happen."

"Maybe he shouldn't work here if he is bothering my employees," Grim added.

"No, don't be ridiculous, Grim. Besides, I can handle it." I spotted Jim Gates with his wife Laurel and watched as she hovered around him. She seemed concerned over something. She kept her eyes on her husband and a hand on his arm.

"Come on, girl, I gotta find a proper drink." Brick hauled Minnie off toward the bar.

"Is your dad okay?" I whispered to Grim, who didn't follow my gaze as I nodded toward his parents.

"He's fine," Grim growled and moved me in front of him as a waiter walked by with a big tray of bacon-wrapped dates. The place was packed, but when his free hand landed on my bare hip, and he pushed his erection into my back, my eyes went wide, but no one was the wiser.

He bent down and pressed his warm lips to my ear. He didn't need to say anything. I felt it too, and as much as I wanted to play, I needed to talk to him first.

"I need to talk to you."

"Talk or fight?" He chuckled. "Because either one usually ends up the same way." He squeezed my hip.

"I'm serious, Grim."

"Grim, darling." Her cool voice sent a shiver down my spine, but what was worse was Grim's reaction. He flinched, but at least his hand didn't leave my side. A gorgeous, five-foot-eight blonde bombshell in a sleek yellow dress draped her arms around him. She slid between us, and he had to break contact. "I'm so glad you wore the red tie we discussed the other night." She swept her arm down her dress. "I promised you I'd wear my yellow gown. You like?"

"What are you doing?" He dodged her question.

"Mingling." She turned and looked down at me then looked me up and down. "I don't think we've met. I'm Jenelle Borrows."

I figured she'd be pretty, but she was a fuckin' top shelf model. A flawless beauty.

"Kenna Lodge," I somehow pushed by my lips.

"Oh, the girl on the phone last night. You really were persistent."

"I was doing my job."

"And part of your job is calling your boss at four a.m.?" She chuckled at Grim, but I held my own.

"That's right."

"Four a.m. or four p.m., Jenelle, what difference?" Grim scanned the room. "Work never stops in Vegas. You should know that. She did the right thing by calling."

"Grim?" Leo called, and Grim looked at the two of us and shrugged. I could practically feel her claws from where I stood.

"Give me a sec." He left us, and I turned to go find Minnie, but Jenelle grabbed my arm.

"Kenna, can we just talk a moment?"

"Sure." *Oh, kill me now.*

"I'm just going to give it to you real," she walked us a few steps away so her back was turned in the direction Grim left, "because I wouldn't want you to find yourself in the middle of something awkward."

"I can respect that." I nodded for her to go on even though my back inched up higher.

"Grim and I have a long history. We've been on and off again because of our jobs. This time Grim is back, and I am too. When he came home, we reconnected and are dating again." That was news to me. "We're not exclusive yet, but that's what we were discussing when you called last night." She seemed genuine with her explanation, and it made me uneasy.

"Grim's still kind of stuck in his twenties, if you know what I mean." She gave a little laugh. "But I can see he's starting to realize life isn't slowing down for any of us." She paused a moment then looked me directly in the eyes. "Kenna, we're getting married." Her words echoed in my head, and I shook them clear and thought how strange it was that Grim never hinted that he was thinking of marriage. She gave me a small smile then put her hand gently on my arm. She glanced over where Grim stood in conversation with his brother. I could see by the way her face softened she meant what she was saying. "I'm not trying to be a bitch or anything."

Ugh, I hated the passive bitch comments.

"Well, I can assure you we certainly aren't dating," I told her.

"I know." She smiled widely. "Grim doesn't actually date. He just plays around until he gets bored then comes and finds me."

"Doesn't that bother you?" I seemed to have landed in the middle of something complicated.

"I'm putting the time in. I have since we were young, but I can see how he is with you and I'm just saying, Grim's wild and fun, but at the end of it all we'll be together. I guess I'm just trying to save you from getting hurt." I saw she was making an effort to be nice about it, but I could sense her claws rested below the surface, ready to pop out.

"I appreciate the honesty." I tried to look casual.

"Do you want to get something to eat?" She switched the subject so fast I was caught off guard. "I hear the crab cakes are amazing." She smiled.

"No. Thank you." *I would rather cut out my own tongue than share something to eat with this woman.* "You really should go and enjoy some, though." *Lord knows you could use the calories.* I suddenly wanted to punch a wall. I mean, I was going to lose some amazing sex. People like me don't often find sexual partners who fit.

I searched the room for Minnie and saw Grim on his way back. *Damn.* I felt incredibly uncomfortable and just wanted to get out of there.

"Hey, darling, we should find our table." She

smiled at him, but Grim pulled his arm away and took a step toward me.

"Kenna, you wanted to tell me something?"

Fuck, no. I couldn't risk Jenelle making a scene here at such an important fundraiser.

"There you are, Kenna." Minnie saved the day. "Mr. Hong is looking for you."

"Work calls once again. I gotta go." I shrugged and forced a smile at Grim. I could kiss Minnie.

"Jizz-elle." Minnie nodded at her. "I had no idea they would make a dress that color." She turned to me as Jenelle's face turned red. "Let's go."

I stepped back and avoided eye contact with either Grim or Jenelle. I forced myself to walk away at a normal pace toward the exit.

"What just happened?" Minnie asked once we were alone.

"I—" The words caught in my throat, and I looked at her, lost. What was wrong with me?

"You need to get out of here?"

"Yeah."

"Look, Wet and Wild room number one is open for the next two hours. That always fixes you right up. I'll cover for you here. Go do your thing, wear a shower cap or something, reapply fresh makeup, and come find me when you're done."

I looked over my shoulder and saw Grim speaking

to Jenelle. I noticed her arms were at her sides, and he looked pissed.

"Yeah, thanks."

"Anything for you, babe." I rushed away, not wanting to be stopped by anyone else. I made it into the elevator, and when the doors closed, I took a deep breath. It wasn't like I was in love with Grim, for God's sake. I wouldn't know what that feeling was like if it smacked me in the face, but I knew what he was capable of, and that loss alone was enough to make me cry. Shit, I'd been enjoying myself too. I couldn't even let myself have a bit of fun without causing some kind of damn heartache.

Shore dropped me off at Minnie's club and said he'd be glad to stay until I was finished, but the truth was I didn't want a timeline.

"You go back, but thank you."

"You sure, Kenna? I really don't mind."

"Yes, I'm sure. I appreciate the offer, though." I squared my shoulders and attempted to look confident. "I promise to call you as soon as I'm finished."

"Okay." He looked uneasy but left.

I opened the door, waved to the bouncer, and half ran down the back hallway to my favorite room, where I could just be me.

I slipped off my dress, turned Sam Cooke up loud, and stepped into the box where the lights, water, and music took me away.

TWENTY-THREE

GRIM

"**W**hat did you say to Kenna when I stepped away?"

"Nothing. Just a little girl talk." She finger-quoted and batted her lashes at me. I stepped close and lowered my voice.

"I'm not in the habit of repeating myself."

"Relax, Grim," she dropped the act, "I was just letting her know I saw you first, that we have something special, and let her know you and I will end up together."

"Oh, really. So, you feel you have a right to speak for me?" She just blinked as I seethed. "First of all, we aren't even dating." I glared down at her. *This woman was in-fucking-sane. Who was she to speak for me!*

"Are you dating Kenna?" She made my head hurt.

"If I was, that's my business."

"Look," she looked around, "I just explained that you and I have something and that things are happening between us."

"Again, I'm lost on the part where you think things are happening here." I tried hard to curb my temper as so many people were around us.

"Grim, we just talked the other night, and I told you I would wait for you to be ready. I thought we had an understanding." Her eyes were hurt. "It's clear you're playing around with that girl. I know we're not exclusive yet, but she's got puppy dog eyes for you, and it's only a matter of time before she falls in love with you. That just wouldn't be fair to her. I only hope it hasn't gone that far."

"Love?" I laughed at the idea. What Kenna and I ran on was pure venom and hot flame. All either of us wanted was sex. The kind of sex that repelled most women. It wasn't easy to find a partner who could take what I needed to give.

"Yes, love. Because after our talk, she couldn't even look at you. Regardless, it's only fair that she knows the truth."

"Can you hear yourself?" I grabbed her arms and held her against me. "If you ever," I squeezed hard enough to get her attention, "speak on my behalf again, we're over. This little song and dance I do, mostly for your father, I might add, is over."

"I was only—"

"You're a beautiful woman, Jenelle, but you have too much going on upstairs." I referred to her crazy head. "So, find some self-respect and go look for someone else to lust over."

"Aren't you forgetting your pattern with women, Grim?" She scrunched up her nose and rubbed her arms. "You play with them, chuck them, then you call me." I wanted to lash out, I wanted rip her head off for even thinking she could talk to me like that, but there were too many eyes on me, including her father's.

I heard her father earlier as he name-dropped about people who he thought we should have invited. I couldn't care less who he thought was a better fit; we were way past our goal and the night was far from over. I only humored him because he was a good man to know in this city. He knew a lot of people who were connected to my people. I played extra nice with him, but I could see now what a mistake that was.

"Grim, we're going to marry." She looked at me with melty eyes. "You can run from it all you want, but we're meant to be together. I'm being patient. I know you still want to have sex with other people, and I'm okay with that. But I don't want you to hurt someone while you do it."

"Are you fucking mad, woman?"

"It's what you do when you love someone, Grim."

"Fuck me." I stopped talking before I did something I'd regret. I tuned in to my brother's voice.

"Grim!" Leo called, "Tom Harris is on his way here!"

"What?" My head spun.

"He just called looking for Kenna, he wants to sign, and so do four friends!"

Holy shit, she did it.

"Where's Kenna?" I looked around and scanned the crowd. "Min," I called, "where's Kenna?"

"She left." She gave a pointed look at Jenelle, who shrugged and gave me a look that said *I told you so.*

"Why would she leave if she didn't care?" Jenelle smiled and blew me a kiss over her shoulder as she headed toward her father.

I grabbed my cell and punched in her number, but it rang and rang.

"Shit." I closed my eyes for a second and tuned out the room. When I opened them again, I spotted my dad at their table. He watched my mom as she laughed at something someone said. Now, that was the face of someone in love. I made my way over to him and sat down.

"Hello, son." He smiled, but up close he couldn't hide that he looked tired.

"You okay?" I kept my tone breezy; the time wasn't right to pry.

"I just spun your mother across the dance floor, and now I'm taking a breather." He patted my hand. "Now, enough small talk. Who are you looking to kill?"

"Besides Cameron Tame?" I made him chuckle. "I need you to text Kenna to come to the twentieth. Because of her, Harris and his friends want to sign on with Secrets."

"Son, that's wonderful, but why can't you text her?"

"Let's just say Jenelle was pissed at me, and Kenna somehow got caught in the crosshairs. Just a misunderstanding but Kenna took off and won't take my calls."

"I see." He tried to hide his smile as he pulled out his phone and handed it to me. "Do what you must, but I never gave it to you."

"Thanks." I sent off a quick text and waited, but there was no response. That was odd. She always texted my father right back. I stood and buttoned my jacket, and Dad pulled my arm to get me to sit down again.

"When have I ever stepped into your love life and commented?"

"Never."

"There's a first time for everything. Be careful with Jenelle. She's in love with you, and her father's a powerful man. She knows it and will use it to her advantage, and so will he. Just make sure you know what you really want, son. Jenelle just might crawl inside that head of yours and create a fog so you can't see anyone else."

Jesus. Money, sex, and power were dangerous in a world like ours.

"Ten minutes too late." I snickered.

"They're just another family to watch."

"Understood." I got up and looked for Leo. Dad had always been careful not to comment or impose his views on our love lives. At least not unless we asked for his advice. So, the fact he had done just that tossed me for a loop.

"Leo," I waved when I spotted him, "let's move."

We got some champagne and top-shelf bourbon all set up in the office, along with some Cuban cigars to celebrate the contract.

"Harris is set to arrive in forty," Leo glanced at his watch, "and Kenna should be here any moment."

"Good."

"Ah." Leo paused, and I looked up.

"Out with it." I clipped the tip of the cigar.

"Have you noticed anything yet? Like we discussed on the flight?" I set the cutter on the table and tapped a finger next to it as I thought.

"I have my suspicions, yes."

"I think it's time we talked, Grim." Leo chewed his lip. "I'm concerned things are even worse than I thought."

"I agree we should, has dad spoken to you?"

"No." He looked at me oddly.

"Now's not the time. Let's just focus on getting through this. We get the contract signed, then we'll talk."

My phone vibrated, and I saw a text.

Jesse: Still no sign of Kenna.

Grim: Keep your eyes open.

What the hell?

I quickly called my father.

"Dad, can you try Kenna again. She's still not here."

"Really? Yes, I'll do that right now." We hung up, and I tapped the phone screen as I thought.

I called the kitchen and was glad someone picked with such a busy event downstairs.

"Kitchen," the girl answered.

"This is Grim. Put Chef Dale on."

"Right away, sir!" She didn't miss a beat, and a moment later a frazzled chef answered.

"Mr. Gates, what can I do for you?"

"Dale, have you seen Kenna tonight?"

"No, sir, I've been crazy busy in the kitchen the whole day." *Fuck.* "Have you checked with Minnie? She often goes to her club. Especially if she needs to let off some steam." He seemed to key in to my concern.

"If you see her, tell her she's needed on the twentieth." I didn't wait for his response and hung up. A strange feeling washed over me.

"Let's go. Leo. Something's not right." I waved for him to follow. We raced down the hallway, and just as I pushed the button to call the elevator, the doors parted.

"Holy shit, Kenna!" Leo called out and everything around me went red as her battered body stood rigid against the railing.

I snapped.

"Leo! Shut down the floor!" I boomed. "Steven, find out exactly where she came from," I ordered the security guard who already had his radio in his hand. "You," I pointed to Freddy the second guard on duty, "find me a fucking head!" His eyes went wide then he whirled and ran.

Kenna's eyes latched on to mine, and I saw the moment she let go. I jolted forward and caught her, then lowered her to the floor.

Someone was going to fucking die before the night was done, or blood would spray across the city of Vegas until the truth showed its ugly face.

"Grim," she whispered, and I looked down at her, "I'm so sorry."

The End

ACKNOWLEDGMENTS

To my mother, who chuckles at all the dark stuff I do and for being a badass role model for me and my sisters.

To my girls, Liz Clark and Jamie Johnson, for always having my back and being there for me especially when I'm in spin mode.

To my betas and proofers, Rachel Womack, Maggie Savarese, Mandy Freeman, Jamie Johnson, Liz Clark, Kim Kelchner, Veronica Nelson, and Kasey Griffin. You're all rock stars!

To my editor Lori Whitwam, thank you for going above and beyond for my books. I love that I can reach out at any time and ask you for help.

To my reader group, like I've said a zillion times, thanks for being my safe place.

To anyone who has taken a chance on my books, I thank you!

J.L. Drake, born and raised in Nova Scotia, Canada, later moving to Southern California. Though she loves the weather in Cali, she would sell her left kidney for a good rainstorm. Jodi's love of the seasons back home in Canada definitely appear in her books.

When she's not writing, you can often find her sitting somewhere along the coast of Huntington Beach, reading, or at home curled up on a couch with her two children and husband, binge watching a good movie.

AUTHORJLDRAKE.COM

FOLLOW ME ON SOCIAL MEDIA

facebook.com / JLDrakeauthor
x.com / jodildrake_j
instagram.com / j.l.drake
tiktok.com / @authorjldrake
bookbub.com / profile / j-l-drake

Alpha

Tango

HAVOC OF SINS

Grim

Havoc

Sins

DARKNESS SERIES

Darkness Lurks

Darkness Follows

Darkness Falls

STANDALONE BOOKS

Behind My Words

Christmas At The Cabin

Omerta

STONEWALL TRILOGY

Extraction

Embedded

Breached

For the suggested reading order, please scan the QR code: